A DEADLY GAME

Doris Redhead

Raider Publishing International

New York London Cape Town

Cover Images Courtesy of iStockPhoto.com

ISBN: 978-1-61667-270-6

Published By Raider Publishing International
www.RaiderPublishing.com
New York London Cape Town
Printed in the United States of America and the United Kingdom

A DEADLY GAME

Doris Redhead

1

Buttoned up to her chin, the thick grey jacket enveloped her small frame, and the attached hood blinkered her view of the world but still she turned to look back. The lights of the town twinkled hazily through the drizzle and mist; clouds of smoke curled sinuously from factory chimneys, and the warning beacon atop the massive Manilaw building pulsed out its watery red beam to alert low flying aircraft of its towering presence. This massive edifice housed laboratories where new and exciting innovations in medicine, were researched and manufactured.

Even at this late hour, the night shift was beavering away, possibly even now having *eureka* moments as some momentous discovery was uncovered. The rows of windows, like numerous rectangular light boxes, were illuminated on every level. It meant nothing to her and she quickly resumed the climb, limping slightly in her black leather boots, the tattered wicker basket firmly clasped in her right hand. The rough, muddy road with its steep incline up to the trees made her breathless and water dripped from the fringes of her hood on to her face. Her energy levels were low; she had eaten nothing all day. It didn't matter any more, relief was at hand, and her worries would soon be over. She would not be alone any more.

Reaching the first of the trees, she pressed on until she found the narrow path, knee deep in rotting russet and black leaves and with branches of shrubs and bushes flapping noisily in the wind, camouflaging the opening. She pushed through the discarded foliage, the deciduous debris of winter, trudging through the damp undergrowth, and then, recognizing the place, she turned off to the right, doubling back on an untravelled route, parallel to the path. Perhaps fifty yards on, the shrubs began to thin out and the trees were less densely packed. Here was her refuge, a small leaf strewn glade, a sanctuary which she had selected weeks before as the place where she would end her life.

A large and ancient oak dominated the place, its huge gnarled roots running tortuously across the earth before plunging through leaves and twigs into the firm ground to form a root ball mirroring the tree itself. It was majestic and strong, even now, with its skeletal form and its leafless branches. The cold wind did not penetrate this sanctum. She kicked the downed leaves towards the base of the oak and then, satisfied that there were enough, she settled down between two of the massive splayed roots. For a while she sat with her back propped up against the great trunk, scooping bundles of leaves over her legs, and then she pulled the wicker basket towards her, its contents which hitherto had been hidden by the long blue woollen scarf, spilling out.

Five small packets of pills and a litre bottle of cider lay now exposed within the much used and worn basket. She reached for the nearest packet, prised it open with her numb fingers, and punched out fifteen white pills into her palm. The decision to end her life had been definitively made and preparation carefully planned. Resolutely, one by one, she popped the pills into her mouth and crunched them to powder. The taste was unpleasant and she stretched over for the cider, unscrewed the top and swallowed several large mouthfuls of the amber liquid. Feeling a little nauseous then, she capped the cider bottle and slid down amongst the rustling leaves, her hooded head resting on the slight incline at the base of the tree. She would wait for a bit and then swallow more pills. Heaving a deep sigh of relief and resignation, she let her body relax into the ground. Dressed for the winter's night in her thick blue cord trousers, a red sweater which her mother had knitted for her and her three quarter length woollen coat with its attached hood, she soon began to feel warmth creeping into her chilled bones, the leafy blanket provided adding insulation and the oak's huge roots protecting her from even the slightest draught. An inner warmth and peace swept through her as she snuggled down, the damp moss and fallen foliage exuding a musty, earthy aroma.

It was a good night to die; all the arrangements had gone according to plan, the money for her outstanding month's rent was sitting in an envelope propped up by a glass on the table in her room. Inside the envelope too was a suicide note, thanking Mrs. Maltby for all her support over the last year. It was only fair that Mrs. Maltby knew the truth. She had been a pillar of support and kindness and she should feel no responsibility for what was about to happen.

Even the elements seemed to be supportive of her resolve, providing a background symphony as the high winds buffeted the trees, causing them to creak and groan. The sleety rain had increased and was now pelting the ground outside her sylvan resting place. Leaves rustled around her, twigs cracked and the intertwined branches of the trees wrestled and jostled noisily. It was pitch black all around her but occasionally a shaft of moonlight penetrated the thick canopy overhead, illuminating briefly the intricate mosaic of bejewelled spiders' webs spanning adjacent branches, sparkling decoratively where raindrops were captured in the delicate handiwork. Then the tunnel of blackness extending up to the sky was like a kaleidoscope of sparkling colours leading up to the very top. It was after midnight and the sky was dark now. Only the marbled moon and a few intrepid, cheeky stars peeped intermittently through the canopy and twinkled at her, as if beckoning to her, drawing her up to some paradisiacal afterlife. The rain had started early in the evening with gentle drops spattering the pavements, but as the darkness descended it had escalated to a heavy downpour and was now falling steadily outside the confines of the trees. But here she was-dry, under the thick umbrella provided by the ancient oak's branches, and sparse autumnal foliage. In any event, getting wet was not really a significant issue at this time.

She sighed deeply, gazing up at the treetops. There was a gentle rustling noise as the variegated leaves wafted around in the breeze and small nocturnal creatures foraged for a night time snack, but there were no other extraneous noises to distract or intrude. It was a beautiful and peaceful place, a perfect place to die. People would say that it was here, that Nicky Partington's body was found, amidst the fallen leaves on the woodland floor.

Content now, at one with nature, her thoughts began to drift. There had never been any difficulty in choosing this way out and no problem about the execution of the deed. No-one really cared whether she lived or died, least of all herself. She should have died at the scene of the accident a year ago, along with her parents and her brother, Patrick. She was never in any doubt about that. She belonged with them. The reunion with her family had just been delayed but that would be remedied tonight.

She slithered deeper between the gnarled roots of the great tree, enveloped by the quilt of reddish and gold leaves, unwavering and resolute, ready to complete her mission.

Her final resting place was a small clearing, surrounded by majestic old trees, many now losing their foliage in the October chill. It was located at the top of Mansion Hill, a desolate spot on the outskirts of the town of Edgerley. It was a place she had selected a few months previously, an unfrequented and secluded hideaway, free from intrusion, away from the well-trodden public footpath through the wood. It was the 30th October 1995, the anniversary of the accident, one year ago exactly to the day. Yet, it seemed like yesterday to Nicky, her memories acute and painful still. She could so easily conjure up the image of her mother who, that night, was wearing a beige cable sweater, her short wavy grey hair tidily brushed back off her pretty face. Nicky remembered so vividly her mother's smile, as she turned towards the back seat of the car where her son and daughter sat, concentrating on the game. Her father, whose strong profile was etched so clearly on her memory, focused on the road ahead, both hands firmly holding the wheel. It was late and raining; visibility was not good, the spray from passing traffic obscuring the road ahead but her father was a careful driver and had slowed to a safe speed. They were playing the number plate game, in which each player took it in turn to make up an acronym to fit the letters or numbers on the passing cars. There had been FPA 693, the Family Planning Association and 693 squadron unite, her brother, Patrick's contribution, then NFR 512, five hundred and twelve Not for Resuscitation, from her mother, and then Nicky contrived for SHP 005, Sherlock Holmes's pipe and smoke rings to follow. They approached a large roundabout and her father stopped at the thick, white line on the road, awaiting the passage of vehicles coming from his right. They were all laughing as Patrick had reeled off for MWF 1, my wife's the fat one, and trying to make out the letters on a passing van when suddenly they were aware that a huge lorry was hurtling uncontrollably and at great speed, across the lanes of the roundabout, crashing into unsuspecting cars in its path and heading straight towards them. Looking over his shoulder, her father searched frantically for a way to manoeuvre out of the path of the oncoming monster and did succeed in pulling away into a ditch at the side of the road, but in the last few seconds, the lorry turned its great evil bulk in an unexpected change of direction, plunging with all its terrible weight and force into their car.

She had regained consciousness in Edgerley General Hospital two days later where medical and nursing staff had fought magnificently and tirelessly to save her life. Her battered body was swathed in bandages, the white cocoon of dressings punctuated by intravenous drips, drains and metal rods splinting her broken arm and leg. Bleeding in her chest necessitated an emergency operation to stem the flow, and shortly afterwards, an operation on her abdomen was performed to deal with further bleeding in her pelvis. Her survival had been a matter of touch and go.

During the first few days of her admission, she was anaesthetised in Intensive Care and unaware of the heroic efforts, which were being made to preserve her life, and later, when she was stable and able to breathe for herself, she could barely speak. It was almost ten days later, when, in answer to her questions, the doctors told her that, sadly, her parents and her brother had all been killed outright at the scene of the accident. Death must have come instantaneously for them, she was told. She had been lucky, they said, that she had been thrown from the vehicle during the violent collision, landing in a field nearby. Passing motorists had tried to help her until the paramedics arrived and whisked her off for emergency care.

It had taken months before she was on the road to recovery from her near-fatal injuries. The constant flurry of white coats around her gradually diminished as she made steady progress. Physiotherapists embarked on a rigorous programme with her to restore movement in her damaged limbs and with it, her independence.

In the days that followed, she had a number of visitors. A lawyer came to advise her of her financial situation. Her father had been in the process of selling one house and purchasing another. The sale fell through, debts had been incurred and after all had been settled, there was little money remaining for her. The kindly man asked if he could do anything to help her and so she asked him to contact the university to let them know that she would not be able to continue with her degree course, which she had barely begun.

A pleasant lady from the Social Services came to let her know that she would be entitled to some disability benefits and that they would assist in finding a suitable place for her to stay since her old house had been sold and she was, in effect, homeless.

The friendly hospital chaplain visited regularly, encouraged her to thank God for saving her life and tried to convince her that clearly she had some divinely selected job to do. In due time, *He* would convey, in *His* own way, exactly what *He* required of her, even if that was not apparent to her just yet. He had been adamant and so well intentioned. The Lord would show her the way; she should just be patient and wait for a sign.

She leaned up for support on her elbow, swallowed down another handful of tablets with the aid of the cider, lay back again, gathering another pile of papery leaves over her body, and resumed her reveries.

The depression which followed the accident was a natural reaction, they said. Time is a great healer, they said, and in due course, she would snap out of this state of mind and regain her zest for life. They had certainly tried hard to lift her spirits and towards the end of her hospitalisation, with no improvement in her inexorable depressive state, she affected an outward patina of self assurance, strength and even happiness, which belied her inner turmoil but gave her carers some false gratification that she was responding to their efforts.

In due course, a room was found for her in a grand old multi-storey terraced house on Chalmers Street, close to the town centre. There were five leased rooms in the old building, all provided at reasonable charge by the owner, Mrs. Phyllis Maltby, an elderly widow who, herself, lived on the premises on the first floor. She was reputed to be a kindly, caring person who provided basic and inexpensive accommodation, suitable for those with low incomes, and from time to time, she assisted the Social Services by accommodating someone in need of a little special support. Here, Nicky would meet other people and begin to get her life back together, they said.

The house at 23 Chalmers Street had an impressive entrance with nine deep steps up to the spacious foyer and a supporting wrought iron railing at each side. Nicky's room was on the second floor, up a further fourteen steps.

In the first few months, just out of hospital, it was a major struggle for Nicky to climb the stairs up and down every day, even with the help of the banisters and railings, and she did ask Social Services if they could find a room on the ground floor somewhere, but they told her that inexpensive accommodation was hard to find in the town and encouraged her to persevere in this house where Mrs. Maltby would help her if she was in difficulties. It would be good for her to use her muscles and it would get easier in time, they said. The room itself was quite generous as regards space with, at one end, an integral kitchen area with a microwave and single electric hob where she could make simple meals and at the other end an en suite bathroom, all neat and clean. It was warm and she had privacy.

During the following weeks, she was occupied with more physiotherapy sessions and clinic appointments. She had had no time to enlist with a new GP in this town although it was something the hospital had encouraged her to do at her earliest convenience.

The daily struggles with the stairs gradually did become easier, as predicted, and as she became stronger, and coped with the meagre allowances, she had come to know the other tenants in the building. The ground or basement area was used for storage. On the first floor, in addition to Mrs. Maltby, stayed an elderly widowed lady called Mrs. Rose Parkins, an octogenarian who was confined to her room on account of previous strokes and severe arthritis. Mrs. Parkins seemed to have daily visitors, district nurses, meals on wheels and attentive do-gooders from her church, always bearing gifts of candy, books and flowers, but she enjoyed having other visitors dropping in. Nicky occasionally knocked on her door and entered, to say 'hi' and to offer Mrs. Parkins any help she might want. Here was someone with greater physical problems than she had. The old lady always welcomed her, never tired of her company and listened eagerly to any news she might have. Mrs. Parkins always seemed to save a small task especially for Nicky to do, whether it was a letter that required posting or some item of clothing that needed attention or perhaps a photograph which she particularly wanted to find in the back of a drawer. Nicky was sorry for the old lady confined to her room, dependent on visitors and was pleased to help. In the room above Nicky's, lived a young couple, Gemma and Andy Symington, both of whom went out to work every day and were scarcely ever in evidence during the week. Even at weekends, they were occupied with shopping, visiting friends and relatives and so Nicky knew very little about them, although they exchanged pleasantries when they passed on the stairs.

Another couple stayed in the room opposite the Symingtons on the top floor, Marion Wood and Steven Beattie. Extrovert and friendly, they had invited Nicky for supper on several occasions. Marion was a secretary in a building society office and Steven was employed selling double glazing units. They were always cheery and happy, always looking forward to something. Whether it was a holiday or promotion or getting married, they always seemed to be preoccupied with the forthcoming events in their lives. Nicky liked the couple, although their perpetual exuberance was somewhat wearing when she herself had nothing to look forward to. She didn't burden them with her woes either as she felt she could not intrude too much into their busy schedules.

In the room opposite Nicky, stayed a single man aged 45, Calum Masson who was recovering from a nervous breakdown and kept himself very much to himself. She did make an effort to engage him in conversation from time to time but with little success. Indeed, he seemed self absorbed, shy and retiring and did not express any interest in getting to know Nicky, beyond polite exchanges in passing. On occasion, he would open up and answer her questions but the events which had conspired to elicit the breakdown were not imparted to Nicky and she felt no curiosity or interest in the matter, having enough problems of her own without taking on board those of a complete stranger.

Mrs. Maltby proved to be all that Social Services had painted her to be, kind and thoughtful with an innate desire to help everybody. Since the entrance to her flat was adjacent to the main door, she invariably left it ajar and would emerge fairly regularly to have a friendly word with her tenants as they came and went on their daily business.

From time to time, she would invite one or other into her cosy apartment and press tea and cakes upon them, as she enquired how things were going. She had taken a great maternal interest in Nicky from the beginning, was well aware of her life shattering and near death experience, having been appraised by the Social Services, and regularly caught her for a chat to ensure that all was well. Mrs. Maltby encouraged her to talk about her family and her future, frequently making use of the phrase '*It will all work out in the end*'. Nicky didn't want to talk about her family as this stirred up the worst memories and she was of the opinion that things did not work themselves out. Someone had to work them out. Nevertheless she liked Mrs. Maltby, trusted her and had genuine respect for her. If she did need help, she was certain that Mrs. Maltby would do whatever she could to put things right. The problem was that Nicky felt that she had failed to pull herself out of the depths of despair, that somehow it was her own fault and that there were too many things wrong in her life to put right. She could not impose on her landlady.

Nicky knew that she had received a great deal of help from a variety of sources, over the last year and perhaps she should have pulled herself together, overcome her problems and resumed a normal life, but she had known from the day she had heard the tragic news of her family, that she would never rally. Her body had healed but her mind would not, could not. As far as she was concerned, it was all over; she had no-one and nothing, no reason to live.

Groggy now, and fumbling awkwardly in her basket, she pulled out another handful of pills from the packets, dropped a few in the leaves and prepared to swallow the rest, when, somewhere in the depths of her clouded brain, she registered a change in the level of the woodland orchestral sounds and thought that she heard an engine noise in the distance. She knew that there was a small airfield at Channing's, a small village situated a few miles south of Edgerley, a place used for military purposes, and occasionally a small plane or helicopter would be seen in the vicinity. It was risky for a plane out in this weather, she thought, and at first, she paid little heed, dismissing it as a small aircraft, but then as the drone became clearer and began to sound more like a car engine, she registered the sound but still dismissed it since she knew that there was no road up to the wood, only a muddy farm track which ran alongside the perimeter and used only rarely by farm vehicles on their way to or from Standing Farm on the other side of the hill. She was confident that the vehicle would turn off soon, and the noise would recede. Yet, still, the purring of the engine seemed to become louder and louder until it was decidedly unwelcome and frankly intrusive. Try as she may, she could no longer ignore it.

2

Compelled to investigate the unwelcome noise, she reluctantly heaved her weary body up the tree trunk, and turned her head shakily in the perceived direction of the vehicle, straining her eyes in the gloom, to see what was going on. There were no car lights although the engine noise had been quite close but as she listened, and peered through the darkness, she heard the sound of a car door opening and realised that the vehicle had stopped, the engine cut and the lights were out.

Whatever was happening was being done furtively and suspiciously. She had no interest in the goings on and just longed to lie down in peace. This was an unwelcome and unexpected interruption to her plans and she hoped that the vehicle would simply turn round and disappear.

Straining to see, she could just discern the shape of a long, dark car. A tall man was standing by the driver's door. He was wearing a dark coat with the collar upturned to protect him from the high wind and driving rain but his head was bare. Then the passenger door opened. A girl emerged. She was carrying a large box. She walked towards the woods and suddenly alarm bells rang in Nicky's mind, as she realized that she was in danger of being discovered. Anxiously, she watched as the girl, of slight build and with a pony tail which bobbed up and down, walked into the trees. Nicky could hear snivelling and after a while she realized that the girl was crying. As the footsteps approached, Nicky kept absolutely still, flattening herself against the rough tree trunk, trying to meld into it, increasingly apprehensive that her hiding place would be discovered and she would have a lot of explaining to do. But eventually, aware that someone was pushing back the tree branches a few yards away, and heading off in a different direction, she relaxed a little. Nicky felt light headed, her knees threatened to give way and she longed to lie down in the leaves but she daren't make a noise until the intruders had left so she continued to press her body to the tree leaning on it for support. Leaves rustled and twigs snapped as the girl made her way through the dense undergrowth and continuously, there was the sound of sobbing. Time seemed to stand still, it seemed to take the girl an inordinately long time to do what she was doing but finally the rustling of the leaves ceased and the girl stumped back out of the wood. Nicky could hear louder crying now as she walked back to the car.

When the girl emerged from the wood, she was no longer carrying the box. She exchanged no words with the man. They didn't even share a glance and as the girl opened the passenger door and stepped inside, he looked all around as if checking that there was no-one else about before he got in. It was clear that they did not want anyone to witness their actions. After a few seconds, the car made a u-turn and began to roll slowly and silently down the muddy incline; the engine had not been triggered and there were no lights apparent. Nicky's befuddled brain was struggling to comprehend what she had seen and found that she had been holding her breath as the events unfolded.

As the car rolled off slowly down the muddy slope, a shaft of moonlight illuminated the rear of the vehicle for an instant. Even in her somewhat hazy state of awareness, she glimpsed the number plate- ESG 492.

Reflexly, she thought *Ever so Good,* one of her

mother's favourites and then a few seconds later, she murmured *1492, Columbus sailed the ocean blue,* just take one away and you have 492. She smiled cynically to herself, thinking that she was indeed in the process of taking one away, so her acronym was quite appropriate. She imagined that her mother and her brother would have approved of her effort for the final game.

Nicky slipped down the tree again to rest on her side in the thick bed of leaves, trying to regain her dreamlike peace but her thoughts were confused and unsettled now. She tried to re-focus on her days at Chalmers Street, to re-live the conversations with the other tenants but it was no use. She couldn't help thinking about the strange interruption. It seemed very odd for two people to come up to Mansion Hill in the middle of the night to leave a box. The deliberate attempts to minimize noise and lights made it all the more strange and suspicious. She tried to tell herself that it didn't matter any more, it was no concern of hers, but the niggling thoughts would not go away. Whatever it was, she decided that it had to be illegal and certainly something that they wished to conceal from others. It was none of her business, she told herself. Now comfortable and almost asleep, she dismissed the whole episode and let herself surrender to the soporific effect of the pills. But then it occurred to her that the box might be a drop of drugs or money and someone else might come along to pick it up. It was worrying to think that someone else might come to search this part of the wood and, although on the verge of sleep, she knew that she would not settle again until she had satisfied her curiosity and investigated the contents of the box. Reluctantly, she resolved to locate it, examine it and then return to complete her mission. It would be a short diversion but would rid her brain of the distraction. There might be a simple explanation, that the family pet had died, but then why didn't they bury it in the garden? Perhaps the cat had delivered a huge unwanted litter of kittens. but then, why not go to the vet? No, there was more than that going on.

She heaved herself up and hanging on to tree branches for support as she picked her way to the place where she had seen the girl, she felt queasy and lightheaded. Tripping over a straggling root, she fell awkwardly landing flat on her stomach. The impact made her nauseous but she pressed on to find the box. It wasn't immediately obvious; the girl had hidden it under a large rhododendron bush and had smothered it with piles of leaves for camouflage. Bending under bushes and reeling giddily, Nicky eventually found the box and pulled it out of its hiding place, brushing the leaves from the top.   It carried something solid but wasn't very heavy. She knelt down beside it and listened. There was no sound from the box, no mewling or whimpering. She would just have to open it up and see what was inside.

The cardboard box was about 2ft square, with its lid neatly folded into place, not tied or sealed, merely closed. She gently pulled the lid apart, teasing out one section after another. In the pitch darkness, she could see nothing inside but blackness. She dragged it further away from the overhanging bushes and waited for a shaft of light to help define the contents. She felt sick again and hoped the spasm would pass but another quickly followed and she could not control it. Turning away from the box, she vomited copiously into the undergrowth, her stomach painful and cramping. The spasms continued for a few minutes, draining her of every ounce of energy. She knelt wearily beside the container. The overwhelming sleepiness signified that some of the medicine had already been absorbed but would it be enough? Remembering that she still had another two packets of pills in the basket, she collected herself and concentrated again on the box's contents.

At last, pulling the box even further away from the large bush, she glimpsed what lay within it. It looked like a doll, a male doll, naked and still. It wasn't at all what she had expected and she rubbed her eyes in disbelief. She couldn't understand why the girl would secret away a doll in the woods. Could it be stuffed full of drugs or money? As she stared inside the box, it occurred to her that there was something odd about the doll. It had an umbilical cord and this, tied off with a piece of yellow ribbon. Could it be a baby, a dead baby that had been hidden here? The infant lay as before, unmoving and silent. It was hard to imagine why someone had chosen to dispose of a dead baby in this way. It had to have been an unwanted child, a concealed pregnancy but why, in this day and age of easy morals and an *anything goes* society, did this have to happen? She gasped incredulously and felt tears accumulate in her eyes as she gently put her hand in to touch the child. He had curly, dark hair which felt smooth and soft to her touch. He was cold. She gently prised open the small fingers and wondered at the perfection of the tiny hands. Suddenly the baby shivered. She blinked and peered into the box, thinking that her eyes were playing tricks on her. She was certain that he had shivered and watching spellbound, she waited for some other sign of life. The baby began to wriggle in the container waving his small arms about jerkily. He was alive! Shocked by this revelation, Nicky forgot the heaving cramps in her stomach and lifted the baby gently into her arms, cuddling him to her chest, aware that he was much too cold and in need of warmth and love. She unbuttoned her jacket and pressing the baby into her warm red sweater, she refastened the coat to protect him. His face was nuzzling into her neck, making wet sounds, and his small fists clutched on to her sweater as though his very life depended on her. The tears flowed down her face and she found herself having feelings that she had not experienced before.

"What on earth brings you out here in dead of night? You should be tucked up, all cosy and warm in your cot," she whispered, gently cuddling the child.

"Why have you been brought here? Was that your Mummy in the car? Maybe she thought you were dead but even so, why would she put you in a box and bring you up here? She could have gone to the hospital to get help. Why here?" she asked the child.

The baby responded by making snuffling noises at her neck.

'What is your name, I wonder, little one?' she asked.

Her thought processes were now quite incoherent but somehow a maternal instinct was kicking in and she did recognise that this child was a priority and must be kept warm and fed at all costs. Her own well-thought out plans seemed to have suddenly evaporated as something else took their place in her brain. Her plans would have to go on the back burner for the time being, she realised. There was an obligation, indeed a moral duty, to ensure that this child was safe from harm. The reason for his rejection was a mystery. The same thoughts went through her mind again and again. *Why did these people want to murder a baby? Could it be that the girl had mistakenly thought the baby was dead? Surely they had not deliberately planned to terminate his life! Why would anybody secret the body in the woods on Mansion Hill in the small hours of the morning?* It was all incomprehensible to Nicky.

She stumbled back to the oak tree, supporting her small bundle with one hand, brushing branches away with the other, and then sat between the roots again, cradling the child, kissing his cheeks.

'Well, I will have to call you something, won't I?' she said, starting with the first letter of the alphabet, Allan,

Archie, Andrew,... No, let's try B... Bobby. Billy, Bertie, Barnaby,... no...how about Calum, Charlie, Connor, Colin...Oh I know, Columbus! I'll call you Columbus Partington,' she told the boy, her mind recalling her previous thought processes in figuring an acronym to the letters of the number plate.

Looking down at the baby, she smiled to herself and then said, 'Well, that's a bit too much, isn't it, but his first name was Christopher. Christopher, yes, Christopher Partington, that sounds just right. From this moment on, you will be Christopher Partington.'

The baby was gnawing his little hands hungrily and getting progressively distressed and she knew instinctively what she had to do.

Righting the wicker basket and wrapping the baby in her long, blue scarf, she gently placed him along the bottom of the container, pulling the woollen garment over his head as a protection from the cold night air. The basket proved to be exactly the right length to accommodate his small frame. The pill packets and cider bottle, she wedged at his feet and rising unsteadily from her intended deathbed, she yawned widely and began to make her way out of the wood.

3

It had been a six mile walk up to this hill and at the time, feeling purposeful and full of desperate thoughts, it had not seemed very far, but now here she was, hurtling erratically down the slope, splashing in puddles, slipping on muddy stones, her precious cargo held in a vice-like grip. The return journey had not been in the equation and now thoughts of what she was doing and how she would manage, flooded her befuddled brain.

She would have to go to the police. They would be able to find the owner of the car with her help and it shouldn't be too hard to find the people responsible for the attempted murder of this child. This was definitely a punishable offence. Of course that would mean she had to explain what she was doing up the hill in the middle of the night. She smelled of drink and couldn't even walk in a straight line. Would they believe her story? Was it illegal to attempt suicide? What would Mrs. Maltby think of all of this? She couldn't answer her own questions and felt giddy just thinking about it all. She would have to think this all over later when her mind was clearer. The immediate goal was to get back to Chalmers Street as quickly as she could and see that the baby was warmed up and fed. Nothing else mattered now. The other issues could wait.

It did seem to be a long way home to warmth and food for the infant. As she ran down the hill she was so light headed that she almost fell headlong and had to pull up and concentrate on walking more carefully, taking care to avoid the deep ruts in the rough track. At the bottom of the hill, she finally reached the main road, and fumbled in her coat pocket to see if she had any money. There were a few coins so she kept an eye open for a late bus as she hurried along the deserted streets. From time to time she tried to run but her coordination was less than ideal and she weaved about the pavement in a drunken-like state, slowing down, or stopping occasionally, and then marching on as quickly as she could, her mind racing with thoughts of what she ought to do-, whether to go to the police or not, how to get nappies and food when she was penniless, what to do for the best- for Christopher and for herself. Her head ached and her feet felt leaden. What she would do for a cup of tea. The envelope with a month's rent was sitting on her table. If she could get that, there was an all-night chemist a block away from Chalmers Street. There, she could doubtless get all Christopher needed for a day or two. After that, she had no idea how they would manage. She would have to take it one day at a time.

Half way home, a blue bus rounded the corner. There was no bus stop but she signalled wildly to catch the driver's attention and luckily, he stopped. The automatic doors slammed open and she stepped gratefully aboard into the warmth, where only one other passenger, a young dishevelled man, sat, slouched against the window, almost asleep. The middle-aged, Asian driver eyed her suspiciously and she suddenly realised what a sight she must look after lying in the leaves and then running down in the mud and wet. She must look very odd. Luckily the baby was quiet and the driver would not know what her basket contained. She thanked him for stopping, dropped the correct coinage into the box and made her way to a seat, placing the basket on her knees. The warmth and comfort of the bus was a welcome relief and soporific. Her jacket smelled like a wet dog and she longed to get dried off. She glimpsed at the baby and saw that he was sound asleep, wrapped in the woollen scarf. After a short ride, she alighted close to Chalmers Street, and jogged along to number 23 where she quickly climbed the nine steps to the front door. Mrs. Maltby's sitting room light was on even at this hour. She was a light sleeper but this was one night when Nicky did not want to stop for a chat. It worried her that Mrs. Maltby might have been up to her room where the envelope containing her month's rent and suicide note had been left propped up against a small glass on the table. It would be embarrassing and awkward if she had to explain what that was all about, but worse, much worse, how would she explain the baby's appearance? Suddenly she felt guilty- guilty of worrying Mrs. Maltby and letting her down, guilty of being in possession of a child who obviously didn't belong to her, guilty of sneaking into the house like a thief in the night.

Cautiously turning the Yale, Nicky silently unlocked the front door, and slunk inside, stepping on the edge of the stairs to avoid the predictable squeaks of the floorboards. Mrs. Maltby hadn't heard her. She reached her own room and quietly opened it, shutting the door behind her, placing the basket on her neatly made bed and quickly looking at the table to see if her note was still there. She heaved a sigh of relief. It was still there, apparently unopened.

Christopher was asleep, swathed in the warm scarf and looking angelic in repose. The central heating radiators were on, still hot and making occasional clanking sounds, and so she placed the basket gently near one of them to ensure that the baby felt its warmth. She quickly tore open the envelope and pocketed the money. The all-night chemist, Allen's, would be open and was just one block away. She would be quicker if she went by herself but what if the baby cried while she was out? That would be hard to explain and so she decided that she would have to take him with her.

In the bathroom she glimpsed her wan face. Suddenly feeling extremely thirsty, she filled a glass with water and drank eagerly. There was nothing in the room to eat or drink since she had cleared out the fridge and the cupboard before leaving earlier that evening, with plans never to return. Even her clothes, apart from those she was wearing, had been tossed into the local dumpster. She had nothing. She drank another two glasses of water and then, picking up the basket again, quietly closed the door behind her as she set off for the pharmacy.

The cool drink and the sense of urgency seemed to have awakened her senses and she was beginning to feel less confused as she hurried along toward the lights of the store. It was raining lightly now but the large, wet droplets dripping down her cheeks were of little concern to her as her mind raced with thoughts of the night's strange events. Passing a rubbish bin awaiting the morning's uplift, she tossed the pills and the cider bottle inside.

When she arrived at the pharmacy and pushed through the large glass doors, the place was quiet save for some romantic background music and she could see no other customer at this late hour. The uniformed security man, sitting relaxing in a corner with his foot propped up on a large crate, and reading the sports page of a newspaper, looked up enquiringly at the latecomer as she entered and then nodded, acknowledging her presence. The young girl behind the counter was busy filing her nails and looked up only with casual interest as Nicky walked along the aisles. She found the baby section and picking up a bottle, teat, a packet of formula mixture designated for newborn babies and a pack of disposable nappies, she approached the desk and placed the items on the counter.

'We are not really open for anything except emergency

medication at this time of night,' said Angela, the pretty, dark haired pharmacist, bearing a name badge and attired in a pristine white uniform, stretched rather tightly across her ample midriff.

'I'm sorry,' said Nicky, 'but it is a sort of emergency. Please can I have these things?' she asked, pleadingly.

Angela could see that the girl looked sick, pale and drawn and was in some clear distress so she obligingly rang up the purchases on the till, without asking any more questions. It wasn't wise to confront customers late at night. You never knew what could happen.

'I see that there is an offer on the babygros,' remarked Nicky, looking longingly at the *two for one* package of blue and white garments, propped up beside the till.

'Yes, it's a good offer. That's the last set, actually. Do you want them?' Angela asked.

'Yes, please,' said Nicky, rummaging in her pocket for more money.

Angela wrapped up the items neatly and placed them in a plastic carrier bag, smiling as she handed them over to the girl. Pregnant herself, Angela couldn't help but wonder how such an emergency could occur at this hour, after three in the morning, requiring the basic essentials for a baby. Tomorrow, she would have to explain to her boss, her reasons for allowing this customer to buy the goods during an emergency service evening. However, she knew that Hannah Leicester, her boss and Martha Hoe, the deputy, would not question her judgment. They would understand and would have done the same thing in the circumstances, she was sure. In fact, she thought that Martha, who could not resist the opportunity to be of assistance to anyone, would probably have asked the girl how she could help.

Delighted with her purchases, Nicky thanked the girl, gently put the bag at Christopher's feet and ran all the way back to the house.

She hurriedly entered the building, doing her best to be quiet and had almost reached the bottom stair when a voice called out, 'Is that you, Nicky?'

Her heart in her mouth, Nicky put the wicker basket by the stairs and went over to answer Mrs. Maltby's call, hoping that it would be a short conversation. 'Yes, Mrs. Maltby, it is me. I apologise for disturbing you so late. I have been out with friends and lost track of the time. How can I help you?' she asked.

'Oh, you haven't disturbed me at all, Nicky. I am still wide-awake and have very little chance of sleep tonight,' she said, appearing fully dressed in her dark green, woollen outfit and casual slippers.

'What is the matter?' asked Nicky, noticing how stressed she seemed.

'I have had some bad news and I need to talk to you about it. Can you spare me a few minutes before you turn in for the night? I realise it is late and I am asking a lot of you. You must be very tired. I suppose it could wait until morning but I would so like to sort things out as soon as possible,' she added, running her hands through her greying hair.

'Yes, I'm happy to come and talk with you. Would you mind if I just changed out of my damp coat and dried my hair a bit? It is raining and I don't want to sit around and catch a chill,' Nicky said, hoping that she could get back quickly to deal with Christopher, before becoming embroiled in Mrs. Maltby's troubles.

'Of course, my dear. That's very kind of you. Do take as much time as you need and just drop in whenever you are ready. I'll leave the door open for you. It will be a great relief to talk to you. I do appreciate it, you have no idea,' Mrs. Maltby said, patting Nicky's arm.

Nicky grabbed the basket and raced up the stairs. She could hear snuffling little cries as Christopher tried to make his presence felt. He had tossed the woollen garment aside and was wriggling about in the basket, sucking on a piece of wicker which was loose and jutting out of the woven material. He was obviously starving, poor, wee soul. She tossed her sodden jacket onto a chair, and carried the basket into the kitchen. Here she quickly read the instructions on the formula packet, prepared a bottle, and tested the temperature of the liquid carefully as she removed it from the microwave. She had no experience of dealing with babies and was simply going on instinct.

Picking Christopher up gently, she cradled him in the crook of her left arm and, sitting on the edge of her bed, offered him his very first bottle. At first he tossed his little head about from side to side in a frantic search for the teat and eventually latched on to it and began to feed. Nicky watched the hungry child sucking furiously for a few minutes. Suddenly, he stopped and searched her face with his large eyes, blowing bubbles. She thought her heart would burst with love and tears gathered in her eyes. He began to suck again, his eyes never leaving her face, and she watched him adoringly as the bottle was drained dry. Inexperienced with babies, she tried to recall what mothers did, and lifted him up to her shoulder, patting his back. The reward came almost immediately in the form of a loud burp. With her free hand, she managed to open the packet of nappies and the babygros while holding him and then laid him gently down on her bed where she applied a nappy with as much skill as her inexperience allowed and gently eased a new blue outfit on to his little frame. He had soft dark wavy hair and she pushed it back with her fingers, admiring his beautiful little face. Pulling the pillows and bedspread around him to prevent him from falling off the bed, she went to the bathroom to towel dry her hair and splash some cold water on her face, reluctant to leave her boy but anxious to get back downstairs to see what Mrs.

Maltby was worrying about. Her reflection in the mirror still looked pale and tired and so she rubbed her cheeks vigorously trying to raise some colour before leaving the room. By the time she had finished, Christopher was sound asleep, snug and relaxed, under the covers.

4

'Come in, come in, Nicky,' the landlady said, bustling her plump frame to the door and closing it quietly behind them.

'Sit there by the fire, dear. I've just made a pot of hot tea and there's some of my chocolate cake. Just help yourself,' she said, generously, directing Nicky to a well upholstered armchair by the fireside, in the somewhat over furnished room.

Nicky sat by the open fire, glad to feel the warmth on her body and salivating at the sight of the large slices of cake arranged on a plate in front of her. She hadn't eaten all day and very little on the previous day, saving enough money to pay the rent before she left everything in order. It was tempting to dive in straightaway and demolish the whole plate but she politely restrained herself.

Mrs. Maltby poured two mugs of tea and offered Nicky the milk jug.

'I hope you enjoyed your evening with friends, Nicky. It's good to see you out socializing.'

'Yes it was good,' replied Nicky hoping there were no more questions about her fictitious friends. 'Just went on a bit late.'

'Thank you so much for stopping by. I really need to talk over my problems and especially with you, Nicky. Just you carry on, help yourself now, dear, while I tell you all about my day,' she said, pushing the chocolate cake in Nicky's direction.

'Thank you,' said Nicky, taking a large slice, her mouth watering.

'I wonder if you remember last summer when my sister, Marjorie, came over from New Zealand to stay?' Mrs. Maltby began, sitting herself on a well stuffed chair opposite Nicky.

'Yes, of course,' answered Nicky, trying to swallow a large mouthful of the delicious cake. 'A very nice lady. I spoke to her on several occasions.'

'Well, today, I received a phone call from Carol Kingdon, my sister's neighbour in Auckland. Marjorie had a stroke yesterday, quite a serious one by all accounts.' Mrs. Maltby's voice started to break and Nicky could see how upset she was at this news.

'Oh, I am sorry,' said Nicky, polishing off another mouthful and trying to take in this development.

'She has lost the power in one side and can't speak, apparently. I asked Carol if I could speak to her but she wasn't able to talk to me at all,' Mrs. Maltby continued, tears beginning to gather at the inner corners of her eyes.

'What a shame! You must be awfully worried about her,' Nicky interjected. 'It is so difficult when you live poles apart.'

'Yes, that is the problem, and so I have decided that I have to go to New Zealand and see her for myself. I may not be able to look after her but I must try. We have only each other now. We both were married once and are now widowed and neither of us has any children so we live for each other now,' she continued, dabbing her eyes with a lace handkerchief. 'I feel very close to her and it would be dreadful if I didn't go to her and then she didn't pull through. I just wouldn't be able to forgive myself.'

Mrs. Maltby slurped a mouthful of hot tea, her hand shaking a little as she held the cup.

'I understand. Of course you must go. You have been

over there before, haven't you?'

'Yes, I've been on two occasions. Marjorie has a lovely home overlooking the beach, just on the outskirts of the town. It's not the long journey I'm concerned about, but of course, if I go, there will be no-one to look after this house and all of the tenants,' she said, with a worried look on her face.

'We're all pretty sensible and get along quite well,' said Nicky reassuringly. 'I'm sure that we can manage to hold the fort while you are away. You shouldn't let that hold you back. We would all help each other.'

'If I do go, I think it will have to be for at least a month, Nicky. With strokes, it's hard to know, isn't it? I expect Marjorie may take weeks to regain her mobility and independence. There's no knowing how long she will be in the hospital but I would like to be there to help her until she can cope again. There's just no way of knowing how long that will take.'

'Don't worry about Chalmers Street. Really, it is more important that you go to your sister. I would be happy to look in on Mrs. Parkins every day,' said Nicky, trying to be helpful, 'I know you keep a close eye on her, so don't you worry about that. We get along quite well and I'm not working so I'm here all the time to see that she has her regular visitors.'

'That's very kind of you, Nicky, I do worry about Rose, but there are lots of little chores which would need to be done. What I was going to propose to you, if you don't mind me making such a proposal, was that you should take over temporarily as landlady. As you are not employed at the moment and everyone else is working, except Mrs. Parkins, of course, and you are also the most sensible and reliable of my tenants, in any event, it occurred to me that you would be the ideal person to take up that position. I have been sitting here all evening writing a list of all the things which would need to be done, and keeping an eye on Mrs. Parkins is top of the list.' Mrs. Maltby paused for a moment, perusing the notes on the paper before her.

'This must sound like a real imposition and I have absolutely no right to ask you to do this. I don't want you to feel that I am using you but you are the only person I can think of, who could help me out,' she added, looking pleadingly at Nicky.

'It really is no bother, Mrs. Maltby. I'll do my best,' said Nicky, thinking that everything ticked over quite steadily and that it wouldn't be too much trouble to chat to all the tenants now and again.

'It would be like having a job, actually, and of course, you would have to be paid in some way. My mind has been working overtime, and I thought that it would be best if you moved into this flat and stayed here while I was away. You would be living here rent free too. It would be a relief for me to know that someone was caring for the flat, able to take all the phone calls and answer the doorbell during the day and so on.'

Nicky suddenly realized what was being proposed and excitement grew within her. To move into this warm flat and to be paid too-that would be a major step forwards for Christopher and herself. She munched the cake and thought about the possibilities of moving into Mrs. Maltby's well maintained flat.

Mrs. Maltby picked up her list of things *to do* and said, 'The electrician is coming next Tuesday to fix that immersion heater in Calum's room and I have arranged for the painter to come on Thursday to start redecorating the hall. It's all in need of freshening up. There's also the mail to sort and take round to everyone each day. Then, Mrs. Buchanan from the Social Services is due a visit. They have to inspect the premises periodically, you know. I have it all written down here. What do you think, Nicky? Is it too much to ask?' she said, laying the paper down and pouring Nicky another mug of tea.

'If that is what you want me to do, I'll gladly do it,' said Nicky, the proposal sounding very appealing to her. 'As you have said, I am free and have no job pending at the moment. It would be good for me to take some responsibility. I'm happy to do this.'

'Oh, you are so good. What a relief it is to know someone reliable will be around! It has been worrying me all evening. If you didn't want to do it, I wouldn't know where to turn. Have more cake, dear. Did you like it? Please eat up.' Mrs. Maltby said, pushing the plate of chocolate cake towards Nicky.

'Thank you,' said Nicky, helping herself to another slice and thinking how wonderfully warm and comfortable she and Christopher would be in Mrs. Maltby's cosy domain. 'When were you thinking of setting off?' she asked, munching the soft moist cake.

'I phoned the travel agent earlier on today and it seems that I could probably go at the end of this week if I am prepared to take a cancellation which has become available. The flight would be leaving London on Saturday night so I would have to leave Edgerley, take the train to Manchester and fly down to Heathrow on Saturday morning. It's all a bit sudden but the sooner the better, really. I told the lady that I would confirm things tomorrow as I had to talk to you and be certain that you would be willing to cover my back.'

'This is Wednesday so you have two whole days to get your bag packed and make the plans. That should be plenty of time,' said Nicky, thinking that she would be rent free and have more money for Christopher.

'Yes, there is time. Oh, my dear, what a great relief to know you will help! Thank you so much.'

Nicky quickly scoffed the cake, drank the remains of

her tea and then rose to return to her charge upstairs.

'You should try to get some rest, Mrs. Maltby. You will have a busy day or two ahead of you, and if you think of anything else for me to do, just add it to your list,' she said.

'Would you drop in tomorrow afternoon to go over things again, Nicky? I may think of something else in the meantime.'

'Yes, I'll come in about 3 pm tomorrow, if that's convenient, and you can tell me how you are getting on with the plans,' she said, wondering how she would ensure that Christopher was settled at that time.

'That would be perfect. I'll know whether or not I have been able to confirm the flights and we can discuss all the details again.'

The thought of seeing Christopher's sweet face, made Nicky run up the stairs again. He was still asleep and lying spread-eagled on the bed, his little arms and legs thrown out from his sides. She couldn't help but smile at the peaceful infant.

'You have brought me luck, Christopher. In two days, we will move downstairs into a lovely home and I will be able to buy you some clothes and toys with the extra money,' she said, kissing his forehead. Looking round her room, she knew that the move would be very easy. Her belongings had all been tossed out over the last few days, as she had anticipated no further need of them and her cupboards were bare. For two days, she would have to keep Christopher quiet and hidden. If Mrs. Maltby knew about the baby, she might have concerns about trusting her with the business and her home.

Still excited about the prospect of being interim landlady and having extra cash, she showered and, wearing the only underclothes she possessed, slipped into bed beside the sleeping child, putting her arm around his small body and feeling the softness of his hair against her cheek.

Tiredness overtook her as she lay reflecting on the massive change in her fortunes over the last few hours, having moved from a desperate state of emptiness and depression, to a position of hope with a job, extra funds and, most of all, someone who needed her, a child of her own. For the first time in an entire year, she fell asleep with a smile on her face. All thoughts of going to the police had evaporated.

5

It was past noon when she awoke the next day, an intermittent gentle thump on her back reminding her of Christopher's presence, and she turned to see the wriggling infant, excitedly flailing all his limbs and pursing his lips in the expression of a kiss. She laughed at his antics and he accentuated his efforts as though he knew that he was the centre of attention. She lifted him up and carried him through to the kitchen, whispering to him affectionately all the time. She made up a bottle of the formula and taking it from the microwave, returned to the bed where, absolutely mesmerised by his every move, she fed the hungry child. His warm little body cuddled into her and she knew that she would hold on to this child with every fibre of her being. Everything seemed to be happening so quickly. Little had she imagined that Mrs. Maltby would entrust the place to her and even pay her for the small amount of work required. She was looking forward to moving into Mrs. Maltby's flat with its warmth and comfort. She showered and dressed again in her blue cords and red sweater, the only clothes she possessed, and settled Christopher safely amidst the pillows and bedspread. It was almost three o'clock.

'Hello, Nicky dear, come on in. I'll just put on the kettle and we can sit by the fire.' Mrs. Maltby greeted her warmly.

Nicky took up the same seat beside the fire where she

had sat on the previous evening, enjoying again the blazing hearth and awaited Mrs. Maltby, who entered a few minutes later with the teapot, mugs and a plate of biscuits on a tray.

'Have you made any progress today?' asked Nicky.

'Indeed, I have, dear,' she said smiling and beginning to pour the hot tea. 'I have purchased my tickets for the trip to Auckland on Saturday night and I have also booked the train up to Manchester on Saturday morning, so I am well ahead with the arrangements. It's all very exciting but at the back of my mind, I am worried about Marjorie. I phoned her neighbour, Carol, this morning and she tells me that she is holding her own, much the same as yesterday. I don't suppose I can ask for much more at this stage.'

'No, but at least she is no worse. I expect Carol has told her that you are coming so she may be trying hard to get better, glad to know that you will be arriving soon,' said Nicky, reassuringly.

'I do hope so,' said Mrs. Maltby, her face reflecting her concern.

'Anyway, you have done well today. It was very lucky that you managed to get a cancellation so soon. Now, have you thought of anything else you would like me to do in your absence?' Nicky offered, accepting the mug of tea and the biscuit proffered.

Yes, there is, Nicky,' Mrs. Maltby answered. 'Tell me, are you familiar with a computer?'

'Yes, I used one through secondary school so I am fairly computer literate. Why do you ask?'

'I have a laptop. It's over there in the bureau,' she said, pointing in the direction of the highly polished writing desk. 'I was wondering if I left that here, could you perhaps keep in touch with me every so often by e-mail? My sister and I regularly e-mail to each other so I can use her machine when I arrive, and I'll give you the address. That way, you could get in touch with me quickly if there was any problem at all.'

'That is a great idea. I can drop you a little message every day or two to reassure you that all is well and to let you know how the painter is progressing and so on.'

'That is just the ticket,' said Mrs. Maltby, looking relieved. 'I can always telephone you and you me, but email is very handy especially when there is a thirteen hour time difference, and if I've forgotten to tell you something, I know that I can get you that way.'

'Yes, that's a very good idea. I didn't know you even had a laptop.'

'Well, I'm no expert but I can do basic things. Now I'm just going to leave the fridge and freezer as they are. There is plenty food and you must just use it up. There's no point in any of it going to waste, dear. I will restock the place when I get back.'

'Thank you. I will not let it go to waste, I can assure you,' Nicky said, trying not to appear excessively pleased although the thought of all that food made her mouth water.

'There is another thing- the jumble sale clothes. I have packed two black bin liners with old clothes for St Martin's jumble sale. Mrs. Carruthers is coming round on Monday evening at six pm to collect that. It's over by the door there- just some clothes I don't use any more. Can you make sure that you are in when she calls?'

'Of course. Have you made a note of that on the list?'

'Yes, it's all there and I have called her to say that you will be here in my absence.'

'I'll definitely be here for her,' said Nicky.

'Now, regarding the newspapers and milk. I get a pint of milk delivered every morning from Grant's and a Telegraph from Watt's the newsagent. I have put some money into two envelopes to pay for these throughout the coming month. We might as well just continue with that arrangement for the few weeks that I am away. If you could pay the delivery boys on Monday morning, that will keep things ticking over. There's no point cancelling for a few weeks. If it turns out to be longer, then we can discuss that.'

'That's fine,' said Nicky, already planning to cancel the paper and milk and keep the money for more important things.

'Now dear, drink up that tea or it will be cold,' said Mrs. Maltby. Everything is falling into place, and I wouldn't be able to do all of this without your help. How very fortunate I am to have you here! What a godsend you are! By the way, I have also put some money in the envelope here for you as payment in the meantime.'

In spite of Nicky's protests that she was happy to do it for nothing, Mrs. Maltby pressed it on her. Tea over, they pored over the laptop for a while, making sure that Nicky was au fait with the machine and the relevant addresses she would need. She was appraised of the times and dates when the painter and electrician would arrive and had a tour of the flat.

'There are two bedrooms, a single and a double one, which I use. Feel free to choose whichever you like. The telephone is by my bedside so it is probably best if you use this one but you must just feel free to do whatever you wish. I know how careful and tidy you are so I have no qualms at all about leaving you in charge,' Mrs. Maltby said confidently.

With all the details discussed, Nicky returned to her flat just in time to hear Christopher's cries. Red in the face and throwing himself about amongst the pillows, it was obvious that he needed a nappy change and more milk so Nicky quickly picked him up, talked soothingly to him and prepared another bottle, hoping that no one else in the house had heard him.

Happily replete again, Christopher was placed on the floor while Nicky ran a shallow bath. She undressed the giggling child and holding him tightly, immersed his firm little body into the warm water, enjoying his obvious delight at this new adventure, his little legs kicking vigorously. With the baby clean and dressed again, she sat on the bed, talking to him about the plans for Saturday, their pending move, the kitchen full of food and the warm fire.

'There's a nice big double bed and in the sitting room a lovely warm fire. Best of all, the fridge is full of food and for the first time in ages, I'm going to eat properly. I'm going to cancel the milk and the papers so we will have more money to spend on your wardrobe and your food. I'm going to take care of you, Christopher,' she promised, cradling the sleepy youngster in her arms, and kissing his brow.

The following day passed quickly and Saturday arrived. Then, a little tearfully, Mrs. Maltby set off in a taxi for her long haul to New Zealand. Within the hour, Nicky and Christopher moved downstairs to the comfortable and well-appointed accommodation which had been left in her care. It had taken only minutes to collect her few belongings and the items which she had already purchased for Christopher. She laid the little boy on the living room floor in front of the fireplace, while she explored the rooms, opened the cupboards and smiled at her great good fortune.

In the kitchen she found plenty of food. In the fridge, she found shelves full of fresh meat, salad, bread, butter, milk and eggs as if Mrs. Maltby had deliberately stocked up for her. Having eaten little in the last two days, Nicky set about preparing a large plate of ham sandwiches, adding slices of tomato and layers of crispy lettuce to each. She made a pot of tea, placed everything on a tray and carried it through to the small table by the fireside where she could enjoy the warmth of the fire, the plentiful food and, at the same time, watch Christopher as he rolled around happily, sucking the collar of his babygro and making soft baby sounds. She hadn't been as happy as this for a long time and had almost forgotten how good life could be.

Contemplating the flat and the duties required of her, she planned to take her responsibilities very seriously and made a mental note to pop in to see Mrs. Parkins that very night, to reassure the old lady that all was well. She had counted out all the money for the milkman and the newspaper boy and would cancel these deliveries on Monday, saving her additional funds. She began to formulate a list of things which Christopher would need, a pram, a cot and a bath of his own as well as clothes and toys. Acting as locum landlady was a most fortuitous occurrence and it had presented itself at an opportune moment. Her mind was filled with plans to acquire all the essential items for the child and in so doing, she would be making a new beginning for herself. No thought of taking the child to the police or to the social services entered her head.

At the end of the month, she knew that she would have to review her situation and seek out new ways and means of continuing to accrue more money and security for them both, but in the meantime she was going to make the most of her new circumstances.

6

As the days followed, Nicky kept busy popping in to see Mrs. Parkins, sorting out the mail, accompanying the electrician to fix Calum's immersion heater and making tea for the two painters who were busy redecorating the large hall. Mrs. Carruthers came to collect the clothes for the jumble sale but not before Nicky had raked through the bags and removed two warm sweaters which she found quite suitable for her own paltry wardrobe.

Every evening she sat with the laptop and wrote to Mrs. Maltby, itemising the work that had been done and reassuring her that things were ticking over without any difficulty.

Mrs. Maltby responded regularly, advising Nicky of her sister's progress and the wonderful weather in New Zealand, which allowed her to sit out on the deck and enjoy long afternoons in the sun.

A week after Nicky's move into Flat 1, Mrs. Maltby wrote to say that she had decided to ask the painters to proceed with the repainting of Nicky's room too, since it was vacant at the present time and this provided a good chance to carry out the work without inconveniencing anybody. She was also considering extending her stay with her sister as Nicky was obviously coping admirably and her sister, still in hospital, was making slow progress. She thought that she might delay her return until the New Year if Nicky didn't mind. Nicky was sorry for Mrs. Maltby but also relieved to have an extension of her comfortable status, having as yet, not decided on a future plan of action.

She made an effort to catch the other tenants as they left or entered the building, to ensure that they could convey any difficulties or concerns to her and to let them know about Mrs. Maltby's plans. It was on one of her encounters with Marion Woods and Steven Beattie, that she learned that Marion was pregnant. The couple was, as usual, in a state of high excitement, thrilled with the prospect of the new baby and was discussing finding another place to stay, preferably on the ground level, where it would be easier to use a pram and it would be less arduous to bring in shopping and the paraphernalia of young babies.

Nicky was happy for the couple and offered warm congratulations but was sorry to hear that they would move away as they were the most congenial of the tenant group. She so wanted to share her baby stories with Marion but had to keep them secret. The irregular circumstances of Christopher's arrival meant that she could discuss him with no-one and in all her conversations with other people, she was constantly on guard to ensure that she did not let any clues of his presence become known to anybody. However, the extraordinary love which she felt for him and the joy which he brought into her life were so overwhelming that she felt this was a small price to pay. Christopher was, in her mind, her salvation, her reason for living. Thoughts of him and their future together filled her with excitement and optimism.

On the following morning, she conveyed the news of Marion's pregnancy and the possibility of their imminent move, to Mrs. Maltby who seemed delighted and uncon-cerned that she might lose two of her paying tenants. Indeed she seemed to see it as a further opportunity to redecorate another flat. No mention was made of advertising for new tenants and Nicky did not broach the subject.

It wasn't long before Marion and Steven found the accommodation they were seeking and presented a month's notice to Nicky, to pass on to the landlady. Mrs. Maltby wrote back that she would instruct the painters to proceed with redecoration in that flat too and so the afternoon tea and biscuits ritual for the men continued. There had still been no mention of seeking new tenants and Nicky wondered if Mrs. Maltby was already dealing with that issue.

One afternoon, a young girl rang the front doorbell. She was a blonde, Polish student who was looking for temporary accommodation as she was attending a course of study at the local technical college. Her name was Esme Podalski. Nicky explained that there might be a flat available in a few weeks but currently, as she was only serving in a temporary capacity, she did not have the authority to agree to such action and encouraged the girl to seek accommodation elsewhere. The student was very disappointed and asked Nicky if she could contact the landlady on her behalf and try to persuade her to take a new lodger for a six week period. She left her name and contact telephone number with Nicky.

The following day, Nicky raised the subject of taking in new tenants in her communication with Mrs. Maltby and was surprised when she was told that the future of the house was in some doubt, Mrs. Maltby having decided that at her stage in life, she might be better to continue living in the warmth of the New Zealand climate with her dependent sister and to put the house in Chalmers Street on the market. She therefore did not want to embark on any new leasing agreements. However, she promised Nicky that she would not be making any impulsive decisions and advised her that she was unlikely to make any definite move on that issue until the summer, in six month's time, so there was no immediate need to worry. In any event, Mrs. Maltby had to contact the Social Services and give them plenty of time to find alternative accommodation for Mrs. Parkins, for whom she felt a great responsibility. In the meantime, she planned to redecorate the whole house gradually and slowly make it ready for sale. She intimated that she would return in the summer and consider a sale at that time.

Nicky was in two minds regarding the news. On the one hand, she was pleased to have even more time to enjoy the comforts of Mrs. Maltby's flat and her rent-free status but this news did imply that by the summer, Nicky and Christopher had to find somewhere else to stay.

Esme Podalski, the young Polish student phoned on the following day, explaining that she had failed to find a place locally and was hoping that the landlady had agreed to her request of a short lease. Nicky decided to allow the girl to have her own room which had been freshly painted and decorated. Mrs. Maltby was clearly not returning until the summer and Esme required only a six week stay. She negotiated a weekly rent from the girl, to be paid directly to herself. Esme was delighted but Nicky worried about her decision, feeling guilty at deceiving Mrs. Maltby who had always been truthful and honest with her but she rationalised that she needed the money and what Mrs. Maltby didn't know about, wouldn't hurt her.

Marion and Steven moved out, much to Nicky's disappointment but they promised to keep in touch and let Nicky know when the baby was born. Their room was refurbished and the painters had then been instructed to clear out and paint the basement area. A few days after Esme had moved in, she knocked on Nicky's door and told her of a fellow student who also required a short term stay. Since Steven and Marion's room was now free, she wondered if that could be offered to her friend. Nicky decided to avail herself of the opportunity to make extra money, and arranged for the flat to be leased, to Monique Carlin, again with a direct weekly payment to herself.

Mrs. Maltby wrote to the remaining tenants advising them of her decision regarding the house sale and soon the Symingtons were busy seeking a new home and even Calum was asking around to see where he could go. The Social Services found a place in an old people's home for Mrs. Parkins and Nicky could see that in a short time, she would be the only remaining tenant. She felt sorry for the old lady having to move at this stage in her life but her health had deteriorated and she certainly would benefit from more regular care than she currently had in Chalmers Street.

Two weeks later Calum moved out. He had very little to say and Nicky was not sorry to lose his company. He obviously was a loner and had not fitted in very well with the others.

After six weeks, Nicky found herself alone in the house now apart from the painters who were working their way round the place, preparing it for sale. Nicky had little to do except think about her own future and had been turning over in her mind all the options available to her, bearing in mind that she now was in the position of a single mother with responsibility for a little boy.

Before the accident which killed her parents and her brother, she had secured a place at university to study history and looking to the future now, she wanted to get a good job with enough money to look after Christopher, provide him with the best education possible and see that he lacked for nothing. Events seemed to be conspiring to direct Nicky towards a new job and new accommodation. After a lot of soul searching, she decided to approach the university again and request that they re-consider her previous application in the light of her recovery from the accident. She informed them too that she would like to switch her chosen course to law, thinking that this would provide her with a solid foundation to get a well paying job in the future. It would soon be summer and Nicky had to have her plans ready soon.

The university response was very understanding and positive, offering her, on the basis of her previous exam results, and the unfortunate events which had prevented her from continuing with her course, a place to start a law degree in October of that year, some six months away. In the numerous leaflets, which accompanied the university offer, she saw that she could apply for a student loan, and for students with children there was a crèche available on site. A plan was beginning to take shape. She would find a job to finance the two of them until October and then apply for a loan to take effect thereafter. Accommodation would also be a consideration. She needed to find a place to stay, preferably close to the university campus and conveniently placed for the crèche.

Over the past months after Mrs. Maltby's departure, she had saved a significant sum, considering her benefits, her money from Mrs. Maltby and the weekly rental of two students, at a time when her outgoings were minimal. She was sure that she would have sufficient funds for a few months rent but the money would not last for ever and some additional source of income would be imperative until her student loan became available.

She was perusing the accommodation sites in Edgerley on the Internet one day, when a knock sounded on the door. It was Marion Woods who had popped in to say hello. Nicky found herself in a tricky situation, as Christopher was lying peaceably on the floor but she invited Marion in and told her, 'I'm looking after my sister's baby for a few days. She is suffering from post natal depression and I have offered to give her a break.'

'How wonderful for you, not for your sister of course,'

exclaimed Marion, her own pregnancy now very apparent. 'I didn't know you had a sister.'

'Yes, Susan. She is older than me,' Nicky lied.

'He is lovely. May I hold him? I need the practice. In another three months, I will have to deal with one of these, too,' she said, laughing and picking up the contented child.

'He seems to have a slight tan. Has he been jaundiced? Apparently small babies can have jaundice for a few weeks or months, can't they? See how little I know,' Marion commented.

Nicky looked at Christopher and noticed how different his skin colour was compared with Marion's pale arm. She hadn't noticed that before and quickly said, 'I don't know. He is certainly darker skinned than you are.'

'He looks well anyway; a wee gem,' Marion continued, rocking the giggling child.

'I'm sure you will be a great mother, Marion. You are the maternal type and Steven looks like a useful sort of chap to have around. He will probably take on the nappy changing and feeding, too,' she said, trying to change the subject away from her imaginary sister. She was also now concerned at Christopher's colour. He did look a healthy, happy, wee boy but now that Marion had drawn attention to the skin colour, she began to worry that he was, in fact, ill. She had not yet purchased a pram and had never taken Christopher outside so she had judged his skin colour only inside and mostly in artificial light. Feelings of guilt began to fill her mind. She had not taken him to a doctor. The implications of discussing his origins had made her apprehensive about such a move, but suddenly she knew that somehow she would have to deal with these necessities for his sake.

'It's all so new, isn't it? There's so much to learn about babies, not just the feeding business but the vaccinations, the childhood diseases, the milestones they are meant to achieve and all the rest. We've been reading books about it. You almost need a degree to have a child,' said Marion.

Nicky suddenly felt very inadequate. She hadn't really thought about all the issues Marion had raised. What a fool she was, to think she could raise a child on her own!

'Well, I'm quite green on these issues, too, but I have offered to keep him until my sister is better. I don't know for how long that will be, but I will have to deal with him meantime. I can see that I will be running to you for advice soon. How is your new place?' she quickly asked.

'Oh it's so good; on the ground floor in Melville Place, number fourteen, a very small flat but good enough for the time being. We have two bedrooms so the baby can have his or her own in due course. I came in today to give you the address and phone number. Please come and visit. Once the baby arrives, I will be on my own and lonely.'

'You won't be working then, will you?' asked Nicky.

'Not until after the birth but then I will have to go back, I suppose; perhaps part time. We can't afford to live on Steven's salary alone. Mind you, we will get allowances for the baby and free milk coupons and, so on, so that will help.'

'Do you have to apply for the allowances?' asked Nicky, wondering how she could make use of this information.

'Yes, once the doctor or the hospital has given you a form confirming the baby has been born, you can get a birth certificate at the registrar's office and then you can use this to apply, at the council offices, for the allowances and all the free care that is on offer. It's just a lot of form filling but every bit helps, doesn't it?'

'Of course,' said Nicky, acutely aware of her lack of knowledge and thinking that she had probably lost out on free utilities, had she but known and been in a position to apply.

The afternoon passed quickly as the two girls chatted and when Marion left, promising to drop in again, Nicky spent the evening on the Internet looking for information on *Bringing up Baby*. The issue of Christopher's skin colour preyed on her mind and she felt increasingly guilty that she had never taken him to see a doctor or considered what health checks he required. It was exigent, she knew, and she determined to amend that somehow in the coming weeks.

A letter arrived informing her that she had successfully managed to negotiate a student loan, but she was anxious not to overstretch her budget and in looking for a new flat, she was very aware of her restricted financial position. She sat at the sitting room table counting out her savings, amounting now to a sizeable sum what with the earnings from Esme and Monique's rents, the money saved from cancellation of the newspapers and milk as well as curtailing the spending on her benefit by eking out all the food in Mrs. Maltby's cupboards, fridge and freezer.

She had to buy essentials for Christopher and her first purchase was a pram. Free from prying eyes of other tenants and the landlady, she felt safe pushing the pram around the streets of Edgerley. She looked at flats for rent and kept an eye open for any temporary employment advertised, which might suit her before she began her University studies in October.

Finding accommodation was less easy than she had imagined as very few places were willing to accept a child as well, anticipating, no doubt, periodic screaming fits and complaints from neighbours regarding their sleep disruption. Consequently she spent a great deal of time walking from one place to another, frequently returning home despondent and weary. However, eventually she did find a one bedroom flat on the first floor of a terraced building. The rent was higher than she really wanted to pay but as she was exhausted with her searching and increasingly concerned about the imminent return of Mrs. Maltby to Chalmers Street, she agreed to the terms, paid for three months in advance, and arranged to move in the following week.

Later that evening, she wrote to Mrs. Maltby to let her know the date of her departure and promised to call round to visit on her return.

7

The new flat was small but furnished adequately. She knew that it would take her time to accumulate a few things of her own.

Each day she visited the local library and perused the *jobs* columns of the local newspapers and after many days of searching, she came across a temporary clerking post, which was available in a lawyers' office in town. It involved helping with filing and general clerical assistance, the post having arisen on account of the maternity leave of a member of staff. No previous experience was required and the post was available immediately.

Nicky was concerned as to how she would deal with Christopher when she was working but decided to make enquiries about the position.

Placing a call to the offices of Bradbrook, Kemp and Armstrong, a cultured female voice invited her to attend for interview on the following day at 2 pm.

For a year, Nicky had taken no interest in her appearance or her well being. She had never been a fat person and over this period, she had lost more than two stones. That evening she stared at her naked body reflected in the full length wardrobe mirror. She was stick thin, she thought, her pelvic bones and ribs projecting so obviously from under her thin layer of skin. Her pretty face was gaunt and her dark, wavy hair shapeless and dull. With a change in her outlook and a goal in mind, she decided that it was time that she started taking her appearance more seriously. At least there had been no shortage of food in Mrs. Maltby's house and she had been eating regularly and healthily but she was still rather thin. There was still some money she had kept from the rent she had retained and she decided to invest in a basic smart wardrobe and a visit to the hairdresser.

First thing in the morning, she dressed Christopher and together, they set off. As they left the flat, Nicky carefully humping the pram down the steep flight of stairs, she met the couple who stayed below her, Jean and Harvey Morrison, a retired couple who, on receipt of a winning smile from Christopher, chatted with her amiably. Jean was a slight person with pointed facial features and wispy, beige coloured hair. She was wearing a floral coverall while Harvey, who was rotund, wore a long green cable cardigan over a checked shirt and baggy brown cords. His hair was totally white and he sported a large white mustache below which hung a smouldering pipe. An alert white Scots Terrier peered at them all from the sitting room door. He was joined in a few minutes by a large lumbering grey coloured bulldog whose slack skin and doleful expression made him look the picture of misery.

Christopher had been trying to grab Harvey's pipe but the sight of the dogs fortunately diverted his attention from that dangerous pursuit. He pointed excitedly at the two canines and attempted to say *dogs*.

'He likes the dogs, doesn't he?' remarked Jean.

'That big lump is Tyson,' added Harvey, 'and the wee one is Caspar.'

'Gosh, they are very different, aren't they?' said Nicky.

'That's the idea. With these lazy bulldogs, you have to have another one that gets them moving, so Caspar here is pretty good at giving Tyson exercise, chasing him around,' Harvey said, removing the smoking pipe from his mouth.

'A bit like people, I guess. You can see which one is Tyson in this family,' he chuckled.

'They are both fond of children so don't worry about your little one,' Jean said reassuringly, giving her husband a friendly nudge in the ribs.

As Nicky pushed the pram outside, Jean called after her, 'Why don't you park the pram in the common hallway? It will save you the stairs each time.'

'Thank you,' called Nicky, grateful for the consideration. She could see that Christopher's charismatic ways were proving to be an asset.

In one of Edgerley's large stores, she purchased two short sleeved blouses, one white and one pale blue, a pair of smart, grey court shoes with Cuban heels, a well cut, grey suit which was two sizes less than she usually wore and some white underwear. Pleased with her purchases, she phoned Marion to ask if she could help by looking after Christopher for a couple of hours that afternoon. Marion, now struggling with her gravid pregnancy, but bored and at a loose end, was delighted to help out. Christopher was also bored with the shopping and had fallen asleep in his pram. Nicky noticed the hairdressing salon situated at the rear of the large store and approached the reception desk to enquire if a quick cut and blow dry would be possible. Luckily, the girls could fit her in almost immediately and so she relaxed while her hair was attended to. She bought some new make up and a small bottle of Jean Patou perfume, called Joy, the name reflecting how she was feeling. The makeover had improved her self esteem enormously. A few months earlier, she would never have believed that life could change so dramatically.

She hurried back home with her acquisitions and leapt into the shower before trying on the new outfit. Christopher watched her through the glass panelling, laughing as she directed the nozzle towards him and sprayed the water at his face. Wearing her dressing gown, she made Christopher's lunch and spent a little time with him, telling him that he was going to visit Marion while Mummy looked for a job. He seemed quite pleased and swallowed his lunch enthusiastically. His nappies were changed and Nicky looked out more nappies, a couple of bibs and a few rusks to take with her.

She dressed in her new clothes, applied some makeup and admired herself, feeling a boost in her confidence as she approved the mirror image. Her hair was soft and lustrous, her model-like slim figure showing off the new suit to advantage. She could barely remember when she had even thought about her appearance with such interest.

Leaving Christopher with anyone, even with Marion whose maternal instincts were buzzing, was hard. They had never been apart, not for a day. However, it was a necessity now and Nicky was glad that she had kept in touch with Marion, and grateful that she had accepted her lies about this baby belonging to her depressed sister, Susan. She told Christopher that she wouldn't be long and kissed him gently.

'Don't worry about him. We'll get along just fine,' said Marion comfortingly, 'and *good luck* with the job.'

Nicky took a bus to the law firm which was on the other side of town in an unfamiliar area. The wide roads and grand old buildings served to make her even more nervous than she already was. However, she was confident with her smart appearance and was sure that she would make a good impression at the interview.

Ushered into a small office, she was offered a seat in front of an immaculate desk, all papers and accessories arranged tidily. In due course, a middle-aged woman entered and immediately apologised for keeping Nicky waiting.

'That's quite all right.' said Nicky politely, admiring

the smartly dressed lady, who reminded her of a school teacher with her erect bearing and perfect makeup. There was not a hair out of place, her short grey hair styled and shaped expensively around her oval face. If she had any makeup on, it was subtle and natural looking. A pair of rimless spectacles hung from a pearl chain at her neck. Her green woollen dress outlined a trim figure. She wore a delicate and likely expensive gold watch which drew Nicky's attention to her hands where well manicured nails completed the picture of elegance.

'My name is Cynthia Gladwyn,' she said as introduction, smiling kindly at Nicky, 'and I'm the Secretarial Manager in Bradbrook, Kemp and Armstrong. Thank you for coming today… Miss Partington, isn't it?' she said, looking down at her blotter on which lay a white sheet of paper, apparently containing the information on Nicky gleaned over the phone.

'Yes, Nicky Partington.'

'As you know, we are looking for some immediate help with the general work here in the office. One of our employees has gone off on maternity leave rather sooner than we had expected. She has blood pressure problems, and so we have been thrown into a bit of difficulty. Tell me, what is your situation at the moment?' asked the interviewer, who sat with her graceful hands now folded in front of her, studying Nicky.

Nicky explained that she was awaiting the start of her University course in law in October and said that she would be free immediately, if found suitable. She did not elaborate on the past, hoping that Miss Gladwyn would not be too curious.

'I have recently acquired accommodation in Rowland Street, close to the University, and now have six months before I take up the course. Naturally I was hoping to find some gainful employment meantime. I have secured a student loan but obviously I would like to limit the debt that I incur over the next three years.'

'Have you been in employment since leaving school, Miss Partington?' Miss Gladwyn asked.

Nicky told her that she had been acting as locum landlady and caretaker of a property in town for some months and offered Mrs. Maltby's name as a reference, should one be required.

Miss Gladwyn's face seemed to soften as she heard about Nicky's plans for the future and her immediate availability. Nicky went on to say, 'If you would like me to submit a formal CV, I would be happy to do that.'

'No, that won't be necessary. I would, however, like you to complete this form, if you don't mind.' She handed Nicky a three page document.

'Is there anything you would like to ask me about the job?' Miss Gladwyn enquired.

'May I ask the hours of work involved?' asked Nicky, her mind always on Christopher's situation.

'Of course. The office is open for business from 9 am until 5 pm and certainly, initially, I would like you to be here during these hours in order to show you the ropes and to introduce you to the other employees here. Is that a problem?' she asked, her eyes surveying Nicky's neat attire.

'I should tell you that I am a single mother with a small son and obviously I will need to make arrangements for his care while I am working,' Nicky explained, trying to sound organized and efficient.

'How old is your son?' asked Miss Gladwyn, a frown appearing on her previously lineless forehead.

'Almost six months now,' Nicky replied.

'I see,' she said considering the implications of this complication. 'Well, once you have shown competence in the job, I'm sure we could allow you to have flexi time which might suit your own commitments. Are you prepared to give it a try?' she asked, looking a little concerned.

'Yes, I'll do my best to organise my home life around the job. I am very interested in obtaining gainful employment and it would be an added bonus for me to work in a legal setting which may be of value in view of my career choice,' Nicky replied.

'Very well, then. Will you be kind enough to complete the form and I'll discuss the matter with one of the partners.'

Miss Gladwyn handed Nicky an expensive silver pen and busied herself at her desk, while Nicky answered all the questions. One of these asked if the applicant had ever been charged with a criminal offence. Nicky quickly wrote *No*, but a sense of dread filled her when she reflected on the irregularity of her relationship with Christopher and the lies which she had had to tell since his birth.

She passed the form back to Miss Gladwyn who checked each answer carefully. After a few minutes, she rose and announced, 'I'll be back shortly. Would you mind waiting in the reception area? We'll not keep you long.'

Nicky sat in the entrance hall, feeling as though she had just sat an exam and was waiting for the results. It was strange having to provide some information about her own situation for the first time and although she hadn't directly lied to Miss Gladwyn, she had a feeling of guilt, nonetheless. There was no doubt that she had to be on her toes and ready with plausible responses when asked personal questions. The office seemed very spacious and some sections had obviously had a recent refurbishment, for the smell of paint hung in the air. The plush, thick, pile blue carpet in the entrance hall suggested the firm was on a successful footing. Nicky hoped that she would be offered the post but she did wonder if her single mother status would be a hindrance. It also concerned her that she would have to pay for someone to look after Christopher and she wondered how much money she would actually make after the overheads were paid.

Within twenty minutes, Miss Gladwyn returned, smiling and said, 'That's settled then. I have discussed this with Mr. Pettigrew, one of our team and he thinks you should be given a chance. It is a short term position, possibly just three months, and the work is very basic. I hope it will be mutually agreeable. Now, let me show you around and I'll discuss the terms of the employment, outline the wages and the method of payment. They walked up a flight of stairs to the upper level. Here there were two old style desks facing each other in the centre of a large open plan room, with two young girls busy at computers, their desks piled high with paperwork and scrolls. Each turned to acknowledge Nicky's presence with a nod and smile. Situated around the area were five individual rooms. Miss Gladwyn pointed these out as the personal offices belonging to the senior legal team, and told Nicky that she would meet all of the staff when she began working.

'The first office over there belongs to me,' she said, raising her hand to indicate her personal domain. 'If you ever should need help, please come and ask.'

Nicky was shown round a magnificent board room containing a huge oval mahogany table and eight matching chairs with green leather upholstery, and the coffee room where everyone popped in at some point during the day to relax and socialise.

'Downstairs in the main filing room is where we keep all the files and legal papers, and that is where I want you to start. There is a great deal of sorting out to do. We have accumulated a large backlog since Sandra left. She hadn't felt well for several weeks and was falling behind rather badly so it would be very important to get these files in order as a priority,' she explained. 'Then we may ask you to make copies using this machine, here,' she continued, tapping the top of the large grey copier.'

Nicky thought the basement was rather dingy and stuffy but the post was well paid and since she could start immediately, there was a chance to sustain her income for the next few months. It would generate extra money provided she did not have to pay out too much for babysitting, and working in the well known law firm offices, would be beneficial to her CV.

As they climbed back to the entrance hall, Miss Gladwyn asked, 'Can you start tomorrow at 9 am, then?'

Nicky replied cheerfully, 'Certainly. I'll see you tomorrow.' Her positive answer hid the concern she was experiencing regarding Christopher's care.

She caught the first bus back to Marion's house, anxious to see how Christopher had fared and found Marion enjoying a quiet cup of coffee and watching the television while Christopher lay asleep on the mat in front of the fire.

'Hi there!' said Nicky, 'How has he been behaving?'

'Just look at the wee darling. He has been absolutely no trouble at all, played for a bit and then just fell asleep. I haven't really had to do anything, haven't even changed a nappy,' Marion remarked, 'Anytime you need a babysitter, just call.'

'Well actually, on that subject, Marion…I have a big favour to ask.'

'Did you get the job, then?' she asked excitedly.

'Yes, that's the problem. I'm supposed to be there from 9 am until 5 pm for the first few days anyway, and then the Manager rather hinted that I might be able to have a flexible arrangement, which might be easier. I think they are desperate for some help so maybe she will be agreeable to less stringent hours. I was wondering if I might ask you to help for a few days. Is that at all possible, Marion?'

'You have come at the right time. I was just thinking how bored I was and that I could do with something to occupy my time. Of course it is OK. You must take the job. Surely your sister will be able to take Christopher back soon, too.' replied Marion. 'She can't expect you to look after him for ever. Your job is important, too.'

'I don't think that will happen any time soon,' said Nicky, bluffing her way through the situation. 'She is still feeling very depressed and feels unable to cope. However, hopefully in the next few weeks, she will be able to take him back even if it is for a few days in the week. Thank you so much for offering to help. I will pay you, of course,' she said, 'the going rate, whatever that is. At least this week it is only three days, tomorrow being Wednesday.'

'No worries, Nick. I'm happy to help. I'm here every day until this wee one arrives,' she said, patting her distended stomach. 'Will I see you at around 8.30 am tomorrow, then?'

'Yes, that would be wonderful, thank you so much,' Nicky said, picking up the sleeping baby and placing him in his pram, ready for the trip back to the new flat in Rowland Street.

She spent the evening playing with Christopher, giving him an extra long bath time and leisurely giving him his evening bottle, feeling guilty at having left him in the afternoon. She told him all about her day and the plans for tomorrow. He was happy and didn't seem at all perturbed by her news.

In the morning, she had Christopher bathed, fed and dressed ready for the day, tucking a few nappies and extra bottles in the pram beside him. She had written the name, address and phone number of the law office on a piece of paper just in case Marion had a problem. She set out early, found Marion in her dressing gown and slippers but ready to deal with Christopher.

On reaching the office, and again wearing her new, grey outfit, she rang the main doorbell and was greeted by Catherine Jepson, one of the secretaries, who ushered her in and took her to Miss Gladwyn who immediately led her to the filing room, offered her a white apron to protect her clothes against the dust and gave her a quick lesson on the filing system.

'If you have any questions, just pop upstairs and ask one of the girls or knock on my door. We are here to help and I don't want you to feel isolated down here. In fact, you will find that we all pop down here from time to time to retrieve files or to copy something,' she said, 'and so you will have company intermittently. Then, at ten thirty, we will all have a coffee break together so we can chat more then, and you can meet the other members of staff,' she said in a motherly way.

'By the way, in case you were wondering, we have two young partners here, Mr. Amos and Mr. Pettigrew. They are both building their empires and work seven days a week. Mr. Bradbrook, whom you will meet later today, is the senior partner in the firm, of course.

Mr. Kemp is on holiday right now in Barbados and Mr. Armstrong passed away last year. We have retained the firm's name because it is a well-known and highly reputable one but in due course I expect the two younger members will want their names up there, too. Any of the team may require files and no doubt you will meet everybody in the course of the next few days.'

'Thank you,' said Nicky, putting on the white overall and setting to work. There were numerous piles of documents lying loose on the floor and on the table, all of which had to be matched with the correct file. She spent a few minutes trying to read the names on the files and inserting them in the correct order. From time to time, she came across a file or document which had been misnamed or misfiled and so she made sure that the names were easily read and in correct alphabetical order. Not infrequently, she found that the outer jacket was so worn and tattered that the name on the file cover was obscured and in addition, loose sheets of paper hung partly outside, making it all appear very untidy. Seeing a pile of new file covers in a large box in the corner, she began to change the tattered ones and write in thick, black ink, the appropriate name as apparent from the documents inside. This strategy helped a lot as the stiffer fresh covers, stood up better instead of curling up, and so she began to sort out some of the existing files by renewing the outer cover, reinserting the loose leaves and soon completed a whole shelf length. Her white overall became progressively greyer and she could see that the documents and the shelves were all covered in a thick layer of dust. Clearly no-one had cleaned this filing area for many months. She began to take all the files out in small piles, stacking them on the floor, and having noticed that there was a small antiquated toilet area at the back of the room equipped with some cleaning utensils, she selected an old towel, soaked it in soapy water and proceeded to wipe down the metal shelving prior to replacing all the files tidily in order. Time passed quickly and she was surprised when footsteps clattered down the stair and Catherine appeared. 'Coffee break, Nicky. Come on up,' she announced cheerily.

'Thanks,' said Nicky, sneezing, and followed her upstairs to the communal room where all of the secretarial staff had gathered and a corpulent older gentleman attired in a pinstripe three piece suit was dunking a rich tea biscuit into a mug with the title *boss* inscribed on the side. His Pickwickian appearance, long grey sideburns and white wavy hair gave a comical and amiable impression.

'Nicky, this is our most senior partner in the firm, Mr. James Bradbrook. Mr. Bradbrook, this is Nicky Partington.

She is helping us sort out the filing chaos downstairs,' announced Miss Gladwyn, looking a bit flustered and red in the cheeks.

Mr. Bradbrook rose stiffly and extended his warm, doughy hand.

'Ah, Nicky, God bless you, my dear. We are all delighted to have you on board and I wish you all the luck in the world with that humongous task. Actually, I need a file with the name *Dunning* on it, *Myrtle Dunning*. I don't suppose you have come across that this morning in your travails?' he asked.

'In fact, I have seen that,' Nicky replied. 'It is an unusual name and sticks in my mind. I'll go and get it right now.' She set down her mug and rose to retrieve the file.

'No, no Nicky, have your tea. I'll go and look,' said Miss Gladwyn, rushing out of the room.

She was gone for only a few moments and returned with the newly bound file in her hand.

'Well well, well,' said Mr. Bradbrook, 'how's that for service?'

'Nicky has done a marvellous job down there and she has only been here for five minutes. What a difference! Tank you,' she said, patting Nicky's hand.

'Brownie points already,' said a younger male voice, as Mr. John Amos, a handsome, dark haired man with his shirt sleeves rolled up, entered the room.

Nicky was introduced to the dashing young partner in the firm and noted how quiet the other three girls had become during his brief visit to collect a cup of coffee.

'I'm sure you don't generally have a grey hair in your head at your age,' he remarked, 'but right now it looks like you had a grey rinse, all that dust has aged you considerably,' he said, flicking some of the dust from Nicky's hair.

Nicky felt her skin tingle and was a little embarrassed

by his familiarity, but smiled congenially, running her own fingers through her hair and shaking it.

'I think it is my fault, I stirred up the dust when I was cleaning the shelves.' she said, hiding her blushes.

'I think the firm will have to cough up for a hairdo at the end of the week if the poor girl is to be immersed in a dust cloud, Miss Gladwyn,' he continued.

Miss Gladwyn, turning towards him, agreed, saying 'Absolutely right, Mr. Amos. That's something to think about.'

As the young man left, coffee cup in hand, Christine whispered 'Quite a dish, isn't he, Nicky?'

'Now, we'll not have any of that talk,' said Miss Gladwyn firmly, scowling at Christine and nipping the conversation in the bud. 'Mr. Amos is a high flying corporate lawyer and you should show him respect. In addition he has a wife and two children, so please, don't forget that. We must all behave professionally.'

Christine looked a little cowed but winked at Nicky.

After the break, Nicky returned downstairs to her duties, pleased that Miss Gladwyn had noticed the work she had accomplished earlier.

The day passed quickly and she was beginning to derive some satisfaction from the job she was doing, gradually making inroads into the large pile of files, which lay stacked carelessly on the floor. The room was warm, the windows sealed for security purposes, but she was becoming accustomed to the clouds of dust. Her thoughts of Christopher were never far away. Leaving him with Marion was hard but she knew that this job an opportunity to increase her finances and ultimately her efforts were directed at supporting Christopher and herself.

On the following two days, breaks were uninterrupted by Mr. Amos's presence and Nicky had begun to make conversation with Andrea and Lynne, two of the other secretaries who joined Christine and herself at these times. Miss Gladwyn did not always come through but when she did, she was relaxed and chatty. The general atmosphere in the office seemed friendly and congenial. The secretaries were all around Nicky's age and there was a pleasant camaraderie. In other circumstances she could see herself joining them for a drink or a party and chatting about fashion, boys and celebrity gossip, but things had changed and she could not allow herself to become too friendly with anyone. It wasn't something she regretted. Not for a moment did she feel that she had done the wrong thing in keeping Christopher for herself but she was aware that so much of her life was now embroiled in a tissue of lies. Christopher was her pride and joy. Nothing could change her feelings for him and all her planning was for their future together. Even if she wanted to give him up, it would be difficult to explain how she had found a baby on the top of Mansion Hill and kept him for almost a year. No one would believe the story. She thought of the feelings stirred inside her by John Amos and pondered on how she would act supposing he was single and interested in her. She could never explain to him or to any young man the unlikely turn of events which led to her have a little boy. Any relationship would flounder if she exposed the truth and she could not risk losing Christopher. He was her world and nothing else was of any importance now. She had no regrets and felt that in time, as she perfected her explanations and other people accepted her situation, the worries of inadvertent exposure would lessen.

On Thursday evening, she began to think about speaking to Mrs. Maltby, who would be at Chalmers Street by now, and she felt that she could not leave that relationship without thanking her personally for all her help. She wondered if she could prevail upon Marion to keep Christopher for a little longer but when she saw how exhausted she looked, she decided against it. Christopher had been playing all day and was clearly tired. She considered taking the pram with her to Chalmers Street and parking it outside on the step, or perhaps telling Mrs. Maltby that she was babysitting for a friend. After many conversations together talking about her family and her brother, Patrick, she knew that Mrs. Maltby had been told that Nicky had no family and would not buy the story of a sister with post natal depression. However, when she arrived home, another possibility presented itself to her. She found Jean Morrison, clad in a grey trouser suit and blue pinafore, sweeping leaves from the front doorstep. Caspar was not helping, trying to wrestle with the brush as she worked. Tyson lay motionless on the small patch of lawn at the front. Caspar started to bark as the pram trundled in the gate and was quickly shushed by his owner, who turned her attention to Christopher. 'How's that wee darling today?' she asked.

'He's almost asleep. I think I'll leave him in his pram for a while so as not to disturb him.'

Jean peered into the pram where Christopher's eyes were practically closed and the blanket had almost covered his face.

'Isn't he just perfect?' she said, clearly enamoured with the lad. 'You must allow me to baby-sit for you some time when you need a break.'

'Actually, Jean, if it wouldn't be too much trouble, I would appreciate your help this evening. I need to go the see my last landlady to finalise things and will only be a couple of hours. Would you mind looking after him? I think he'll sleep anyway.' she asked.

'Of course, just pop him inside. Harvey is off to his bowling this evening so I have all the time in the world.'

Nicky hurried to Chalmers Street and was pleased to see the sitting room light on. She rang the bell and was greeted effusively by Mrs. Maltby who looked tanned and thinner than she had been before the trip. In addition to the rumpled patterned skirt and lemon coloured twin set, she was pulling a chunky knit black cardigan around her as though she was feeling the change in temperature from New Zealand.

'Come away in, Nicky,' she exclaimed. 'I'm so glad to see you and my, you do look well.'

'Yes, I'm much better, Mrs. Maltby. I'm in a nice flat in Rowland Street with some very agreeable neighbours. I'm all set for university in October and meantime I'm doing a temporary clerking job in a law firm. It's all coming together for me. Actually, I really want to thank you so much for letting me stay in your home and for the money you gave me. You have no idea what a difference that made. I do hope you found everything in order.'

'You did a great job, juggling the tenants' comings and goings as well as being around for the painters. I want to give you this by way of thank you,' she said, handing Nicky an envelope.

'There's no need, really.'

'There's every need. You stepped into the breach in the nick of time and I appreciate that, too.'

'How is your sister?' asked Nicky politely.

'Well, she's coming along but she will need help for the foreseeable future so I am returning there shortly and will stay now in New Zealand. It's no hardship, I assure you- sandy beaches, sun and friendly people. What else could one want?'

'Sounds good to me,' replied Nicky.

The two sat and chatted over a cup of tea and a slice of cake, Nicky relating what she knew of the other tenants' whereabouts and the imminent delivery of Marion's baby.

Nicky was anxious to return to Christopher and when she thought it polite, she stood to take her leave.

'Before you go, Nicky, can I give you this?' Mrs. Maltby said, handing Nicky her laptop with the associated cables, all tidily arranged in a carrier bag.

'No doubt you will need a laptop for your studies and I don't need this one. I use my sister's as she is no longer able to do that sort of thing and you would be doing me a favour if you would take it.'

'That's wonderful, Mrs. Maltby,' said Nicky, genuinely delighted with the gift. She knew that she would need one for her studies in the coming months. 'I do need one and have put off buying until nearer the University term. I am so grateful.' She hugged the kindly woman and said, 'I'll e-mail you every so often to let you know the news of Edgerley, if you want.'

There were tears in her eyes as she left Chalmers Street and she set off for home, planning all the things she would be able to do now that she had a laptop. Ten minutes into the journey she stopped and set the bag down. She extracted the envelope which Mrs. Maltby had given her and counted the notes therein. Continuing through the centre of town, which was busy with late night shoppers, she perused the shop windows, looking for bargains and treats for Christopher. Outside a camera shop, she surveyed the array of different devices and their prices, finally deciding that if she had a camera, she could record Christopher's antics and begin his first photo album. She purchased a small silver digital camera which was on sale and tucked it into the bag with the laptop. Pleased with her purchase, she had no thought of spending any more money but seeing a lemon polo-neck sweater in a smart boutique, she changed her mind and added that to her bag. Further along the road, she entered a toy shop and bought a red Ferrari and a ball for Christopher.

Thinking of Jean Morrison's help this evening, she bought a colourful porcelain pot containing six hyacinth bulbs as a token of gratitude, from the florist's next door.

On the following day, she wore her new sweater under the grey suit and was pleased with the reflection in the mirror. Each day she seemed to spend a little more time titivating her hair and makeup. She knew the reason for this, her attraction to John Amos, even although she knew that there never would be any relationship with him. Somehow, she wanted to look smart and attractive to him. He seemed to bring out the best in her.

When five o'clock came round on Friday, she found herself almost reluctant to leave her task. She had made great inroads into the reorganization of the files, had settled into the firm and was pleased to be earning a little money. She was also looking forward to having a weekend alone with Christopher.

Miss Gladwyn came down to admire her handiwork and to urge her to get off home.

'You are working a miracle in here. It is such a relief to get this stuff sorted out. When these chaps want something, there is some urgency about it and recently we have really been struggling.'

'It's quite pleasing to see it looking better. Actually I'm quite enjoying it,' said Nicky.

'Tomorrow is, of course, Saturday, Nicky. I shall be coming in to draft some documents for Mr. Bradbrook. It is your day off, I know, and you can say *no* to this of course, but I wondered if you would like to make some extra money by coming in for a few hours on Saturday or Sunday? The sooner we have the files sorted, the sooner we can move you to more challenging jobs.'

'I would be happy to do that, but I have to consider Christopher, my son, too.'

'Ah, yes, of course you do. Forgive me for asking, dear,' Miss Gladwyn turned to go.

'No, I'm pleased you asked. Can I make a suggestion,

Miss Gladwyn? Could I bring Christopher with me? He is still very small and will just lie about contentedly in his pram beside me. He hardly ever cries. If you don't mind me bringing him, I will happily come in,' she offered.

'Well, now, why didn't I think of that? That's what to do. Come in whenever it suits you and bring in that son of yours, too. I would like to meet him.'

The following morning, Nicky dressed Christopher in a new red and white outfit she had bought for him and set off early to walk to work. It was a good forty minute walk but Christopher enjoyed being in the pram and she was saving money this way.

When she arrived at Bradbrook, Kemp and Armstrong, there were few members of staff in evidence. The receptionist, Catherine, smiled curiously and Miss Gladwyn seemed genuinely quite enamoured with the little boy, admiring his good looks and his easy going temperament. She commented that Nicky was obviously coping admirably with her son and Christopher smiled obligingly at her, trying to grasp her dangling spectacles, much to her amusement.

Nicky lifted the carry cot section of the pram down the stairs and positioned Christopher where he could observe her at work, setting out a few toys to keep him busy. She worked away steadily, interrupting her labours from time to time to feed or change Christopher who seemed quite at home in the dusty environment, happily kicking his legs in the air and cooing softly. Nicky was glad of the opportunity to supplement her basic earnings and especially pleased that Miss Gladwyn had allowed her to bring Christopher into the office, since this obviated the need for a costly babysitter as well as allowing her to spend time with him, too. She wondered if Miss Gladwyn would permit her to bring Christopher on week days. At break times, she ran upstairs to make a cup of coffee but brought it downstairs with her to be with Christopher.

In the afternoon, Miss Gladwyn appeared, bringing a large box of letters for filing. 'How is that little man getting on?' she asked, smiling at Christopher.

'He's settled in well; seems to like looking around at a new place, I suppose,' Nicky replied.

'I haven't heard so much as a cheep from him. What a good boy!' she said, beaming adoringly at him.

'Thank you. Yes, he is good. He hardly ever cries- only if he is very hungry and I haven't got the bottle ready.'

'He's just adorable. I could take him home with me,' she said, handing Christopher a soft toy which had become distanced from his play area.

'Would you like these filed?' Nicky asked, taking the box of letters.

'Yes, but there's no hurry for them. I do need to find *these* files urgently though,' she said handing a long list to Nicky. Mr. Amos has come in, too, so I'm quite busy upstairs. How long can you stay today, Nicky?'

'I have no other jobs to do so I'm happy to stay as long as you want today,' she answered.

'I have quite a bit of work to do so I'll be here until maybe 7 pm tonight. If you want to stay until then, I can lock up after we go, but do take a break at lunch time,' she said.

'Thanks. I will.'

Nicky quickly located all the files on the list and took them in two piles up the stairs where she placed them on Miss Gladwyn's desk. There were voices from an adjacent office and she assumed that Miss Gladwyn was in conference with one of the lawyers.

At lunch time Nicky picked up the cot and took Christopher for a walk in the fresh air. Bradbrook, Kemp and Armstrong was situated in an upmarket area with rows of impressive Victorian homes, many now converted into office blocks. It was a quiet street with little traffic and an enclosed garden area situated centrally. She bought a tuna sandwich and carton of orange juice at a small corner store at the end of the road, then returned and sat on a park bench to enjoy her meal. Christopher fed too. She pointed out the pigeons and squirrels to him and he watched with great interest and made his own unintelligible comments. By the time she returned to the office, he was fast asleep.

Nicky worked on until 7 pm at which time she heard Miss Gladwyn coming down the stairs.

'Are you ready to go, Nicky?' she asked.

'Yes, just coming,' she said, removing her apron and picking up the cot. Suddenly, heavier feet clomped down the stairs and Mr. Amos appeared, carrying a buff file.

'Nicky, this file belongs to Jonathan Mitchener. I need Jacob Mitchener's, his father's, file.'

'That's my fault, Mr. Amos, I just put J. Mitchener on the list,' said Miss Gladwyn.

Nicky put the cot down and worked along the row of files, taking only a few seconds to find the correct one and handed it to him. 'Sorry for the error,' she said.

His good looks were disarming and in particular, his piercing dark eyes which found hers and for a moment, Nicky held her breath, locked in his penetrating gaze.

'Right, thank you.' he said brusquely, taking the file in one hand and lifting the cot in his other.

'I can manage,' Nicky said, but he climbed the stairs in front of her and she found herself following with Miss Gladwyn bringing up the rear.

Christopher had awakened and stared at the stranger, looking quickly round for Nicky.

'Good looking lad, you've got there,' Mr. Amos remarked, placing the cot securely in its base.

'Thank you,' said Nicky.

'I suppose you will be bringing him in every day?' he

enquired, again locking his eyes with hers.

'I'm not sure if that is permitted,' she began.

'It's OK isn't it, Cynthia?' he asked Miss Gladwyn who looked nonplussed.

'He seems to be no trouble at all so if that suits you, Nicky, please do just that. It will save you having a minder, won't it?'

'That's very kind,' she said delighted.

'Can I count on the help of you two girls tomorrow again?' asked John Amos. 'I have a lot of work to get through and it will be all the quicker with your help.'

'I'll be in by ten, Mr. Amos. What about you, Nicky? Can you manage that?' Cynthia Gladwyn asked.

'Yes, I can manage ten o'clock. That's no problem.' she said, finding herself decidedly drawn to the man with the hypnotic dark eyes.

It was growing dark but she walked home, chatting all the while to Christopher, telling him that he would be going to work with her in the morning and telling him how pleased she was with his behaviour.

During the ensuing weeks, she packed in as much overtime as she could and now that it seemed to have become acceptable for her to bring Christopher along too, she felt much more relaxed.

By the end of the first month, she had cleared the backlog of files and the filing room looked immaculate. Only the daily workload required attention and with the tidy system, this was becoming easier. Miss Gladwyn had instructed her in the operating system of the copier and from time to time, she was asked to provide copies of clients' documents or legal papers.

She didn't see much of John Amos, but one afternoon, he came down to the filing room to make a copy of a particular paper and said, 'You are working very hard, and it is much appreciated. The last girl we had in here wasn't really interested and latterly not very well, so the difference is noticeable.'

'I need to pay the rent and save as much as I can before starting the university course,' Nicky said. 'I am pleased to have the opportunity to work in a law office, too, and being allowed to bring Christopher in is an added bonus. Have you any children?' she asked.

'Yes, I have two, a boy, Bobby, who is 5, and a daughter, Gill, who is 3 years old,' he replied.

'They are at an interesting stage, aren't they?' she remarked, casually.

'Interesting and sometimes a bit of a handful,' he said, finishing the copying and heading up the stairs.

Hesitating on the bottom stair, he turned to ask, 'Is there anything you think would improve the efficiency of this system?'

'I suppose ideally air conditioning or a ventilation system is really what is required. It is stuffy and very dusty here,' she offered.

'Anything else?'

'An intercom system or even a telephone. The person down here is rather isolated from the rest of the staff. I don't mind it, but of course, I'm not here permanently. It would be good to have better communication with the people upstairs. That would save us shouting to each other, or running up and down when a file is required,' she suggested.

He turned and went back upstairs. Nicky found herself trembling a little. John Amos was handsome and had a rangy, muscular physique. If things had been different, she could have so easily fallen for him. However, there was no future in such dreams. He was happily married and she was not in a position to get involved with anyone, so she dismissed the thoughts and carried on with her work.

The efficient reorganisation was a two edged sword as

Nicky could see that her overtime would not be required and at the end of her second month with the firm, Miss Gladwyn stated that she could have a rest, that she would not be required at the weekend.

On the walk home, Nicky stopped at the pharmacy to purchase nappies and food for Christopher. She noticed that Angela, the pharmacist who had served her on the night Christopher came into her life, was talking to a customer. Nicky's appearance had changed a lot since that night and she doubted that Angela would make the connection. Nevertheless, she steered the pram away from the girl to avoid any embarrassment. A red plastic truck was on display, having been reduced in price, so she added that to her shopping basket as a reward for Christopher's agreeable cooperation and easy temperament.

Taking a short cut through Meredith Lane, she found herself passing the registrar's office where births, deaths and marriages were recorded. She had passed this way on many occasions, perhaps in the hope that a miracle would happen and someone would offer her an easy way to sort out the birth certificate issue which loomed larger each day.

Without a birth certificate, she could not easily register with a GP nor could she claim the allowances which would normally be available to a single mother.

The grimy windows were usually covered with notices, giving an air of mystery and dejection to the place but today a young and obviously newly married couple, smiling and excited, was departing the building. Friends and relations were showering the happy couple with multicoloured confetti and laughing noisily. Nicky observed the activity and pointed out the pretty bride and the carpet of confetti to Christopher, as they made off in a small car, adorned with tin cans, silver horseshoes and *Good Luck* stickers. Other passersby had also stopped to enjoy the happy moment and admire the bride's cream outfit. While Nicky paused, allowing others to pass by, she looked at the office, thinking how much she needed a birth certificate for Christopher but unsure as to how she could go about it without disclosing information which might seem suspicious. The dull frontage of the building was, as usual, adorned with numerous notices and advertisements, but one, in particular, caught her attention.

Due to the merging of this office with the George Street branch and the expansion of these premises into No 22, part-time temporary office help is required, flexi time negotiable.

Nicky noticed that the office already occupied numbers 20 and 21 Meredith Place and the adjoining accommodation was obviously vacant, the windows opaque with an internal, white, masking paint. The cobbler had seemingly gone out of business and clearly the merger had required a takeover of the adjoining property. Perhaps because she desperately needed to sort out the birth certificate issue and also because she needed all the additional income she could get, she impulsively, pushed open the door and went in. A rather flustered, plump, middle aged lady with tightly permed pepper and salt hair and thick lens glasses, told her politely that they were actually closed for the day.

'Is it something urgent, or could you call again tomorrow, perhaps?' she said squinting at Nicky and her pram, over the top of her glasses.

'It's about the part-time work you have advertised in the window. I just wanted to express an interest,' Nicky said in reply, turning to go.

'Gosh, that was quick. I have only put that notice up an hour ago. Please come in. I'm sorry to have spoken so abruptly. It's been a busy day and we were glad to get to the end of it,' she said, smiling and locking the door to deter any further visitors.

'Come through to the office. Just bring the pram with you,' she said, leading the way into an overcrowded room, occupied predominantly with four large square polished tables pushed together to provide a massive working surface, and piled high with heavy hard-covered register books, computers and numerous boxes. A young lady, very obviously pregnant, was slipping into her coat in preparation for leaving for the day.

'Hello,' she said cheerily, 'I'm Alison. What a gorgeous, wee boy!' She hurried over to take a closer look at Christopher and try to initiate a baby speak conversation with him.

'I'm Nicky,' Nicky replied as she followed the older lady through to a dingy office, which Nicky thought had probably served as a large cupboard in the past.

'Where's Ted?' she shouted over her shoulder to Alison, ushering Nicky to a seat in front of the desk.

'Out the door like a shot,' replied Alison. 'See you tomorrow,' she continued, collecting her handbag and setting off for home.

'Bye, Alison,' said the lady, dropping heavily into the large chair behind the desk, and pushing piles of paper across it. The pram barely fitted into the room but Nicky managed to park it alongside the desk and Christopher, curious about this new face, stared around him, eyes agog.

Nicky noticed the lady's maroon jersey suit was decorated with numerous small particles of confetti and in her hair too, the small colourful fragments of paper had lodged, giving her a careworn and comical appearance.

'My name is Mary Marshall,' she said introducing herself, 'and I'm the registrar here.'

'Nicky Partington,' Nicky offered, 'and this is my son, Christopher,' she added, nodding towards the child, now fixated on the overhead fan.

'Well, Nicky, you can probably see that we are up to

our eyes here in complete chaos. Two registrars' offices have been merged and this one has had to expand to cope with the influx of material and stuff. It is all rather a shambles and has added greatly to our work. After a great deal of frustrating negotiation,' she said, scratching her untidy and thinning hair and dislodging some of the small pieces of coloured paper, which floated on to the blotter, 'I have succeeded in getting some money to pay a part-time helper in the hope of getting things straight. It is very basic clerical work that is required, with a lot of filing and arranging of books and documents, which need to be merged with our own. All of this will eventually be on a computer system which we do currently use, but it is time consuming to get the previous data introduced and will take us many months, I expect.'

'I am used to filing,' Nicky said, explaining to Miss Marshall that she was working at the offices of Bradbrook, Kemp and Armstrong and that she was awaiting the law course at university in October.

'Ah, I see,' said Miss Marshall, so your time is already fairly well occupied.'

'I am free most evenings and weekends for the next four months, if that is of any use to you. I suspect that my temporary post at Bradbrook, Kemp and Armstrong will not continue too much longer so I may have more time available shortly,' she said, hoping that the registrar would look favorably on her situation.

'How are you placed this weekend?' she asked.

'Quite available,' replied Nicky.

'Well, how about coming along tomorrow about nine o'clock and I can begin to show you what is required. If you can see what needs to be done, then there is no reason why you can't come in when you are free, on a flexible basis. One of us is usually here. Actually, in many ways, it will be easier to work when it is just you and me, so we can give that a try if you are happy with that,' she suggested.

'That would be fine with me,' said Nicky, wondering if she should broach the issue of Christopher when her availability was already in question.

Miss Marshall went on to explain the hourly rate of pay and issues of confidentiality.

'If you require a reference, I'm sure that Miss Gladwyn at Bradbrook, Kemp and Armstrong would provide one,' said Nicky.

'Oh, if you are good enough for that law firm, you are good enough for me,' Miss Marshall answered, smiling. 'Now, is there anything else?' she asked, scratching her head again, the frizzy locks standing up untidily and residual coloured paper fragments perched precariously here and there.

'Ah yes, we have to fill in this form, just your address and so on.' She rummaged in a drawer, handed the form to Nicky and then found a pen for her.

Nicky began to complete her details and hesitantly asked, 'As you can see I have a small son and I have been very fortunate with the law firm that they have allowed me to bring him in to work with me. He is no trouble at all and of course it saves me having to pay child minders. How would you feel about my bringing him to work? If you would prefer that I didn't, then, of course, I won't do that,' she asked hopefully.

'Oh, that's a difficult one. It would be setting a precedent and as you saw, Alison is pregnant. The next thing will be that she will want to bring in her baby.' She pondered for a few minutes, rubbing her chin with her wrinkled hands. 'However, you are not going to be earning a fortune here and I can well understand that you would prefer to avoid paying for a babysitter, as well as having him near you. They are so adorable at that age.'

She looked at Christopher, her hands clasped in front of

her, beaming at the happy little boy. 'Well, Nicky, why don't we give this a try? Bring him in tomorrow with you and we can see how we get on. That's fair, isn't it?' she suggested.

'More than fair. That's very good of you,' said Nicky, warming to the older woman.

'If we don't get some help soon, I think we'll all keel over,' she said, rising stiffly from her chair.

Nicky weaved the pram round the desks and set off for home, excited to have seized the opportunity of a job at the registrar's but wondered how difficult it would be to get a birth certificate. She decided that she would play it by ear, observe how the forms were filled out and see whether she could supply the requisite information without raising suspicions. If she had a certificate, she could apply for child allowances and free childcare. It would be easy to roll up at a general practice and register her child. Christopher was almost nine months old now and she was increasingly aware that he should be receiving regular checks. In later life, he would undoubtedly need a birth certificate. Somehow it had to be done.

8

On the following day, the weather was fair and she pushed the pram along to Meredith Lane at 9 am. Christopher having been up since 7 am, had had his bath and morning bottle. He was almost ready for a snooze when they arrived at the registrar's office. Mrs. Marshall let them in and spent a few minutes admiring the dark haired little boy who, sleepily smiled back, enjoying the attention.

The registrar, today wearing an unflattering green trouser suit, a pale yellow blouse and navy lace-up shoes, showed Nicky through to the new premises where a hardwearing light grey carpet and numerous varnished wooden shelves had recently been installed. Some daylight entered through the cracks in the white paint which had been used to hide the renovations and activity from the public but it was a much brighter and airier room than the basement area at the Bradbrook, Kemp and Armstrong Office.

Half of the room was occupied with huge packing cases all bearing the registrar's address in two feet high bold lettering. Nicky parked the pram in a quiet corner where Christopher could nod off to sleep, while Mrs. Marshall instructed her on the requirements of the job. All of the large boxes had to be emptied, their dusty and heavy contents wiped down and arranged alphabetically on the new shelving.

It seemed to Nicky that most of the contents had been

around for many years and some were now in a fragile state. She removed her jacket and set to work while Mrs. Marshall went to her own office to clear some of the week's accumulated paperwork. 'I'll be next door, so if you have any queries, just pop in,' she said amiably.

Left to herself, Nicky ploughed through the work, making steady inroads into the mounds of boxes. Many were thick registers, with old fashioned graphics emblazoned elaborately on the outer leather covers and containing old certificates and documents. As she lifted each one, she glanced inside to gain some knowledge of the format of the certificates and the information contained therein. In some, the ink had faded and the writing was illegible. An hour later, her arms ached from lifting the heavy tomes, and Christopher had awakened, but was kicking about contentedly in his pram.

She was just about to take a break when Mrs. Marshall came in, bearing two steaming mugs of coffee. 'Oh, that is beginning to look better already,' she exclaimed, surveying the tidy row of books and the pile of folded cardboard containers. 'I'm sure you are ready for a break,' she said, offering Nicky a mug.

'Thank you,' said Nicky, grateful for the interruption.

'It would be good to get some of the empty boxes and crates out of this room. You will see the progress more clearly.'

'You're absolutely right. There's hardly room to swing a cat here. I'll ask Ted to put these out on Monday for recycling. The whole place is so cluttered at the moment. All the cartons on the desks and on the floor through there are all filled with more stuff. It's impossible to work in this mess. I'm quite angry the way we have been put upon, but what can you do? Anyway you are here, thank goodness, and I'm sure that will be a great help. Tell me, do you want to carry on through the afternoon, Nicky?' she asked.

'Yes, I have no other commitments this weekend. If you are happy for me to carry on, then I am very willing to do so,' she replied.

'Oh, I would be thrilled. I'll tell you what, in a short time, I'll pop across the road to the deli and pick us both up a sandwich. They do some great sandwiches! Any preferences?'

'That would be very nice, thank you. Ham or chicken salad would be fine. I'm not fussy really and I have Christopher's lunch here, so I can settle him, too.'

'He is well behaved, isn't he?' she said cooing at Christopher, wriggling about and trying to sit up to see where he was today.

When Christopher had had his bottle, Nicky put him on the play mat, which she always carried with her, and let him roll around the floor where he could see her working. He was curious about his new surroundings, staring at the window and the shadows of people passing by. A cardboard box proved to be a fascinating toy for quite a while.

At lunch time, Mrs. Marshall came in with the sandwiches and more coffee. She flopped down beside Christopher on the mat and played with him while consuming her sandwich. 'He is a fine boy and so cheerful. That's a credit to you. He must feel loved and secure.'

'Thank you. He has a very nice nature.'

'I guess he takes his colouring from his Daddy,' remarked Mrs. Marshall.

'Sorry?'

'Well, your hair is dark and wavy but his is quite different, isn't it? Tight curls and his dark eyes and lovely tan, that didn't come from your side, so I'm guessing his dad has passed these features on to his son.'

Nicky stared at Christopher and as with Marion's observations, she saw what Mrs. Marshall had seen right away. He did have a darker skin than she had and his eyes were such a deep mahogany, that it should have been obvious his father must have been the same.

'Yes,' she said finally, 'he takes after his father. Sadly we are not together any more.'

'Oh, that is a shame. So many young people don't stick together. Life is so hard and demanding, isn't it? You will have a difficult road ahead of you bringing him up by yourself. What about your parents? Are they close by?' she asked.

'My parents died in a car crash almost two years ago,' she said, thinking that at least that was true.

'My, my, what a tragedy. Well, good luck to you, Nicky. You have a mountain to climb but you seem tough, and you know, you will be stronger at the end of it all. These difficulties often bring out the best in people. You are having a rough spell just now but there are *ups* and *downs* in life and you will definitely be due for an *up* in the near future.'

Nicky lifted Christopher and propped him up by an empty crate. Now, almost sitting unaided, he enjoyed the support from the wooden box and tried to grasp nearby objects, giggling as he failed and fell over.

'Well, I could watch his antics all day, but I must go and do some more work. I think we should go home about 4 pm today. Enough is enough.'

Nicky worked away contentedly, making steady progress while Christopher entertained himself with the box. All the while, she was thinking about Christopher's father, wondering what nationality he was and where he was now. It wasn't jaundice then, she thought; just a normal skin colour. Why had she not thought about that before now?

At 4 pm, Mrs. Marshall appeared with her coat on and announced, 'Time to go home, Nicky.'

'Would you like me to come in tomorrow?' asked Nicky, putting Christopher back in his pram and tucking him in. 'I can come back one evening after work at Bradbrook, Kemp and Armstrong or next Saturday if you prefer.'

'I won't be here tomorrow, myself. I must have a rest, but if you would like to do that, I could give you a key. The reception area and my office will be locked for security reasons but you seem quite trustworthy to me, so if you want to do that, you could just keep a note of the hours you put in and give it to me when you come back on Monday evening. You will have to ensure that you lock up when you leave. Would that suit you?' she asked.

'Yes, that would work well,' answered Nicky. 'You have my address and phone number if you need to ask me anything,' she added.

*   *   *   *

Early the following morning, with rain threatening, Nicky walked smartly through the streets, pushing the pram. Christopher was wide awake, and although the hood was up, he tried to pass comment on everything he saw. Nicky, in turn, told him where they were going and promised that they would have a day at the park soon. They arrived at the registrar's office as the rain started.

She immediately noticed that an expandable metal gate had been pulled across the reception area preventing access to the desk and cupboards, and the door to Mrs. Marshall's office had also been securely locked. She guessed that the new certificates would be in reception and consequently, she could not acquire one at this time. However, she determined to work hard, gain Mrs. Marshall's confidence and hopefully in time, an opportunity would arise to allow her access to the document she so desperately wanted. She needed to be as familiar as possible with the process of registration and this was her chance.

She had brought plenty of bottles of milk, jars of baby food and nappies for Christopher as well as a packet of sandwiches for herself, planning on a full day's work. Although the rain pattered on the windows, it was warm in the office and she was glad that she would be saving on the heating bills, too, while she worked there. She put Christopher down on the floor mat and he happily practised his paediatric aerobics, happily chattering to himself. Nicky began by lifting the boxes from the office tables, bringing them through to the new room, hoping to create an obvious improvement for the staff when they arrived on Monday morning. She piled the empty containers in the foyer. Hopefully, Ted would dispose of them on Monday morning. The day passed quietly and peacefully. Nicky spent some time studying the birth certificates in the registers again, noting that some had written *Unknown* in the box reserved for *Father's Name*. She decided that she would make a similar entry when the time came. There were other questions which bothered her, questions such as *Place of Birth, Where and When Born, Signature of Person Informing, Place and Date of Registering* and most importantly, *The Signature of the Registrar.*

As she wiped down the large, black registers, she contemplated how best she would fill in the boxes. Eventually she decided that she would insert the name of the local hospital as the place of birth, as so many entries seemed to have, and enter twelve thirty am as the time of his delivery into the world. It seemed highly unlikely that anyone, on seeing the certificate, would check whether this information was true or false. She required her parents' names, mother's maiden name and the date of their marriage and then there was the informant. That was usually the father of the child but she could register the baby herself. What was absolutely essential, however, was the signature of the registrar and her seal. Nicky knew that she could never ask Mrs. Marshall to sign the document and it seemed likely that the seal was kept safe under lock and key, either in Mrs. Marshall's office or in the reception area. In the next few weeks, she would try to find out exactly where the seal was located but in the meantime, she could practise writing Mrs. Marshall's signature which was appended to many of the documents in her charge. She had no choice but to forge her signature. Strangely she didn't feel guilty about her deviousness, only a building anticipation that soon she would have a birth certificate for Christopher, but as the day passed, she thought about the criminal act she would be committing- forgery- and the repercussions should anyone ever challenge the information. She wasn't sure exactly what the punishment would be but she could see no other way to acquire the document which would make so much difference to her and to Christopher. Every time she took a break to feed or change him, she spent a few minutes copying Mrs. Marshall's signature and folded one certificate up and popped it into her handbag, so that she could take it home and continue to practise her forgery there. No-one would miss one certificate from the mountainous collection, she was sure.

It was almost midnight when she locked up, leaving the office a changed place; the desks dusted and cleared, the piles of papers neatly piled by each computer, and all the remaining boxes stacked in the new room, ready for shelving. She had written a note for Mrs. Marshall, giving the number of hours worked and to say that she would be working at Bradbrook, Kemp and Armstrong until 5 pm but would come along to the registrar's later, hoping that her availability would have increased. She didn't want to lose this job at the registrar's office. This was more than a job. It was a means to an end.

9

At Bradbrook, Kemp and Armstrong, the hours required for the job of filing and copying had gradually declined as Nicky was on top of the backlog and was efficiently dealing with the day to day work. Her time had become split between working downstairs and helping in the offices upstairs where Miss Gladwyn introduced her to other tasks. But even with the additional chores, the hours had been reduced to three days per week. This proved useful as it allowed her more time at the registrar's and much as she enjoyed working at the firm she needed to earn as much as she could, and most importantly, she needed a birth certificate for Christopher.

She took a great interest in the legal documents which passed over the desks of the secretaries, and was able to ask questions about basic legal matters as they arose. Miss Gladwyn, mindful of Nicky's plan to become a lawyer, went out of her way to teach fundamental rules and regulations of the job where she could and Nicky eagerly absorbed the information. She could see that she had chosen an interesting career and looked forward to starting the course and perhaps after graduation, working in such a successful group as Bradbrook, Kemp and Armstrong.

Occasionally, John Amos invited Nicky into his office when he was interviewing a client or discussing issues of corporate law. He was very professional towards her at all times but she knew that she was attracted to him and found it difficult to behave in a completely normal manner. It was hard not to study his handsome face when he turned away from her, or not to observe his strong hands when he handled the documents but she knew that there was absolutely no future in any relationship with him. Her situation now, as a single mother with a son whose origins had to remain completely secret, excluded her from having a normal relationship with any man. Besides, John Amos was also married with two children. She wasn't sure if the attraction was mutual but he certainly was always friendly and supportive. In a way she was pleased that this job would come to an end in the near future and she would not have any further contact with John Amos, whose very presence unnerved her. There was no point at all in getting too friendly with him. She was not in a position to exchange confidences or let her guard down for a moment. This was the price she paid to remain as Christopher's mother, and one she gladly paid. She began to realize too that whether he was married or not, she would never be able to enjoy a close relationship with any man. There were too many secrets she could not divulge. She would never have the warmth of a loving relationship, a close bond with anyone, male or female. No-one could ever know the circumstances of his birth. To Nicky, the loss was minimal as her relationship with Christopher was of paramount importance and a total joy to her.

One afternoon, a man came to the office to cost the work of installing an air conditioning unit downstairs and Nicky knew that John Amos was the instigator of this. He was thinking of all the people who had to work downstairs, not just of her. She did her best to believe that he was doing it for the benefit of the firm and that it was not a personal gift but somewhere inside her, she hoped that he had made the gesture for her.

Michael Pettigrew, one of the other partners, whom

Nicky thought was something of a fop with his gaudy cravats and long sideburns, was kind enough to talk her through some conveyancing documentation and although she found that somewhat tedious, she knew that in due course, she would have to deal with this sort of work.

Overall, it was a congenial place of work and Nicky felt that a great part of that was due to the firm and fair management of Cynthia Gladwyn. Almost three months after starting with Bradbrook, Kemp and Armstrong, Miss Gladwyn took Nicky aside and told her that her temporary post would no longer be needed. A new full-time member of staff had been appointed. Miss Gladwyn expressed genuine thanks and confided in Nicky that she had been a popular member of the team and would be missed. Nicky, in turn, thanked Miss Gladwyn for her kindness and tolerance particularly with regards to Christopher.

She put on her jacket and went round the office to say good bye to the girls. The door to John Amos's office was ajar but she hesitated to enter and was surprised and pleased when he suddenly appeared at it proffering two large textbooks, the corners dog-eared from much use.

'Nicky, you can see that these are well thumbed and I would like you to have them. They will be fundamental to your course and I'm sure you will find them useful,' he said, handing them to her. Their hands brushed as the books were exchanged and Nicky's heart raced even more.

'That's very kind of you,' she said, taking the books. 'I appreciate all your help.'

She found herself blushing as she made her way out with Christopher in his pram, the books safely under the pillow out of reach of his small hands. The sun was shining. She seemed to bounce along the road and for some reason, she couldn't stop smiling. The whole experience at Bradbrook, Kemp and Armstrong had been financially and educationally successful. The feelings she had experienced

when in John Amos' presence had been an added bonus but
now she had to turn her attention to the birth certificate
issue and she strode out as she made her way to Meredith
Lane.

When she arrived at the registrar's office, she was
greeted warmly by Ted, Alison and Mrs.Marshall.

'I can stay for a while tonight, if you like,' she offered.
'My job at the law firm is now finished so I'm free to come
here any day you wish.'

'It's Alison's turn to stay late tonight so she will be
here to keep you company,' announced Mrs.Marshall,
dressed again in her maroon outfit which seemed even
more dowdy than before.

Alison did little work that evening, happy to play with
Christopher, and asked Nicky all sorts of probing questions
about childbirth and looking after a new baby. She was a
pretty, blonde girl with a vivacious and convivial nature
and Nicky found herself telling her that she had had
Christopher at the local hospital, that her son was the result
of a careless one night stand and that she was enjoying
looking after him by herself. She regaled Alison with tales
of her imaginary labour and the joys of motherhood.
Somehow the lies flowed more easily as time went on.

Alison, now six months pregnant with her first child,
chatted to Nicky about her husband Gordon, an insurance
agent, and her plans for the new arrival, the baby's room,
the preferred choice of pram and the different theories
about feeding regimes.

Nicky worked away while Alison chatted to her.

'Will the registrar have a temporary assistant when you
go off on maternity leave?' asked Nicky.

'I don't know. We do have another member of staff,
Tom Scarfield. He had a nervous breakdown about three
months ago and is getting better apparently, but we don't
know when he will be able to return. I think Mrs. Marshall

is hoping that he will come back soon and then when I go off, at least he will be here to keep things ticking over.'

'I see,' said Nicky. 'She does seem to work very hard, doesn't she?'

'Yes, she does far too much. She is really pleased with you. At least she can see some light at the end of the tunnel with regard to all this filing.'

'Perhaps I could learn to do some simple work on the computer?' asked Nicky.

'Yes, I'll ask Mary. There are a lot of forms to be completed. I could show you that sometime,' offered Alison.

In the days that followed, Nicky worked long hours to complete the filing amalgamation and gradually became involved with some of the office work. Alison did explain some of the entry data which required transfer to the computer and Mrs. Marshall was not averse to her learning to do some of Alison's job. It seemed to Nicky that Alison had lost interest in the position at this late stage in her pregnancy and was marking time until the baby arrived. She had confided in Nicky that she might not return to the office at all after the baby was born.

In the evenings when Nicky was on her own, she completed as many forms as she could on the computer and these were all checked by Alison or Ted the following day. Ted proved to be a quiet, rather dull colleague. He was aged around 30, Nicky guessed. He was wiry and slim with balding, auburn hair. He wore glasses which made him appear nerdy, was invariably dressed in a brown tweed suit and checked shirt, and looked very serious. Living with his elderly mother, he seemed to be content with his job and his home life, and had no ambition to widen his horizons. He had no major hobbies other than watching television and reading. Nicky found him extremely boring, lacking in motivation and rather careless, but he was quite knowledgeable about the work in the registrar's office, and so she tried to glean as much information from him as she could. In a way, it was just as well that he was not curious about her and Nicky was glad that he didn't ask her anything personal.

By the time Alison was ready to go on maternity leave, the following month, Nicky was ready to take over a large part of her job as there was no sign of Tom Scarfield returning, although Mary Marshall had been in communication with him. Mary was delighted for Nicky to increase her hours and Ted shared Mary's relief at having an extra pair of hands because he was not a man to go the extra mile for anybody. He took shortcuts when he could and rarely stayed one minute past his scheduled time. He could see that Nicky was fastidious and tireless about her work and after a few weeks, he had stopped checking her entries as they were always very carefully and accurately completed. After almost two months in the job and her mission to obtain a birth certificate for Christopher still not completed, Nicky was invited to join Mary Marshall in reception to see how each certificate was processed. Nicky was excited and pleased that she would finally get to understand the registration system and sat beside Mary as several certificates were completed and entered on the computer. Each form had a number and when complete, the Registrar's seal was stamped across it. Nicky learned where the seal was kept- in a drawer under the reception desk. The drawer was secured with a brass key, which Mary Marshall kept in a locked drawer in a desk in her own office except on those occasions during the day when certificates required its use. She knew that time was running out for her. The university course began in two weeks' time and she was apprehensive that she might not achieve the main aim of her employment, namely, the acquisition of a birth certificate.

In the evenings she continued to practise writing Mary's signature until she had it perfect and all the other answers to the questions on the certificate were decided. She first needed to steal one of the thick blue certificates and every day in the office, she waited for an unguarded moment when she might purloin one without being observed, but it was uncommon for the reception desk to be unmanned even for a short time.

On two days per week and on Saturday mornings, Mary performed marriage ceremonies in the small chapel in number 20, Meredith Place and although Ted helped to some extent, he clearly did not enjoy that aspect of the work and loathed working at weekends. Saturdays were, of course, the favourite choice for weddings and so throughout the peak marriage times of spring and summer, Saturdays could be busy. Nicky knew that the registrar's seal was required on those occasions and it could be found in reception. Working through the week, she did not customarily work on Saturdays and so she found that her access to the seal was very limited. She was beginning to think that she would fail in her mission to acquire a birth certificate for Christopher.

The moment presented itself one Friday afternoon when two weddings had been scheduled in the adjoining chapel. Mary was rushing around organising the music, the flowers and the small, noisy crowd of people who accompanied the first bride and groom. Mrs. Anstruther, an upright and well known member of the town council, served as the regular witness and was punctilious and reliable with regard to this task. She was a buxom, middle-aged lady with thinning, grey hair and spectacles. She had a loud, booming, singing voice which was an asset when it came to the hymns as most of those attending the ceremonies, sang quietly and tentatively if at all. Mrs. Anstruther's daughter had telephoned Mary Marshall in the early afternoon that day to inform her that she was unwell, suffering from influenza and would not be able to attend. She had submitted two other names of reputable people who might help out in her absence but Mrs. Marshall had not been able to make contact with either of them. Ted had been relegated to the task of witness. Unlike, Mrs. Anstruther, he was a poor singer and loathed being in the public eye. It was a job he disliked intensely, a fact which was reflected in his sullen and sulky demeanour. Nicky was working away diligently at the computer when Mary rushed in breathless, her cheeks flushed and said, 'Nicky, I would like you to lock the offices, sit in reception and make sure none of these hoodlums wander about. Is Christopher OK? They seem like an unruly bunch and could quite easily wreak havoc in here. I want them out as soon as possible. We are running late as it is. If anyone requires anything urgent, ask them to come back at 4 pm or to come back on Monday, if possible.' She sneezed violently and removed a paper handkerchief from her jacket pocket to blow into it.

'Christopher is sound asleep. Are you OK, Mary?' Nicky asked.

'I have a fierce headache and these people are not helping much. It's all the stress but I'll survive,' she answered, blowing her streaming nose again.

Nicky closed and locked the inner doors, pocketed the keys and went to sit at the reception desk. Several young people, shouting and laughing, came into the foyer. Mary appeared, looking even redder in the face and quickly ushered them into the chapel area, giving Nicky a look of consternation as she propelled them firmly through the door.

When the first hymn began, Nicky gently slid the drawer containing the new blue certificates open, slipped the top sheet out, hid it under the large desk blotter, and noiselessly closed the drawer again. She listened as Mary

A Deadly Game 97

launched into her marriage ceremony spiel. The registrar's seal was not locked in its drawer because it was required for the wedding certificate. Nicky was tense and anxious as she began to remove the brass seal, senses on high alert. Mary was still working her way through the marriage ceremony and there was still a second hymn to be sung. Nicky knew that when that hymn ended, the register would be signed and then there would be a rush of people making for the door, and someone would come for the seal.

As quickly as she could, she extracted the seal, tested it on a notepad by the telephone, and, satisfied that it was stamping well, lifted the blotter and stamped the rubber seal firmly at the bottom of the blank birth certificate. With her heart beating fiercely and her hands trembling, she returned the seal to its rightful place, scrunched up the paper she had used for testing, and replaced the blotter over the stolen form. In a matter of seconds, the newly married couple and their attendant following burst out into the foyer with Mary Marshall and Ted in close pursuit. Mary came round the desk and removed the seal, pressing it firmly on the wedding document which she handed over to the retreating groom, who was being roughly pulled away by his inebriated pals.

As the wedding party all quickly piled into waiting taxis, Mary urged Ted to tidy up the chapel and rearrange the chairs for the next ceremony. 'I need an aspirin,' she said, holding her head in her hands.

Nicky handed over the office keys and when Ted had disappeared, she slipped out the birth certificate and quickly entered the office, secreting the document under a cardboard box, while Mary was washing down her pills. Some violent sneezing and a great deal of nose blowing followed.

'You don't sound very good, Mary,' said Nicky, 'It's just as well the weekend is here. You need to have a rest and get rid of that cold.'

'You're right about that,' said Mary emerging from her office, her facial colour matching the tone of her weary maroon suit.

The second wedding proved to be a more sober affair. Mary looked less stressed and Ted looked distinctly relieved when it was all over.

'Right, I'm going to head for home early for once. I'm not feeling too well,' announced Mary, taking the key to the seal drawer into her office with her. 'Ted, could you tidy up the chapel and make sure that you check Nicky's work before you go home? Remember to lock everything up carefully, and hopefully, next week will be a little less hectic for all of us,' she added, turning the key in her office door as she headed off.

'Yes, Mary,' answered Ted, who saw only an opportunity for him to get away early, too.

'Shall I help you with the tidying up, Ted?' Nicky offered, seeing that Ted was looking rather glum.

'Thanks,' he said, and they both went back to the chapel. Nicky found the vacuum and started to clear off all the confetti while Ted rearranged the chairs and removed the flowers from the vases, since they would not last over the weekend. With two of them working together, and Ted anxious to get away, it didn't take long to put the place to rights again.

Since Mary was out of the door, Ted said, 'You don't need to have anything checked. You're more careful than I am, so we should just get off, too.'

Nicky would not normally succumb to such a suggestion but today was special. She needed to get home to complete the certificate, and agreed decisively with him.

As Ted went to collect his grey flannel coat from the cloakroom, Nicky slid the certificate into her bag, pocketed one of the blue-ink fountain pens from reception, and slipped on her jacket. She collected Christopher, still asleep in his pram, and tucked the bag carefully under his covers. On Monday evening, she would enter the data into the computer, record the entry date as 30th October of the previous year and the data would be saved.

All evening, she had a single thought on her mind but it was only when she had Christopher safely in bed, that she brought out her trophy and studied it to ensure that the seal had produced a clear stamp. She was nervous and excited at the prospect of having a completed birth certificate for Christopher and meticulously practised everything she would write on it.

She carefully placed the certificate on a magazine, taking her time to make sure it was flat, and checking and rechecking every detail, as she filled in the boxes with the blue ink pen. Finally, she added Mary's signature, which she was sure, would pass scrutiny now.

She waited while the ink dried, admiring her handiwork. Her delight at having successfully acquired the form was tinged with guilt, as she reminded herself of the criminal act she had performed. She respected Mary Marshall and hoped that she would not ever suffer repercussions for her actions. It seemed unlikely, however, that anyone would question the details, and as time passed, the risk would diminish.

Bringing up someone else's child was obviously a crime in itself but there had been no choice in the matter. Christopher's own mother had not wanted him and surely, she could not be punished for taking the course she had done, she rationalized. The lies and deceit, which followed had been necessary to continue the façade but that would stop now that she had the certificate. It was all above board now. Christopher Partington was legally *her* son.

10

As the University course got under way, Nicky was relaxed and ready for the next stage of her life. The money she had accumulated over the summer months, had allowed her to purchase a comprehensive wardrobe for Christopher, now a year old, as well as several high quality items of clothing for herself. The new flat was very adequately furnished, Christopher was enrolled in the crèche and her student loan became available. Everything was coming together.

In the days following the acquisition of the birth certificate, Nicky lost no time in taking Christopher to a GP's surgery, informing the staff that she had only settled here recently after parting from her boyfriend, and Christopher had a thorough check as well as his due vaccinations. Her application for child allowance had been accepted on production of the blue certificate and her registration with the local GP. A heavy weight seemed to have dropped from her shoulders.

The lectures were interesting and Nicky concentrated on every detail. Some of her colleagues were still youthful, carefree and unsettled, but for Nicky this would be her career, and she wanted to make a success of it for Christopher. She couldn't wait to complete the course. Each evening she took out John Amos' books and read a few pages, which always triggered memories of her feelings for him. Her student colleagues were pleasant, friendly and fun, but with the responsibility of Christopher, she could not participate in their nightly revelry and long chats over coffee although she did join in the general camaraderie when it was convenient. She felt relaxed and happy, regaining some of her old confidence and self esteem. It seemed a lifetime ago that she had started on her history degree with no cares in the world. Several fellow-students had tried to date her but she had just laughed, brushing off the advances casually. Some were immediately disinterested when they heard that she had a son but she knew, deep down, that a relationship was out of the question; her past had to remain firmly closed to others. She had made her choices and she loved Christopher as much as she would have, had he been her own child. He completely filled her life and brought her total happiness and joy.

She passed the end of year exams with flying colours and allowed herself two full weeks off, spending each day exclusively with Christopher, going to the park, the zoo and the local swimming pool. They were complete together. No-one else was needed. Life was beginning to move ahead and her worries were behind her.

During the second year of her course, the students visited a number of sites for educational purposes. They rotated in small groups through the hospital pathology laboratories, witnessed part of a post mortem examination (an experience which reduced some of her colleagues to a ghastly grey colour), and attended lectures by local forensic pathologists. Every aspect added to Nicky's knowledge and she read extensively on every subject.

On one occasion, the students visited the local police station and were appraised of the role of the police working hand in hand with the lawyers. A tall, well-built and middle-aged, local police inspector gave a number of lectures to the groups, outlining the close cooperation of the police force with the legal fraternity. Crime statistics were outlined and future plans for improvement in dealing with the most challenging areas of work, discussed.

Further tutorials described the numerous means at the disposal of the police to catch criminals- fingerprint databases, DNA sampling as well as the use of closed circuit cameras, computer technology and the use of informants.

Nicky had teamed up with two of her male peers, Jonathon Brooks and Clark Baird on a police station visit. After the lectures and workshops, a young sergeant was designated to show them where the interviews with prisoners and witnesses took place, where blood samples and medical examinations were performed and where the officers collaborated in piecing information together. He was verbose and humorous, cracking jokes about the differences between lawyers and the police while describing the routines and procedures which were strictly adhered to. Several on-going cases were briefly discussed and the direction of the investigations outlined. The three students were fascinated by the complexity of the facilities and eagerly asked questions of their tour guide, who was only too pleased to show off his knowledge.

As they passed through a busy office where officers sat glued to computer screens and paperwork overflowed from desks, the sergeant stopped at one workstation and asked the young constable what he was working on.

'This particular case is a mugging, Sergeant' the constable explained. 'A young man was walking home, along Broad Street, last Tuesday night, around midnight, minding his own business, when three men jumped him. They ripped his jacket off him, stole his wallet, credit cards and a valuable watch and also punched and hammered him on the head. He ended up staying in hospital for three days. We are trying to identify his attackers at the moment.'

'Any leads?' asked the sergeant.

'Yes, we are examining CCTV footage which captured images of the three men coming into Broad Street from Montgomery Place and we are trying to enhance these images at the moment. It's difficult because they are all wearing hoods which cover a large part of their faces. However, yesterday somebody used one of the credit cards in a store in town, so we are trying to get a description of that person, too.'

'That's good. Anything else of use?' persisted the sergeant.

'There is one other possibility. A man who was returning home after the night shift at a local factory, thought that at about the same time as this crime was committed, he saw three suspicious men getting into a car in Farnby Way, which is at the end of Broad Street. He described the car as an old Mondeo, coloured green and cream. He recognised it because he owned a Mondeo himself, so we think that his information is likely to be accurate.'

'Did he notice the number plate by any chance?' asked the sergeant.

'He thought it had an L and two sixes in it but unfortunately that is not very helpful. However, we are checking out the owners of all green and cream Mondeos in the area.'

'Thank you,' said the sergeant, moving the group along.

'Identifying vehicles is a vital part of our work and, of course, may yield valuable information in certain cases. In this case it may turn out to be a stolen vehicle, of course. We can very often obtain useful information from the DVLA, if we have the whole or any part of the number plate,' he added, stopping by a large machine, with flashing green and red buttons along its frame. Let me demonstrate that to you,' he said,

'Give me a vehicle registration number, any number,

yours, a friend's?'

Jonathon and Clark joked that they were not rich enough to own a car. As the Sergeant pointed to Nicky, she blurted out *ESG 492* without really thinking,. From the moment the number escaped her mouth, she regretted it and wished she could retract her words. Why on earth had she suggested that number? Did she have a secret wish to know who owned that car? Suppose she was asked how she knew that particular plate? She quaked as the Sergeant punched in the numbers and waited an anxious few seconds until a sheet of paper spewed out of an opening into a tray.

'Unlike your impecunious colleagues, you must have plenty of money. This is a Jaguar. It has changed hands in the last year, I see, and here,' he said, handing the sheet to Nicky, 'you can check to see if it is accurate.'

'A Jag, eh? Where have you been hiding that?' asked Jonathon Brooks, jovially.

'Not mine, I'm afraid; my uncle's,' she said quickly, nodding to the police officer that the details were correct, and casually slipping the paper into her pocket. She reproached herself inwardly for what she had done and yet she felt so excited about the information, she could not even read the details provided. An hour later, the tutorial was complete and Nicky tried to behave nonchalantly as if nothing of any note had occurred. Feeling a need to show how relaxed she was, she opted to join the others for a drink at the local inn and talked over all the points which had been raised through the afternoon. They chatted cheerfully, but she could think only about the piece of paper which was burning a hole in her pocket and her own surprise at the extraordinary and almost automatic memory of the number she had seen almost two and a half years ago. She had thought little of it in that time, indeed, tried hard to forget the whole episode on Mansion Hill but somehow it was ingrained on her memory. Jonathon and

Clark tried to persuade her to join them in visiting a second pub but Nicky, already late, had to pick Christopher up from the crèche.

'Ah, Miss Partington, we were beginning to worry about you,' said the nursery superintendent, as she greeted Nicky at the door. 'Christopher was a little tearful waiting for you. I think he is tired today.'

'Mummy, Mummy,' shouted the little boy, 'Mummy ....lost,' he said, with big tears in his eyes.

Nicky hugged her precious son and said, 'I'm sorry I'm late. I was held up tonight. It won't happen again,' as her own eyes filled with tears.

She spent the next few hours playing with Christopher and asking him about his friends at nursery school. She allowed him to stay up late that night, and decided to take the following day off, to spend with him. It was Friday so she would have a long weekend spoiling her child. She couldn't bear to see him crying and wanted to make up for taking her eye off the ball.

Once he was asleep, she sat in the armchair with a mug of cocoa and allowed herself to remember the night of October 30th 1995, when Christopher came into her life. She pictured the car, a Jaguar, she now knew, and the two people who had brought the child to Mansion Hill. Only then, with trembling hands, did she unfold the piece of paper, which she had brought back from the police station, and read the information on it.

The black Jaguar, registration ESG 492, had belonged to a Mr. James Randall of Beaulieu, Cherrybank Avenue, Edgerley until April 1996, at which time, Ian Goldsmith of Eaton Crescent, Manchester had purchased it.

Nicky found herself trembling and a heavy lump seemed to form in the pit of her stomach, as she lay back and let the information sink in. James Randall was the man with the car. Was he Christopher's relative? Should

Christopher be called Randall? Where was Cherrybank Avenue? It was not a street she knew in Edgerley. A sick feeling grew in the pit of her stomach and more memories of that night flooded into her mind.

James Randall must be the name of the man who had driven Christopher to the woods that night; the man who had brought the girl, the man who had colluded with that girl to conceal or to kill a baby boy. Was the girl his lover, his wife, a friend? She knew that Christopher was of mixed blood now. Marion and Mary Marshall had opened her eyes to that. Was that the reason James Randall wanted to be rid of the boy? Surely he could not be so prejudiced that he didn't want to acknowledge the child because of that? Did he just want to get rid of an inconvenience?

Nicky felt exhausted and a little frightened at her discovery. Why had she offered the number? Did she subconsciously want to know the truth of Christopher's rejection?

She wasn't sure if she really wanted to know.

As she lay in bed, recounting the whole sorry episode, again and again, she decided that at some point in the near future, she would have to follow up on this information, and find Cherrybank Avenue.

11

The following day brought sunshine and warmth and Nicky decided to take Christopher to a nearby park and spoil him all day. She had purchased a comfortable baby walker for him as he had outgrown his first pram, and quite frequently he wanted to walk by himself or to push the walker. She showed great patience allowing him to try whatever he wanted to do. The park was quiet on this weekday and Christopher spent a couple of hours on the swings, sliding down the chute and heaving himself up on the climbing frame. By lunch time, he was exhausted with all his exertion and sat on the mat with her, playing with daisies and watching various dogs as they passed by with their owners. Nicky had brought a snack lunch with cheese, salad, fruit and crisps. Christopher munched away happily leaning on his mother affectionately. While he was content and distracted, Nicky examined her local map and finally located Cherrybank Avenue. It was several miles north of the town, in an area she had never visited.

She heard a young boy shouting, 'Daddy, Daddy, look at me.' She turned to see the boy pedalling a two wheeled bike propped up with stabilizers, clearly proud of his newly gained balancing prowess, in spite of the bike wobbling precariously over the path and endangering pedestrians and animals in his way. It occurred to her then, that Christopher would never be able to shout for his father. He would grow up wondering why he didn't have a father and at some point he would ask her what had happened to him. She was filled with concern but resolved to be the best mother and father that he could ever wish for. When the time came, she would tell him the truth. That was his right.

Lunch over, Nicky suggested to Christopher that they went on a bus ride, an experience he particularly enjoyed, so they set off to find one heading northwards. Information on the routes through the town was displayed on the shelter and she perused the destinations searching for Cherrybank Avenue. the number nineteen bus route looked to be the best one and while they waited, Nicky amused Christopher by drawing pictures on the dirty, glass shelter until the bus arrived. They clambered aboard with the baby walker. Christopher stood on the seat near the window with Nicky's arm supporting him, and peered out excitedly at the passing scenery. It took over half an hour to reach the beginning of Cherrybank Avenue. Then the bus turned off. It seemed that there were no bus stops in the Avenue. Nicky jumped off, carrying Christopher and the buggy and began to walk along the road. Immediately, it was obvious why it was named Cherrybank Avenue as a row of well-established and flowering pink cherry trees lined the wide road on each side. Some blossoms had already fallen and the pavements were carpeted with the delicate pink blossoms.

'Snow,' exclaimed Christopher pointing to the thick layer of flowers.

'Yes, it's like pink snow, isn't it?' replied Nicky, 'Lots of flowers have dropped from the trees. Isn't it lovely, Christopher?'

The little boy nodded and wanted to walk on the pink carpet, keen to kick the blossoms around. Nicky waited until he had trudged along, picked them up and torn the small florets into pieces, then led him onwards up the street, all the while checking the house names.

It was a most exclusive part of the town and on each side of the street, there were large palatial residences, long winding driveways and exquisite gardens. It was quiet too. Not a single car passed her as she made her way up the long avenue. She stopped at the entrance to one mansion and gazed through ornately carved gates at the meticulously manicured lawns, the weed less stone drive and the three expensive cars parked near the house. She wondered if this was Beaulieu and suddenly began to feel shaky. What if someone came out and spoke to her, admired Christopher or asked her what brought her here? What if James Randall appeared, out for a walk? What would she do or say? *This is your son, the boy you threw away in Mansion Hill Woods. Do you see a resemblance?*

She walked on, passing perfectly trimmed hedges, gently swaying pampas plants and buildings of magnificent architecture, but all the time growing more and more uneasy thinking that the Randalls lived somewhere here.

It occurred to her that Christopher should be living in one of these luxurious homes, lacking for nothing, financially secure for life. She could not offer him this sort of life, however, and began to feel embittered and angry. How could these people have thrown Christopher away like so much rubbish? Had his presence been so inconvenient, so embarrassing, such a mistake, that the only way to deal with the problem was to put him in a box and hide him in the woods? A white Mercedes cruised out of the electronically controlled wrought iron gates on the opposite side of the road. She stared at the driver, a young man of around eighteen years. She noticed that the house was called *Greenacres*. The thought occurred to her that Christopher's mother might have more children. Perhaps she was married and had a legitimate child. Christopher could have a step brother or sister. All sorts of possibilities flooded her mind.

Christopher struggled into his chair and lay down, tired and a little irritable.

'Home, Mummy?' he asked wearily.

'Yes, darling, we'll turn round and get the bus back to town in a few minutes.' She handed him a small apple and said 'Have a little rest while Mummy looks at all these pretty houses.'

She speeded up her pace and carefully studied the house nameplates which were often discreetly hidden or only placed up at the house where they were difficult to read from the street. It was almost at the very top of the tree lined road that she caught sight of a huge fountain playing cascades of water from bugled nymphs into a large rippling pond. It was stunning, and for a few minutes, she and Christopher watched the display. As she reached the entrance to this castellated home, she noticed a small lodge off to the right hand side. It was petite and bijou, only suitable for one or two occupants but its quaint design and the festoons of colourful blooms which decorated the garden, gave it a magical look, like something out of a Disney movie. A garage was attached to the far end of the small house, its white doors immaculately painted. Sitting in the driveway was a sparkling blue Astra. Opposite the quaint house were rows of beautiful flowering rhododendrons lining the wide driveway, and as she gazed, she noticed a sign, partly hidden by rhododendron foliage. She knew then that she had found Beaulieu, the home of the Randalls and Christopher's real home. Standing in the entrance, she let her eyes sweep over the distant house, the large turning area in front of a massive Gothic style wooden front door and the rolling lawns, punctuated by the softly playing fountain and elaborate flower beds. There was no sign of life, no Jaguar in the parking area.

She could imagine Christopher having fun running down the green banks and dabbling in the water. Whatever happened here, she asked herself; some dreadful tragedy which compelled the residents to dispense with a child, a wonderful child like Christopher. Her heart broke and she felt tears in her eyes. Suppose she went up to that great front door now and announced their presence. What would they say? What sort of reception would she get? But even as she stood there, rooted to the spot and filled with emotion, she knew that she could never do that. She might lose her son. They might decide that they wanted him, after all. It was time to go home.

'Would you like to live here, Christopher?' she asked.

There was no reply. She looked down at the pram and noticed the half eaten apple which had rolled down the side of the walker and the occupant leaning to one side, now sound asleep.

Nicky turned around and made her way back down the floral pavement, sobbing her heart out and glad that Christopher was unaware of her deep unhappiness. Thinking about the past induced a physical pain inside her which all the blossoms in the world could never alleviate.

12

The second year of her law degree completed, Nicky began to turn her attention to the future. Perhaps because John Amos had specialised in Business Law, and had encouraged her to take an interest, she found that this area of the work appealed to her and she decided to focus on the courses being offered in that field. She had decided to draw a line under the past and lock these memories away in a secure place in her mind. Periodically she had unlocked the thoughts surrounding Christopher's appearance in her life, and depression had ensued. Maybe in twenty years she would be able to look at it all dispassionately and calmly, but not now.

She threw herself enthusiastically into her work, read into the small hours of the night and eked out their meagre funds carefully, always neglecting her own needs if a choice between Christopher's and hers arose. Her days were full and all her free time was spent with Christopher. She was content with her lot.

Towards the end of the year, a three day conference was to be held in Manchester focusing on corporate law issues and Nicky was very keen to attend. One of Christopher's favourite carers at the crèche, Charlotte Brown, had offered to baby sit if Nicky needed help so she decided to ask Charlotte to stay in the flat with Christopher for the three days while she was away. She knew Christopher would be happy and well looked after. Luckily

Charlotte was free and willing to stay with Christopher.

It was the first time she had really been alone for over three years and there was a sense of freedom in her mood. She met with other attendees and enjoyed the first day lecture programme thoroughly. On the second day, she was surprised and a little thrilled to find that John Amos, was on the list of participants as a speaker. She hadn't seen him for almost three years and was looking forward to renewing his acquaintance. She looked around for him in the crowd but he did not seem to be in the audience and she concluded that he would simply come just prior to the lecture and return to Edgerley directly afterwards. There may not be any opportunity to speak to him, after all. After a bit of thought, she wasn't really sure whether she wanted to meet him again or not. It was too complicated. He was the one person she had met who made her feel uneasy, a little out of control and she could not afford to lose her grip when things were going well. When he finally stood up on the podium to speak, her heart lurched and a tingling warmth spread over her. Her face felt hot and she didn't seem to breathe normally. She concentrated on his talk and after a while she settled down again but there was an undercurrent of excitement which persisted. He was a handsome man, smartly dressed and his delivery was well practised and impeccably delivered.

After his presentation, he left the hall and she was relieved to see that he had not joined the audience. Presumably he was off home. It was best this way.

On the second evening, there was a dinner dance in the hotel where all the delegates were staying. Nicky had splashed out and bought a figure-hugging red dress for the occasion and the whole experience of being free, of feeling young again and the expectation of launching her own career, made her giggly and girlish. She joined several acquaintances for dinner and later they all gravitated to the bar and the dance floor. It was a long time since Nicky had danced and she threw herself into it with enthusiasm, joining the noisy crowd jostling on the floor and enjoying much hilarity. They all knew that this carefree student behaviour would come to an end soon and they would have to join the ranks of those in the serious, responsible, legal profession. As the evening wore on, the music mellowed and more romantic melodies were played. The group she was with, made sure that drink was in plentiful supply and Nicky knew that she was happily inebriated, but they were all staying in the hotel so it would be easy to fall into bed when the time came. She could relax for once. She didn't have to worry about Christopher; he was in good hands.

The band leader announced that the next waltz was *an excuse me* and Nicky went up with one of her student colleagues, Arthur Keithly. After a few minutes, her partner was gently pushed aside and she found that his replacement was none other than John Amos. Her inhibitions had been eliminated by the alcohol and although she was amazed to find herself dancing closely with him, she was so drunk by that stage that it was easy to joke and laugh, to compliment him on his interesting lecture and to chat in a carefree fashion about Bradbrook, Kemp and Armstrong. The light seemed to have dimmed and John Amos's arms were pulling her towards him. His closeness might normally have perturbed her but now, relaxed and uninhibited, she chose not to worry about it, to relax and be casual. However, as their cheeks touched and his arms drew her ever closer, a powerful surge of longing overwhelmed her and she knew that she was out of control and reluctant to extract herself from his embrace.

The music faded and there were shouts for more. John Amos whispered to her, 'Let's go somewhere less crowded,' and taking her hand, led her out of the room and to the lifts. Two other couples squeezed inside with them and it was impossible to speak to each other while the elevator rose to the third floor. John took her hand and led her to room 310. He swiped the lock and they went inside.

'How about another drink?' he asked, making for the mini bar.

'No thanks, I've had too much already,' she answered. He pushed a button and quiet music filled the room. Then he drew her to him and they danced again to the music, swaying together, cheeks touching and hands restlessly entwined.

'I've missed you, Nicky,' he whispered.

'It's been nearly three years,' she said, leaning her body into his. Her feelings for him had not changed in all of that time. The attraction was still there, even perhaps stronger than ever. Normally she would have held back and checked herself from getting involved, but now her resolve was weakened with the drink and his clear message of desire for her served only to enhance her feelings of want and need.

'I saw your name on the list of delegates and was so hoping that we would meet.'

'We shouldn't be here alone like this, should we?' she asked half heartedly.

'If you don't want to stay, I'll take you to your room.' he said, 'but I want you to stay, Nicky. Please stay.'

She released herself from his arms and sat down on one of the two single beds.

'I don't want to go anywhere,' she said, and lay down on the blue, quilted bedspread.

He came over to her and lay down beside her, gently kissing her neck, her face and then her lips. She fondled his hair, touched his face and slid her arms around his shoulders. Kicking off her shoes she wound her legs around his. It was all wrong, she knew that, but the feeling of his hands on her, the softness of his kisses triggered an explosion of feelings which could not be curbed. She had dreamed of this and yearned for him but had never thought it could come to fruition. From the moment she had met him, there had been an instant desire and longing. No other man had had this effect on her. She wondered if he had sensed her vulnerability and was using her for his own ends. Perhaps he was a heartless philanderer, exploiting the power he possessed over many of the women, he met but somehow it didn't matter. If this was a one night stand, so be it. It would be a night to remember, a night when she felt loved, a night she had thought she would never experience.

For an instant he broke free and looked into her eyes,

'Are you OK with this, Nicky?' he whispered.

It wasn't clear in her mind, at that point exactly what he was implying, but she knew that at that moment in time, she wanted John Amos with all of her being, and nodding, she made no move to resist him. Gradually, between kisses and caresses, he removed her clothes and adeptly threw his own on the floor. They explored each other tenderly and sensitively amidst words of endearment, breathless gasps and loving expressions. For a long time, they lay together, fondling, touching and taking everything slowly but as the tension heightened and gentle caresses became more urgent, John Amos leaned over to his jacket and extracted a condom. He applied it expertly and as Nicky hazily considered the thoughtfulness of this act, he entered her with practised expertise. It was her first encounter with sexual intercourse, her first exquisite climax and for the first time in her life, she reached extraordinary and hitherto unknown heights. She clung to him, her nails gripping his back, reluctant to let the moment pass. Gradually they both relaxed with his arms round her, lying like spoons. She knew that what had happened had been wonderful, something she had dreamed about, but she needed to think carefully about it all when she was more alert. Now her brain was too weary to give anything much thought, and she quickly fell asleep.

Several hours later, still befuddled and half drunk, she wriggled from his embrace to stumble to the toilet. Thinking that a shower would waken her up, she stepped in and let the warm water cascade down her body, her skin still tingling from the passionate lovemaking. She was suddenly aware that she was not alone in the shower as John stepped in beside her and began to rub the shower crème all over her.

She responded by soaping him and within seconds, they were entwined and inseparable. Now there was no time for a condom; his thrusts were desperate and needy. As they stood together after, he apologized and kissed her.

Dried and wrapped in soft, downy towels, they lay on the bed and slept again. It was almost nine o'clock when the noisy delivery of breakfast trays, awoke them. Nicky was practically sober and couldn't believe what had happened. The warmth and loving they had shared had been, for her, an incredible eye-opener. To have shared John Amos's most private feelings, filled her with awe and love.

He rolled her round, the towel dropped and in seconds, he was on top of her again, gasping as he plunged inside her, their synchronous ecstasy prolonged and beautiful.

'I have a lecture to attend,' she said, lying naked on the top of the rumpled bed.

'And I have to go home,' he said.

They looked at each other and smiled.

'Please don't let me lose you, Nicky,' he said, his hand holding hers tightly.

She looked at him. 'I'm not going anywhere.'

He rubbed his eyes and said, 'I need you.'

Nicky brought her hands up to touch his face. 'I'm not going anywhere,' she repeated.

13

The passionate liaison with John Amos lingered in her thoughts but she was glad that he had not been in contact. It had been a one night stand for him and she was not too surprised. It could never be more than that. He was married with two young children and Nicky had secrets which she could never share with him. She had to concentrate on her career and building a good life for Christopher. As the third year came to an end, Nicky pondered on the future for herself after university and carefully researched the schools which Christopher would attend in due course. The private schools were costly but she was determined to enroll Christopher in the best. His interests had to be given top priority. It would be imperative that she took up employment immediately after graduation. She had a student loan to pay off and Christopher's fees to pay in due course.

Her hard work and diligence paid off and she graduated amongst the top five students of the year. With this record of achievement, she had little trouble obtaining offers of employment and was amazed to find that a note of interest had appeared from Bradbrook, Kemp and Armstrong. She considered this offer long and hard. It would be easy to slot back into a firm with which she was familiar and she could be assured of support from the more senior partners but something made her hesitate- her attraction to John Amos. After a lot of thought, she wondered if it had been his idea to forward an expression of interest and that thought concerned her even more. Prestigious and successful though the firm was, she knew within herself, that there would always be an unspoken bond between John Amos and herself and although she was strong willed and resolute in many ways, these attributes did not apply to her feelings for him. There was no future for them together. Too many secrets and lies lay between them, to say nothing of his own family. To be aware that John Amos's office was but a few feet away and that he had once held her like a man deeply in love, was a disaster waiting to happen. The baggage which she carried with her would destroy both of them and she could not embark on that route.

She wrote a letter of thanks to Mr. Bradbrook for his kind offer and tried to explain that she wanted to gain a few years of experience before settling into such an established company. She should have written *I love John Amos, and to work beside him, knowing that he would never be mine, would break my heart,* for she knew that that was the truth. It was safer for both of them if she kept her distance from him.

Instead, she accepted a position in a rival firm with the name Martin and Ainslie, the office being located in the centre of town and in a rather dingy unprepossessing building in spite of the fact that it had as large and as prestigious a clientele as Bradbrook, Kemp and Armstrong. The offices were dimly lit and the whole place was in need of some fresh paint. But the actual premises, were not of great importance to her. She would work hard and earn a good income. That was her goal. Scott Martin, the senior partner, had started the firm on his own, twenty years previously, and had built up a reputable and solid business. Now over sixty years of age, an ebullient extrovert and humorist, he spent a great deal of time on the golf course as he anticipated the imminent culmination of his successful working life. His three children had grown up and left home, and he felt content with his achievements, now relishing some well earned relaxation with his wife, June. He was a round, jovial character, always dressed in a smart three piece suit but he had no airs and graces, proved a most affable colleague, easy going, and ready to advise Nicky where necessary. Gordon Ainslie, in his forties, was a slight man and still had a full head of hair, unlike Scott who was totally bald. Gordon was quiet and had a more serious demeanour and had a reputation as a hard working and ambitious lawyer. The two men had worked closely together for ten years and together had developed the business. Here, Nicky could learn from two experienced lawyers and perhaps develop her own special interests. Apart from the substantial opportunities which this new post offered, its location was also very convenient, being close to her flat. She determined to beaver away under their guidance and advice and try to build a solid foundation for her future career, putting all thought of John Amos aside.

During the first year of her employment with Martin and Ainslie, Nicky settled in happily. Her personal secretary, a young girl called Marilyn Crawford, always smart and efficient, became a trusted friend. She had worked in the office for three years already. She was an attractive, dark haired young lady, interested in fashion and jazz, but in the office, she dressed demurely and always behaved with the decorum appropriate for a legal office. The receptionist, Martha Landry was in her thirties, married but with no children and was easy to talk to, polite and personable, always ready with a smile. There were two other secretaries, one, Mrs. Agnes Corrigan, a middle aged lady, had been personal secretary for Mr. Martin for many years and had a wealth of experience behind her, and Grace Wilson, in her fifties and single, who worked with Gordon

Ainslie, was most congenial and helpful too. It was, without doubt, the wit and joviality of Scott Martin which kept the company in good spirits, for his gregariousness and camaraderie, pervaded the atmosphere and it wasn't long before Nicky felt that she was one of the family.

On Christopher's fifth birthday, she took him along for an interview to an elite and very expensive school. It was five miles out of town and would add significantly to her daily travelling but she was prepared to undertake this to provide Christopher with the best education she could. In due course, he was accepted into the school and the daily routine of travelling back and forth became an integral part of Nicky's life. She was proud of her handsome little boy and pleased to see that he enjoyed the new environment, made friends easily and soon settled in. In these early days of his schooling, a great proportion of Nicky's salary was siphoned off for school fees and extracurricular activities for Christopher but that was no hardship to her, she rarely spent money on herself except to maintain a very smart wardrobe for work and her evenings out were far and few between.

The work at Martin and Ainslie was interesting, her experience with business law increased over the following years and she rapidly became the firm's authority in that area, attending meetings and lectures on the subject at every opportunity. She avidly watched the stock market and read every journal she could get hold of.

As Scott Martin announced his intention to retire at the age of sixty five, the three partners held meetings to plan for the future. Scott had accumulated a large clientele and some well known and wealthy business people in the town. It was clear that a replacement partner would be required to carry the workload but Scott was anxious to assure his most important clients that there would be a seamless transfer to the care of Gordon or Nicky rather than being foisted upon a junior and inexperienced colleague.

'If we can't provide a continuous first rate service, these clients will shift their business elsewhere.' he said to Gordon and Nicky in the boardroom.

'How many of these elite people are we talking about?' asked Gordon, anxiously.

'Well, I can whittle the list down to three major players, the rest are less demanding and fairly tolerant,' Scott said, 'I have the three files here and I think we should go over their portfolios so you are familiar with their backgrounds because they are all complex and require a bit of thought.'

'OK' said Gordon. 'Fire away.'

'The first is Conrad Barclay. You'll know his name. He owns the large hotel chain which bears his name and various other smaller companies with which you will be less familiar. I'll pass along a copy of his assets to you. Conrad is now in his early seventies and has more money than he will ever need. His will is in order and a copy of that is also enclosed. It is complex because he was married twice and has children from both marriages. He also has a son with whom he does not communicate for some reason, and he is excluded from the inheritance. Conrad is quite fit for his age but he's getting on like the rest of us, and it is likely that one of you will be called upon to handle the will in due course so it's best if you familiarise yourselves with his wishes so there is no difficulty at the time.' Scott handed a copy each of Conrad Barclay's folder to Gordon and Nicky.

Gordon, who had seemed increasingly nervous as Scott's retirement loomed closer, flicked through the contents and remarked, 'I think this is more up Nicky's street than mine.'

'That's OK with me,' said Nicky, 'I don't mind taking this on. You'll be around for a while to keep us right, Scott, so perhaps we can spend some time together discussing the details before you go and perhaps meet the clients in the office. It takes time to get to know the full picture and you have the advantage of knowing the personalities as well.'

'Yes, of course, you're quite right. We will have to introduce you to the clients over a period of time to allow them to get to know you and to have faith in my successor. The introductions are not likely to be in the office, however. These three guys never darken our door. They are all control freaks, expect a personal home service, at the flick of a wrist, but it is worth it financially for the firm, so don't balk at that.'

'Who is your second biggie?' asked Gordon.

'Christian Telfer, the owner of the Telfer's Plant Hire Company. He's another one who has diverse interests, a company in Brussels as well as here. I liaise with a Belgian lawyer, Marcel Fourier, to keep tabs on his European interests but he has his finger in a number of pies and is forever buying and selling his holdings when he judges the time is right. Here is a copy of his portfolio, as at the end of last year.'

'Again, this is Nicky's territory,' said Gordon, testily, 'However, I don't want to inundate Nicky with all of this work and clearly she will need more time to manage these high flying businessmen. Perhaps I can take a larger share of the more routine work, the less problematic clients. I think that would suit me better in any event and it will allow someone with experience to take over that aspect of the business, which is clearly vital to the firm.'

'Yes, I agree,' said Scott, 'and actually I was going to ask Nicky to take number three in any case. He is another big businessman who can be very demanding but once he knows that you are up to date and keeping on top of things, he will relax. The third man is Jack Randall.'

It was as if a thunder bolt had hit her. Nicky suddenly shivered, her mouth opened and closed and a sense of dread filled her. Perhaps there were several Jack Randalls. Surely this was not the one who resided in Beaulieu?

If Scott had noticed Nicky's expression of alarm, he ignored it and continued,

'Jack Randall initially owned only the steel mill here in Edgerley but he steadily bought shares in the Manilaw Pharmaceutical Industry and now he owns a major share in that company, certainly has the controlling hand and that is where he has made most of his money although he has many other smaller interests. I've known Jack for a long time and we grew together as he acquired more and more shares and properties, so I know his assets pretty well. I'll give you his portfolio, Nicky, as I think Gordon is right, these people will all require your particular expertise.'

He handed Nicky Jack Randall's folder and she quickly perused the contents, her heart beating rapidly as she noted the address on Cherrybank Avenue. She wished then that she had accepted the offer of a post at Bradbrook, Kemp and Armstrong. This situation would not have arisen. Her initial enthusiasm for picking up Scott's most precious clientele, faded in an instant and she held on to the papers tightly because she knew that her hands were shaking.

'Now, in the course of the next few weeks and months, I will introduce you to all of these men and we will meet regularly to ensure that you are au fait with the details. Do you, by any chance, play golf, Nicky?' Scott asked.

'No, I'm afraid not,' she responded hesitantly.

'Pity, because they all like to chat during a round and in the clubhouse after. Never mind. That's probably a bloke thing, isn't it? We'll work at it one bit at a time, OK?'

'Yes, that sounds fine. Give me a day or two to go through the details and then set up a meeting.' Nicky said, wondering how she would ever deal with meeting Jack Randall.

14

Nicky was anxious and alarmed at the prospect of meeting Jack Randall face to face and wondered how she could ever develop a business relationship with this man, a man who had collaborated in the attempted murder of Christopher, but she had no choice in the matter. Gordon clearly was not prepared to take on these giants of industry and she had the knowledge and experience to do so. There was no one else available to take over Scott's three celebrities.

As the days passed, she studied all three portfolios in detail, particularly the one belonging to Jack Randall. She took the folder home with her and continued to deliberate and memorise every one of his holdings. She had to be well prepared when she met each of them but Jack Randall would be the biggest challenge because she knew that she would be emotionally unhinged when they eventually met and she would struggle to be calm and rational in his presence.

Almost two weeks after Scott had passed on the folders of his three elite clients, he came into Nicky's office and said, 'How have you been getting along with Jack Randall's folder?'

'I have been through it pretty thoroughly,' she replied.

'That's good, because I spoke to him on the golf course yesterday and told him about you. I have told him how good you are and he is happy for me to bring you along at our next meeting, which is Thursday afternoon. Can you make that, Nicky?'

Butterflies began to swarm in Nicky's stomach but she said, 'No problem.'

'Right, we'll leave about two thirty and be there around three pm. He has a magnificent house. You'll be impressed, I'm sure.'

Nicky smiled, she already knew that he had a magnificent house, but inside, she was far from happy. She wanted to run away and hide. How could she avoid a meeting with this man?

She had dismissed all thoughts of Beaulieu and its occupants since the day she had taken Christopher to the blossom-strewn street. Her curiosity had turned to anger and sorrow that day and she had concluded that it was something that should not be pursued, could bring nothing but heartache, but now, unexpectedly and unavoidably, she was about to meet Jack Randall and admire his luxurious home. She wondered if Christopher's mother would be there and how she would cope with that. The more thought she gave to it, the more worried she became. Her body trembled at the thought of being in Jack Randall's presence. However, one thing gave her strength. He didn't know who she was. He didn't know that she had been there that night and he didn't know that Christopher was alive and well. There, she had the advantage. For the occasion, she would be an actress, play the part of the astute lawyer, the perfect successor to Scott Martin but at the same time, she would be observing the man and trying to detect some clue, however small, that would confirm that he was indeed the man who had collaborated to hide Christopher in Mansion Hill Woods in a box, the man who was the driver of ESG 492 on that dark night of 30th October 1995.

The following days passed swiftly and all too soon it was Thursday. Nicky, who had been in a perpetual state of anxiety, had dressed in a dark navy trouser suit with a pale blue blouse just visible at the neck, and had been to the hairdresser. It was power dressing, she knew. She wanted to impress Jack Randall and she determined to act in the way he would expect, as a smart, efficient, business woman. Her knowledge of his portfolio was perfect. Indeed, she probably knew more about his holdings than he did, so thoroughly had she researched his interests. She could probably suggest a few changes too but she had to focus on the conversation and not miss a beat. It was imperative that no-one could suspect that she had more on the agenda than was planned.

At 2.30 pm, Scott Martin appeared and asked, 'Ready?'

She rose, collected her briefcase and joined him.

'You are looking pretty stunning, if I may say so,' said Scott admiringly.

'Must make the right impression, mustn't I?' she replied, smiling.

'You'll certainly do that, lass,' he said, 'I wouldn't say he was a ladies man, Jack, but he has been married before. His first wife died about ten years ago. She was a very pretty lady and they had one child, a daughter, Felicity. She must be, what, maybe twenty-five-ish now and she looked like her mother, blonde and slim, from my memory.'

They walked to the car and hopped in.

'Why do you use the past tense regarding Jack's daughter? What happened to her?' asked Nicky, trying to appear only vaguely interested.

'Well, unfortunately, the girl had a breakdown in her teens. It was very sad and Jack was dreadfully upset about it. She was a fragile, delicate creature and I suspect her temperament was on the delicate side too. Something happened to upset her. Nobody knows, or says, what triggered the change in her but it seemed to be a major mental breakdown from which she has never fully recovered. I believe that she is looked after in a special clinic and I don't think she comes home much at all now. I don't bring up the subject unless Jack does. It is, of course, a major source of disappointment to him. It broke his heart, and if I were you, I wouldn't mention anything about *children* while we are with him. He had such high hopes for her. I remember once when June and I attended a charity ball at which the Randalls were present, many years ago now, Felicity was there looking quite delightful, a waif of a creature. Jack spent a lot of time with Earnest Guild, an entrepreneurial individual who was reaching giddy heights and making a fortune at the time. He had his wife and son with him. The son, Jason Guild, must have been a year or two older than Felicity, a handsome and very intelligent young man., looking very striking in his dinner suit that evening, I may say. I think Jack did his best to foster that friendship in the hope that Jason and Felicity would get together but that didn't seem to happen.'

'Oh, thank you for giving me the *heads up* on that. I wouldn't want to put my foot in it on my first encounter,' Nicky said, trying to digest this new information. She clearly wouldn't be meeting Jack's daughter then.

'This is such a beautiful part of the town, isn't it, Nicky?' Scott remarked as the car drew into Cherrybank Avenue.

'Quite lovely and only for those with plenty of money.' replied Nicky.

The car turned into the stony driveway and approached the impressive carved centre door. Nicky recognized its arch-shape from her previous visit, and on the lawn, the ornate fountain was still spewing out cascades of bubbling water. A heavy feeling fixed itself in the pit of her stomach, as she stepped out of the car.

As they approached the main door, it was immediately opened by a smartly attired butler, dressed in a black suit and white shirt. He bowed respectfully, ushered them inside and asked them to wait for a moment in the hallway while he went off to ensure that they were expected and to be admitted to Mr. Randall's office.

Nicky was immediately awestruck by the grandiose foyer with its carved woodwork, its wide theatrical staircase and the intricate chandeliers which dangled from various points in the high ceiling. The central stairway rose to reach a huge, arched window, mirroring the shape of the front door, and from that point, it divided, curving symmetrically on each side, to form a gallery above the entrance hall. Ornately carved newels adorned the banister ends and a thick pile red carpet covered each step. It reminded Nicky of the hall depicted in Tara in the movie *Gone With the Wind*.

Suddenly the butler re-appeared and guided them through a long corridor, wood-panelled and carpeted in the same lush red covering.

They passed two closed doors and then the butler knocked firmly on the third door, which already was ajar. 'Mr. Martin and his associate, Mr. Randall.' he announced loudly.

'Come in, come in, Scott,' a deep voice said. As they entered, Nicky barely took in the shining mahogany desk, the leather swivel chair and the fitted bookcase along the whole length of one wall. She could hardly take her eyes from the tall man who stood up from his seat and came round the desk to shake their hands warmly and politely.

'Jack, this is my shining star, my brilliant colleague, Nicky Partington. Nicky, meet the great Jack Randall,' gushed Scott Martin, beaming.

Jack laughed and shook Nicky's hand firmly. She had to smile at Scott's extravagant introduction. Had it not been for the undercurrent of anxiety she was experiencing, it might have been a warm enough reception to break the ice with this important client but Nicky was picturing this man standing by a car on a cold, October night. It was hard to believe that this apparently warm hearted, amiable man could have been the same person.

'Sit down, please sit down,' he said, as he seated himself behind the large desk.

Scott's joviality continued unabated. Jokes were cracked and Nicky was regaled with numerous amusing golfing reminiscences. It was clear that the two men were close friends and had a strong bond. The conversation turned to business and Nicky periodically contributed or asked questions but most of the time, she sat, observing and listening. She snatched a brief glimpse through the window on her right and saw the spacious well kept garden, the summer house and marble figures, but for the most part she couldn't take her eyes off Jack Randall. In her mind, it was another place, another time. Memories of that night flooded in. She wanted to say, *'I was there that night. Christopher is safe,'* but more than anything she wanted to ask, *'Why, why, why did you do it?'*

She restrained herself, battling the parallel trains of thought and forcing herself to listen to the discussion. Having said little up to that point, she decided to proffer her suggestions for the future in several areas and obviously impressed Jack with her knowledge and judgment.

'That's interesting,' he remarked. 'You're right, Nicky. We may have to watch what happens there and if necessary, make a move. I see you have your finger on the pulse. Thank you for that.'

The butler brought coffee and the conversation proceeded without any embarrassment or hiccough. There was no mention of Jack's daughter. Scott expertly directed the discussion, oiling the wheels with his easy manner and humorous remarks.

'Well, we'll leave you in peace, Jack,' said Scott, rising. 'I just wanted to let you and Nicky get to know each other. As I told you, my retirement is imminent and I want to assure you that Martin and Ainslie will continue to look after your interests as well as before. In fact, probably a greater deal better. Nicky has considerable experience in Corporate Law now; she is much more up to date than I am, and I think she has demonstrated that today. She won't let you down.'

Jack Randall rose from his leather chair and nodded. 'Thank you both for coming. I'm sorry you're going, Scott. We've had a lot of laughs as well as having a productive business relationship. I hope you are not going to give up golf, too. You're the only person I can beat nowadays.'

'I'll get so much practice in, you'll not be able to say that any more,' said Scott as they made their way out to the foyer, laughing and shaking hands again.

Facing the great wooden door on the way out, Nicky caught sight of two huge portraits, hanging on each side, one of an elegant slim, blonde lady, her hair swept back into a chignon, wearing an off-the-shoulder white evening gown and sparkling diamond necklace and the other of a much younger version, an attractive blonde girl with a pony tail wearing a pale pink polo neck sweater and beige riding jodhpurs.

Nicky's knees felt like jelly and she could hardly bear to look at the smiling innocent face. This had to be Jack's daughter, Felicity, and Christopher's real mother. She quickly sped out to the car before her feelings became apparent to the others. Stomach cramps gripped her and she wanted to hold herself tightly in case she should vomit, but she did her best to hide her anxiety and hurried into the car.

'Well, that went well, didn't it? What did you make of Jack?' asked Scott, once they were in the car and moving slowly down the drive. He was oblivious to Nicky's discomfort.

'He seemed very charming, astute, affable.' replied

Nicky, trying hard to appear relaxed.

'Yes, he can be all those things but he can also be bad tempered and vitriolic. If things are not going according to Jack he can be quite abrasive. I must say, though, that he has mellowed over the last few years, perhaps because of his daughter's illness, I don't know. I suppose he has made his fortune and there is less stress for him now. He has nothing to prove any more. He certainly took to you like a duck to water.'

'Do you think so? I do hope that's true if we are to work together,' Nicky said, trying to behave calmly although her insides were churning painfully.

Scott didn't seem to notice Nicky's unease and told everybody in the office how impressed Jack Randall had been with her. She acknowledged his remarks and laughed but escaped as quickly as she could into her own office where she collapsed in her chair, cradling her head in her shaking hands. She tried to hold back the tears in case someone popped in but inside, her heart was breaking. Christopher was almost six years old now. It seemed that his mother was Jack Randall's daughter, Felicity; a beautiful girl who had suffered a breakdown and had never recovered. Nicky turned that around in her mind and wondered if the breakdown could have been related to the birth of her son or if it had occurred earlier. Something tragic had happened that night in Beaulieu. The whole business just filled her with sorrow. She hadn't wanted to know any more but circumstances had determined that it wasn't over and as luck had it, she was destined to become Jack Randall's personal lawyer. There seemed no way out. For a moment she considered changing law firms. She could ask John Amos if she could go back to Bradbrook, Kemp and Armstrong, He would agree, she knew, but that was another problem, something else she wanted to avoid. Life was suddenly becoming very difficult.

Marilyn came in with a cup of coffee and Nicky pulled herself together. Scott Martin was still in post for a few months yet and she would throw herself into work to keep her mind occupied. This had always worked before. A replacement would have to be found for Scott in due course. Perhaps they would be lucky enough to attract an experienced, golfing lawyer who suited Jack Randall's needs and she would be able to bow out. She still had to meet the other two magnates, Christian Telfer and Conrad Barclay, but these men posed no problem for her, there was no personal involvement and she was not going to worry about them.

15

The following summer, the firm planned a grand party to celebrate Scott Martin's pending retirement. A suitable venue was selected, some two hundred invitations were printed and a catering company chosen, but it was a great sadness when Scott died unexpectedly of a heart attack on the golf course only days before his last day at the firm. Almost sixty five years of age and so full of life, it was hard to believe he had gone. His cheerfulness and ebullience were sorely missed in the office. No longer did he bounce in with his jovial greetings, his quick wit and his easy going manner. The atmosphere in the office changed overnight. Nicky was devastated, not only because he had been such a friend and support but because now she would be plunged into her role as Jack Randall's adviser.

'Nicky, you must be strong,' said Marilyn one morning as the girls met for coffee. 'You are the one who may end up holding the fort here.'

'What do you mean?' she asked,' Gordon Ainslie is fit and well, isn't he? I expect he will take over the role of senior partner with no problem and be around for a long time to come.'

'Oh, you don't know, then,' Marilyn continued, 'Gordon had a bit of a health scare several years ago. He went blind in one eye for a while. At the time, he had lots of tests and ultimately, the doctors diagnosed multiple sclerosis. He has been pretty well since then but he was told to take things easier and not to get too stressed. It was difficult for him because he is an ambitious, clever chap and his wife had just had a baby girl. He has been cutting down a bit on his workload over the last few years and in fact, it was because of his illness, that your post was created to help ease the work he was doing.'

'No, I didn't know that,' said Nicky, concerned at the news, 'We should get another person in post as quickly as possible then. I will be taking on some of Scott's clients but it won't be good for Gordon to carry the brunt of the additional clientele as well as his own workload.'

On the following day, feeling that there was, more than ever now, a pressing need to fill the vacancy which had become available through Scott's unexpected demise, Nicky approached Gordon Ainslie to discuss the matter but he had already anticipated the problem and asked her,

'Nicky, do you know of any suitable graduates who might be prepared to come to work with us? What about friends in your year? Have they all settled down already?'

'I'm not sure, but I can ask around. There were several who were bright and easy to get along with. I'll explore the situation. It will be good to get someone else in post as soon as possible. In the meantime, please don't hesitate to delegate anything you can. I'm happy to work longer hours for a while until there are three of us again.'

'The girls have told you about my MS then?' he asked.

'Yes, I'm sorry to hear about that, but you seem to be OK at the moment, don't you?'

'Yes, I've actually cut down on the work since you've come. I get very tired sometimes and stress seems to make it worse so I have to keep things steady and calm. I have put a pile of problems over here,' he said, pointing to a large collection of folders and documents on the edge of his desk. 'I would be grateful if you could take on some of these clients but you can't do everything. If you feel it's too much, just say so. We may have to turn some business away for the time being.'

'That's fine,' said Nicky, gathering up all the papers into her arms, 'I'm glad that you are using me; that's what I'm here for. Please don't overdo things. I'm sure we will cope in the short term. At least Scott had prepared us for what was to come, and if we advertise in a week or two, we may get lucky and attract some hard working experienced partner to the firm.'

'You're a great help, Nicky. I appreciate it. You're right, of course. We must try to expedite a replacement for Scott, although, in many ways, he is really pretty irreplaceable. By the way, his funeral is on Thursday afternoon at 2 pm and I think we should all go.'

'Yes, some of the girls have worked with Scott for years; the office can close for the day, maybe Friday, too, and all the staff can attend. I'm sure they will want to pay their last respects to Scott. He was very popular and a great leader.'

'Let's do that. Close Thursday and Friday. That's a good idea. I'm going to say a few words at the church. Can you make sure the girls all get there?'

'Of course, I'll pick them up personally and take them there. I'll tell them right now so that they all know what's happening,' she said, gripping the bundle of papers.

As Thursday came around, Nicky arranged to meet all the girls at the office and drove them to the church.

The small chapel was almost full when Nicky arrived with Marilyn, Martha, Agnes and Grace. They filed down the aisle to the front pew where Mrs. Martin sat, tearful and slumped between two tall, handsome lads on one side and a tearful young girl on the other, whom Nicky presumed were her children. They each solemnly offered their condolences and then slid into the second row. The girls were sincerely upset at Scott's passing; all were tearful and quiet.

Nicky sat at one end of the little group, deep in her own thoughts about Scott Martin's replacement and Gordon Ainslie's illness. The enjoyable honeymoon period was at an end. Now she would find herself taking on more and more work. Her sphere was expanding. The added responsibility did not bother her, she would embrace that, but it concerned her that Gordon might at any point, suffer a relapse, and she could find herself drowning in the work. She didn't mind working hard but she had Christopher to consider too and it was imperative that someone else was taken on soon.

Absorbed in her own thoughts, she was only vaguely aware of someone moving along the seats towards her and as he took the adjacent seat, she looked up to see that it was John Amos who had chosen to sit beside her.

'Hi,' he said, quietly. 'Sorry to hear about Scott. You must be sorry to lose him. He was a good man.'

'Did you know him well?' she asked, her eyes drifting over him and a familiar longing filling her.

'Yes. We had known each other for a long time. We discussed clients periodically and I have played a round or two of golf with him on occasion.'

Nicky wondered if John had played golf with Jack Randall too. It seemed likely.

'Yes, he will be sadly missed. His presence was always so positive, so calming, so welcoming. He has taught me a lot and I'll miss his guiding hand.' she said, so aware that his proximity made her body tingle. All her resolute decisions to keep her distance from him began to crumble. She wanted him to hold her hand or to make some gesture of affection, and yet, she didn't. Life was hard enough without John Amos in her life.

The organ music played quietly as Scott Martin's coffin

was brought solemnly in. The 23rd psalm was sung and then the minister began his text and the congregation fell silent apart from the gentle sobbing of close relatives and friends. Nicky watched the grieving widow and her stalwart sons and daughter cling together as tributes were paid to their nearest and dearest. Gordon Ainslie, looking rather pale, made a moving and apt speech about his beloved colleague and the girls sitting beside Nicky dissolved into more tears.

The ceremony over, and the music fading, Mrs. Martin and her children rose stiffly to walk down the aisle to a place where friends and relatives could shake their hands and express their sorrow. The congregation rose to follow. John Amos turned to Nicky, his coat brushing her sleeve as he said, 'There will always be a place for you at Bradbrook's, you know.'

Nicky raised her eyes to meet his and all the emotions which he triggered, welled up inside her. How easy it would be to agree to his proposal and forget the problems which beset her! Why was life so unfair? Eventually, she replied, 'That's nice to know, John, but right now Gordon will need support and I must stay there. It wouldn't be right for me to jump ship at this moment. We will take on a third person soon and hopefully things will settle down again. It's a good place to work and Gordon is an agreeable colleague, too.'

'OK,' he said, 'but I'm there if you need me.' He moved on, following the mourners up the aisle, with Nicky close behind him. She looked up at his dark hair, a few strands curling over his pristine white collar and wanted to touch the soft wool, navy coat which hung so perfectly from his broad shoulders. She watched him as he took Mrs. Martin's delicate hand in both of his and told her of his great admiration for her husband. Nicky followed and could barely speak to the woman; she was so filled with emotion. Once out of the chapel, she herded the girls together and made for the car, keeping a casual eye out for John Amos, and it was with a sense of relief that she saw him getting into his own BMW.

'We have all been invited to the house for drinks so I think we must do that out of respect, are you all in agreement?' she asked the girls.

'Yes,' they chorused.

'We'll not stay long, maybe just an hour, if that suits you all and I'll take you home afterwards.' she promised.

The short journey to the Martins' residence gave the girls time to collect themselves, and the hankies were finally dispatched with.

The Martins' house was beautiful with well kept gardens and a mini golf course tucked away at the back. The interior décor was expensive and of high quality but comfortable and homely. A local catering firm served canapés and champagne while the guests milled around. The majority of the guests were legal and business acquaintances and several were anxious to quiz Nicky and Gordon on the future of Martin and Ainslie. Gordon stood with Nicky and together, they showed a united front, supporting the continuance of the firm and talking of plans for the future. It was an opportunity to put out feelers about possible suitable new colleagues and the conversation moved on to that topic.

'I keep trying to entice her away from you,' a voice said, 'but she will have none of it.'

'Hi, John, how are you?' said Gordon as John Amos entered the group.

Nicky looked at him, her heart immediately beating more rapidly.

'We are looking for a new member of the team, so if you happen to know of someone good, perhaps you can let us know,' she said, trying to be calm and objective but she feared that her blushes would tell him what she was really feeling.

The conversation continued, others joined the group and Nicky eased away. She found Mrs. Martin surrounded with friends but gradually pushed through to chat to her. 'You can see that we are all here today. The girls were quite adamant that they had to come and so we closed the office for a couple of days. It's amazing how much one person can affect so many. Scott brought out the best in everyone and gave us all a bit of fun every day. He was such a joy to work with and we are all going to miss him dreadfully.'

'He loved going to work too, you know. He started up that business twenty five years ago and it meant the world to him. Agnes and Grace have been very loyal to him for many years. He was lucky to have found such good colleagues. I hope you and Gordon will keep it afloat,' Mrs. Martin said.

'We intend to do that, June, and if we can help you in any way at all, please, just let us know,' she said.

Another friend pushed through to embrace June Martin and Nicky extricated herself. Time was moving on and she decided to find the ladies room and then collect the girls.

The toilet was situated down a long corridor painted off-white, the thick pile, aqua carpet lending a cool air to the place. There were numerous framed photographs of Scott with various colleagues and golfing buddies hanging on the walls. She noticed one picture of Scott with Jack Randall, both smiling, arms around each other, and she wondered why she had not seen him at the funeral.

It had been an emotional day and John Amos's presence made her feel like a lovesick teenager. Each time she thought that he had moved on out of her life, he was suddenly back. She splashed her hot face in cool water and then spent some time carefully re-applying her makeup and trying to regain her composure.

As she stepped out of the room, she saw that John Amos was walking slowly towards her, as if he had been waiting for her to emerge. As they neared, he took her arm and led her gently into an adjoining room. It was a small study with heavily embossed wallpaper, well-filled bookcases, a large desk with red leather inlay and a matching upholstered chair. He gently pushed the door shut, stood close to her, too close, and whispered to her, 'I don't know what to do, Nicky.' He drew her to him and she found that her resistance had disappeared. She should be walking away, telling him to move off, but she stood rooted to the spot, letting him melt into her, his arms encircling her, their bodies entwined. Their cheeks touched, gently at first and then pressed urgently together and soon his warm moist mouth sought and found hers. Their bodies moulded together as one and she was unable to restrain herself, holding him with the same fervor as he held her, an overwhelming need enveloping her whole being. It was where she wanted to be, where she belonged and only slowly and reluctantly did she withdraw from the embrace.

'You know how I feel about you, Nicky,' he said, his voice cracking with emotion.

'This is why I can't work at Bradbrook's. You know that, don't you?' she said quietly.

'I just want to have you near,' he said, holding both of her hands in his.

'It wouldn't work, John. We would hurt your wife and children and in the end, we would hurt each other. It wouldn't do the firm any good, either.'

He held her close again and said, 'I love you, Nicky. I have always loved you.' She could hear the need in his voice and so wanted to tell him it would be all right, that she felt the same way but images of a cardboard box in a wood came into her mind, memories of falsified documents, a birth certificate and a lifetime of lies and she pushed him gently away.

'You don't really know much about me, John. If you scrape the surface, you might find that you feel quite differently about me. Whatever feelings we have for each other can't lead anywhere. We can never have a future together and we have to accept that. Please don't make it more difficult than it is.'

He stepped back a little way and said, 'When you say that I don't know you, do you mean I don't know about Christopher, his father, the way it was then for you?'

She thought for a few minutes. 'Yes, that's exactly what I mean.'

'But it's in the past, years ago. A lot of water has run under the bridge for both of us; it's not important now.'

She looked into his moist dark eyes, caressed his cheek gently and said,

'The past and the future are not dissociated, at least not for me. Christopher is my life, my reason for living, nothing will ever change that.'

'I know how much you love him but you have a life, too. He won't always be with you. He'll grow up and get married. He may emigrate. Who knows, kids move on. Eventually you will be on your own again. You can't deny yourself a loving relationship, can you?'

The answer had always been clear to Nicky. No-one could ever know about the past. There could never be an honest relationship with anyone, male or female. There had been too many lies. There were no words she could think of to answer him and she turned to go.

'You're still in love with him, aren't you? Is that why you can't get close to someone else? Are you thinking that one day he will come back into your life?'

'Who?'

'Christopher's father.'

'I haven't given him any thought for about six years,'

she said, thinking that at least that was true, and trying to edge away from him. The questions were getting too hard to answer, too near the truth.

'Can we at least be friends, Nicky?' he said grasping her hand again, reluctant to let the matter rest.

She looked at his face and his soft eyes and she longed for him so much.

'I hope so,' she said and slid her fingers from his grasp.

16

Work was all consuming over the next few months and Nicky took on as much of Scott Martin's load as she could, partly to keep herself well occupied and partly because of her concern for Gordon Ainslie's health. Three month's after Scott's death, a new partner was appointed, a young man, called Peter MacDonald, three years graduated, who had been working in London and found the travelling and pace of life unacceptable there. Peter was married and had two children. He was a family man and a keen angler. During the first year without Scott, Gordon Ainslie suffered periods of tiredness and lethargy and from time to time, he was forced to take prolonged breaks, but the three of them worked well together and the firm showed a steady profit.

Money was ploughed back into the business and a major refurbishment was carried out, up-to-date computer networking was installed and more clerical staff employed. There was an all pervading atmosphere of success and productivity about the place. Nicky worked tirelessly and with Gordon Ainslie's medical problems and Peter MacDonald's inexperience, it was Nicky who became head of the firm. Two years on, a fourth partner was appointed, a new graduate called Gavin Ross, a single man, and a source of much admiration by the girls in the office. The business was on a roll, and it was Nicky who engineered the direction of its progress.

In spite of all that was happening, she selected a new

apartment in an up market part of town and furnished it lavishly. Christopher was enjoying school and she had more time to concentrate on the business. She wrote articles for recognised journals, lectured at various conferences and social gatherings, took work home with her and accepted all the business that came her way.

Nicky became well-known in legal circles, and when she had been with Martin and Ainslie for twelve years, she was elected to the chairmanship of a prestigious national corporate law group. She was not yet thirty five and had risen to great heights through her relentless dedication and hard work. Christopher had reached the age of seventeen, had excelled at school and was embarking on a university degree in engineering and computer sciences. Throughout his youth, Nicky had devoted all of her free time to helping him, to supporting his interests and guiding him towards a useful career. As he matured, their close bond and trust, built over the years, had only strengthened.

Nicky was proud of her son and never regretted the decision she had made to keep him. Often, she forgot that he wasn't her real son, the lies and cover-ups had been effective with her, too. Time had passed without further difficulties and she had begun to feel safe and secure. The initial questions asked about him as a child, were no longer a problem. She had all the answers and had put all thoughts of the past out of her mind. She did meet with Jack Randall regularly but she had succeeded in maintaining a professional relationship with him, leaving behind the thoughts which troubled her and had determined to let sleeping dogs lie. His wife, Sylvie always greeted her in a friendly fashion too. Nothing good could come from pursuing the past.

Christopher had never asked about his father, accepting what she had told him at the start, that he was the result of a brief liaison when she was young. He was secure in her love and had never felt the need to discover any more.

Her peace of mind was disturbed, however, when, one afternoon, she had scheduled an appointment with Jack Randall and on arrival, his wife Sylvie, met her in the foyer. Sylvie, as usual, was dressed expensively with a designer outfit of pale turquoise.

There were ladders everywhere, white covers over the banisters and a team of decorators at work. 'Oh, Nicky, I do apologise for all of this mess. I am having a makeover of the entrance hall. It is too dark and dim. Jack has finally allowed me to make a few changes but of course, it takes weeks and is associated with a great deal of inconvenience.'

'Don't apologise, Sylvie. I'm sure it will all look wonderful when it is finished. No pain, no gain. Isn't that what they say?'

'Absolutely. Listen, when you and Jack are through, let me show you what's happening upstairs. I would value your opinion.'

'That would be lovely,' said Nicky, following the butler to Jack's office.

It was a short meeting, Jack seemed preoccupied and after signing a few papers, he thanked her for coming and she rose to leave.

As she reached the foyer, Sylvie grabbed her arm and said, 'Come on, Nicky. Mind the stairs. Don't trip.' And she led her upstairs along the balcony. Here there was a marvelous view of the garden through the Gothic style window and Nicky found herself enthusing about the architecture, the décor and the unique design of the house.

'Yes, when I brought Scott Martin up here, all he could say was, *'Is that the golf course over there?'* She laughed at the memory as she pointed away into the distance.

'Scott enjoyed his golf. We really miss him.'

'Jack was very close to him. They were friends long

before I met Jack and they played golf almost every week together. He was a delightful man and we were very sorry to miss the funeral but we had just flown in to Switzerland for a short break and we didn't know about it in time. We have a house over there.'

Nicky remembered that the Randalls had been missing from the funeral. Now she had the explanation.

'So, what colour is this section to be painted?' asked Nicky, pointing to a denuded wall on the balcony.

'I've chosen an exquisite fleur-de-lis patterned wallpaper, mainly a light cream colour so that will brighten up the balcony. Look, here is a sample,' she said, unfolding a long roll. 'What do you think?'

Nicky admired the choice of paper and complimented Sylvie on her courageous alterations.

'It hasn't actually had a coat of paint in years. Jack never wants to change anything. He likes everything to stay the same. I have such a problem getting him to agree, but for some reason, he is allowing me free rein this time,' she said excitedly.

'It's a huge undertaking. Are you doing the whole house?' Nicky asked.

'Almost,' she laughed 'While Jack is in a good mood, I'm getting on with it. He can't stand the intrusion of workmen and noise so I'm setting everything in motion and then we are going off to Switzerland to our house there so that when we come back in a few months, it will all be finished.'

'That's a great idea. You will miss all the upheaval and mess.'

'That's the plan.'

As they walked along past bedrooms and bathrooms which all seemed to contain a paint pot or roll of wallpaper, Sylvie provided a running commentary of her plans. 'This room will not be changed, unfortunately,' she said, opening a large, curved, wooden door.

'This is Felicity's room. It is all pink because she liked this colour scheme when she was here. Pink drapes, pink carpet, pink bedspread, it's all so little girly but Jack won't have it changed.'

'Doesn't she come home any more?' asked Nicky innocently.

'No, she stays in a special clinic. You know that she had a breakdown years ago and it seems that she is unlikely to get much better. However, she is happy there and well looked after, so I think we should just redecorate but Jack won't hear of it.'

Suddenly there was a light knock on the door and the maid appeared.

'Yes, Esther, what is it?' enquired Sylvie.

'Mrs. Davidson is here. It's about the fete. Do you wish to speak with her, Madam?' she asked politely.

'Oh, yes. Please excuse me, Nicky, I'll be right back. We are organizing a money raising event for needy children.' She left with Esther leaving Nicky alone in Felicity's bedroom.

Nicky felt ill at ease and walked over to the grand bay window framed with pink, silk drapes, and looked out at the view. It was a magnificent panorama but far in the distance she could see the woods on Mansion Hill and her stomach lurched. How could Felicity ever look out of this window, to be reminded every day of what she had done? Nicky turned away and began to examine the delicate ornaments sitting on the dressing table. Gently opening the top drawer, she found only white, lacy underwear was contained therein. She closed it and opened the next drawer. Inside were more undergarments and on top, a photo frame face down in the lingerie. She slipped out the photograph and turned it up. Facing her was a happy couple- Felicity, looking radiant and smiling broadly, leaning against a very handsome young man, a coloured man with dark eyes and even white teeth. He was wearing a naval uniform and in the background of the picture was a ship with the name *HMS Newark* on it. Nicky looked at the man, his features so like those of Christopher, and she knew that she was looking at a picture of Christopher's mother and father. She quickly unclipped the back of the frame and slipped the photograph into her briefcase. Closing the drawer nervously, she left the room. Downstairs, Sylvie was just saying her goodbyes to Mrs. Davidson as Nicky reached the doorway and so she said, 'Thank you so much for the tour. It's all going to look wonderful, I'm sure. I must get back to the office. Have a lovely time in Switzerland. Bye.'

She couldn't wait to get to the car and away from Beaulieu. She had a photo of Christopher's parents. She had never known who his father might be and having a photograph provided a piece missing from the jigsaw of events- Christopher's father. Some day she would have to tell Christopher everything she knew. Perhaps she would leave him a synopsis in her will. He had a right to know who his parents were but he didn't need to know about the problems which beset his family and which led them to rejecting him and she knew that she couldn't ever have the courage to tell him that.

It was lunch time and she decided to stop at a favourite bistro, L'isle du paix' situated near her new flat. It served French cuisine and unusual fish dishes, but apart from the delicious food it was well designed with discreet bays where customers could converse in relative privacy. She wanted to be alone with her thoughts and selected a quiet table by the window. The head waiter, Georges, knew her well and after exchanging pleasantries he took her order for the Dover sole with herb sauce. For a while she watched the passersby and thought about Felicity, a pretty girl who had been in love with this man in the photograph. That was clear. What had gone wrong? Why was the photo secreted away in a drawer, face down? Had Felicity put it there or did Jack want to hide the past. Did he not want a constant reminder of Felicity's connection to this man? Christopher should be with them, living a privileged life in that mansion on Cherrybank Avenue. She couldn't give him such luxury but she could give him love.

She picked at the sole and then pushed the plate aside. Opening her briefcase she withdrew the photograph and stared at the couple, searching their eyes, studying every feature. They made such a handsome, happy couple. She turned the picture over and read the message inscribed on it: *To my beloved Felicity with all my love. Yours always, Alex.* Printed at the bottom, it read *HMS Newark, April 1995.* Nicky turned the picture over again.

So you are Alex, Christopher's father, she thought. His face was familiar now, perhaps because of the resemblance to his son. For a long time, she gazed at the man.

Something had happened between April and October 30th 1995, something which split this lovely couple, Felicity and Alex, and ended in disaster. A feeling of great sadness overwhelmed her. Christopher's parents should have wanted him, loved him, protected him. Why hadn't they?

Each piece of new information brought feelings of sadness and Nicky really didn't want to think about it any more. It was too hard. She slipped the photograph back into her briefcase, paid the bill and set off back to the office.

17

'Your next appointment is here, Miss Partington,' Marilyn Crawford announced, as soon as Nicky crossed the threshold.

'Oh, thanks, Marilyn. I had forgotten that I had agreed to an extra appointment. Do we know anything about this man?' she asked, taking the thin folder from her secretary.

'His name is Jeremy Ratcliffe and he says that he is representing Star Magazine.'

'OK, Marilyn, ask him to come in,' said Nicky, sitting behind her large walnut desk, placing the briefcase at her feet, and collecting her wits.

A few minutes later, Marilyn returned, a short, slim middle-aged man in tow. Nicky took in at a glance the unpressed grey suit, the cheap shirt, the unkempt greying hair and the smell of alcohol. She hoped that whatever he wanted, he would not stay long.

She stood up and shook his hand, which seemed limp and damp. 'How can I be of assistance to you, Mr. Ratcliffe?' she said, sitting down again and trying to appear interested in this client, whose appeal was definitely waning.

'It's very good of you to give me a little of your precious time, Miss Partington.' he said, patronisingly. 'I am a freelance journalist and from time to time the Editor of Star Magazine invites me to write an article for them. You may be familiar with our publication?'

'Yes, I have seen it and read it on occasion. Indeed you may find a few copies in our waiting room.' she said politely.

'Excellent,' he said. 'Well, you will know then that the magazine features eminent business people who have achieved a great deal in their careers. The article, of course, brings with it, publicity, and this in itself may be good for business. The public has an appetite to hear about successful people and I'm here today because the editor has been following your career with interest and was impressed with your recent elevation to the chairmanship of the National Business Group. He thinks that this would be an opportune time to have a story about you. Being a woman, your success appeals to businesswomen as well as men, and being a single mother, as I understand, is an added bonus. It sets you up as a great role model for working women. So I am here on the Editor's behalf to seek your permission to write an article about you, your career, the university you attended, the efforts you have had to make and so on. We would like to include a few pictures, perhaps with you sitting here at your desk, if that is acceptable to you.'

Nicky was flattered by this offer and despite her negative feeling about the journalist, she said, 'That is very complimentary.'

'Well, if you are agreeable, Miss Partington, I would begin to put together the broad bones of the story and then come back to you for editing and confirmation and perhaps some photographs. Your academic achievements are listed in the university press and I can no doubt pick up some quotes from your presentations which are well publicised. Essentially, I shall be highlighting your rise to great heights and the success of the firm here. I believe you worked with Scott Martin who started this firm and it is a great credit to you that it has gone from strength to strength since his death.'

'That sounds perfectly all right with me,' she replied, pleased at the recognition it would bring to the firm.

'That's wonderful. I will make another appointment then, with your secretary, for next Thursday and, if you don't mind, bring along the magazine's photographer so we can snap a few pictures of you here at your desk. Is that OK?' he said.

'Yes, speak to Marilyn. She will give you a convenient time.' She stood up, shook his limp hand again and returned to her work at the desk.

The week seemed to fly past as her desk was constantly piled with work. Gordon Ainslie had taken two weeks off at short notice and although her colleagues Peter and Gavin picked up some of the pending work, she found herself under more pressure than usual. By Thursday, she had almost forgotten that the creepy journalist was paying her another visit. Before she knew it, Thursday came around and Marilyn reminded her that Jeremy Ratcliffe and a photographer would be coming at 3pm. She hadn't had time to give his article much thought and hoped that he would produce an acceptable story. It was, as he had said, good for business, and so she greeted the two men amicably at 3 pm. The photographer, a man in his thirties called Malcolm Lees, had shoulder length thinning and dyed blonde hair, a pair of khaki pants, and a green shirt with sleeves rolled up. He carried in various cameras, lights and tripods as he smiled pleasantly at her, making suggestions regarding her position at the desk, trying a photograph with her holding a pen, reading a paper or answering the telephone.

Ratcliffe stood back, giving the photographer room to stage his shots. Nicky sat compliantly in different poses, and tried to look relaxed. After innumerable flashes, Malcolm seemed satisfied with his work and packed up his gear, saying that she would receive a copy of the pictures in due course when they were developed and they would select the best ones together.

As he left the room, Ratcliffe pulled up a chair opposite the desk and sat down. Nicky didn't like his behaviour. The faint smell of alcohol reached her and she sat back in her chair, but she knew that he would want to go over his article with her. She asked him, 'And how are you progressing with the article?'

Ratcliffe pulled a sheaf of papers from his worn satchel and, crossing his legs, balanced the notes on his knees. 'I have collected quite a lot of information, Miss Partington, and it is just a question of putting it all together now. However, there are a few points which have confused me,' he said, rubbing his chin with his long fingers.

Nicky waited patiently, trying to appear relaxed and interested in what he was saying.

'When I researched the university records, I discovered that you had actually started a history degree in 1994 and then a year later, you started your law degree.'

'Yes, my initial studies were interrupted by an accident,' she said helpfully.

He nodded. 'Further delving into this brought forth the story of your car accident in 1994, a tragic disaster for you and your whole family. I was going to include this in the article as it shows even more, your great survival instinct.'

'How did you find out about the accident?' asked Nicky, beginning to feel nervous.

'The university records include the reason for your interrupted course and so I went on to look at local newspapers and actually there was a long piece in the Guardian in 1994 describing the horrific accident and your multiple injuries. It was obviously a dreadful time for you.'

'This is ancient history, Mr. Ratcliffe, and I don't think your readers need to hear about the accident in any detail. I would prefer that part of my life was skipped over,' she said quickly.

'Yes, I understand,' he said, and Nicky hoped she had curbed his interest in her past, but he went on to say,' There was, of course, a bit of a conundrum.'

'What is that?' she asked.

'Well, I did go along to the registrar's office to read the details of your son's birth, to get the date and so on, and I was surprised to find that he was registered on 30th October 1995.'

Nicky's heart sank and she asked, 'Why did that surprise you?'

He raised his reptilian eyes to meet hers and said, 'Because I also searched the hospital records at the time of the accident and found that the hospital notes say that you had a hysterectomy in November 1994.'

He paused and continued to stare at her, waiting for a reaction.

Nicky felt an adrenaline rush and the sweat on her hands, as the man delivered his findings.

'Hospital records are confidential, Mr. Ratcliffe. You had no right to access my medical history. It is illegal.'

'Absolutely. You are right and I apologise for doing so, but you will see that I am in a dilemma now.'

'Why, you can write your article without reference to the accident or anything that pertains to it,' she said, hoping to bluff her way out of this.

'I could do that,' he said. Nicky picked up on the insincerity and cynicism in his tone, but she remained silent.

He continued, 'You're right, of course. My methods were less than acceptable. However, if we proceed a little further with this, we find that your actions were not entirely legitimate either. Is that not the case, Miss Partington?'

'To what are you referring now?' she enquired, sullenly.

'Your son's birth certificate.'

'What about it?'

He fingered the papers on his knee and read from them.

'It states that you delivered a baby boy in the local hospital on October 30th 1995. However, that is not the case. There is no hospital record of that delivery and that could not possibly be the case if you had a hysterectomy a year prior to that date.'

He paused, wringing his hands in a disconcerting way that made Nicky feel that she was up against a conniving and devious person.

'It occurred to me that, if you had not been the person to deliver that particular baby, then there must have been some mistake, or... some wrongdoing with the birth certificate.'

He paused for effect and swung his legs one over the other. Nicky picked up on his apparent discomfiture- or was it that he was enjoying hers?

' I visited the registrar's office, as I told you, in Meredith Lane, and spoke with Ted Innes, a most helpful young man who said that he knew you quite well because you had actually been employed in that very office during the months of May until you started university in October. He remembered how proficient you were with the computer and he also recalled that occasionally, you brought your young son along to the office with you. When I asked him if he recalled the registration of your son's birth, he could not recollect that, but he suggested that, since Mrs. Marshall was working in the office as registrar at that time, and had since retired, it might be worth my while speaking with her.'

Nicky was not surprised to hear that Mary had by now retired from her position and wondered what she had thought of these enquiries.

'Mrs. Marshall was positively effusive, singing your

praises. She said that she was extremely proud to have known you and not at all surprised that you had achieved such success. She always rated your ability very highly.'

Nicky wondered where all of this was heading. How much did he know about Christopher's birth? Could he have any inkling of his parentage? She couldn't believe that he had worked that out. There was no trail leading to the Randalls.

'She, like Ted Innes, had no recollection of you registering your son's birth and could not recall any conversation with you about that. I asked her if anyone could forge a birth certificate and she was quite adamant that that was not possible, given that it required her signature and her personal seal on each form. I pointed out to her that her signature and seal were appended to that certificate. To cut a long story short, she disliked my insinuations regarding your integrity and more or less shut the door in my face.'

Good for you, Mary, she thought. 'Is that it?' she asked.

'For your information, Mr. Ratcliffe, I adopted Christopher in a private agreement.' she hastily contrived.

'I'm sure you did, and that was very noble and generous of you. However, the fact then remains that the birth certificate is wrong and likely fraudulently obtained.'

'The information you have gleaned has been obtained in an underhand way and consequently, would not stand up in court, Mr. Ratcliffe.'

'Oh, I have no interest in going to court, Miss Partington. You're right. I would not wish to put my misdemeanours on show in an attempt to expose yours. However, I do have information, which I suspect you do not wish to be made public, you being a respected lawyer an' all, and it occurred to me that you might be willing to recompense me for keeping silent on the subject.'

Nicky saw immediately what he was up to, and for

once, had no slick answers. 'Blackmail is a dirty business, Mr. Ratcliffe,' she said, fuming at his arrogance, and dismayed at his research activities.

'Let's not think of it in those terms. I have a cash flow problem. It's entirely my own doing, liking the gee gees too much, and right now, I need to pay off a rather aggressive debt collector before he breaks both of my legs. I'm in desperate straits here and this seemed to be an opportune moment to use my trump card with you, otherwise I would never have pursued the matter, I assure you.'

'So how much are you expecting?' asked Nicky, her anger and resentment building.

'I need fifty thousand pounds,' he said bluntly.

'That's absolutely ridiculous,' she said.

'Yes, it is, but it's what would get me out of a deep hole.'

She looked down at her blotter and considered her situation. If she didn't give him the money, he would probably relay his discovery to the police or to another newspaper reporter. The police would easily discover, as he had done, that Christopher was not her son and questions would have to be asked. If this should explode into the public domain, Christopher would find himself confronted by unexpected news. If anyone was to tell Christopher about the circumstances of his birth, then it had to be her.

If, on the other hand, she did give him the money, there was every chance that Ratcliffe would return for more. He would see it as a continuing and easy source of revenue. She was between a rock and a hard place.

'It's really a matter of how important this information is to you. Clearly, if you don't mind the general public or the authorities reading about this irregularity, then there is no point in my pursuing it.' he said, mockingly submissive.

'I will have to think about this. You will have to give me some time,' she said.

'Very well, but I can't wait too long, you understand. I have my own deadlines, Miss Partington. Suppose I make another appointment for next week. I'll ring the office when I have a free moment. Will that do?' he said, smiling.

'Right.' she said, and was already pretending to study the papers on her desk as he left.

However, once he had closed the door, she shivered and a surge of fear swept over her. She knew that Ratcliffe would not leave this alone. He had found a goldmine and, worst of all, she had practically invited him to do so. She was so angry with herself for not thinking things through. Work had been busy and she had foolishly gone along with him. He would keep digging away, trying to find out where Christopher had come from. She believed that there would be no records of his birth to find, no adoption papers and no link between herself and the Randalls. The photograph, which she had purloined from Beaulieu, was safely hidden in her handbag. Nevertheless, she felt anxious and for the first time in many years, she began to feel that the truth might have to come out after all this time. She had worked so hard, had built a successful career and was respected and admired in the law profession for her work. Christopher had enjoyed a happy, secure upbringing and schooling and was now a man, ready to embark on his own career and mould his own life. Children did not stay at home forever. She knew that, and she had always wanted Christopher to be an independent and confident man in his own right. He was already showing that he was intelligent and self-reliant and she had every confidence that he would have a promising future. His girlfriend, Bobbi, was something of a fixture and perhaps he would want to cement that relationship in marriage in a short time. She would not stand in his way. There was a lot to think about. This shabby journalist had brought her to a watershed in her life. Perhaps she had been unrealistic in believing that the truth need never come out. For seventeen years, she had kept her dark secret, shared it with no-one, confabulated explanations as they were required. It had become second nature and she had assumed a sense of security in the matter. However, now, someone had breached her security system and the burden which she had borne with fortitude, on her shoulders for all of these years, was now weighing heavily.

There was a short knock on the door and Marilyn popped her head in.

'Would you like a cup of tea, Miss Partington?' she enquired.

'No thanks, I'm just heading off home. By the way, Marilyn, could we just look at my schedule for the next two weeks? Something has come up and I would like to take some time off,' she said, 'I know it's inconvenient, but Gordon should be back next week.'

'Is everything all right?' enquired Marilyn, 'I have never known you to take time off.'

'Oh, yes, just a small family matter. By the way, did that horrible man Ratcliffe make another appointment?'

'No, he slunk out, sneering at me, as usual.'

They perused the diary together, and rearranged several appointments, delegating others to the most recently appointed member of staff.

'I'll phone round and change these dates. You haven't had a holiday in a long time. It will do you good. Perhaps you could telephone and let me know exactly when you will be coming back?' she said.

'Yes, of course, I will. Thanks, Marilyn.' she said, retrieving her handbag and briefcase.

18

As she turned the handle to the door of her flat, she had a sense that something was different. It was an intangible feeling that someone had been there, or perhaps was still there. She walked from room to room, checking on her personal papers, her files brought back from the office and her drawers and cupboards. Nothing was missing, even a five pound note which she had left on the mantelpiece, was still there, but she still couldn't shake the feeling that someone had violated her space. She studied each corner in turn looking for something out of place. By nature, an extremely tidy, almost obsessively tidy person, she always lined up the books in her bookcase so the spines were parallel and the small books were at one end of the shelf, the taller ones at the other. Suddenly she noticed that one book was slightly out of alignment with the others and when she came to extract it, she noticed that it had been replaced upside down on the shelf. There was little doubt that Mr. Ratcliffe had paid her a visit. She hurried through to the kitchen and flung open the cabinets. There was nothing to suggest that he had checked in here. She anxiously selected her cookery scrap book where she filed recipes of interest and from the space between two foolscap sheets on which there was described a recipe for *salmon en croute*, she pulled out Christopher's birth certificate and a message from the DVLA intimating who was the owner of ESG 492 on October 30th 1995. The documents had not been touched. Ratcliffe had not found them. The certificate and the car details had cost her a lot in terms of courage and ingenuity and she had hidden them amongst her cookery books, after much thinking, since having cooked the books in some way, she considered that these formed an apt addition to the collection. Had he discovered the car data, he could have explored further the Randall family history. There was nothing else in the flat, which could help him in his search, but clearly he was looking. No doubt he had deduced that Christopher's father would be someone else who might pay him some money to keep quiet.

Her uneasiness persisted. She felt restless, increasingly depressed, as uncomfortable thoughts filled her mind. She paced about the house and then, finally, she decided she had to get away, away from Jeremy Ratcliffe and into a place where she could spend some time thinking it all through. In the bedroom, she threw her blue suitcase on to the bed and began to fill it with clothes, toiletries and personal items, including her laptop, which she had brought back from the office with her.

By the time she had completed the packing, it was late afternoon. She wondered if Ratcliffe was watching the house even now, hoping to tail her every movement, and looked out of the windows to check on suspicious vehicles or people behaving oddly, but saw none.

She trailed the wheeled case to the car and placed it in the boot, again checking around her.

With no definite plan, she drove around the town, constantly checking in the rearview mirror to see if she had a tail but there did not seem to be anything definitive. The sign towards the motorway appeared and she exited the town streets, heading south in the steady traffic, the rush hour in full flush and the evening drawing in. The long lines of vehicles grew, but in no hurry, and with no specific destination in her mind, she contented herself creeping along slowly in line. At first, the radio's music and chat distracted her mind but after a while, she switched it off to focus on thoughts she knew were buried deep, enmeshed in a network of pain and blackness. For a year following the accident, she could think of nothing other than the death of her family and the losses she had suffered. Driven into a desperate mindset, she had been pushed to the edge of suicide. It had been the worst time of her life, an experience, which had been so traumatic and filled with anguish, that it had a profound and everlasting effect on her. Driving on automatic pilot, she took herself back to the beginning, the point where one life had ended and another, so fragile and tenuous, had begun, up there, in the dark woods on Mansion Hill. The turbulent, black thoughts which had engulfed her then, returned now, and the depressive sense of doom, brought her back down, reuniting her with the familiar feelings of despair, as though an unseen hand was pulling at her from the depths, beckoning to her to revisit that hell. Over the last seventeen years, she had, on one or two occasions, tried to open the door to these thoughts, but it was too painful and she had always managed to close the door again, partitioning off these unwanted secrets.

The rain started to spatter the windscreen as darkness fell, the wipers swept from side to side hypnotically and with both hands firmly on the wheel, her expensive Mercedes hummed quietly along. The traffic moved steadily and she lapsed into her own world, going over and over every detail of the past once again.

The baby had been unwanted, secreted away where no-one would have found him. Had she not been there that night, Christopher would not have survived. She was not in any doubt about that. For some reason, he was not wanted, not loved, an embarrassment, a problem, dead or alive. She had never understood the reasoning or emotions, which had forced his mother or his grandfather to make the decisions they had but it was preferable to believe that they had thought he was dead when they disposed of him in the manner they had chosen. The alternative was unthinkable. On that fateful night, her own brain had been clouded by suicidal thoughts and the drugs and alcohol she had consumed, and she had initially thought the baby dead, too. Looking back, it was hard to remember exactly what was happening in her mind, so many issues had blended into a thick morass of confused ideas.

Perhaps she had been unstable, unhinged, unfit to make the choices she had made. Perhaps she should have taken the child directly to the police where he would have been cared for by social services and foster parents. Knowing the number-plate of the car, which had transported him, the police would have sought out those who had carried out the deed. Jack Randall and his daughter would have been arrested. Felicity had been in the Fairfax Clinic for seventeen years, off and on, without having been charged but she had lost her freedom in any event. The responsibility for her actions had been too hard for her to rationalise. How would she have fared in prison, exposed to public outrage and condemnation? And Jack- would his business empire have folded, his reputation marred? Would his marriage have been destroyed? Did Sylvie Randall know anything of her step daughter's child? Would that have been a better outcome for them? For Christopher? How would he feel in later life that his mother had been sent to prison for concealing her pregnancy and trying to hide a newborn baby?

Nicky could have taken the child to the hospital, left it on the steps for some passing visitor to find. She had seen on the television from time to time, appeals for a mother to come forward when this sort of event occurred. Would Christopher have fared better if she had chosen one of these alternatives? She couldn't believe that, loving him as unconditionally as she did. No-one could have loved him more. No-one could have supported him and been there for him, any more than she had.

The night had drawn in and only the blinking of car lights registered in her mind. A major junction was looming, a choice to be made, continue on south towards Southampton or veer east towards the capital. The Mercedes remained in the southbound lane.

These early days when she and Christopher had lived in Mrs. Maltby's flat had been idyllic in so many ways after months of misery and hopelessness. Christopher had been a joy from the beginning, his every smile and antic had raised her spirits in a way that nothing else in the world could have done. His presence had transformed her life, brought her a reason for living, a reason to seek employment and a future for them both. Tears ran down her cheeks as she remembered how she had taken him with her to Bradbrook, Kemp and Armstrong, her delight when he started to walk and talk. No mother could have felt more emotion than she had. Perhaps her feelings were more acute because of the circumstances of his birth and her own infertility. The news that a hysterectomy had been required had not initially seemed too important but as the realisation penetrated, she knew that she had assumed that she would have children, liked children, and would have wanted to have children when she met Mr. Right. To have Christopher was a miracle and bringing him up had been an unexpected gift. But looking back now, she recognised the shadow, which had always been lurking somewhere at the back of her mind, a shadow which had followed her, had waxed and waned over the years but which was rarely absent. Now it had grown to enormous proportions and was threatening to overwhelm her life as she had come to know it. She had moved mountains to reach the comfortable, secure situation she was in, had worked so hard, so many hours, denied herself close friends, denied herself the love of a man, kept up her guard all these years, and now there was a possibility that it might all come tumbling down around her. Christopher was not hers and somewhere in her mind, she had always worried that he would be taken from her, but that had not happened in seventeen years and she had grown to assume that she was safe from enquiries and questions.

The combination of the rain and the rhythmic movement of the wipers obscured everything except the two white lights of the preceding car. As her mood darkened, it occurred to her that she could drive into an oncoming vehicle and end it all. Christopher was old enough to manage by himself and she had left him a sizeable legacy. He would get over her death and move on. Ratcliffe would have nothing worth selling then. Christopher had done nothing wrong. Perhaps this was a good way out. She wouldn't need to face all the questions when the shit hit the fan.

The wipers started to screech as the rain had subsided. She switched them off and drove on, thoughts of her death filling her mind. She thought of her parents and her brother. She needed their help now. For hours, she drove on, in a zombie-like state, her heart broken.

The signposts for Southampton appeared and she slowed down to make her way into the city centre. A few minutes later she caught sight of the Excelsior Hotel with its flashing neon lights and followed the directions to the car park. It was almost ten o'clock. She felt exhausted and it was time to rest. The city was new to her. She had never visited, had had no reason to, and even now, she could not face the reason for arriving here this night.

Removing her suitcase, she pulled it down the ramp and entered the luxuriously appointed foyer where several smartly clad receptionists stood, poised in readiness, with welcoming smiles.

'Good evening,' she said, handing a young man her business card, 'I would like a single room, please. It may be just for one night but I may be here for several days. I have some business to attend to and I'm not sure just how long I will require to stay.'

'That's no problem, Miss Partington,' the man said politely, completing the details on the computer, and handing her an electronic keycard and hailing the lift attendant.

'Room 986,' he instructed the porter who grasped Nicky's case and ushered her towards the lift.

The view from the bedroom window would have been stunning but the darkness and rain obscured most of the city at this late hour. In the far distance there were ships with illuminated masts and rigging. She wasn't far from the harbour and the naval base.

She showered and prepared for bed, still numb with so much thought of the events of the day and the repercussions which had ensued. The mini bar reminded her that she had not eaten all day and she snacked on a healthy oat biscuit while pouring a brandy with ginger ale. She drank the brandy and sat in the quiet room, gazing out of the window, contemplating what she was doing.

How do you deal with a blackmailer, she asked herself? It was a dangerous pursuit. She had heard of people who had killed the person extorting money for secrets. Killing him was not on her list of options although she wished he would drop dead. No-one else knew what he knew, as far as she could tell, although he may have placed the information on a computer file or elsewhere. There was no way of knowing. The only other way to handle the situation was to expose the information first so that Ratcliffe had nothing to gain, but was this really what she wanted?

Tiredness overwhelmed her and she downed a second brandy.

Exposing the truth meant telling Christopher of his beginnings. It meant telling Jack and Felicity Randall that their secret was about to be exposed and it meant finding Alex, Christopher's father. She knew why she had come here. She had come to find Alex.

19

Weak sunlight filtered through the thin lace curtains when she awoke the next morning and the brightness lifted her mood. She called room service to provide a light breakfast and dressed in her casual brown trousers and cream sweater as she waited. She wasn't hungry but she forced herself to eat some of the scrambled eggs and a slice of toast with some orange juice, before leaving the room.

She phoned Marilyn and told her that she would be staying at the Excelsior hotel in Southampton for a few days. Then, she walked along the street, hardly noticing the shops and offices which she passed. She bought a mug of coffee from a stand in the square and sat down on a bench to drink it. It would have been nice just to sit here all day and do nothing but she had come to Southampton for a purpose, a hazy ill-defined and alarming purpose. Somewhere in the depth of her brain she knew that the thought had occurred to her that it was here that Felicity's lover, Alex, had been stationed all these years ago. The likelihood of his being here now was absolute zero but there would be records and just maybe she could find a clue as to who Alex was. It was far fetched and irrational but it was the only clue she had to discovering who Christopher's father was. In her subconscious, the idea had grown but she had never really faced up to the fact that one day she might actually come here and try to find him. But now it was at the forefront of her mind. If Ratcliffe did spill the beans, and if the police investigated, testing Christopher's DNA, who knows what they would find. If she were questioned, how would she react? She would have to tell the truth. It was becoming urgent that the Randalls knew what was about to happen and if possible, Christopher's father should also be informed. He might be completely ignorant of his son and of the events which had placed Felicity in a special clinic, but he needed to know.

She had never wanted all of this to happen but Ratcliffe had precipitated it. She could pay him off. She had enough money, but he would return some time and bleed her dry. No, she couldn't have that. She had worked hard for her money. It was Christopher's money, and Ratcliffe was not going to take it all from him.

She went back to the hotel, taking note of the street names and the notices directing people to the dock area. She poured herself another brandy, downed it quickly and then changed into a smart, pale blue suit with a cream blouse. She picked up her bag and left the hotel once again.

Crossing the road, she glimpsed the fluttering pennants of nearby ships and walked on in that direction, emerging close to the harbour where traffic and crowds of visitors milled about the roads.

Suddenly the throng of people moved forward and Nicky found herself caught up in the general melee. As she was propelled along, she saw a large sign intimating that *HMS Windsor* was open for viewing. The long line of visitors was moving in the direction of the ships and although she could easily have excused herself to avoid the line up, she allowed herself to be caught up in the laughing, happy group of adults and children, all eager to see the fine ship.

After a few minutes, they were all ushered towards a gangplank where two smart naval officers were chatting and answering the numerous questions, put to them by the visiting party. She embarked behind a middle-aged couple who engaged her in conversation as they walked along.

'It's a huge ship, isn't it?' the lady stated.

'Beats me how they stay afloat,' said her husband.

'Our son is in the navy,' the woman added, 'and he told us we should see this ship while it was still in dock.'

'Yes, it's quite something,' Nicky contributed, admiring the perfectly clean decks, the sparkling, varnished woodwork and the shining brass portholes.

'Pity they didn't keep their own rooms as tidy,' the woman went on, laughing.

A senior officer gathered a group together and proceeded to indicate various areas of interest, gave details of the numbers of staff normally aboard and told then about the innumerable voyages this particular ship had embarked upon. Nicky followed the group around as they were taken into the boardroom, the dining room and the magnificently polished kitchens, half listening to the commentary. Having to descend a narrow stairway on to the lower deck, she was helped by a handsome young officer, who seemed rather taken with her. He followed her around, pointing out items which he thought might be of interest and not missing an opportunity to hold her elbow.

'What brings you here today?' he asked politely.

'That's a good question.' she thought, wondering what really had brought her there that day.

'Actually, I thought this was an opportunity to see round this magnificent vessel but I am here in town on business, in a way,' she said.

'Business with the navy, Ma'am?' he continued.

'In a way,' she said. 'I am a lawyer and I have a client who met a young sailor in Southampton about eighteen years ago. He served on the Newark, an American vessel which was docked here for some months at that time, I believe. I am trying to find out something about him and it occurred to me that the navy might keep records of personnel back many years. Do you think that might be the case, Captain Denny,' she asked, checking the man's name badge.

'I am not familiar with that vessel, Ma'am, but it may be worth asking at the main office, over there.' he said, pointing towards a huge, red brick building, swathed in scaffolding.

'Thank you,' she said straining her eyes to see exactly where he was indicating.

'I will be happy to take you over there, when this tour is complete,' he said, enthusiastically, 'if you can hold on for a few more minutes.'

'That's not necessary but it would be much appreciated if you can spare the time,' she said, giving him a smile.

The tour complete, Captain Denny gently took her elbow and helped to direct her to the administrative offices, some hundred yards away.

Arriving at the main entrance, he gallantly held the door open for Nicky to enter. Three ladies in smart white blouses and navy skirts were sitting behind a long reception desk, working away at computers. Nicky noticed the blushes of the two younger women when they saw that it was Captain Denny who had arrived. The oldest lady, middle aged and rather serious, stood up and stared at them. 'How can we help you?' she said, matter-of-factly.

'Good morning, Mrs. Hudson. This lady is Miss Partington. She is a lawyer and is trying to locate a member of American naval personnel who was docked here eighteen years ago. Can you be of assistance?'

'Do you know to which vessel this man was attached?' she asked, sitting down at her desk and pressing a few buttons on her keyboard.

'Yes, the Newark,' said Nicky, turning to Captain

Denny to thank him for making the introduction.

He turned and left the room clicking his heels, his every move noted by the younger girls.

'Now what exactly do you require?' she asked Nicky rather officiously, the previous apparent helpful attitude evaporating as Captain Denny left.

'I am trying to find an officer who was working on *HMS Newark* in 1995, probably in the early part of that year. The ship was in dock here around that time, I believe,' she said.

Mrs. Hudson turned somewhat reluctantly to her monitor and asked 'What is his name?'

'Well, I only know that his first name is Alex. I do not have his surname.'

Mrs. Hudson looked up at her with an exasperated expression on her face and said, 'Do you have any idea how many men work on a ship that size?'

'I'm sorry, it's the only clue I have,' said Nicky. 'I realize that this is a long shot but it is important. I was hoping that I could find out where he is at present so I can get in touch with him.'

'Presumably this is a legal case he is involved in. Really, I don't think it is appropriate for me to give out personal information in this way, even if I knew who he was. You would have to go through proper channels, and speak to the commanding officer on the base. I am not at liberty to give you what you need. I'll give you the name of the senior officer and you should contact him and provide him with the exact details.' she said, handing Nicky a card and rising to move towards the rear of the office. 'I'm sorry, Miss Partington. Good day.'

She then turned to address the two girls in the office, 'I'm going to the meeting now. I'll be back in half an hour.' And with that she disappeared out of the office door.

Nicky was very disappointed and started to walk

towards the exit, clutching the card in her hand but as she reached the door, one of the girls said, 'Miss Partington, don't pay any attention to her. She's always very grumpy. Perhaps we can help you. It was, after all, eighteen years ago. Now, I have the Newark personnel here for 1995. Was this man an officer?'

'I'm sorry. I don't know. His name was Alex, presumably Alexander,' she said.

'The only things I know about him are that he was called Alex, that he was 25-35 at that time and was African-American.'

The keys clicked away again and Nicky looked anxiously at the door in case Mrs. Hudson returned unexpectedly.

'There are 5 men called Alex registered with the Newark in the first half of 1995. Do you know where he came from? One of them was from Chicago, one from New Orleans and another from Boston, and two from Tennesee,' she said.

Do you know where he came from?' she asked again.

'No, I'm afraid not.'

'Would you recognise him?' the girl asked.

'Possibly,' said Nicky 'Why do you ask?'

'There are photographs attached to the records. Come round here and look,' she said, lifting the wooden flap of the reception desk allowing Nicky to enter the office area.

The first photograph showed a white man with a high forehead and narrow face. 'No, that's not him,'

A second photograph appeared. It was a coloured man but much older than the *Alex* she had seen in the photograph.

Nicky gasped as the third photograph appeared. Immediately, she recognised the face of Alex and saw that the surname was Sanderson.

'Yes,' she said. 'I believe that is the man I am looking

for.'

'You may have seen him on TV. He's quite famous now, a high flier; works with NATO or something.'

'Really? That's interesting. I may have seen his picture on the news. He is definitely familiar. You have been very helpful,' said Nicky. 'I had so little information to go on. I'm surprised to have been able to find him. Thanks again.'

She smiled politely and turned to leave when the rear door flew open and Mrs. Hudson appeared.

'What is going on here?' she asked angrily. 'I hope you have not been coercing my staff into giving you confidential information.' She stormed quickly round to the desk where a photo of a coloured naval officer was filling the screen.

'What have you been saying, Muriel?' she asked accusingly.

Nicky felt sorry for the girl and said, 'It's my fault entirely. Muriel was just trying to help. Really, it is not her fault, Mrs. Hudson.'

'This is quite out of order,' she shouted. 'I will have to report this immediately.'

She pressed a buzzer on the desk and within seconds, a smartly uniformed officer appeared. 'Captain Nicholson, we have a problem here. This lady, Miss Partington, who says she is a lawyer, came to ask about the whereabouts of a naval officer on *HMS Newark* in 1995. I have already told her that we cannot give out such confidential information about personnel and yet she went behind my back and persuaded Muriel here to give her what she wanted. It is a breach of confidentiality and I don't want my staff being accused of this sort of behaviour. I think it requires a bit of investigation.'

'Perhaps you will come with me, Miss Partington,' he said, politely, holding the door open.

Nicky followed him as he led her to a small windowless

room containing only a centrally placed wooden table and two upright chairs.

'Please have a seat, Ma'am. Someone will be with you shortly,' the officer said.

Nicky was lost in thoughts about Alex Sanderson. She had found Christopher's father. Suddenly she had to pull herself together as she was to be interrogated about her visit. At first, she thought that the enquiry would have been brushed over, that Mrs. Hudson was acting too cautiously but gradually she realised that it wasn't going to be so easy.

After some time, the young officer re-appeared, a more senior colleague in tow. He greeted her politely, introduced himself as Captain Torrance, apologised for keeping her waiting and then sat opposite to her across the table.

'May I begin by confirming your name, date of birth, place of birth, current address, occupation and place of business please?' he asked.

Nicky obligingly gave him all the answers he required, trying to appear no threat at all to the navy.

'I understand, Miss Partington, that you made enquiries about some naval personnel. This included gaining access to information regarding one of our most senior figures and that should not have been made available to you. I'm sure that your reasons for making these enquiries were perfectly reasonable and expect that you were quite oblivious to the high ranking of that particular individual, but nonetheless, we have to ensure that personal information does not fall into the wrong hands. Because of the ongoing NATO meeting in London, we are all on a high alert and any suspicious behaviour has to be checked out.I'm sure you appreciate that.'

'Yes, of course, I do.' said Nicky, trying to appear calm.

'Now, as I understand it, you were trying to locate someone called Alex?'

'Yes, that's right. I had the name from an old photograph and no more information to help locate him.'

'You identified this person as Commander Alex Sanderson?'

'Yes, but I didn't know who he was. I had no idea how important a figure he was.'

'What is your particular interest in Commander Alex Sanderson?' he asked staring at her.

She wondered how to answer and could see that whatever she said, she could be in difficulty, so she opted for a part truth.

'As a lawyer, my work has to be confidential, Captain. I can only assure you that I bear no ill-will whatsoever to Commander Sanderson and have no intention of hurting a hair on his head. You can, of course, check my records and you will find that I am a bona fide practising lawyer with no criminal record to my name. This interrogation is out of order and completely unnecessary,' she said firmly.

'That is for me to decide,' he retorted.

They sat for a few minutes in an awkward silence.

'Miss Partington. I'm sure that your visit here was completely innocent and there's nothing would make me happier than to dismiss this as trivial and of no importance. All you have to do is to give me a plausible explanation for the visit. You are an intelligent person. Surely you can do that?'

'My work is confidential, like yours and I cannot disclose my client's details in this situation. All I can tell you is that my client wishes to find Commander Sanderson to give him some information which may be of interest to him.'

'I'm afraid that answer does not satisfy my questions,' Miss Partington,

'I need to have a bit more information. Who is your client and what information does he or she wish to impart?

'If we think it is of sufficient importance, we may be able to pass it on to Commander Sanderson on behalf of your client but we have to be assured that it is neither dangerous nor suspicious. Surely you can understand that.'

Nicky couldn't figure out how to escape the situation, and said, 'I'm sorry but I really can't tell you any more.'

'You will not divulge to me the reason for your enquiries today?' he asked.

'I have explained to you, Captain. I cannot give you anything else,' she said.

'Is there someone else you would give it to?' he asked.

'I can only tell Commander Sanderson the reason for my enquiries, no-one else.'

'I can't promise that he will take the message when he is tied up in a meeting of national importance but I can try to forward it to him,' he said gruffly. 'But under the present circumstances, I will have to detain you here until the NATO conference is over and perhaps you will reconsider your answer. If you clarify the matter, you will be allowed to leave immediately. Surely that is some incentive to give a truthful explanation?' he said firmly, rising, folder in hand. 'If I were you, Miss Partington, I would give it some thought.'

She studied her hands and wondered how she would manage for several days in custody. But what could she possibly say to appease the man? As he left the room, she said, 'Tell him that it concerns Felicity Randall.'

20

Nicky was escorted to a secure room by the young officer whom she had met. The small room was stuffy and drab with a small, sparsely covered cot and basic toilet facilities in one corner. On the ceiling were 6 small lights embedded into the plaster. Only 4 were lit and these only dimly. She sat down on the worn, grey blanket, on the edge of the cot, leaned forwards and held her head in her hands. The weight of anxiety was unbearable. She had not anticipated the rapid escalation from being reprimanded by the office supervisor to incarceration in this oppressive cell and the potentially catastrophic prospect of having to explain to someone the genuine reasons for her enquiries. She cursed herself for not being more cautious but what had started out as a straightforward mission to locate all the men with the name *Alex*, who had served on *HMS Newark* in April 1995, and identify Felicity's lover, had turned into her worst nightmare. In a couple of hours, her secret and very personal life was on the point of exposure. It seemed to her that someone was holding a massive hammer up in the air, poised to smash to smithereens everything she held dear. Of course, she was acutely aware that she had brought it all on herself. If she had left things alone and paid off Jeremy Ratcliffe, she could have averted or, at the very least, stalled all this heartache. She wracked her brain in an attempt to manufacture a credible story which would extricate her from her predicament. Could she make up a story to satisfy their curiosity? She had become an expert in confabulation over the last seventeen years, after all. Could she begin by retracting her words- 'I *can disclose my reasons for being here, only to Alex Sanderson himself. Tell him it concerns Felicity Randall.*' Why in heaven's name had she done that? She had been cornered. It was almost as though she had stopped trying to hide the intricate web of deceit which she had spun for the last seventeen years. Was it all really so fragile and vulnerable? She had built her life round lies and omissions and had almost come to believe them herself. The stories she had told about Christopher's birth were well practised and perfectly honed to be credible to all she met. They flowed so easily now, had been so believable that for years, she had felt secure and safe from prying eyes. It was her fault that things had come to a head. Her success in business law and her elevation to chairman of the National Business Group, so gratifying and rewarding, had in fact led to her downfall. Glowing with pride, basking in the spotlight of her achievement, she had made a mistake, sanctioning a journalist to write a short piece about her for Star Magazine, but she yearned for her fifteen minutes of fame, like everyone else. The award had seemed to be something she had earned and for just a few days, she had let her guard down. Overconfident and assured, she had felt that nothing could stop her at this stage. Yet, here she was now, her past in imminent danger of being displayed to the world for judgement and condemnation, her future going up in flames.

She kicked off her black, patent, high heel shoes and rolled down on her side on the hard cot, facing the wall. It seemed appropriate, facing the wall. Wasn't that what people did when they had given up on life? She shut her eyes in an effort to blot out all the wild thoughts ricocheting around in her brain, but her thought processes were working overtime, conjecturing every possibility and consequence of her actions. She had pressed the self destruct button once again and however much she wanted to, she wasn't able to alter the consequences of her action.

She sat up and fumbled around in her handbag for her mobile. Perhaps she could phone Christopher and reassure herself that he was OK. Just chatting to him could help. She knew that he was in London with his girlfriend, Bobbi, and her parents. It was to be the first time he was meeting her parents and he had been nervous about the trip. They would adore him, she knew. He was so handsome, so charming and polite. Whatever happened, they couldn't help but approve of him; she was certain of that. Christopher was on the threshold of his own future and Nicky knew that he would not be taking this relationship too seriously, although they did seem to have plenty in common and got along well. It would be his choice when the time came. She would not interfere.

She fumbled around with the buttons on the mobile, numerous thoughts flooding her mind. Perhaps in time, Christopher would start to question his own roots. So far he had accepted blindly the theories she had fed to him. He believed that Nicky had had a brief relationship with the man who was his father and he had never probed further into that, most likely out of respect for Nicky. He believed that his grandparents and his uncle had died in the car crash in October 1994. Perhaps the tragic event and Nicky's reluctance to talk about that fateful night, had diverted any questions to date, but in time, when he married and began to have his own children, he might begin to seek more answers. She was convinced now that Jack Randall was his true grandfather, Sylvie Randall was his step grandmother and Felicity was his birth mother. She was also aware that Christopher was the only grandson of Jack Randall and with Felicity being so indisposed, it was not likely that there would be more grandchildren.

The Randalls were financially very successful and lived a privileged lifestyle. Christopher was legally the heir to the Beaulieu estate. How could she deny him that right? If she were to die before he knew of his heritage, he would lose out and although his own personal prospects were very promising, she would have denied him knowledge of his real family and the chance to inherit a substantial fortune. In her heart, she knew that this would be unjust. However painful it might be, she had to disclose the circumstances of his birth to him before it became too late.

The mobile beeped and informed her that there was *No Signal*, which was hardly surprising in the confines of the solid building in which she was now a veritable prisoner. There were 3 voice messages.

The first was from Marilyn, her secretary, sent at 2.15pm that afternoon.

'Hi, Nicky. Just had Christopher on the phone wondering where you were. I have told him that you are meeting with clients in Southampton and will be in touch. Hope that is OK. Maybe you could ring him? Also, that horrible man, Ratcliffe, phoned. He wanted to see you today but I told him that you would not be back for two weeks and to make an appointment then. He didn't make an appointment and put the phone down on me rather abruptly. I don't like that man! Nothing else. Keep in touch, bye.'

The second message was from Christopher, timed at 2.30pm.

'Hi Mum. Well, I've met Bobbi's Mum and Dad. They are quite nice, if a little pompous. Tomorrow they want to go shopping with Bobbi and have booked seats for the ballet in the evening. I have politely opted out of that and that leads me to my next point. Marilyn tells me you are in Southampton and I had noticed that *HMS Windsor* is in dock and open to the public tomorrow. I would love to take a look round that great ship and was wondering if we could meet up, maybe for lunch? I could get the train down. We could see the Windsor together or if you don't want to do that, at least we could have some time together. Give me a ring when you are free.'

There was a third message, sent only an hour ago.

'Mum! Phone me.'

Nicky switched off the mobile and lay back on the bed, the tears flowing down her cheeks.

Where am I? Oh Chris, what am I going to do? She lay on her side, her thoughts of Christopher, their first meeting in the woods on Mansion Hill, reliving for the millionth time, her anguish and distress at that time, the loss of her Mum, Dad and brother. *'Oh God, Mum, see what has happened to me; see what I have become. What would you do now? What would you have done if you had found Christopher? Should I have given him up?'* she asked, the tears streaming as images of her family came vividly to mind.

She tortured herself, going over again and again every detail of that night, the night that was meant to have no end. If Christopher had not come into her life at that precise moment, she would not have enjoyed the years with him, watching him starting to walk and talk, ride his bike, excel at school and make friends. No, she knew that she would do it all again. Even supposing it were all to fall apart now, Christopher had brought her unimagined and totally unexpected pleasure and happiness. For almost eighteen years, the two of them had bonded and formed a solid friendship. Had he been her own son, she could not have loved him more; she was in no doubt about that. Her success at work had been thanks to him. She had put everything into the jobs she had done because she wanted to give Christopher the best upbringing a parent could provide. She had been both mother and father to him, as well as his best friend. There was nothing she would not have done for him. He was nearly eighteen and at university now. Soon he would fly the nest and make his own way in life. That was the way it happened. She was resigned to that and in some ways welcomed his growing independence. It reflected his inner confidence and strengths and affirmed that she had brought him up with all the tools necessary to fly solo. It wasn't as if they needed to be together all the time. The desperate need to love and be loved had diminished as they had both climbed to a higher level. She was content in her job, financially secure and she too would be making her own way as he explored his horizons. She didn't resent that at all and had already recognised that in a way, he didn't need her now as much as he did when he was younger. He was a young man with his future ahead of him and she knew that whenever they could meet up, they would do so. They would always be there for each other; she knew that. The parent-child bond of almost eighteen years would not be wiped out overnight even if revelations of Christopher's birth reached him.

Their relationship and trust had a strong foundation, she reassured herself, but she began to wonder if the news would shake Christopher's total trust in her. Would he disown her and adopt his true kin? Would she lose him, lose the person she loved most in the whole world? Would she survive the rest of her life on her own? It was then that her thoughts turned to John Amos, a man she knew had a deep affection for her. Admitting that the feelings were mutual was not something she wanted to do and she had done her best to cool the relationship. They had shared a special night together, a stolen night which should not have happened. John was married with two children. Catherine had told Nicky that his marriage was rocky but she didn't want to be instrumental in sealing its fate. In any event she had been brought up to believe that husband and wife had no secrets from one another and already she had spun her usual stories about Christopher's origin, to John. He really knew nothing of her past and if he did learn that she had been party to the goings-on surrounding Christopher's upbringing, he would steer well clear, she was sure. As a revered lawyer of integrity and good judgement, he could not afford to be associated with her complex criminal past. If only things had been different, she would have valued a friend to lean on, a man of her own to love. With John, she had glimpsed what could have been, but sadly, things were as they were and any hopes and wishes for their relationship were fantasy and were doomed to come crashing down when everyone knew what she had done.

For a while the tears trickled down her face but eventually, emotionally spent, sleep came. It was a troubled sleep with vivid and alarming dreams catapulting her into a dark and deep abyss. The room was poorly ventilated and overheated. She thrashed around restlessly.

It seemed that only a short time had elapsed when she felt someone touch her shoulder. She jumped reflexively, at first thinking that it was part of her dream, but then the hand shook her more forcibly. She opened her eyes and turned to see who was there, dazzled by the bright light which had been switched on. She was disorientated and mentally exhausted. Her face was tear-stained and blotchy from crying and her hair mussed from tossing about on the cot. Her clothes were rumpled and in disarray.

A young female naval officer was the one doing the shaking. 'Miss Partington, I have been instructed to take you to the interview room. Will you please follow me?' she said authoritatively.

Nicky was still trying to remember the events of the day and at first was confused, but she picked up her handbag and jacket and followed the girl. She was returned to the same drab interview room and was invited to be seated again. She put her bag on the floor and folded her jacket on top of it. The bright light was too much and she put her elbows on the table and covered her face with her hands. She would have fallen asleep again but a few minutes later, loud footsteps tramped across the wooden boards, a chair scraped across the floor and someone sat opposite her again. She imagined it was the same interviewing officer but a different voice spoke, a deep and masculine voice, 'Good evening, Miss Partington.'

Half asleep and rubbing her eyes, she looked up and said 'Oh Chris.....' and then stopped herself as she realised that the man in the room was older, slightly darker skinned than Christopher and had some grey streaks in his dark wavy hair. He was ruggedly built and was dressed impressively in his impeccable uniform adorned with the regalia of a most high ranking official.

'Miss Partington,' he began again, 'I am Commander Alexander Sanderson. I understand you have something to tell me.'

She couldn't take her eyes off him. His face was exactly like Christopher's; his mouth, the set of the teeth, his ears and his dark brown eyes. Even his hands, now clasped in front of him had the same shape, the nails just the same configuration. It was uncanny. He was Christopher all over again.

'Let's get this over, Miss Partington, shall we? We are all busy people,' he said firmly.

'My name is Nicky Partington,' she said, dazed and taken aback by this unexpected encounter.

'I know who you are, Miss Partington. I just want to clear up the reason for your enquiry about me. I received a message which said that it had something to do with your client, Felicity Randall. Is that correct?'

'Felicity Randall is not a client of mine.'

'Then she is a friend?'

'No, I have never met Felicity Randall.'

Commander Sanderson pulled back his shoulders and breathed in deeply. 'Miss Partington, I came to Southampton to have a brief meeting with some colleagues today and I have plans to return to London shortly. Captain Torrance persuaded me to spend ten minutes helping to sort out this situation which has arisen because of your visit here. If you have brought me here on a wild goose chase, then there will be serious repercussions,' he said, angrily.

Nicky stared at him, taken aback by his tone.

'You now have five minutes, Miss Partington. Make the most of it.'

'What I have to tell you, Commander, does concern Felicity Randall. Indeed, she is central to the story and this is far from being a wild goose chase. I believe when you have heard me out, you will understand that.'

'I'm all ears,' he said, leaning back on his chair, his arms folded, looking very serious. It was a pose, which Christopher took when she began to tell him something he didn't like and Nicky couldn't help but smile.

He stared at her with mounting curiosity.

'I believe that eighteen years ago, in 1995, you were assigned to *HMS Newark* and you were stationed here,' she began.

He didn't move, just sat alert, listening.

'You met a young lady called Felicity Randall and struck up a relationship with her.' She paused and said, 'Commander, what I have to say is a family matter, a private matter and you may prefer it if we are alone when I tell you,' nodding at the young officer standing at attention by the door.

Commander Sanderson thought for a minute, then turned and said,

'Perhaps you could wait outside, Captain.' The officer withdrew, closing the door quietly behind her.

'Thank you,' said Nicky.

'Carry on, Miss Partington.' he said, turning to face Nicky again.

'Please call me Nicky,' she said.

'Very well,' he replied, but not surprisingly did not reciprocate that she called him Alex.

'This is very difficult for me to talk about, Commander. I haven't talked about it ever in almost eighteen years but I will tell you everything, now that the situation demands it. It's hard to know where to begin.'

'Why don't you start at the beginning?' he suggested, looking at his watch.

'The beginning for me was on 30th October 1995 but the beginning for you was much earlier that year, when you were based here in Southampton.'

He said nothing but she sensed concern now and he was certainly paying attention.

'On 30th October 1994, I was in a car accident, an accident which killed my parents and my brother. I, myself, was seriously injured and was in hospital for months. When I was eventually discharged, I was still in a poor state of health and suffering from depression. To cut a long story short, I became suicidal and decided to end my life.'

She paused, looked up at him and saw that he was listening. She concentrated on the table top and resumed her story. 'On the 30th October 1995, a year to the date of that accident, I took a number of pills and some alcohol with me to the woods at the top of Mansion Hill in Edgerley with the intention of killing myself.

'I had swallowed quite a number of pills and was lying in the leaves when I heard a car engine. I was afraid that someone would find me and so I hauled myself up and peered through the trees to see what was happening.'

A hard knock sounded at the door and the Captain returned,

'Excuse me, Commander, your car is here.' With that

announcement, she left the room.

The Commander looked at his watch again and said, 'Miss Partington, time is of the essence. It would be helpful if you could outline the story in a few sentences. Can you do that?'

Nicky leaned back on the chair and took a deep breath, 'You have a son.'

'I have a son and two daughters. That is general knowledge. What has that to do with anything?'

'You have a son called Christopher, a son you have never met. He is almost eighteen years old. He is Felicity Randall's son, born on 30th October 1995.'

Alex Sanderson had no immediate answer to her revelation, but after a few minutes, he asked, 'What nonsense is this? What is it you are after?'

'I don't want anything from you. I need you to know about this now. Please hear me out.'

'Have you any proof of this story?'

'I can show you a photograph.' she said, reaching down into her handbag to retrieve the small pocket photo album which contained several pictures of Christopher.

Finding it, she opened it at a recent photograph of Christopher taken near the University on his first day. She handed the whole album to him.

The commander picked it up and studied the picture, then flicked through the others. Nicky thought she detected a change in his attitude, a slight drooping of his shoulders.

He said, 'This could be anyone.' He placed the album on the table, one plastic holder still open in front of him.

'This is Christopher, your son. The resemblance is uncanny. Surely you can see that for yourself?'

The commander sat pensively for a while, and then stood, making for the door. She overheard him telling the young captain that he was delaying his departure by one hour and asking that his wife was contacted and informed of this decision. He returned and sat down again, facing Nicky.

'Continue with your story. You were telling me that you were in the woods on Mansion Hill and you heard a car coming.'

Nicky leaned forwards again, relieved to have won some leeway.

'It was pitch dark and the car had no lights on. It stopped close to the edge of the woods. A tall man stood by the driver's door and then a young girl got out of the passenger side. She was carrying a box. I couldn't see their features but the girl was not particularly tall, though she was slim and blonde with a pony tail which bobbed about as she walked into the woods.

She tramped through the leaves and I could hear that she was crying. After what seemed a long time, she emerged out of the trees and was no longer carrying the box.'

Nicky looked up at Alex Sanderson. He had frown lines on his brow and was looking worried but he did not interrupt.

'After this intrusion, I felt unsettled and decided to explore the box, find out what was so important that it had to be secreted in the woods in the middle of the night and then I would return and finish off what I had set out to do in the first place. It took a while to find the box. It had been covered with leaves and pushed under a large bush, but eventually I did find it and opened it. It was dark and at first I couldn't see what it was and then as a ray of moonlight penetrated the darkness, I thought it was a doll, a male doll. But then it moved and I realized that it wasn't a doll at all, it was a baby, a newborn baby boy.'

Alex Sanderson leaned forward and said, 'Nicky, this is an interesting story, and may be that's exactly what it is, a story. You have already stated that you were suffering from depression, you had taken pills and alcohol. Perhaps this is all a figment of your imagination.'

'It's true that I was depressed and that night, yes, I was under the influence of the drugs, but I assure you that this is true.'

'So, you are going to suggest to me that the bearer of the box was Felicity Randall, who had a ponytail like so many other young girls. Supposing we accept that the story is true, this girl could have been any one of hundreds of girls.'

'I didn't know who she was at the time but I believe it was Felicity, yes.'

'How can you be sure?' he asked, 'It could have been anyone.'

'No, it couldn't have been anyone, Commander. You see, I saw the car number plate and memorised it. It was ESG 492.'

'You said it was pitch black. How could you see the number plate and memorise it in the state you were in?' he said, almost laughing now.

'When we were young, my brother Patrick and I played the number plate game. That's where you make up acronyms using the letters or numbers on car number plates. I was good at it. It was a reflex thing for me to memorise plates. Yes, it was dark, but the moon occasionally peeped through. I can swear to you that this was the number on that car.'

'OK, so that was the number. How did you find out whose car it was?'

The door opened and the young naval officer brought in a tray with a cafetiere full of steaming hot coffee, two cups, milk and sugar.

'Thank you,' said the commander, as she set the tray down on the table between them.

The officer poured two coffees and then left the room.

'For a long time, I didn't pursue that fact partly because I believed that the owners of that car, didn't want Christopher and also because I dreaded anyone taking my son away from me. However several years later, during my university course, I was visiting a police station and the opportunity arose for me to find out who the owner of that car was.'

'Hold on a minute,' he interrupted, 'Who is Christopher?'

'When I found that baby boy in the box on Mansion Hill, I picked him up and cuddled him. He was cold and hungry. My desire to commit suicide had to wait. The baby had the right to live and so I brought the baby home with me. Perhaps it was wrong; perhaps I should have taken him to a police station but I needed him and decided to keep him, to call him my own son and I named him Christopher.'

'You just liked the name?'

'I liked the name but it stemmed from the number plate. It was ESG- so I made up *Ever So Good* and the numbers were 492, so I thought *1492, Columbus sailed the ocean blue.* That's why I called him Christopher, from Columbus.'

'So let me get this straight. You kept this little boy, called him Christopher and brought him up as your son?'

'Yes.'

'So he is now, what, seventeen years of age and still living with you?'

'Yes.'

'Are you trying to blackmail me? Is that what this is about? You think that I will buy this story and pay you to keep quiet?'

'I don't want your money. I don't want anything from you. I just want you to know that you have a son,' she said.

Commander Sanderson sighed deeply. 'So tell me about

this, Christopher.'

'He is going to be eighteen this October and just started at University doing engineering and computer studies.'

Alex Sanderson was sitting forward again, leaning on the table. Nicky sipped the hot coffee. It was good.

'Let's get back to the ESG 492 then. How did you find out whose it was?' he asked.

'I became a lawyer. Did they tell you that?'

'Yes.'

'While I was a student, we had workshops in various places. One was in a police station. We were being instructed on the identification of vehicles and our guide asked for a number to demonstrate how the details were obtained. I stupidly gave him that number and in a few seconds, I had the owner's name and address.'

'It wasn't Felicity Randall's. She didn't drive,' he said.

'No, the car belonged to her father, Jack Randall, residing at Beaulieu, Cherrybank Avenue.'

'She could have met someone else after I left and had his baby,' he suggested.

'The timing of his birth suggests that she was pregnant when you left and was at full term in October. In any case, Commander, he is your son. He is your spitting image. When you came in here tonight, for a brief moment, I thought it was him.'

'Oh, Chris. That's what you said.'

He studied the photograph again, looking very sad and tired.

From her handbag, Nicky extracted the other photograph which she kept with her constantly, the photo taken in front of *HMS Newark* in April 1995, a picture of two people so much in love.

'Where did you get this?' he asked, wiping away tears.

'I stole it from the drawers beside Felicity's bed when I was visiting the Randalls. On the back, you wrote, *With all my love, Alex.'*

'You have visited the Randalls? So they know all about this?' he asked, incredulous.

'No, I'm a lawyer, Al....sorry...Commander. I work for a firm called Martin and Ainslie. Scott Martin was the senior partner when I first started there and Jack Randall was his client. I didn't know that until Scott was planning to retire and then he passed on several clients to me. One of them was Jack Randall. So I became Jack's lawyer. It wasn't a position I sought. He knows absolutely nothing of this. We have a professional relationship. I told you that I hadn't spoken of this to anyone for the best part of eighteen years and that is a fact.

For a few minutes, Alex Sanderson was speechless and unable to talk for tears which, seemed to flood out. Nicky waited patiently, looking at the man who was responsible for bringing Christopher into the world. She felt a great affection for him and wanted to put her arms round him, as she would have, had he been Christopher. How easy it had been to tell him about the events which had changed her life. He had made it easy, he had not been judgemental and now she had broken his heart, she could tell.

'How is Felicity?' he asked eventually, controlling his tears.

'She had a nervous breakdown some time after the baby was born and has not been right ever since. She lives most of her life in the Fairfax Clinic where she is cared for. She doesn't seem to get home much now as far as I can tell. I don't know why she had the breakdown but it seems to have happened shortly after the baby was born.'

He looked crestfallen and did not talk for a while.

'I'm sorry to have landed this on you at this point. You seem to be very busy and it was amazing that you agreed to see me. I suppose it reflects the fact that you cared about Felicity and the mention of her name was enough to entice you to speak to me.'

He looked up at her and looking at his watch again, said, 'I think we should get away from here and find another place to talk in private. There is no reason to keep you here and it's late.'

He rose and disappeared out of the room. Felicity finished her coffee, put on her jacket and retrieved all the photographs from the table.

When he returned, he said, 'Right, I have straightened things out here. Come along. Where are you staying?'

'The Excelsior.'

A chauffeured limousine drove them the short distance to the hotel. They did not converse en route. Alex seemed deep in thought.

'Do they have an all night coffee lounge in the hotel, do you think?'

'I doubt it.' she said.

'Excuse me, Sir, there is an all night place along the street, it's called Nola's Lounge', interrupted the driver.

'Thanks. Just drive there please. Is it reasonable?'

'Yes, Sir, and quite up-market.'

'We'll be half an hour, maybe an hour. I'll call you if you like.'

'Right, Sir.'

They entered Nola's Lounge with Alex holding her arm. The heavy, red flock wallpaper darkened the place but the atmosphere was cosy and warm with quiet music playing in the background. A smart waiter appeared and smiled at them. 'We have a quiet corner for two over here, Sir,' he offered.

'Perfect,' said Alex, 'and could you bring a menu? We would like to eat.'

They settled into the red velvet-clad booth and perused the drinks list handed to them.

'A gin and tonic for me please,' said Nicky.

'Make that two, then,' Alex added.

'I can't believe what's happened tonight. You have no idea what has been going through my mind. I thought I was in the brig for the foreseeable future. It's amazing to meet you and see how alike you and Christopher are.'

'Tell me why, Nicky, after almost eighteen years, you have decided to find me now? What triggered that search?'

'I am being blackmailed. That is why.'

She told him the story about Jeremy Ratcliffe and his finding that Nicky had to have a hysterectomy after the accident in 1994 and then had discovered that Christopher's birth certificate stated that he was born to her some twelve months later.

'It's amazing that he was able to find hospital records so far back.'

'Amazing, and unlucky for me.'

The waiter returned with their drinks and they ordered sandwiches and fruit.

'And the birth certificate? How did you get that?'

She told him about her job in the registrar's office and how she had forged the certificate. 'So you see, when he decides to spill it all, I shall lose my job, be disbarred by the Law Society and worst of all, Christopher may disown me, I have lied to him over the years, too.'

'But no court would convict you after what you did. You saved his life, brought him up well, by all accounts, and anything you did, was done to help him.'

'I hope everybody thinks like that, but I did commit various crimes throughout the years and there is no just cause. I could have taken him to a police station that night.'

'Yes, but then Jack Randall and Felicity would have been in trouble. He would have gone to a foster home but you gave him everything, probably a great deal better than a foster home.'

'I would like to think so.'

The sandwiches and a fruit bowl with grapes and pears, was placed on the table and Nicky found herself starving after the long day.

'May I ask what happened between Felicity and you? The photograph is such a happy one. You looked so much in love then.'

'We were in love and I asked Felicity to marry me. She accepted and suggested that I broach her father on the subject. That was a terrible night. He was so angry and accused me of everything you can imagine. He told me in no uncertain terms that his daughter was not going to marry a common sailor nor was she going to marry a coloured man. He was furious and told me that I had to leave and never see or contact Felicity again. I retaliated and then he said that he would make a formal complaint about me to my commanding officer. He said he would accuse me of unwanted advances, obscene behaviour and anything else he could think of. That would have finished my naval career and he knew that.

Felicity and I thought about running away but that was not going to work. Jack could still have ruined me, so we parted. It was a dreadful time. I didn't know she was pregnant, believe me. She certainly never told me and I suspect that she would not have found it easy to tell Jack either. I wonder what happened there. Poor girl! I feel so responsible for what happened.'

'Jack has suffered for his actions too. He has lost his daughter and has no other children. At the moment, he is unaware of Christopher's existence but now I shall have to let him know.'

'His reputation will be seriously damaged if all of this becomes public knowledge.'

'Yes, he won't be happy about it. I wondered what to do with this man, Jeremy Ratcliffe. Perhaps Jack would prefer to pay him his money and take his chances. I have to give him the chance to make a decision.'

'If he takes his information to the police, they will ask you what you know, so Jack will be discovered as the man who drove the car. Felicity seems to be ill and probably will not face charges.'

'I wondered too if, when they did a DNA test, if that would yield anything. I don't suppose Felicity's DNA is on record, although they could easily do it to confirm that she is his mother. But I also wondered if yours was on some naval database?'

'Yes, mine is on record, perhaps not readily available to the British police, but yes, it's available.'

'What do you think I should do, Commander?'

'Call me Alex, please. We are practically family, it seems.'

She smiled at him. It was such a nice thing to say.

'You are doing the right thing but it is a balance. The only way to deal with a blackmailer is to call his bluff and to ensure that he has nothing to hold against you. However, you also have to count the cost and the cost to you, to Jack and Felicity is pretty high in this case.'

'Perhaps I should just pay him off.'

'No, I think he should be exposed. If you tell Jack all about this, I think he will be prepared to put his money somewhere safe. He could go to France or to Switzerland. He has homes in both of these places.'

'Yes, I know but he can't leave Felicity.'

'No, he would have to take her with him. I wonder how she really is. Would it help if I went to see her?'

'I don't know, but maybe you and Jack will have to discuss the situation with regard to Ratcliffe so you can ask him how she is.'

'Maybe. That won't be any fun, but one thing I am longing for, is to meet Christopher. When can I see him, do you think?'

Nicky took out her mobile and said, 'I had a message from him earlier but couldn't reply.'

She studied the messages and said, 'He has sent me 2 text messages today, the first is from this afternoon. He is in London with Bobbi, his girlfriend. They were meeting Bobbi's parents and going to the ballet or something. He had phoned Marilyn, my secretary, and she told him that I was in Southampton. He is asking me if he can join me here for lunch tomorrow. He isn't interested in the ballet and would like to visit *HMS Windsor* as he has heard that it is open for visitors. The second call is just, *Mum, call me.*'

They sat in silence for a while and then Alex said, 'Nicky, I would just love to meet my son. How about having lunch with me tomorrow on board *HMS Windsor*? I'll make the arrangements. Tell him we are friends and over lunch we can tell him the truth. What do you think?'

'He needs to know everything and I know he will be so elated to know that you are his father. He has never been curious about that but when he knows that Commander Alex Sanderson is his father, I think he will leap with joy. I love him so much and will always love him. He has been everything to me all this time, my reason for living and the only son I will ever have. What we have shared has been wonderful and I wouldn't have missed it for the world. However, he isn't my son and I don't possess him. I have to let him have his own life. I can't hold him. Perhaps he will feel that I did the wrong thing, that I should have told him all of this when he was younger. Perhaps he'll feel cheated. I don't know… but I have to let him go now, I know that. However hard it is, he has to be free to make his own choices.'

'I can imagine that it's a difficult thing for you to do and I'll be there to help you. Thank you for your appraisal of me. I hope Christopher is equally impressed. I have let him down all these years. I have a great deal to do to make it up to him. One other thing I should tell you, Nicky. After Felicity, I met and married a fellow African-American called Jo. We have three lovely children, all obviously younger than Christopher so he has a step brother, Joseph who is 15 and two step sisters, Caroline who is 14 and Clementina, who is 12.'

'That's wonderful. Gosh! What will he think about that?'

'Jo is here with me. We drove down and we're staying at the Belvedere.'

He looked at his watch. 'It's three o'clock. She will be wondering what on earth has happened. I told her about the message which you sent and of course I had told her about Felicity. We have no secrets. She knows that Jack pushed me out the door. She will be quite taken aback when I tell her all of this, but she will take it all in her stride. She is a most amazing person. You will like her and she will be a great asset tomorrow. She is very good at talking when other people are shy or retiring. She will put Christopher at his ease in no time. Believe me, she can talk for America.'

'OK, I'll text Christopher now. What time shall we meet?'

'Let's say 1.15pm lunch, so arrive at the ship at 1pm. I'll arrange that you are picked up as my guests so you get through the barrier without any problem. So the car will pick you up at 12.45. Can he get down here by then?'

'I presume so, since it was he who suggested lunch.'

Nicky sent the text telling Christopher to come to the Excelsior hotel by 12.30 pm if possible, that she would make lunch plans.

'That's great,' sighed Alex. I was going to drive back to London tonight but I can go tomorrow night instead. Meeting my firstborn son has to be my top priority.'

21

Once back at the hotel, Nicky felt buoyed up and excited. A huge weight had been lifted from her shoulders. She had actually shared all of her dark secrets with a complete stranger, but Alex Sanderson did not seem like any stranger and her heart had warmed to him. It was past 4 a.m. when she had returned to her room after a long emotional discussion with Alex in Nola's Lounge. There was little chance of sleep now. She showered and sat in the armchair, gazing out of the window at the cloudy sky, anticipating all the questions that Christopher might have, knowing that once again, she would have to go over the whole story.

At 6 a.m. the breakfast room was already serving and she decided to enjoy an early meal. Somehow her appetite had returned and she felt the need for sustenance for what would be a significant day in her life. For the first time in weeks, she ate a hearty breakfast of grapefruit, scrambled eggs, bacon, toast and orange juice, surprising herself at her upbeat mood in spite of the traumatic and sleepless night that she had experienced. She couldn't help but think over the night's unexpected meeting and everything that had been said. Alex Sanderson's looks, his mannerisms and his softness had been so familiar, so easy, that she had divulged the most private of secrets to him without much difficulty. There hadn't been any choice in the matter, she knew. Perhaps that had been the key. There was no choice now. Jeremy Ratcliffe had seen to that.

Now she had to tell Christopher everything, too. Meeting his father had helped a great deal. Now she wouldn't have to tell him by herself but she didn't want him to read about it in a magazine or newspaper. She had to be the one to tell him. It was something she knew had always been inevitable but she had put it off for so long, reluctant to lose her son's trust, reluctant to admit that he was not her son at all.

It was a bright morning, the sky mainly blue overhead, only a few fluffy white clouds broke the homogeneity of colour. The stores were just beginning to pull up their shutters and open for business. Nicky didn't know the town at all and wandered around the main streets and soon found a small cobble-stoned square lined with smart boutiques displaying expensive and very elegant women's apparel. Perhaps the uncomfortable and sweaty evening in her confined accommodation, had made her feel untidy and dirty, but she had decided to make an effort to look her best for the next very difficult meeting. She browsed through the first boutique but found nothing that caught her eye but in the second store, she found a very expensive cream silk suit, a matching top with narrow straps. The whole ensemble was very feminine. It was a good fit and although the price seemed extortionate, today, she wasn't going to worry about it.

Further round the square, there was a trendy shoe shop, and here she purchased a pair of elegant strappy black patent sandals and a matching handbag. Carrying her purchases, she popped into a small lingerie store to treat herself to some new cream underwear and tan tights. So early in the morning, it was not hard to get a hairdresser's appointment right away and this was followed by a full facial, pedicure and manicure. Throughout the morning, she had cleared her mind as she focussed on her attire and her appearance. At least, she thought, she would look smart for this important lunch date with her son and his father.

Returning to the hotel, she passed a men's outfitter and suddenly wondered if Christopher would bring something smart with him. He was unaware of the momentous occasion which was looming. On the off chance that he came unprepared, she went in and bought a white shirt, a striped tie in blue and silver shades and a pair of grey socks.

It was almost twelve o'clock when she returned to the hotel, her stomach beginning to churn with nervousness. Setting out all her purchases on the bed, she showered again and then set about dressing herself in the new outfit, constantly looking in the mirror for reassurance. Finally, she was satisfied that she was looking very presentable for this auspicious occasion, although her hands were shaking, her face was pale and she did look tired. She sighed at the thought of what lay ahead.

Opening the parcels for Christopher, she laid the clothes out on the bed, hoping that he would have thought about bringing a suit with him. She switched her handbag contents and went down to the hotel lobby to wait for Christopher, butterflies turning somersaults in her stomach as she noted that it was already 12.20 p.m.

Since breakfast, she had had only a cup of tea at the hairdressers, so she ordered a cup of coffee and a shortbread biscuit while she waited for Christopher in the lounge, hoping that there was no delay with his train.

At 12.30 p.m, Christopher came bounding through the swing doors and seeing Nicky, immediately came rushing up to her and gave her a warm hug.

'Hi Mum. Gosh, you look great!' he said, dropping his bag on the floor. Nicky saw that he needed to change out of his casual checked shirt and jeans before the day's events.

'Chris, honey, it's so good to see you. I'm sorry to rush you but we have a lunch date in twenty minutes. Can you do a quick change? Have you brought a suit? Here's the key. It's number 986. I'll wait here for you.'

'OK, steady, steady,' said Chris taking the key. 'Lucky I did bring my grey suit. Sounds like this is a special lunch. I'm off; be as quick as I can.' he said, already heading for the elevator, bag in hand.

'You better believe it.' she said to his retreating form.

At precisely 12.45 p.m, the sleek black limousine, Naval pennants flying, arrived at the hotel entrance. The chauffeur parked, entered the hotel and recognised Nicky from the previous evening. 'Miss Partington, good morning' he said politely.

Nicky approached him and apologised for the delay.

'We are running five minutes behind schedule' she said.

'No problem, Miss Partington. I'll wait out there. You just take your time.'

A few minutes later, Christopher appeared. He had showered, his curly hair wet and shining. His grey suit was a little crumpled but he had put on all the new items she had purchased and looked very smart. He was smiling.

'Am I OK, Mum?' he asked her.

'You look very nice,' she said.

'Thanks for the new shirt and things. I needed them.'

They walked through the revolving doors and Christopher suddenly noticed the highly polished limousine waiting by the kerb.

'Nice wheels! I wonder who that is for,' he remarked.

The chauffeur came round the car and opened the rear door.

'It's for us,' Nicky said, easing herself into the comfortable leather seats.

Christopher was clearly very impressed and beaming excitedly, he followed her inside.

'Mum, where are we going? You must have some very

important clients in town. Where are we having lunch?'

'We are going to the naval base and we are having lunch with Commander Alex Sanderson and his wife Jo...'

'Commander Sanderson? Isn't he that American guy who has been in the papers? He's on some mega committee... part of NATO, isn't he?'

'Yes, that's the man.' Nicky said, although she really wanted to say, *'He's your father, Christopher.'*

The car swept smoothly along the streets heading for the gates at the entrance to the base, with Christopher and Nicky feeling like royalty as pedestrians peered in, trying to see who was in the sleek, gleaming vehicle. They sailed through the security gates unimpeded and with a salute from the officer at the entrance.

Christopher, wide eyed and obviously very impressed, gazed out of the window as the car purred its way along towards the dock area and as they approached the *HMS Windsor* and drew up at the gangway, manned by another uniformed officer, he asked, 'Gosh! How long have you known him, Mum?'

'Not long,' she replied, the butterflies now totally out of control in her stomach.

The chauffeur saluted the officer on duty and opened the door to help Nicky alight on the quayside.

'Captain Markham will escort you aboard,' said the chauffeur. Nicky thanked him and found herself being saluted by the duty officer.

'Good morning, Ma'am, Sir. Welcome to *HMS Windsor*. Will you follow me?'

They all made their way up the gangway to the top where another clean cut officer saluted them. 'Miss Partington and Mr. Partington, welcome aboard. I have instructions from Commander Sanderson to give Mr. Partington a tour of the ship before lunch and he has asked that you, Ma'am, join him with his wife in the mess in the meantime.'

'That's great.' exclaimed Christopher, looking at Nicky.

She smiled at him and said, 'See you later, then.'

Nicky found herself being led down spotless narrow corridors, passing numerous doors with shining brass nameplates and eventually reaching a door which had the words *Private Dining Room* in clear lettering. It was a section of the ship which her tour had not included. The escort knocked firmly on the door and a few seconds later it was opened by a smiling lady of Afro-American descent who approached her with open arms.

'Nicky!' she said, embracing her warmly and holding her tightly, much to Nicky's surprise. She was a little taken aback but responded politely, all the while noticing Alex Sanderson was standing near the small bar at the back of the room.

It was not a large mess. The portholes allowed the sunlight to stream in on to the highly polished central oval table on which were arranged, four place settings with heavy silver cutlery meticulously placed around the plain white mats. An ornate flower arrangement completed the table decoration. There were eight carved chairs placed around the table and not a great deal of room around these. At the far end was a small bar complete with numerous bottles and glasses.

'I'm Jo Sanderson,' the lady announced, releasing Nicky from her tight grip, 'and you have already met my husband, Alex,' she said, holding on to Nicky's arm and ushering her towards Alex. Alex also opened his arms and gave Nicky a warm hug.

'Hello, Nicky. I'm so glad to see you. I hope you are not too exhausted after our late chat. What can I offer you to drink?' he said, drawing her to the bar.

'I'll stick with gin and tonic, thank you,' she answered.

'Alex and I have had no sleep at all. We sat up last night talking, talking and talking,' said Jo.

'I must say that you have done a most wonderful thing, finding a baby and bringing him up on your own as well as studying to become a lawyer. I salute you, Nicky, I really do.' she said sincerely.

'I think Jo is even more excited about this meeting than I am,' said Alex,' and that is saying something.'

'I am. I am, too,' she said. 'I was saying to him that it is going to be pretty hard to say thank you to someone for raising your child for you for almost eighteen years. But this is hard for you, Nicky… after all these years to find yourself pushed into this situation. We have been tossing around all manner of ideas and I expect you have, too. Maybe it is for the best. Christopher is almost eighteen, a young man, ready to take the news on board and after eighteen years with you, he will always look on you as his mother. All these years when you have comforted him, helped him, loved him… these are the ties that bind. It is hard to imagine all that has happened but, you know, Nicky, things happen for a reason and we should look on this whole business positively. Alex and I will open our hearts and families to Christopher and to you. We will do everything we can to support you both in the coming weeks or months, if this man decides to spill the beans. We are with you, believe me,' Jo said excitedly, all the while clutching Nicky's arm.

Nicky warmed to Jo Sanderson. She was very attractive with her dark colouring, bright eyes and carefully applied make-up. She was wearing a bright blue dress and jacket, and a gold necklace and matching dangling ear rings completed the ensemble.

'I'm nervous, I admit, and I'm grateful that you are so supportive. I'm also tired, not having had as much sleep as you have obviously had. It's a bit like waiting for a major

exam and I know that I will be relieved when it is over,'
she said clutching her drink.

'It is time for all of this secrecy to end, whatever the
consequences. It is hard to lose a child, even one who is not
actually your own, but now, I have to give him back. The
consequences for me are unimportant. What matters is
Christopher's future and, you're right, he is old enough to
deal with the news of his birth. In a way, I'm glad that he
will know the truth of it all, although I have spent almost
eighteen years avoiding facing up to it.'

'We were thinking that we could let the dinner go ahead
first, chat about the ship, his studies and anything else. Jo is
good at keeping the conversation going. If we can get
through the meal, I feel that we will have put him at ease,
he will know us a little and then we can tell him together.
What do you think, Nicky?' Alex said.

Nicky was shaking and downed her drink quickly. 'If
you want it that way, that's fine,' she said. 'I'm glad to
have you here to help with this. I have had to make all the
decisions by myself up until now. It's such a change to find
someone else offering to help with it all.'

Alex took her glass and refilled it.

'Don't get me drunk, please. I need to be fully alert for
this dinner,' she said, smiling nervously.

'Don't worry, Nicky. Kids are resilient. They look
ahead to their future and what happened before, well, it's
what happened before. We have three kids, a boy called
Joseph who is 15 years old and two girls, Caroline who is
14 and Clementina aged 12. The two girls are almost as tall
as Joseph and twice as astute. The poor boy is pushed from
pillar to post by his bossy sisters but that's what teaches
them how to deal with other people, isn't it? Joseph is like
Alex... very handsome and very kind.' Jo clutched her
husband's arm as she spoke, 'And the two girls are over
talkative bossy boots like me.'

Nicky had to smile at this charming woman and felt that she would indeed open up her world to accommodate Christopher. They were nice people and he would no doubt quickly warm to them. Their whole attitude was one of concern for her and strangely, she didn't feel that she was losing Christopher at all. He was gaining a family that was rightfully his and she felt ready for this change. She had had almost eighteen years to build up her own confidence and felt that she too, was prepared for what lay ahead.

They chatted on for half an hour, the conversation rarely deviating from Christopher's life with Nicky, where they stayed in Edgerley, the school he attended, his interests and then Nicky's career, her University experience and her posts with the law firms. Jo kept the conversation flowing and although Nicky still felt distinctly ill at ease, knowing that her world was on the point of changing, she was gradually adjusting to talking about herself and Christopher's life- topics which she had rarely aired in public before.

The conversation was interrupted when there was a sharp knock on the door and again it was Jo who jumped up and opened it.

'Mr. Partington, Ma'am,' the officer announced.

'Christopher, how nice to meet you,' Jo said, taking Christopher's arm and drawing him into the room. Nicky watched as he quickly took in the surroundings and the fact that his mother was standing beside Commander Alex Sanderson. 'I'm Jo Sanderson and this is my husband, Alex,' Jo said.

Alex approached with outstretched hand and took Christopher's in both of his. 'Hello Christopher,' he said, 'I'm delighted to meet you.'

Christopher was obviously rather overwhelmed by the company, and he nodded to Nicky and then said, 'I'm honoured to have this opportunity to see round this magnificent ship and also to have dinner with you, Sir. I know you have been in London recently in connection with some high power discussions. It is very good of you to allow me this privilege.'

'It's my pleasure, Christopher. Let me offer you a drink and then perhaps you can tell us how you enjoyed the tour.'

Alex, with trembling hands, busied himself preparing a glass of gin and tonic for Christopher and Jo began chatting to Nicky, trying to make everything appear natural and very normal.

'Last year we went all over the place. Alex serves on so many committees nowadays, it's all go. There are always dinners and entertainment and I have to constantly have new dresses and handbags…you can imagine what a chore that is!' She laughed and went on to chatter about their most recent trip to Honolulu. She was full of colourful stories about people they had met and sights they had seen.

After a while, the waiters appeared in pristine white uniforms and dinner was served. Alex moved towards the nearest chair at the far end of the table and Jo took Christopher's arm and gently pushed him to the seat on Alex's left, seating herself next to Christopher. Alex held Nicky's seat for her while she took the one on Alex's right, directly facing Christopher and periodically he smiled or lifted his brows, as if passing familiar messages to her.

The pheasant soup was delicious, hot and served with warm crusty bread. Jo asked one of the waiters to ask the chef for the recipe, and then chatted on about the amazing foreign dishes they had tasted on their travels. Christopher cleared his plate and momentarily glanced at Nicky. She smiled back and said, 'A little different from the university canteen, I expect?'

Christopher laughed and told the group about the abysmal canteen food and then went on to tell them about the lovely food that he had had in London with Bobbi's parents. They had taken him to two different restaurants and both had been quite superb.

'So what are you studying at university, Christopher?' Alex asked.

'I'm doing engineering with computer science as a large part of the course. I've only been there a couple of months but already I feel certain that this is exactly what I want to do. There are so many aspects of engineering and the field is wide open. Every day I learn about sides to it that I have never heard of. There is a lot of course work, workshops, reading and so on but it's all very applied and really it's fascinating and so far, very enjoyable,' he said enthusiastically.

'What interested you in the Windsor? Nicky told us that you had expressed a wish to see her,' Alex asked.

'I'm most grateful to have had this chance, Sir,' he replied. 'It's hard to know why ships interest me. Perhaps it's the size of them, the engineering and construction involved. So many men are involved in their design, their running, their maintenance, it's hard to believe. They are magnificent beasts, to me, and so many of them have travelled all over the world, been involved in conflicts here and there. They all have a history.'

Jo looked at her husband and said, 'Tell Christopher about your decision to join the navy, Alex.'

As the soup plates were cleared and a large roast beef was brought in, Alex talked about the time when he joined the navy, his own university career which was also engineering but without the computer science aspect.

The wine was poured, potatoes and vegetables dished up; waiters came and went and the conversation buzzed with barely a break.

Jo and Nicky chatted about the problems the wives of naval personnel had with their husbands away for long periods and the worries when the men were sent overseas to contribute to dangerous assignments.

A slight lull stimulated Jo to talk about Virginia which was where they lived now. 'We have always to make arrangements for the kids when we go away. We do have a live-in sitter, Kathy- I can't call her a nanny now the kids are older. She's a gem, an older woman; by that I mean in her fifties. She's quite fun and luckily the kids like her but you know we always feel guilty when we are away too long. Sometimes I stay home and Alex goes away alone but actually the kids are getting older and that bit more responsible... What am I saying? Joseph locked himself out of the house just last week. They can do some pretty stupid things still, but Kathy, our sitter, seems to be able to handle them.

Alex talked about his pleasure in returning to Virginia and related stories of previous homes where they had stayed during their marriage. They had travelled widely and moved on a number of occasions. He omitted to mention his visit to England eighteen years previously.

More wine was poured, the main course cleared and a young waiter presented each of the four with a choice of desserts.

'Look at that, Sticky Toffee Pudding, Baked Alaska…. Alex, you're not having that Sticky Toffee Pudding, are you? He just loves the desserts and so do I, but if I eat any more, I shall have to go on a strict diet again. Why is it that most other wives are as thin as a pin?' Jo said.

'What about you, Nicky? Does anything appeal to you?' Alex said. 'And don't listen to Jo. Have what you like.'

'It all appeals to me but I think I'll pass and just have coffee, if I may. I've had a wonderful meal, thank you.'

'I'm with you, Nicky,' Jo said, folding her white napkin and placing it on the table.

'Christopher, please tell me you want to join me in a

Sticky Toffee Pudding?' Alex asked. 'It's embarrassing for me to eat that alone.'

Christopher laughed. 'Yes, it's favourite of mine, too. I'll happily join you.'

'What other favourites have you, Christopher?' Alex asked.

'Well my all-time favourite would be Banoffi Pie. Do you know that, Sir?' he replied.

'Oh, Banoffi pie, of course. Quite delicious! We must ask the chef to get the recipe, and next time we dine, we'll make sure it's on the menu.'

Suddenly the room seemed quiet. Nicky wondered if Christopher was thinking that there was a possibility of meeting again. He glimpsed her way but could not tell what was going through her mind. Her face was impassive. She was giving nothing away.

The desserts came. The women gasped in jealousy as the two men enjoyed the sweet, syrupy pudding. The coffee was served and the waiters cleared the table. Nicky knew that the time was approaching when the reason for this dinner would be explained and her heart jumped a beat.

Alex rose and brought 4 small glasses to the table from the bar.

'Nicky, brandy? Port? What can I get you?'

'A small brandy, Alex, please. That would be very nice.'

'Jo likes a brandy too,' he said pouring a second one. 'And you, Christopher?

'Thank you. I'll have a brandy, too.'

Finally they all sat around the table, glasses in hand.

'Shall we have a toast, Alex?' Jo asked.

'Yes, I think we should toast *the future*.

They each raised their glasses and drank.

'And another toast,' Alex said, 'this one is to Christopher- *success and happiness.'*

They all drank again. Christopher was beaming, obviously pleased with the personal attention he was getting from such a distinguished man.

'Right, well now that we have enjoyed a sumptuous meal in pleasant surroundings and in very good company,' Alex said, 'this is the time when more weighty issues have to be discussed.'

He turned to Christopher and said, 'I must apologise to you, Christopher. You have been at a disadvantage here today because this meeting was set up for a particular purpose and everyone else in the room knows exactly the reason behind it. I want you to know that what you are about to hear is hard for us to talk about at this moment and it is very sensitive. It concerns your Mum, Nicky, and it concerns me.' He placed his hand over Nicky's.

'I'm going to ask Nicky…'

'You're my father, Sir…. You are my father, aren't you?' Christopher suddenly blurted out.

Alex looked at Nicky and then at Christopher. 'Well, you have jumped the gun, and you are correct, Christopher. How did you know?'

Christopher looked elated and tears came into his eyes. 'From the moment I saw you, I recognised the similarities; and your mannerisms, too. They are so like mine.'

'So much for holding back,' said Jo. 'The cat has been out of the bag all afternoon.

'Did you and Mum meet then in Edgerley or was it earlier than that?' Christopher asked.

'Ah, it's not quite that simple, Christopher,' Alex said, seeing the conclusion that Christopher had jumped to.

'We met yesterday, here in Southampton for the first time,' Alex said.

'I don't follow,' said Christopher, his forehead furrowed as he looked at his mother for answers.

'Nicky, last night I asked you to begin at the beginning

because when you told me that I had a son I knew nothing about, I didn't follow either. Last night, Christopher, Nicky and I talked for hours; talked about eighteen years ago, about things that happened then that have come to the fore again. It was only yesterday that Nicky came to see me and she is going to tell you everything now…ok, Nicky?' he said, patting her hand.

'Mum?'

'You remember, Christopher, when I used to tell you about the crash that killed my parents and my brother?'

'Yes.'

'You remember, too, that I had four operations at that time. When you were little, you used to recite them to me.'

'Your left arm, your right leg, your chest and your tummy,' he said obligingly.

She smiled, 'Yes. Well the fourth operation on my tummy was performed to control bleeding in my pelvis. The doctors had to stop the bleeding in order to save my life and to do that, they had to remove my womb… perform a hysterectomy.'

'You're not ill, Mum?' Christopher asked, a worried look on his face.

'No, Chris, I'm not ill. What I'm saying is that from the time of that operation, I could bear no children of my own. I am not your real mother.' Her voice cracked and tears began to form at the corners of her eyes. She could not speak for emotion.

Christopher rose and came round the table. He sat on her right and put his arm round her shoulders. 'You'll always be my real mother, whatever happened,' he said comfortingly.

She wiped away the tears and after a few minutes, said firmly,

'Chris, please listen to me. I have to tell you the whole story.'

He withdrew his arm and sat quietly by her side, pensive and concerned.

Nicky began at the beginning again and related the whole story which she had told Alex only a few hours earlier. Jo was quiet for a change now, listening intently to every word, her eyes moist too.

Christopher sat speechless, his mind filled with confusion and awe. When he heard that his mother, Felicity, was now cared for in a home, he was clearly distressed, and sat with his head in his hands.

'But she is alive? I could see her?' he asked then.

Alex had been waiting for his turn to contribute and took the chance to tell about his relationship with Felicity and his concern for her now.

'Since last night, I have been thinking that we should both go to see her. Who knows, maybe when she sees us, she will remember the past and be able to shut out the thought that she had lost her son.'

'You have to be careful, Alex,' Jo said. 'It might not be advisable. It would be a great shock for her. You would have to consult her medical adviser first.'

Nicky pulled out the photograph of Felicity and Alex which she had taken from the bedroom in Beaulieu. She passed it to Christopher and said, 'This picture was taken in 1995, about 6 months before you were born. Felicity must have been about 3 months pregnant with you at the time.' Christopher held the photo and gazed intently at the two people who were his parents.

'I can't believe this,' he whispered, bringing his hand up to his face.

Jo came across to lean over his shoulder and said, 'I've never seen that picture, either. She is pretty and so young.'

'She was nineteen then and I was twenty five. We wanted to get married but Jack Randall was having none of that, primarily because I was just a sailor, American and because I was coloured. He had great expectations for Felicity's future. I have no doubt that he loved her very much, like most parents. He felt that her relationship with me was disastrous for her and I feel responsible for all that happened. If I hadn't met her, none of this would have come about. She would have married a wealthy businessman and have had a couple of kids now.'

'You can't blame yourself for what happened to Felicity, Alex,' Jo said 'She could have contacted you. She could have gone to the hospital and had proper medical care. No, it isn't your fault at all.'

Christopher couldn't take his eyes away from the photograph but eventually he placed it on the table and said, 'A few months ago, I didn't tell you this, Mum. I had been invited to lunch with Bobbi's parents and during the meal, her father turned to me and said, 'Bobbi tells us your mother is a lawyer?'

'I told him that you were a specialist in business law and that you had recently been elevated to chairman of a major national committee. He then turned to me and asked, 'And your father? What did he do?'

'I told him that I had never known my father and I didn't know what he did, but it made me wonder why I didn't know that. Then he asked me, 'Where did he come from? Was he West Indian, perhaps?'

I had never really thought about the colour of my skin. It had never been an issue and I wasn't sure what to think. It's funny but I was never very interested either, but after that dinner it stayed on my mind and during the holiday week when I was in London staying at Bobbi's place, I went to Kew and looked through the records for my birth certificate. I don't know what I expected to find but in the event, my father's name was UNKNOWN and my mother was recorded as Nicola Partington.'

He looked at Nicky now, 'How is that, Mum?'

Nicky stared at the table and twisted her hands together. 'Do you know the lady who always says hello to you in the street, the one who makes a lot of you and says, 'How's young Christopher?' ...Mary Marshall?

'Yes. Well, Mary Marshall was the registrar in Edgerley for many years and, although you are too young to remember, I worked in her office for some time before going on to university. My official role was in book keeping and as a filing clerkess but I took that job for the express purpose of forging your birth certificate. Without it, I couldn't register you with a GP and I couldn't claim an allowance. Mary knew nothing of that deception and would be horrified to know what I did. There were things I had to do to look after you and to give the impression that you were my child.'

'You had to do it; it was quite justified in the circumstances. After all you had saved Christopher's life and everything you did, you did for his benefit. No court would condemn you for that,' Jo said.

'I'm afraid that might not be the case and certainly the Law Society would frown upon any of its members engaged in devious practices. No, I think, when this information is made public, I will be disbarred.'

'Why would it come into the public domain, Mum?' Christopher asked anxiously.

She told Christopher about Jeremy Ratcliffe and his threat to tell the police that he was not her son.

'He found your birth certificate, too, and he also searched my medical records which told him that I had had a hysterectomy before your birth, so he found himself with information which he could use to blackmail me.'

'How much does he want?' asked Jo.

'He asked for £50,000 but that would only be the first request of many, I expect. How long could I go on paying him? I would prefer not to pay him, to call his bluff.

However, I'm not the only one to be affected if this story is made public and you, Alex, have a right to your opinion too.'

'As I told you last night, I'm against giving him any money, too. Blackmailers are not usually content with only one payment. Felicity could be seen to be guilty of concealing the pregnancy and of attempting to murder her child, charges I find incredible, knowing her as I did, but it would seem to be unlikely that she would be affected greatly by the sounds of it. The police could hardly pursue charges against her if she is as incapacitated as you seem to think. Jack Randall of course, on the other hand would be put in a very serious situation if his role in this is exposed. He could be charged with attempted murder.'

'And rightly so,' contributed Jo. 'He tried to do away with a child.'

'He is a rich man and a bit of a boor but he is also Christopher's grandfather,' said Nicky. 'His actions were inexcusable, as far as we know. We can only surmise what happened that night and Felicity won't be helpful in clarifying things. I think I have to speak with Jack myself and tell him what I have told you. He is unlikely to deny it, given that I was there, that his car was there, and that DNA would prove that Felicity is Christopher's mother. Maybe with the threat of exposure, he will be prepared to open up a bit. I know that's perhaps overly optimistic but I have met him professionally on a number of occasions and he knows me a little. I can set up an appointment with him and give this a try.'

'I'm not very happy about that and I am certainly prepared to accompany you, Nicky… you know that,' said Alex.

'Thank you, but I think I should go alone first. If you came or if Christopher came, he might have a heart attack. After all, he has believed for eighteen years that he got away with it. He believes Christopher is dead and that you have been out of his life for all of that time.'

'You are very brave, Nicky, going into the lion's den alone. You can tell him that I plan to visit soon and discuss what to do for the best.'

Alex sighed and continued, 'Tonight I'm afraid I have to be in London and then tomorrow we are flying to Delhi for another meeting. Nicky, you have my contact numbers and you know that I will do all I can to help you both, so please keep me informed. Important as my job is, my family is more important.'

He reached into his inside jacket pocket and pulled out a small packet.

'Christopher, I have missed almost eighteen years of your life and that pains me but I am determined not to miss any more. I have not been there for you; I didn't know about you. I have let you down but I want to make up for that in the future. You are a Sanderson and my family is your family.'

'Yes, all fifty nine of them, Christopher,' said Jo quickly, seeing that her husband was finding the whole situation very difficult. 'At the last get-together of all the aunts, uncles and cousins, that was the number- fifty nine. You will be the sixtieth. That rounds it up nicely.'

Alex smiled. 'Now you know what your father does and where he comes from. If you want to change the birth certificate, that can be done with DNA proof. If you want to be Christopher Sanderson, I would be very happy but that is entirely up to you.'

'You don't have to make any decisions today, Christopher,' said Jo. 'Goodness me, the poor lad has a lot of thinking to do before he does that.'

'You're right as usual, Jo. But I want Christopher to know that he is part of our family. Joseph, Caroline and Clementina are his half-brother and half-sisters; our home is your home, and that applies to you, too, Nicky. If ever someone was family, you certainly are. If things don't work out afterwards, we will help you. Don't worry about that. We will take care of you, I promise.'

Nicky thanked him and felt an enormous feeling of relief and gratitude knowing that Christopher's father had turned out to be such an exceptionally nice man.

'This is a small gift for you, Christopher,' Alex said, opening the packet.

'I wanted to give you something today. There wasn't much time and this is all I could get before we met. It is an IPhone, I expect you have one already?'

'No, Sir. I have a mobile; a very basic one at the moment.'

'Well, the man in the shop assured me that this was the best. In the list of contacts, you will find my contact numbers and even for the house in Virginia. Please don't use that for a few days. We need to tell the kids all about you first,' he said, handing it to Christopher.

'You will also find my email and Jo's in there, so you can be in touch any time. If you need or want anything or even if you don't need or want anything, please keep in touch. You are my son and I want very much to be your father.'

Christopher rose from his chair and went behind Nicky to shake Alex's hand but when Alex opened his arms, Nicky watched her son throw himself into them. The two men gripped one another, emotions high and tears spilling out on their faces.

'Another brandy would be good,' said Jo, moving to the bar.' Port will be fine, however, since we have managed to finish the brandy. Let's all have another toast.' She poured the glasses, giving Alex and Christopher time to control their feelings.

Nicky found herself crying too, but it wasn't sadness

that overwhelmed her. It was an immense sense of relief as well as the sight of her son so deeply affected by the news of his birth. Christopher extricated himself from Alex's arms and wrapped her up in his embrace. She could feel his soft face against her neck and was reminded of another day, another place.

'Shall we toast the future again, Alex?' she heard Jo say. 'After all, Christopher didn't really know what his future held the last time. Now it will mean something more.'

Jo's voice was the strongest as they raised their glasses once again, *to the future.*

22

Strangely, Nicky felt even closer to Christopher after the emotional meeting on *HMS Windsor* and when they parted company on the following morning, Christopher seemed to have matured and become pensive. He expressed his concern at her proposed visit to see Jack Randall, but she reassured him that if he became too hard to handle, she would leave. If the meeting was held at Beaulieu, Sylvie and the servants would also be around, so it was unlikely in her judgment that he would behave too aggressively. He liked to be in control but in this context, he would have lost control and she anticipated his response could be anger and defensiveness. But if she could get the whole story out, he would be exposed and without any defence. It was hard to watch Christopher leave but the huge weight of secrecy had been lifted from her shoulders and she knew now, what she must do. Almost eighteen wonderful years with Christopher was coming to a close. Her brilliant career was also at an end. She was resigned to these facts now. Perhaps she would go to prison for her misdeeds. It was all hanging in the balance.

Returning to the office on the following Monday, Marilyn was pleased to see Nicky back and passed on the messages awaiting her attention, mentioning that Jeremy Ratcliffe had scheduled an appointment to see her on Friday evening at 6pm. 'This, I may say, in spite of the fact that I told him you would be away for two weeks. I let him make the appointment and planned to contact him if you had not returned by then,' she said.

Nicky thought that it would be best if she could see Jack Randall before that date, since she really wanted to know how he felt about the possibility of an eighteen year old secret exposed. It could destroy Jack's reputation, put his business in jeopardy and might even merit a jail sentence for him. Sylvie might know nothing of the previous episode. It was not something to confide to your young socialite wife whose extravagant parties would lose some appeal. It was possible that Jack might even want to pay the blackmailer, such was the magnitude of his potential loss should Ratcliffe do his worst. Jack was rich, fifty thousand pounds was not going to bankrupt him. He was over sixty years of age and apparently in good health but her news would come as a shock and she hoped that he wouldn't suffer a stroke or a heart attack when she came to confront him with her news. In spite of everything, she had come to respect and even like the man, and had no desire to hurt him any more than was necessary.

There had been a call from John Amos with a message to get in touch at her convenience. Part of her would have rushed into his arms but now that her job and her reputation were on the line, she didn't want to share her burden with him. He was a man of some integrity and a well respected lawyer. The last thing she wanted to do was to put him in the same boat by sharing the knowledge and making him an accessory. It was the wrong time to meet with him again. Reluctantly, she tore up the note and put it in the wastebasket.

She then pressed the intercom button and asked Marilyn to set up a meeting with Jack Randall early in the week, making up a credible reason concerning his shareholdings.

Twenty minutes later, Marilyn entered her office and brought a cup of black coffee with her. 'Mr. Randall was his usual charming self. He says he can see you for ten minutes on Wednesday morning at 8.30am precisely,' she said, mimicking Jack's brusque response.

'Thank you, Marilyn,' she replied, pleased that Jack had fitted her in before her scheduled meeting with Ratcliffe but concerned about the short time he had allocated. Ten minutes was hardly enough to discuss the weighty issues which needed to be aired, but then Jack would just have to reorganise his day, and perhaps his life.

All of a sudden everything seemed to be coming to a head. After all this time, after all the lies and excuses, in a matter of a few days, her whole life was reaching a climax and the outcome did not look promising. Perhaps she should have done things differently, gone to the police earlier, applied to adopt Christopher since no-one wanted him, but she had no money, no house and would have been deemed mentally unstable after her attempted suicide. It seemed unlikely that a court would have allowed Christopher to be adopted into her care, such as it was. The decisions she had made had been made out of necessity and she could not negate them now. That was something she shared with Jack Randall.

At at eight o'clock on Wednesday morning on Wednesday morning she drove up the drive to Beaulieu, passing the lodge at the gate with its adjoining garage and neatly kept borders. As she reached the wide turning space in front of the heavy front door, she saw Jack's red jaguar and Sylvie's grey four by four parked by the far side of the house. They were both shining as though just cleaned and polished. It appeared that both Jack and Sylvie would be at home.

She turned the car to face the exit, parked and walked up to the front door, filled with resolve but her stomach aching with anxiety. The butler, wearing his usual black suit, and white shirt, greeted her politely. She reckoned he was in his sixties, his white hair thinning markedly at the top. He always had a serious demeanour, barely moving his facial muscles as he directed her to Jack Randall's office. He knocked and immediately a loud voice boomed, 'Come in.'

Jack was standing at his filing cabinet, papers in hand. Smartly turned out in a brown check suit, beige shirt and dark brown tie, he turned to face her and said, 'Good morning, Nicky. You're early. Whatever this is about, I hope you will be quick. I have a busy day ahead.' He sat down at his desk and looked directly at her. 'Which shares have you come to discuss? You have exactly ten minutes,' he said gruffly, looking at his Rolex watch.

Nicky felt her whole body trembling but she thought of Christopher and her conversation with Alex, and knew that she had to do what she came to do. She began. 'You have allocated ten minutes to this meeting, Mr. Randall, and I would appreciate it if you would listen to me for at least nine of these minutes without interruption.'

Jack Randall raised one eyebrow. He was not accustomed to people addressing him in this way. He opened his mouth to retaliate but she quickly spoke. 'I am here to discuss the events which took place on the night of the thirtieth October 1995.'

Jack's retort was curtailed and his mouth shut and opened like a guppie. She noticed then how arthritic his hands were as he began to twist them together on the desk.

'What are you talking about?' he managed to blurt out.

'On that night you drove with Felicity to the woods on Mansion Hill.'

'What utter nonsense is this?' he shouted, standing up, towering over her, his face puce with anger.

'I know this, Jack, *because I was there* that night. You drove your previous Jaguar ESG 492 there. Felicity carried a box into the trees and she left it there, covered it with fallen leaves and then the two of you drove away. The car lights were not lit and you didn't trigger the ignition until you were almost at the main road.'

'I don't know what you're talking about and I want you to leave immediately,' he shouted at her, moving around the desk, his stance threatening. Nicky didn't move. She didn't think he would actually hit her although her words had provoked him into a fearsome rage.

'I'm not finished, Jack,' she said firmly. She could not allow him to intimidate her now. She had to finish the story. This was her only chance.

'You most certainly are!' he bellowed at her, reaching for the press button to summon his butler. 'I'll have you thrown out!' he raged, his temper clearly out of control. She noticed that he had not pressed the button on the desk and wondered if he didn't want to explain himself to Peters.

'I found the box, Mr. Randall. I opened that box and found a baby boy. He was cold and hungry but he was alive,' she said quietly.

Jack Randall collapsed into his leather chair and stared speechless at the white blotter on his desk. All colour had drained from his face. Nicky feared that the shock had been too much for him, and waited. After a moment he asked, 'You what?' his expression one of disbelief.

'I took him home and I looked after him. I brought him up as my own son. His name is Christopher and he is now seventeen and at university.'

Jack brought his arms up to the desk and his head fell into them. For a while he was silent and Nicky gave him the time to digest what she had said, now feeling much more in control of the situation. She had delivered the message as succinctly as she could and he knew that she was telling the truth. It had been a direct blow, a bombshell, but Jack had given her little choice.

Eventually he raised his head and said, 'You want to

blackmail me. Is that it? You manipulate your way into my affairs, and then come up with this cock and bull story in the hope that I'll believe you. How did you know that Scott Martin was my lawyer and how did you come to be working with him? What proof have you got to support this ridiculous lie?' he spat at her, frowning angrily, but she could see now that his heart wasn't in the bluff. He knew that the game was up.

'When I finished my training, I applied to Martin & Ainslie for a job. I had no idea that you were a client of Scott's and it wasn't until he was retiring, that I discovered that. It filled me with dread that I would have to meet you and even work with you. It wasn't intentional, I assure you. You are, by the way, the second person to accuse me of blackmail within a week. The first person was Alex Sanderson.'

Jack's face was a mask. He wasn't sure how to deal with this woman. The truth was spilling out too quickly. Nicky could tell that she had struck a body blow. For the first time in his life, Jack Randall was beaten. It didn't feel good to Nicky. She had come to respect the man in spite of what had gone on before. Now, she saw him at his most vulnerable, looking grey and old, his shoulders slumped down as if someone had delivered an almighty blow. She continued while he was silent, 'I found a photo of Alex Sanderson and Felicity in her bedroom when Sylvie showed me round. The name on that photo was Alex and there was a picture of a ship in the background, the Newark. The date was April 1995. It was through that photograph that I traced Alex Sanderson. Commander Sanderson had a relationship with your daughter in 1995 when he was stationed in Southampton. He wanted to marry Felicity and came to you to ask permission but you were having none of it and ordered him from the house in April of that year. Felicity was already in the early stages of pregnancy, obviously something she did not confide in you or Alex. You had forbidden her to contact him, and she never did. Alex Sanderson had no knowledge of Felicity's baby until a few days ago when I told him.'

'How dare you involve Sanderson? He wasn't good enough for my daughter, not then and not now.' he growled.

'Alex Sanderson is happily married with three children. You will have seen his picture on the television and news recently in his capacity as an adviser to NATO. He has done remarkably well and is a most likeable man.' she said, calmly adding, 'He was most distressed to hear about Felicity's illness and if he can do anything at all to help her, he will.'

Jack's head was again bowed, turning from side to side, and he was running his fingers through his wavy grey hair, clearly in some distress.

'It was all his bloody fault,' he mumbled into his hands.

'I was in Southampton last week and we had lunch on *HMS Windsor*; his wife Jo and Christopher, his son too. It was the first time he had seen his son. It was an emotional day,' she said.

Suddenly the buzzer on Jack's desk sounded making them both jump. He pressed it and barked, 'Yes.'

'Mr. Blacklock is here, Sir,' the butler announced.

'You'll have to reschedule. It's not convenient,' he shouted and switched it off angrily.

'I don't believe a word you are saying. It's all nonsense. You won't be getting any money out of me,' he shouted at her again. 'You've never once mentioned that you had a son, not in all the time you have been working for me. Why would you wait seventeen years to tell me all of this, if it wasn't for money?'

She noticed that his bottom lip was trembling and his hands twisting back and forth but he remained sitting and he hadn't thrown her out yet.

'No, I haven't mentioned Christopher to you because I was worried that you would want him back, worried that I would lose him. In all of that time, Jack, you have never talked to me about your daughter, either.' She paused, watching his reaction. 'I don't want your money, Jack. The reason I have had to tell you all of this now, is because a journalist called Jeremy Ratcliffe who works for Star Magazine, is blackmailing me. He was to write a short story about my success in the business sector and unknown to me, he researched my medical history and discovered that I could not have any children. He sought Christopher's birth certificate and that, something I personally forged while working in the registrar's office, stated that I was his mother. His father's name on that is *Unknown*. Ratcliffe has put two and two together. He knows that Christopher is not my child and he knows that the birth certificate is a forgery. He has asked me for £50,000 or he will tell the police about this scandal he has unearthed. He has no knowledge of your part in the story, nor does he know who Christopher's parents are, and frankly I don't think he has sufficient clues to be able to pursue that. However, should he divulge this information to the police, there may be questions I will be obliged to answer.'

Nicky looked at Jack's slumped shoulders and suddenly he seemed to have aged twenty years. Gone was the overconfident brash go-getter and in its place, a man who had lost a major battle.

'I'm telling you about this because if this information becomes public, I will not be the only one to be affected. There could be repercussions which affect others. I wanted you to be prepared in case he decides to spill the beans. I could pay him of course, but I would rather not do that. He is quite likely to come back for more money and at the end of the day, he would ruin me. He may well do that, anyway, by exposing all the things I have done to keep Christopher's origins secret'

'How do I know you are telling the truth?'

Nicky fumbled in her wallet and handed him the photos of Christopher. Jack picked it up and stared at the pictures for a moment. 'He doesn't look like Felicity. That could be anyone.'

'He is your grandson. He looks like his father. You must see the resemblance. He will carry the DNA of Alex Sanderson and Felicity. We can prove this by taking samples from each of them if you are not convinced.'

'I won't have my daughter bothered with this,' he said anxiously.

For a few minutes they sat in silence, Jack trying to think through everything she had said.

'If you were in the woods on Mansion Hill on that night, tell me why. Why would a young girl be out in the dark in the middle of the night? It's not believable,' he stated bluntly.

'One year prior to that night, I was involved in a dreadful road accident, an accident which killed my parents and my brother ...

Someone knocked on the door; the butler appeared with a tray on which two cups of coffee were placed. 'Coffee, Sir?' he said calmly.

'No,' shouted Randall, and then, controlling himself, he said more civilly, 'Yes, yes, bring it in, Peters.'

Peters laid the tray on the desk carefully and handed Nicky a cup of steaming coffee. He behaved casually as if he were accustomed to being on the receiving end of Jack's wrath and had learned to deal with it.

'Milk and sugar on the tray, Ma'am,' he indicated, and then left the room, behaving as though he had not noticed the rude outburst.

Nicky sipped the hot drink and continued, 'I was

seriously injured in the accident and although, after a few months, my wounds were healing, I was very depressed. I had no-one in the world; I had no money because of house payments and other debts; my university career was at an end since I was too unwell to continue, and I had had a hysterectomy to stop bleeding and so I could never ever have my own children. I decided to take my own life on the anniversary of the crash and went to the woods to do that. I had taken numerous pills and was lying in the leaves waiting for death, when your car drove up and I thought for a moment that I would be discovered but Felicity went off in a different direction. When you had gone, I was curious to know why two people would come to the wood in the dead of night and deposit a box. When I found him, I couldn't believe it- a child that no-one wanted, a child left here to die. He was the child I could never have. So you see, Jack, in a way, you saved my life. What has puzzled me all these years was the reason you and Felicity tried to kill him. I just can't get my head round that. Why did you want to kill him?' she asked, her eyes searching his face.

She saw tears in his eyes and the shoulders had fallen even more.

'You don't know what you have done,' he muttered, his hands again running through his hair.

'What do you mean?' she asked.

'*We went back to get him.* We went back and he wasn't there, just an empty box, oh God! That's what caused Felicity's breakdown. She thought he had been taken by foxes and eaten. She was hysterical. We searched for ages but there was no sign of him. Now I know why.'

They went back! Nicky was staggered at this revelation. *They went back!*

What had she done?

'When did you go back?' she finally asked.

'About an hour later. But we thought he was dead. He

wasn't breathing and wasn't moving. He had lost blood because she hadn't tied the cord and I thought he had bled to death. We were just disposing of his body. Felicity had concealed the pregnancy even from me. Sylvie and I were in the house in Switzerland when she phoned, 'Daddy, Daddy, please come home. I need you.'

'We have always been close, especially since her mother died. I told Sylvie that some important business problem had arisen and booked the first flight home, scared out of my wits that something awful had happened to my little girl. When I got home, the house was in darkness. I called to her but there was no reply. Frantic with worry I looked in all the rooms downstairs, then I went up to her bedroom and there she was, lying on her bed, blood everywhere, on the sheets, the bedspread, the rug, and on her. I thought she was dead. She was deathly white. Then when I went to her, I saw the baby at the foot of the bed. Felicity was breathing so I grabbed a ribbon from her dresser and tied the cord but the baby wasn't breathing. I was so worried about my daughter. I held her in my arms and she wept uncontrollably. She felt cold and was shivering, so I ran a hot bath and helped her into it. While she was there, I picked up all the bloodied linen and the rug. I went downstairs to the back yard and put it all in the furnace. Then I came back. The baby was just lying there, unmoving. He looked dead to me. There was a hat box on the floor. I tossed out the hat and placed the body inside. I found new sheets and bedding and cleaned everything up, then went down to the kitchen and made a pot of tea. I was trying to put everything right, you see.

'When I came back, I got Felicity into bed and made her drink lots of tea. She began to perk up and I urged her to go to hospital.'

'Oh, no, Daddy. I don't want anybody to know about this,' she pleaded.

'When she looked around for the baby, I told her that he was dead. I tried to tell her that it was for the best, that she could put it all behind her now, that in a few months, she would be able to draw a line under it. No-one would know what had happened, only Felicity and me. She wouldn't stop crying. I gave her a brandy but she just got more and more tearful.'

'What will we do with him?' she cried over and over again.

'I just didn't know.'

She turned to the window and looking out, she suggested that we took him to the woods where no-one would ever find him. She became insistent and since I didn't know what to do, I agreed. She managed to put her coat on over her nightdress and held the box all the way there. She wouldn't stop crying. Afterwards, when we came home, I thought she would settle and get some sleep but an hour later, she came running for me, shouting, 'I need my baby. I must get him back, Daddy. We can't leave him there. Please, Daddy, take me back to the woods.'

Tears were running down Jack's face now and his whole body was trembling, as he remembered vividly the painful details of that night.

'I drove back to the wood, wondering what on earth we would do with this dead baby but when we got there and she ran into the woods, the box was empty. She started to scream, telling me that the animals had taken him. It was awful. Felicity was never the same again. She behaved irrationally and spoke nonsense. The following day I took her to a clinic outside town where I know the psychiatrist. I told him that she had had a miscarriage and had become crazy. She was admitted, given a blood transfusion and sedated. My little girl has never recovered from that night,' he cried.

Nicky couldn't get the thought out of her head. *They*

had gone back for him. They would have seen that he was alive and then looked after him with the best nannies, good schools, everything he could possibly want. What had she done? She had denied Christopher all of that.

Jack's shoulders heaved as he sobbed his heart out. Tears hit the blotter. His eyes were red and overflowing. This was a side of Jack Randall she had never seen before.

'For a long time, I blamed Sanderson. I told myself that it was all his fault. I wanted to kill him. My only daughter's life was destroyed by him. But after a lot of soul searching I began to see that it was my fault. She loved the man and I had prevented them from being together. *My* pride. *My* prejudices. *My* fault. Now I have lost my precious angel and it looks like she will never be the same again. It is a cross I have borne all these years and one with no end in sight.'

'You have a grandson. He's a fine young man and you will be proud of him. He knows the whole story now and he would like to meet his grandfather,' she said, trying to bring a little hope into Jack's black thoughts and feeling very guilty that she had been responsible for Felicity's breakdown.

'I don't want to see him. All of this pain has eased over the years but you have stirred it all up again. I don't want to have anything to do with him.'

'And Ratcliffe? What shall I do about him? Should I pay him or call his bluff?'

Randall thought for a while, his shaking easing, and eventually, he said,

'I'll pay him. It's my problem. Where does he stay?'

'I'm not sure, somewhere in the Wheatfield estate, I think. His address will be in the directory but wouldn't it be better if he came to my office and it was dealt with there? That way he need never know who you are, what your role in this was. Right now he can't know who Christopher's parents are. Even if he followed me, he wouldn't know. I have official business with you. There is no record of Felicity's pregnancy, no newspaper notice of a child's death late October 1995 and no news of a missing baby. He will hit a brick wall and may give up. The danger is that he will go straight to the police if I don't pay him.'

'What could the police find out?'

'They would question me and take Christopher's DNA. Alex Sanderson's DNA is in an American naval database. Eventually someone might discover that. In any event, Alex wants to acknowledge his son so I suppose he might tell the police about it.'

'Well, we could stall this a bit by paying him just now. When is he expecting the money?'

'He is coming to see me on Friday at at six o'clock in my office and I think he expects to be paid then.'

Randall opened a drawer in his desk and pulled out a cheque book. 'I'll give you a cheque for that sum and you can write one to him from your own chequebook. That way he won't know where the money came from.'

'I have the money. You don't have to pay him,' Nicky said.

'I'll do this for Felicity, not for you. I don't want her to find out any of this. It would kill her.'

He handed Nicky the cheque and she put it in her bag.

'I didn't imagine that this day would ever come. I thought we had buried the past. It was the worst nightmare you could ever contrive and reliving it all is unreal.'

He paused to blow his nose with his white, linen handkerchief.

'I don't want to see this boy and I don't want to see Sanderson. Is that clear?' Jack said firmly, his colour recovering a bit.

'Yes, it's clear,' she said, wondering if Alex Sanderson would accept that. She rose and headed for the door.

Opening it, she looked back. Jack Randall seemed to have physically shrunk. His hands covered his face again. She left without saying good bye. There seemed nothing else to say. She closed the door quietly.

As she reached the hallway, she saw Sylvie Randall talking with Peters, the butler and turned when she heard Nicky approach.

'What is going on this morning?' she asked, clearly agitated, 'Peters tells me that Jack is in a filthy mood. He has two people waiting to see him and I am already late for my appointment at the salon.'

'He has just had some bad news, I suppose that has upset him.' said Nicky, slowly edging to the door.

'So he has lost some money. That's it, isn't it?' said Sylvie, 'How much are we talking about? We have a lot of commitments just now what with the beach house in Cannes and the refurbishments on the boat. I don't want him crying off this weekend either. The Delafoys have invited us to their chateau in La Varenne in Paris. All I need is Jack playing up. How much money has he lost?' she enquired again, staring at Nicky.

'About fifty thousand pounds,' Nicky said calmly.

'Well, it could have been much worse. Was it his shares that let him down?' she asked.

'No, something else. You will have to talk to him about it, yourself,' she answered, making for the door.

'That's exactly what I'm going to do,' she said and stormed off towards Jack's office.

The butler turned to Nicky, 'Do you think his visitors should wait a bit longer or should I tell them to reschedule, Miss Partington?' he asked politely.

'I would ask them to reschedule, Peters,' she advised, and headed out of the door.

She sat in the car collecting her thoughts and then, heaving a deep sigh, drove straight down the drive, on autopilot, her mind a million miles away. She turned right at the main road and headed home. She had only one thought in her mind- *They went back for him.*

It preyed on her mind, eating away at her. She had taken the child and if she had just waited an hour, his family would have returned and found him.

23

The door to Jack's office flew open and Sylvie barged through in her smart white suit, a knitted boucle design with navy trim. She was carrying her navy handbag in one hand and gloves in the other, matching the high heeled shoes she was wearing. 'Jack, what is going on this morning? Has Nicky let you down? She tells me you have lost money. Is that right?'

Jack was seated at his desk, his hands supporting his head, contemplating all that had happened in the last few minutes. He had forgotten completely about the other people who were waiting to see him. He hadn't had time to plan how he would explain what had happened and knowing how persistent Sylvie could be, he opted for the truth. 'Have a seat, Sylvie, we need to talk.'

'Oh my God, Jack, is it that bad? Are we bankrupt? Is that what this is?'

Jack rose and went over to the silver tray where several bottles of spirits were lined up, along with glasses and tonic water. He poured a generous amount of vodka into a glass, added a splash of tonic and handed it to Sylvie. 'No, we are not bankrupt, nor are we in any financial difficulties.'

He poured himself a large whisky and took it back to his seat behind the desk.

'So, tell me what it is.' Sylvie persevered, downing her drink.

'It has nothing to do with money. It concerns something

that happened over seventeen years ago.'

'Before we were married?'

'No, shortly after. I told you part of the story at the time but not the whole story, partly because I was having a tough time dealing with the circumstances myself and partly because I thought it best if no-one knew the entire truth.'

Sylvie finished her drink and rose to help herself to another. When she had seated herself again, Jack said, 'You will recall at that time, we went to Switzerland for about six months. It was after the revelation that Felicity was dating a sailor.'

'Yes, I remember all of that. His name was Sanderson, Alex, I think. You didn't approve of him and you told me that Felicity and you had had a major argument. A few weeks later, we went off to Switzerland but a few months later you were called back unexpectedly on the pretext of a business matter although later you did tell me she had a miscarriage and had some sort of breakdown. I remember all of that; of course, I do.'

'At the time, I didn't know what had happened and yes, I lied to you, saying that I had a business problem to deal with but of course, when I came back, it was to find Felicity here at Beaulieu in desperate straits.'

'I never understood why you lied to me then.'

'I thought you would be jealous of her and angry with me for leaving you alone and going off to help Felicity. The two of you hadn't hit it off too well.'

'God knows I tried, Jack.'

'Well, when I returned home, Felicity was here. She had told us that she was going to stay with her friends, Ruby and Ken Bainbridge in the Lake District and I thought it would be good for her to get away from Beaulieu, away from memories of Alex Sanderson and away from me, too. It was a relief when she went away. As it turned out, she did stay with them for a few weeks and then returned here to stay alone because Peters and Esther were with us.'

'Why would she do that?'

'She was pregnant and didn't want anyone to know about it. She was so frightened that she couldn't confide in me and she probably thought that I would go mad when I heard about it. She knew how much I didn't want her to maintain a relationship with Sanderson. I failed her abysmally. She was missing her mother and I didn't know how to deal with it.'

'She could have told us. We would have dealt with it somehow.'

'As time went on, she became increasingly afraid and the thought of how I would react drove her frantic. She decided to try to get rid of the baby and had heard that drinking gin would induce a miscarriage so she drank gallons of the stuff. When that failed, she resorted to taking drugs, all sorts of things she obtained on the Internet. I found empty bottles and pill boxes all over her room. None of it worked and as time went on, she became more and more anxious.'

'But something did work. She miscarried.'

'No, she didn't, Sylvie. When I arrived here, I found her in her bedroom, out of her mind. She had bled all over the bed coverings and there was a baby lying beside her. She looked awful and my first thought was to get her to a hospital but she screamed at me and refused to go. I was just at my wit's end. I ran a hot bath and helped her into it. She was chattering all sorts of nonsense all the time. I cleared up the room and when I turned to look at the child, it wasn't breathing and wasn't moving. I tied off the cord and put him in a box.'

'Him? Then it was a baby boy?'

'Yes. I hadn't spent much time examining him because

my mind was filled with the state of Felicity. I had never seen her behaving this way before. I made her tea and tried to encourage her to go to the hospital but she was adamant that she wasn't going.'

'I wish I had been there with you.'

'She wouldn't settle and when I told her the baby was dead, she just behaved even more irrationally. She looked out of her window and seeing the woods on Mansion Hill, she insisted that we took the baby's body there and hid it. It was crazy, I know, but since she wouldn't go to hospital, I was wracking my brains, thinking what to do. Ultimately I agreed to it, to keep her quiet.'

'Someone has found the baby's body. Is that it?'

'No, not exactly. Someone found the baby seventeen years ago and he was alive.'

'What? Who?'

'Nicky Partington.'

'Nicky? But how?'

Jack rose to replenish his glass and Sylvie did the same.

'Nicky went through a difficult time when her family was wiped out in a car accident all those years ago. She suffered from depression later and had decided to commit suicide up there in the woods. That coincided with the night Felicity and I were there with the baby.'

'But how is she now acting as your lawyer, Jack? I'm not following this. Is she blackmailing you? Is that it?'

'No, but someone is blackmailing her. You see after the accident, she couldn't have children. When she found the baby, he seemed like a gift from God, I suppose. She kept him and brought him up but in the course of doing that, she had to forge a birth certificate and tell a few lies along the way. She went to university to become a lawyer and worked for Martin and Ainslie where she met Scott Martin. She had no intention of trying to find out who the boy belonged to. Quite the opposite because he was so precious to her, but someone found out about the forged birth certificate after all this time and decided to blackmail her.'

'But how could she know that you had anything to do with this?'

'She had seen the car and memorised the number plate. It didn't take much effort to find out whose car it was.'

'So the boy, where is he now?'

'He is at university and doing very well. Neither he nor Alex Sanderson knew anything of all of this until a few days ago. She found the picture of Felicity and Alex in her room when you showed her around, and followed up the name, Alex, to locate him.'

'Yes, I left her in Felicity's room for a few minutes. She has been a bit devious about this, hasn't she?'

'She has brought him up by herself all of these years. It's incredible. I thought it was behind us.'

'So how much does this man want, to keep the story quiet?'

'He has asked Nicky for £50,000 but she didn't want to pay, believing that he would inevitably come back for more. However, she hasn't done anything yet, just made an appointment with him and I have told her that I will pay the money.'

'My God, so he could keep coming back and bleed us dry?'

'Nicky has a lot to lose if he talks. Her forgery of the birth certificate, amongst other things, might get her a jail sentence and she would lose her job without question.'

'But what about us? We have a lot to lose too, Jack. What will people think about us? How do we know we can trust him?

'We don't. I'm going to transfer more funds to Switzerland and to France. We will have plenty of money to live on. If it all comes out, we may be better off leaving this country. However, I have to think this through. Felicity has to be taken care of. Maybe I can take her with us to a clinic there.'

'How do you know that this blackmailer exists? You have only Nicky's word for it. She might be the blackmailer herself. What proof have you that the baby was alive? Maybe she has made it all up.'

'I don't think so. She showed me photos of him.'

'But she could show you any photos and in your state of mind, you would just believe her.'

'She has spoken to Alex Sanderson and he has met the boy. I believe her.'

'She may be thinking that her son is the rightful heir to Beaulieu. It could all be a ruse to get money.'

'Well, time will tell but she knows so much. Her story is extraordinary but credible. It's hard for me to check up on her without disclosing the reason for my interest. I've known her for some time now and I've come to trust her.'

'You should see the boy.'

'His name is Christopher. She did say that he was anxious to meet his grandfather but I declined. That would be very hard for me, Sylvie, given the circumstances. It was so long ago. I have tried to forget about it. It was the worst time of my life.'

'It was all Felicity's fault. She should have at least told us about her pregnancy. We could have arranged an abortion and had it done discreetly. No-one would have ever known about it.'

'No-one would have known about it if Nicky hadn't been up there that night. I thought it was over but obviously not. Felicity has paid a heavy price for her indiscretion. I don't think we can blame her.'

'All of our married life, I have had to contend with her problems, her needs and now, even now, she is managing to ruin everything for us. You can't blame me for feeling this way about her.'

'She made a mistake. We all make mistakes.'

'Yes, she made a mistake and we are having to pay for it all our lives.

Sylvie knocked back the rest of her drink and turning to Jack, said,

'So where are we now?'

'Now we await the blackmailer and Nicky will pay him off.'

'Who is he?'

'A journalist called Jeremy Ratcliffe. He is coming to see her on Friday evening so she has promised to let me know the outcome of that meeting.'

Sylvie stood and paced the room, her face moist with perspiration. 'I can't believe it, Jack. Our whole world could fall apart.'

'No, it won't come to that. I'll deal with it. Why don't you go and lie down for a bit and let it all sink in. We'll talk about it later.'

'I'll have to cancel my appointment. And what about this weekend? We are supposed to be going to Paris,' she said breathlessly.

'We'll go. Just behave normally. Nothing is going to happen imminently.'

'You don't know that. It could all be in the papers tomorrow, if this man decides to tell what he knows.'

Jack got up and put an arm round his wife's shoulders. 'Take a Valium and lie down. There's nothing we can do at present.'

'Why didn't you tell me all of this, Jack?'

'I was trying to protect you and frankly, I didn't want to talk about it. After all this time, I really thought it was all forgotten and never in my wildest dreams did I imagine this would happen. I'm sorry, Sylvie, so very sorry.'

24

Once Nicky reached home, she flopped into an easy chair and curled up in a ball, going over everything that had been said and trying to rationalise the thought that Christopher might have been with his own family these last seventeen years if she had just waited an hour. The answer phone light was flashing and she wondered if it was Ratcliffe calling to remind her of their date on Friday evening. The plan was now to pay him off with Jack Randall's money but she wasn't in any hurry to discuss the arrangements with Ratcliffe. Eventually, however, she rose and pressed the PLAY button.

'Hi Mum, it's me. Just wondered how you got along with Jack. Give me a call.'

It was lovely to hear Christopher's voice and to hear him call her *Mum*. She knew that she would have to tell him all about her visit to Beaulieu but she was too distraught right now to tell him about it. She wandered into the kitchen but she had no appetite. It was only 11.30a.m and she felt mentally and physically drained. The whole business was sapping her energy. She went into the bedroom and lay down. It wasn't long before she fell asleep.

It was almost two o'clock when she awoke and, feeling guilty about leaving the office for so long, she showered, changed and set off to work.

Marilyn chatted brightly away and Nicky smiled,

listening patiently. Together they prioritised the workload and Nicky dictated a few letters. She felt better when she was busy but as the afternoon wore on, she realised that she was counting the hours until Ratcliffe came on Friday. She was trying to prepare herself as to what to say but it seemed clear that Jack Randall did not want to have his actions publicised or interrogated so she would have to hand him a cheque and tell him that was to be the end of it. At 6.30 Marilyn popped in to say goodbye and a cheery, 'See you tomorrow.'

Nicky worked on, reading mail, answering questions and clearing her desk. It was therapeutic and the time passed more easily while she was occupied with business.

At 8 p.m. she phoned Christopher and told him about her visit to Jack. She told him that Jack had been convinced that the baby was not breathing and was, in fact, dead. Felicity had insisted on returning to get her baby an hour later but by that time, the baby was no longer there. She tried to impress on him that they weren't bad people, just very stressed with the illegitimate pregnancy and the fact that Felicity had not confided in anyone.

Christopher asked, 'Did you believe him, Mum? Do you think he was covering up the fact that he wanted rid of Alex Sanderson's coloured baby?'

'He was very upset … crying, in fact. I think he feels a great deal of remorse and guilt about the whole thing. He did blame Alex for years but now he knows that it was his own pride that was to blame. No, I don't think he wanted to rid himself of Alex's child. He was trying to help Felicity, trying to sort things out in her best interest. She was obviously hysterical and at the end of her rope. Jack had no experience of dealing with this sort of situation and, of course, he loves his daughter so much.'

'When can I see him? Did you ask that?'

'He is in such a state, Christopher, I don't think you

should consider that just now, honey. Maybe when he has accepted the truth, he will come round to that. He was quite stunned when I told him what had happened. He needs time to think it through.'

She couldn't bring herself to tell him that Jack just wasn't interested in making his acquaintance.

'Does that apply to Alex too?'

'Yes, very much so. Are you in touch with Alex?'

'Yes, he e-mails a lot. It's very nice, Mum. I really like him.'

'Yes, you have a very special Dad. I'm glad that you found him, I really am.'

'You found him, not me.'

'Well, you know what I mean.'

'So when does Ratcliffe come round? Are you ready to tell him to shove off?'

'He is due to come on Friday about 6 p.m. but after my visit to Jack Randall, things have changed. Jack wants to buy some time and he doesn't want this to be dug up at all. He has given the money to pay Ratcliffe off so that's what I am going to do. I shall try to tell him that there will be no more but I have little hope that that will be the case. He will come calling again. However, it does delay the exposé and I have to say that I'm not too unhappy about that. For how long of course, who knows?'

'It's interesting that Jack wants to pay him off. Smacks of guilt, doesn't it?'

'He will be worried about his reputation and his standing in the community but I think his main concern is actually for his daughter. He has done his best to bury the whole episode and to protect Felicity from any further trauma. Sylvie will be worried, too. She loves hobnobbing with the elite and the rich, and her parties won't be quite so popular once Jack's history is known.'

'Does she know about it?'

'No, not unless Jack has told her by now. I'm not sure. I left him in rather a distraught state and she knew something had upset him badly. He may confess to her after my visit. We'll see in due course.'

'Will you phone me after Ratcliffe has been, Mum? I really want to know how it goes.'

'Yes, of course. I'll phone when I get home, maybe nine-ish, OK? And Christopher, will you keep Alex informed? It will save me relaying all of this again.'

'Will do. Speak soon then, Mum. Bye.'

That evening, Nicky paced the floor, thinking it all through again and wondering how Ratcliffe would take the deal. She didn't like the man but she had to appear relaxed and more laid back about it than she really felt. Still dwelling on the coming meeting, she went to bed but her sleep was punctuated by vivid dreams, some involving Ratcliffe and some which took her back to the woods on Mansion Hill. Her dreams played out alternative scenarios and disturbed her. When she did awake finally, she had one thing in mind- she had to visit Felicity. Somehow she would have to see exactly how ill she was. Christopher would want to see her even if he could not converse with her and a visit to the clinic could perhaps give her an idea of how possible that might be. There was also the hope that Felicity did have some memory of that night and perhaps could corroborate her father's version of the story. She determined to put her thinking cap on and work out some ruse to visit Felicity, aware that Jack would probably be against such a move.

All Thursday, she worked conscientiously in the office, forcing herself to concentrate on the business and to put thoughts of Ratcliffe out of her mind but his pending visit cast a large cloud over her.

On the following morning, she set off to the office early, and there prepared a cheque for Jeremy Ratcliffe for the sum of £50,000. She put this cheque with Jack's in her office safe, ready for the visit.

All day, she answered calls, prepared tax returns for two of her main clients and advised another regarding an investment portfolio. At lunch she went down to the deli close by and ate a chicken wrap and downed a cup of black coffee. On the way back, the street newspaper vendor thrust a paper towards her and she found some coins in her pocket to pay for it. Back in the office, she read the financial section and whiled away an hour getting up to date with the goings-on of celebrities and politicians. Marilyn came into the office at 5.30 and said, 'I'm going to stay until Ratcliffe has been, Nicky. I don't like to think of you here alone with him.'

'It's OK Marilyn. That's sweet of you but really not necessary. Feel free to get off home,' she said calmly.

'No, I'm definitely staying. I can do some filing and get the schedule ready for Monday in any case. I just came in to tell you that I'll be here,' she said.

'Very well. If you insist. You are very thoughtful and if he gives me any trouble, I'll press the intercom button for your help,' she said smiling. 'You can come in and hit him on the head with your handbag.'

'Yes, absolutely, I'm sure I could knock him cold,' she said, smiling.

Nicky started to sort out files, checked in her legal books on a specific question raised by one of her clients, searched for information on the Net, and checked and rechecked the information, trying to keep herself occupied until 6pm.

There was a knock on her door and Marilyn popped in again. Nicky's heart sank, anticipating that Ratcliffe had arrived.

'It's ten past six and still no sign of him,' she said. 'After all the aggravation he gave me to make this appointment! He really is a piece of work. Should we just go home and let him find us out?'

'No, I'll wait for a bit longer but please get yourself off. I'm sure he'll appear when he's ready. I would rather get it over and then we won't need to see him again,' she said.

'OK, if you're sure, but I'll be at least ten minutes getting ready so maybe he'll appear before I go,' she said, closing the door.

Nicky wondered why Ratcliffe was late. He knew that he had a good chance of getting a large sum of money and she thought that he would have been early rather than late for this appointment. He had told her that he required the money urgently, that someone was threatening violence towards him if he didn't pay up, and it seemed odd that he had not turned up promptly to get it.

Marilyn called, 'Bye' at 6.35pm and Nicky went into the office to make more coffee.

Carrying a large mug, she picked up the mail from Marilyn's desk and took it through to her own office. It had been delivered in the late afternoon and normally Marilyn would sort it out first thing in the morning, locate any relevant files and attach any forms or documentation which was pertinent to save time for the lawyers in the firm.

Now she started at the top and worked her way through the pile, locating files and attaching the letters, and discarding used envelopes. She drank the coffee and persevered with the letters for some time. It was 7.45pm and there was still no sign of Ratcliffe. She had his phone number and considered giving him a ring. However, she didn't want to seem too anxious and dismissed that idea.

There was a legal journal in the mail and she began to peruse this, taking time to read every article in great detail. She made more coffee and settled back with the journal. By 10.30 p.m. she had read the whole issue and her desk looked tidier than it had been in many months. She looked out of the window, searching the street for Ratcliffe but there was no sign of him so she decided to head for home. He wasn't just late; he had failed to turn up, and there had been no communication from him to rearrange the date or explain this change of plan. It was possible, of course, that he was too drunk to come. He certainly looked like a man with an alcohol problem.

Nicky put on her jacket, retrieved her bag, locked the office door and made for her car, looking around all the while for some sign of Ratcliffe. In a way, she was pleased that he had not come but it only meant that the visit was delayed and she would have another day or more of anxiety about it. It seemed increasingly odd that he hadn't come when so much was at stake for him. Had his debt collector caught up with him and perhaps really hurt him? Her imagination ran riot.

Driving home, she scanned the streets for anybody resembling Ratcliffe and when she pulled into her car park at the flat, she wondered if he had decided to call on her at home. However, there was no sign that anyone had been-no note and no message on the answer phone. She was confused and a little disconcerted, having been looking forward to sealing the deal and getting him out of her life, at least for a while.

She phoned Christopher to tell him that Ratcliffe had not appeared.

'Oh, I'm glad you phoned. I thought something had happened,' he said, 'It's almost eleven p.m.'

'I'm sorry Chris. I waited at the office until ten-thirty and then decided to call it a day. Perhaps he'll call tomorrow.'

'OK, sleep well and don't worry. Phone tomorrow if you have any news.'

25

For a week, she heard nothing from Ratcliffe and half expected to see an article written by him in Star Magazine pouring out the details of Christopher's birth and her duplicity, but there was nothing. She kept in touch with Christopher and even dropped a note to Jack Randall to tell him that she had not as yet required his money since Ratcliffe had not appeared. She told him that she would let him know if he did turn up.

Another uneventful week passed and then another. It was Saturday afternoon and she was relaxing at home when the buzzer sounded. Her heart began to beat more quickly as she concluded that Ratcliffe had finally come calling. Reluctantly, she answered, 'Yes?'

'It's Jack Randall here. I would like to talk to you.'

For a moment, Nicky wasn't sure which was worse, a visit from Jack or one from Jeremy Ratcliffe. She buzzed him in and opened the door.

When he appeared, he looked smartly dressed in an expensive mohair camel coat. His grey hair was well combed and overall he looked very distinguished, much more like the Jack she knew. He seemed to have recovered his composure since her visit to Beaulieu and looked in control of his feelings once again.

They walked into the sitting room and Jack sat down without invitation. He opened his coat but did not remove it. Nicky was glad, thinking that meant he would not be staying long.

'Any word on Ratcliffe?' he asked, clearly the first concern on his mind.

'No, he has not been to see me nor has he been in communication. I have not cashed your cheque as yet. It is secure in my office safe. Frankly, I don't know what to make of it at all.'

'Perhaps the Star has sent him off on another assignment,' he suggested, looking worried.

'Perhaps,' she replied, 'but it is odd after all his insistence at making an appointment with me. I can't understand it. It is all a bit of a mystery.'

There was a short silence during which Jack leaned forward with his elbows on his knees, clasping his hands.

'Is that the reason for your visit? Are you worried about Ratcliffe? Did you get my note?'

'Yes, thank you, I received your note some time ago,' he said politely, 'but no, it wasn't that entirely, although that certainly concerns me greatly. I have been giving some thought to our discussion a few weeks ago. It took me aback when you told me exactly what had happened that awful night. It was the worst night of my life but I recognise that you were obviously in a bad way yourself, suicidal and very alone. It's a night that you and I will never forget for our own very personal reasons,' he said seriously, staring at the floor.

Never was a truer word said, but Nicky sat quietly and waited. She knew that he had come to say something. His introduction had been designed to create a bond between them.

'I know that we can't entirely trust this man, Ratcliffe, and even if I continue to pay him off, there may be a day when our worst fears are realised and he discloses everything he knows. I'm ready for that now. I have enough money to look after Felicity and my wife for the rest of our lives. We may fall from grace, as I explained to Sylvie, but we will not be hard up.'

'You have explained everything to your wife?' she asked.

'Yes, after you had left, she quizzed me on my state of mind and I felt that I had to give her all the details, so, yes, she knows everything now. At first she was hysterical but over the last few weeks, we have thrashed things out and adjusted to the idea together, and I have to say she is being very good about it all. She knows that I will see she is all right.'

'That's good, then,' said Nicky. 'Best to have no secrets.'

'I came tonight mainly because I had been thinking about the boy, Christopher. He is my daughter's child and as such, I have a responsibility to him. How to deal with this has been on my mind constantly. If Felicity could discuss it with me, I know that she would want me to make sure he was cared for, too, and I came to tell you that he will be financially taken care of.'

Jack looked up at Nicky who was flabbergasted by this change in his attitude.

'That's very kind of you,' she said.

'No, it's his right. He is my only grandson and there is no chance of any more. I have also been thinking that I should meet him. He may have anger or resentment towards me after what happened but I would like to explain to him that the circumstances that night were so horrendous, that I behaved irrationally and I regret that very much now,' he said. 'I know that I said I didn't want to see him but I've changed my mind. Do you think he would ever consider coming to see me?'

Nicky was awestruck now to hear this mellow, contrite statement from Jack and was pleased that Christopher would, after all, get the chance to meet his grandfather. It had become very important to him.

'He has already asked me if he might meet you,' she said. 'I'm sure he will be open minded about everything. He is young, fit and happy, doing what he wants to do. The whole story doesn't have the same meaning for him now. He can put this behind him more easily than we can.'

'That's good. Well, if you could speak to him and give me a date that suits us, we can make the arrangements,' he said, getting up from the chair rather stiffly.

'What about Alex Sanderson? Could you face him, too? I think he would appreciate acknowledgement and honesty from you too,' she said, hoping that Jack's change of heart would extend to Alex.

Jack stood for a while, his head bowed and then said, 'I treated him abominably. Apologies are not things I do easily. You are right, though. He deserves to see me beg and cringe. Well, if he is available, it may be appropriate if they both come at the same time.' He nodded as he made this conciliatory gesture and turned towards the door.

'Thank you, Jack.' Nicky said. 'I'll discuss it with them both and will let you know.'

Jack nodded again and made his way down the stairs.

Nicky closed the door and sat in the easy chair, contemplating Jack's benevolence and his amazing turn in attitude. She was thrilled that Christopher would, after all, benefit from his grandfather's estate. It was his right and Jack had seen that. At the same time, she felt that Christopher would actually like his grandfather and with this new softening of Jack's stance and a bit of luck, they might enjoy a good relationship in the future. If only they didn't have to worry about Ratcliffe, life would be very promising. Three weeks had passed since his appointment date. She was restless and uneasy, expecting him to appear without warning, so she decided to take the initiative and go to see him.

26

A search through the local telephone directory showed her that Jeremy Ratcliffe resided at No 47, Wheatfield Crescent. The house was located in the Wheatfield estate which was a relatively new build, less than ten years old and sited just at the outskirts of Edgerley. It wasn't an area with which Nicky was familiar although she'd heard and read of the criminal goings-on in that depressing area. It seemed that Ratcliffe couldn't be doing particularly well to be living there and reinforced the fact that his finances were not in good order.

Perusing a local map, she spent some time locating the Wheatfield estate and noting that the Crescent seemed to be a long road skirting the periphery of the complex. The entrance to the Crescent would be easy to find, within a few yards of the main road and she thought that once there, she should be able to find number forty seven.

At around 8.30 p.m. the following Monday evening after, there had still been no word from him, so she dressed in jeans and sweater, donned a short, blue jacket and set off in some trepidation. Prior to leaving the office, she had collected the cheque she had made out to Ratcliffe and placed it carefully in her jacket pocket in order to pay him off when she met with him. It was a thirty minute drive to the turn off to the estate and in the dark she slowed down to ensure that she chose the correct side road.

The estate was comprised of blocks of flats, up to four

storeys high and situated centrally within the site. The Crescent, which was designed rather like three corners of a box, rather than a smooth crescent shape, separated the multi-storey blocks from bungalows situated all around the periphery. The flats were dull grey, concrete monstrosities with a row of balconies at each level. Washing hung from a number of these and rubbish buckets were parked up by the houses like rows of green Daleks. A boy on a bike preceded her into the Crescent but he turned off in the direction of one of the flats soon after.

There were numerous street lamps along the length of the Crescent but their hazy orange glow was not bright and several of the lights were not illuminated at all, either because the Council had failed to maintain them or more likely, because of vandalism. She slowly drove around the Crescent trying to read the house numbers. As she identified the number 25 followed by 27, she deduced that she was heading in the right direction. Approaching number 34 and then 36, she had worked out that the odd numbers had been assigned to the bungalows on the opposite side of the road. Looking for a parking place, she found one behind an overflowing skip, ready for uplifting. There was rubbish on the road and some fragments of glass which she carefully avoided. The cars parked around were all rather dilapidated and rusty, some with dents and scrapes on their bodywork, others deliberately defaced with painted symbols or macho flames. She felt that her new Mercedes stuck out like a sore thumb and she was anxious that it might be a target for bored kids. Switching off the car lights, she sat for a few minutes to see if there was much activity in the street. A lady carrying a cat emerged from one of the main doors of the flats and walked along to the next house, rang the bell and gained admittance. Nicky decided to take a chance and got out of her car. She walked along on the road side of the parked cars, trying to stay out of sight of the windows overlooking the street. At the corner, she saw the entrance door was numbered 46 and in the distance, across the road, situated with a field on one side and an identical house on the other side, was number 47. A green Toyota with rusting sills and a flat back tyre, sat at the door and Nicky thought this might belong to Ratcliffe, suggesting that he was probably at home.

Reaching the small black wrought iron gate, she noticed that it was already half opened and wondered if someone else had come to visit. That would be unfortunate because her business with him was very personal. The outer wooden door was open too, and the glass, internal door, gave off a glow, suggesting that there was a light on inside and further evidence that someone was at home. The green, empty rubbish bin was lying on its side half across the pavement at the gate so she upended it and closed the lid, then rolled it inside to the concrete space to the left of the gate, which seemed to be its home, from the pattern of the other houses. She looked around at the windows opposite and saw a man watching TV in the ground floor flat on the other side of the street, his back to the window, the light from the television screen flashing intermittently. The man seemed to be engrossed in the programme. The rest of the building was in darkness, curtains closed, lights out. She climbed the three steps to Ratcliffe's entrance, stood on the brush mat between the two doors, pressed the bell push and waited, her anxiety level rising. No reply. She pressed again for a longer period, but there was still no answer. Looking round, she saw no-one in the street and the man watching TV, still glued to his programme had not moved. She approached the glass door which was constructed of fifteen small panes, all of which exhibited a whorl pattern so it was not possible to look clearly inside. She knocked loudly on the glass and waited. No reply.

Having come all this way, and geared herself mentally

to the challenge of confronting Ratcliffe, she was reluctant
to leave without doing so. Standing close to the glass door,
she noticed a line of dark colour on the frame. Peering
more closely at it she realised that it was dark red.
Suddenly her stomach lurched and she had a terrible feeling
that she was looking at blood but she pulled herself
together and decided that her imagination was out of
control. Perhaps it was just paint.

She put her hand on the brass door handle and turned it.
To her surprise, the door opened. She stepped into a small
entrance hall and called again 'Mr. Ratcliffe, are you at
home?'

There was no reply. Looking to her left, she could see a
kitchen area with dishes standing on a draining board and a
pair of yellow Marigold gloves hanging over the sink. She
closed the glass door and walked inside. The kitchen was
reasonably tidy apart from a defrosted box of fish fingers
which sat on a plate beside the microwave, the sogginess of
the box and the smell which emanated from it, suggesting
that it was no longer frozen. The adjoining room proved to
be a small storage area with suitcases, boxes and cleaning
utensils filling the space. The next room was a sitting room
with a single, long window at the side. There was no view
from this apart from the blank wall of the next bungalow. A
long, wooden coffee table occupied the centre of the room
and three well upholstered armchairs in various colour
schemes were arranged round it. A wooden sideboard
supported a few photographs of Ratcliffe at some social
occasions and a folded newspaper lay by one of the chairs
on the red carpet. The date on it showed that it was far from
recent. She moved on to the next room. The door was
almost shut and as she pushed it open, a light was evident.

'Mr. Ratcliffe,' she called, pushing the door further and
walking in.

Her eyes widened as she took in the scene and she

gasped in horror. She had found Jeremy Ratcliffe. He was sitting in a curved wooden chair, slumped forwards onto his cluttered desk, his open eyes opaque and sightless. For a few minutes, Nicky stood paralysed, holding her breath, taking in the gruesome sight for, all down the front of his shirt, on the desk and on the carpet at his feet was a river of caked blood. She couldn't take her eyes off him, staring at his rigid, unmoving corpse and half expecting him to come to life. Below his garish floral tie, loosely strung around his neck, was a long, black object entering his chest. Clearly it was the handle of a long knife. Someone had taken Jeremy Ratcliffe's life in a very violent way. Her mind was racing with thoughts of who could have carried out this gruesome crime and thoughts as to what she should do. It was a spectacle she had not anticipated. It seemed odd that the perpetrator had left the weapon and, most likely, fingerprints too. Someone had carried out the deed quickly and made off without considering the evidence left behind. It was a horrific sight and for a long time, she stood and stared, turning over in her mind how to deal with this unexpected and awful situation. Her body trembled and her instinct was to turn and run away. The smell in the room was that of rotting flesh. A few flies were buzzing around the decaying corpse and the blood looked hard. This murder had not taken place recently, she judged. Could he have been dead by the time he was due to come to see her? That seemed likely. Nicky forced herself to look over the rest of the room but it was hard to drag her eyes from Ratcliffe. The small lamp lying on its side on the bloodied carpet, was the source of the light she had seen in the corridor. There had been a struggle. Around the light, the flies buzzed, attracted by the smell of death. A coffee table was tossed on to its side. A two drawer, grey, filing cabinet was also upturned, and numerous green folders were strewn haphazardly all over the stained brown carpet. She needed

time to think about this. Could it have been connected to
the blackmail threat or did he have other enemies? He had
implied that someone was after him for money. Could this
be related to his problems with gambling or had it
something to do with her? Why would a money lender
search through the files? That seemed odd. No, the more
she thought about it, the more she was convinced that this
murder had been committed by someone she knew,
someone who didn't want her secrets to be exposed. There
were very few people who knew about Christopher's
origins, only Alex Sanderson, Jo Sanderson and
Christopher himself as well as Jack Randall, Felicity and
Sylvie. Of all of these people, she could think that only one
had the courage to carry out murder, someone with a
temper, someone who had a lot to lose- Jack Randall. There
was a noise at the front door and her heart leaped to her
mouth. The trembling seemed to escalate. If she were to be
found here in Ratcliffe's house with the body, she would be
a prime suspect in his murder. She had a good motive to
kill him. She waited, terrified that someone was coming
into the house, but no-one entered. After a while, she
cautiously went through to the hall and looked through the
glass door. The hazy outline of a newspaper lay on the
mat. She opened the door a chink and saw that it was a free
Herald and Post and just caught sight of a boy on a bike,
heading off round the corner. Relief swept over her. She
quietly closed the outer door and snibbed the lock. As she
took her hands away, she realised that she was leaving
fingerprints everywhere. Remembering the rubber gloves
she had seen in the kitchen, she went through to put them
on. Still shaking, she half filled the basin in the sink and
squirted in some liquid soap, then taking a dishcloth, she
went back to the door and began to wipe it down, being
particularly careful of the lock itself. On entering, she had
touched the glass door and so she continued to wash every

part of the doorway, even wiping the tiles where her shoes could have left prints. Returning to the sink, she refilled the basin and wrung out the cloth, then took it into the study. For a minute, she stood and thought about where to begin. What had been touched? What would Jack have touched as he came in? She washed down the door, the surrounding woodwork, the door handles and the light switch. She lifted up the overturned coffee table. The lamp had overheated. She switched it off, placed it firmly on the table and wiped it over. Moving to the filing cabinet, she righted it and washed it down, drawing the cloth along each individual metal rail. She perused the titles on each file, searching for one containing any reference to herself, to Martin and Ainslie or to the article which Ratcliffe had been assigned to do. The files contained bank statements, business contracts with Star magazine, household invoices and other irrelevant bits and pieces but there was no file with information connected to her. This made Nicky even more certain that it was Jack who had murdered Ratcliffe. He would have searched for the incriminating file and removed it. The fact that there wasn't one certainly suggested that one could have been removed. She picked up each folder again, checked for some identification or label, wiped each one and returned them neatly in alphabetical order, into the cabinet, closing the drawers. Standing at the desk, she wondered what else to do. The knife drew her attention and she knew that this was possibly the most incriminating factor, the type of knife and perhaps fingerprints too. It would be best to wipe the handle or better still, to take the knife away. Her courage weakened, however, and she couldn't bring herself to touch it.

She could call the police but then she would be asked her reason for being there and she was not keen to disclose that information. There was also the serious possibility that she would become a potential suspect, having motive and being found at the crime scene. Calling the police didn't seem to be a good option. Jeremy Ratcliffe was dead. There was nothing that could save him now. The question was—*Who killed him?*

She tried to think over who else might have killed Ratcliffe. He might have blackmailed lots of people. She could not be the only person to be targeted by this man. He was in financial straits and could well be desperate to obtain some money. Her heart was beating rapidly and she was over breathing. Somehow, she couldn't stop thinking that Jack Randall had a lot to lose if this man exposed the events of 1995. His unexpected recent visit had shown a different, less tense individual. Perhaps he knew that Ratcliffe was out of harm's way because he had something to do with it. Whoever was responsible, it seemed to Nicky that there was a distinct possibility that Ratcliffe's death had some link to her.

She looked round again and thought how careless the perpetrator had been, leaving the murder weapon and most likely fingerprints, behind. If Jack had carried out this deed, then he had been very careless and that didn't fit with her image of the man. He generally planned everything down to the last detail. He had struck her as being a meticulous sort of person. He would not have left the blood on the door frame, the weapon still in situ and probably fingerprints everywhere. Then again, to kill a man in cold blood was bound to unnerve the doer and perhaps Jack had run out of the place as quickly as he could, once he had committed the deed. However, Nicky didn't think that would have happened. He would have wanted him dead perhaps, but the whole idea of that was to avoid exposure, not to invite it by leaving clues everywhere. Looking back, she considered again who the people who knew who Ratcliffe was blackmailing her were and who was in the know soon enough to kill him before his Friday appointment with her. There were only really three contenders, Alex, Christopher or Jack. Felicity was not fit to perform such an act and probably had not been told about Ratcliffe's visit. Sylvie did not know until Jack had informed her, and she was well looked after with no real concerns for her future.

Of course, Jeremy's death was beneficial to Nicky. She could retain her job and her previous misdemeanours need not be publicly exposed in the near future. It was indeed something of a relief, but at the same time, it raised other questions in her mind. As she stood taking in the room, she decided that if Jack had done this, he should not be found out because that would immediately raise the whole issue again and might even make things worse than they were. Strangely, she felt protective of him, even sorry for him. He had lost a lot in his life, his first wife, his daughter who was virtually a stranger from all accounts, and his only grandson.

There were piles of papers and letters on the floor and on the desk, all higgledy piggledy, as if someone had searched through each one. She knew that she had to look there, too, just in case there was any evidence left. Lifting a small pile, she realised that there was too much to browse through quickly and her nervousness was such that she didn't want to stay much longer in this place. Knowing that she had no hope of eliminating all fingerprints from these, she looked around for a container. In one of Ratcliffe's desk drawers, she found a white polythene bag. It contained a few small packets of powder which she deduced were drugs of some sort. She dropped these back into the drawer and picking up all the papers on the desk and on the floor, she folded them all into the polythene bag. That done, she saw that, although there was no computer or laptop around, there were cables, a modem and a mouse on the desk. It looked as though someone had removed his laptop. She carefully wiped the ends of the cables and all around the desk.

Having swatted a number of flies, she flicked their carcasses into the bag, wiping the table over again. Placing the polythene bag on the floor, she returned to the kitchen to refresh the water and came back to wash over the desk and all of its drawers. This was hard because she had to lift Ratcliffe's hands and his face to clean underneath him. For a time she looked at the knife and wondered if she could clean the handle without moving it. She was too uptight to touch it and went round the room wiping all the woodwork, the window sill and even Ratcliffe's shirt, in case his killer had touched him during the process. She went back to the kitchen and wet the cloth again.

Carefully, she went round the room again thinking what else could be incriminating. As a lawyer she knew that the killer always left something of himself, possibly a hair, a button, his own blood. Nicky checked the other two rooms in the house. One was a double bedroom which looked untouched and the other a bathroom. There were no bloody towels and nothing to suggest that the murderer had used the facilities. Standing beside Jeremy Ratcliffe's body, she tried to imagine what could have been left behind. The room looked much tidier since she had set things to right but she was filled with worry that she had missed something.

In the small storage cupboard off the hallway, she had seen a vacuum cleaner and she decided to run it round the study in case any trace evidence had been left. Her mind kept returning to Jack Randall and she felt that she was doing all this to protect him. She plugged in the vacuum and thoroughly went over the carpet around the body and in the hall. She emptied the vacuum sack into the white polythene bag and returned it to its former place, wiping the handle as she left. Still wearing the yellow gloves, she emptied the basin, returned it to its place under the sink and popped the wash cloth in the polythene bag. There seemed nothing else to do and so she retrieved the white bag and made for the door. But something held her back, *the knife*. She stood trembling in the hall, anxious to get away, but finally decided that she had to do it, to take the knife. Gritting her teeth, she went back to the room, quickly slid the long knife blade out of Ratcliffe's chest and wrapped it in the papers in the bag. His body made slurping noises and she trembled in fear, half expecting him to come to life. Finally, she switched off the light, plunging the place into darkness, and, carrying the white bag carefully, she made her way out of the house. Closing the glass door and then after peering out and checking that all was clear, she left the building, firmly shutting the outer door so it would automatically lock behind her.

She had just reached the front steps when she heard footsteps coming down the road and quickly dived behind the green rubbish bucket, terrified that she would be discovered. The steps became louder and she heard a man talking. There must be two of them, she thought fearfully. Suddenly a white Jack Russell dog stuck its nose through the gate and started to bark. Nicky was petrified that someone had come to visit Ratcliffe. She would almost certainly be discovered especially if this dog kept drawing attention to her.

'Quiet, Randy,' a man's voice said and the dog's neck was yanked forcibly away from the gate. The man crossed the road, the dog quietened down, and Nicky heaved a sigh of relief. She waited for a few minutes to let the man move along and while she was crouched by the bin, it occurred to her that she had touched it too. She still had the washcloth and spent a few minutes wiping it down with particular attention to the lid which she had closed.

The gate, too, had been touched, so when she saw that

the TV watcher was still immersed in his programme, she washed down the gate as thoroughly as she could, and then closed it firmly.

Clutching the polythene bag, she walked smartly towards her car, searching the street and the windows for any onlookers but she saw no-one else. The dog walker was nowhere to be seen. Inside the car, she took off the yellow gloves and tucked them in with the knife, the washcloth and the papers she had taken. She found herself shaking and wanted to get as far away from Wheatfield Crescent as she could. Seeing the skip, she considered dumping the bag and its contents down the side of it and then thought that this was too close to the scene of the crime. She started the car and slowly and carefully extricated herself from the parking space. She did not switch on her lights until she approached the main road, hoping that no-one paid her any attention. A black van passed her going in the opposite direction but it was going so fast, she didn't think that the driver would have seen her clearly. Once on the main road, she turned right, away from town and just kept on going, her heart in her mouth. Her speed escalated as she raced along the country roads and at a crossing, a man in a black Volvo jumped the line and she had to brake quickly to avoid an accident. She felt herself shaking again. What if she had an accident now and the police were to find the white bag? She would undoubtedly be the prime suspect in Jeremy Ratcliffe's murder. She slowed down and taking the ring road, headed back to town, all the while trying to decide how to rid herself of the bag. The rain started to spatter her windscreen and she applied the wipers but soon the shower became a torrent and, even at full power, the wipers could barely cope with the downpour. Frightened of getting involved in any accident, however minor, she pulled over to the side of the road and waited. Slumped on to the wheel, she thought over what she had done. She had interfered with a crime scene, and of all her wrongdoings, this was certainly the worst. She could hardly believe how stupid she was. The shaking continued and she felt in need of a stiff drink. She had to get home. Gradually the rainfall eased and she was able to head off again. The roads were almost deserted and as she approached the bridge over the swollen Channing River, she wondered if it would be possible to throw her bundle into its deepest part. A mile from the bridge, she slowed to consider her plan and saw, at the side of the road, a pile of rubble which seemed to have been produced by builders knocking down part of a house. There was no-one about so she got out and chose two heavy rocks. There were also some pieces of twine in the pile of masonry and she picked up two lengths of this and returned to the car. Half a mile further on, she pulled in by the side of a row of houses. Carefully she placed the rocks inside the white bag and used its own ties to twist the top together. She then used the twine to wrap around the package again and again so there was no chance of it opening. Satisfied with her work, she drove on and soon came to the bridge. The traffic lights were in her favour and there was no following car, so she decided to stop in the middle of the bridge and throw the package over. However, just as she was slowing down, a taxi approached from the opposite direction and she was obliged to abort the plan. She continued over the bridge, turned in a side street and started off in the opposite direction. At the lights, she had to stop and a country bus pulled up behind her so again she had to cross the bridge, circle around and return. This time, there was no traffic about and in the middle of the bridge, she stopped, climbed out and threw the white bag into the swirling water below. She ran back to the car and was just starting off again when a four by four towing a caravan, closed in behind her. She casually increased her speed, took a right turn to avert a long spell in front of this driver and then made her way home.

By the time she had parked her car, run up to the flat and shut the door behind her, she was trembling violently. First, she went into the kitchen and poured herself a large glass of whisky. She drank some of it neat but it burned her throat so she added some ginger ale and downed the whole glass. She poured another glass and took it to the bathroom. Peeling off her clothes, she set everything aside to put into a waste bag, ran a hot bath and immersing herself in it, sipped away at the whisky. The heat penetrated her body and gradually the shakes receded. She drained the whisky glass and lay, full length, in the bath with only her face above the surface. She stayed like this until the water began to cool. She topped it up with more hot water and lay thinking about Ratcliffe, filled with guilt feelings as well as fear and anxiety. What was she going to do now? Had her actions merely compounded the problems? How would she ever know if Jack had killed him? Would he confess? No, that seemed very unlikely. It would be up to the police to seek the killer when Ratcliffe was eventually discovered. There had been no sign of a partner or wife living in the flat but she had no idea if he had a family somewhere who might miss him. His employer, Star Magazine, might notice that he had not produced the articles to which he had been assigned. Would someone actually go to his house? Now, instead of having to wait for Ratcliffe's visit, she would be waiting for the police to make enquiries. At the same time, she would have to study Jack carefully and watch everything he said to try to detect any sign that he knew about Ratcliffe being dead. It also occurred to her that the knife must have been taken from someone's kitchen. It had had the configuration of a long-handled kitchen utensil, possibly one of a set. She would have to try to contrive a visit to the kitchen at Beaulieu to see what kind of knives they kept there. One thing was certain: she could not tell

Christopher or Alex about the developments. They would both be extremely concerned. Would it reinforce their suspicions that Jack was capable of murder? He had, after all, possibly tried to get rid of his daughter's child. In the foreseeable future, she would have to be a good actress and pretend no knowledge of Ratcliffe's demise. This part did not concern her. Keeping secrets was something in which she had had a lot of practice.

27

Over the next few days, Nicky focussed on work and did her best to put Ratcliffe out of her mind. Marilyn occasionally reminded her that he had not appeared and she feigned an ongoing concern about it, but she was able to relax a little, gradually, knowing that now, it seemed that the circumstances of Christopher's birth would remain known only to those who needed to know. She filled her appointment book with client interviews, caught up with paperwork which had accumulated over the past turbulent days and lectured at a seminar relating to the management of financial affairs. Gordon and Peter were both very occupied too, and, once again, the office had an air of activity and efficiency.

Alex had e-mailed and she had conveyed to him Jack Randall's apparent remorse and desire to pour oil over troubled waters by setting up a meeting with both Christopher and himself. Alex was very encouraged by the pending reunion with Jack and suggested several dates which would suit his hectic lifestyle. Nicky had also discussed dates with Christopher and since his midterm break was coming up in three weeks time, it seemed that a convenient day could be chosen. Armed with this information, she decided to contact Jack in the hope of confirming the meeting. It was a good excuse to see him and try to determine what, if anything, he knew about Ratcliffe's death. She had promised to keep him posted with regard to her meeting with Ratcliffe in any event, so it was justifiable to have Marilyn phone Beaulieu to make an appointment.

The time allotted was to be 10.00 a.m. the following day.

In the evening, she sat in her comfortable armchair, wondering what questions she could ask to get Jack to drop some clue, just a small faux pas to confirm that he had been the one to do away with Ratcliffe. The hours ticked by and she was still in some doubt as to how to approach the subject. She decided she would just have to play it by ear.

At 9.30 a.m. she drove over to Beaulieu. It was a pleasant day, the sun was shining and the traffic had eased by the time she set off. The possibility that Alex and Jack might be able to move towards a reasonable relationship seemed hopeful although it was still a tenuous and fragile beginning. She hoped that in time, there might be a truce between the two men. Ideally, that was what she really hoped for, but it was early days. It wasn't going to be plain sailing after their previous acrimonious encounter and the disastrous repercussions. If only Ratcliffe had never come on the scene, the cloud which took the edge from her happiness for Christopher and Alex, would not be hanging there, threatening to burst all over her. Yet, had Ratcliffe not appeared, she would not have felt the necessity to locate Alex and so he had served a purpose. Looking back, Nicky genuinely felt pleased about the outcome of her visit to Southampton, although at the time, it had been very traumatic.

She drove up the beautiful rhododendron-lined drive and, turning into a convenient spot, parked and approached the door. The great arched entrance was such a forbidding configuration and, beautiful as the house was, she had a feeling of foreboding every time she went there, her previous experiences colouring her view of the place.

Peters greeted her with a stiff, 'Good morning, Miss Partington' as she entered, and led her directly to Jack's study.

Jack was seated at his desk, poring over a sheaf of papers and his dark framed spectacles perched on the end of his nose. He removed them, placed them on the blotter and came round the desk to shake her hand.

'Nicky, thank you for coming,' he said, welcoming her like a long lost friend.

'Good morning, Jack,' she replied, and sat down in the plush leather chair which he pulled up nearer to the desk.

When he had returned to his chair, he said, 'I have been wondering how things were progressing with you. Tell me your news. Where are we in sorting out a date for meeting with Alex Sanderson and Christopher?'

Nicky thought he looked relaxed and calm, more agreeable than she had ever seen him. The strain which had been evident on her last visit had vanished and she wondered again if he had reason to believe that his secret was safe. His initial concern was not to ask about Ratcliffe, she noted, but to ask about Christopher and Alex. Did that mean that he had stopped worrying about Ratcliffe?

She replied, 'I have spoken with both Alex and Christopher and the best time for them is going to be between May 2nd and 5th. Alex is travelling back from the Middle East at that point and Christopher will be on a break from University. Is that a good time for you?'

Jack pulled the large, brown, leather-bound diary towards him and flicked the pages over. 'Yes, that's good. The 3rd of May is a Saturday. Why don't we settle on that date? Hopefully it will be sunny and we might enjoy a meal in the garden. Although I have to confess that it will be a hard meeting for me. In a way, I am really looking forward to it now, especially to seeing Christopher,' he said. 'He has never been far from my thoughts. I have to say there is some trepidation and yet, on the whole, I have a sense of excitement and optimism about the future, which, frankly, I haven't experienced in a long time.'

'OK, I will inform the others. Would you prefer morning or afternoon?'

Jack thought for a moment and then said 'How about eleven o'clock? Then you can all stay for lunch. We can continue talking all afternoon if we feel things are working out.'

'That will be good,' Nicky said, watching as Jack scribbled something against the date selected in his diary and closed it. It crossed her mind that he might keep details of his whereabouts in the diary, perhaps notes like *Meeting Ratcliffe*. But then she decided Jack would not be so stupid.

'After you left the house the last time, I was in a bit of a state as you know. I can only apologise again for that. Your story dredged up all the ghastly memories of that awful night. Normally, I can keep my counsel and not divulge my worries but Sylvie came in here, as I told you, and insisted that I confided the problem to her and so I found myself telling her the whole story. It was extraordinary really, telling someone else about it after all these years. I hadn't predicted how she would react to this horror story and she was really very upset about it all. Felicity and Sylvie never hit it off. I think Felicity hadn't got over the loss of her own mother. Sadly Alice died of cancer in 1993, twenty years after we wed. It was a blow to both Felicity and me. Fortunately for me, Sylvie came along and I didn't waste time before I asked her to marry me. That helped me to get over Alice's death but Felicity was a bit of a handful for a while, a bit jealous of Sylvie, critical of her and rather objectionable, to be frank. Then, of course, she started dating herself. For some weeks she didn't bring the guy home and I was getting my life together with Sylvie so I didn't pay too much attention. To be honest, I was quite glad that she had found a friend. When she did finally bring Alex home, I was, to say the least, cool with him. He was in the navy and I knew that he would be sailing off in the near future, the fling would end and her heart would be broken. I had plans for her to marry into a family in circumstances similar to our own. Never in a million years did I anticipate what would happen.'

'Did Sylvie meet Alex then?' Nicky asked.

'Yes, she did. When I was telling her about the pregnancy, she was astonished and reminded me that she had met him when he came to the house to see Felicity on a couple of occasions.'

'You said that you had explained the business with Ratcliffe to Sylvie?' she said, trying to draw him out on that subject.

'I had to. She was under the impression that I had lost £50,000 in stocks or shares that day, something you had mentioned to her I believe, so I explained that Ratcliffe had asked for that sum and reassured her that I would pay him off and everything would be fine.'

'She must have been amazed at this development.'

'I think we both have been taken aback by this turn of events but as the days go on as before, we seem to have adjusted to it,' he said. 'It's good to know that I don't have to continue to lie about the events that took place and it's possible to discuss the issue with others after all this time. You must feel that way, too.'

'Yes, I understand exactly. Hard as it is, it does feel like a purge, a load off your mind, just sharing it. I know that's how I feel.'

Jack sat back in his chair, looking relieved. He gave a deep sigh and asked, 'Now Nicky, did you deal with this man, Ratcliffe? Since you did not get in touch, I thought perhaps that you had that done and dusted.'

'Actually, no,' she said, 'the strange thing is that

Ratcliffe did not keep his appointment with me three weeks ago, as you know, and has not been in contact to rearrange a date. I'm not sure what to make of it. What do you think about that?'

She watched Jack's response to this statement. He seemed quite perturbed, as furrows appeared in his forehead and he screwed up his eyes. 'That is strange,' he said. 'What can he be playing at?'

'I did wonder if he had been ill, perhaps in hospital or something. Then again, the Star might have sent him abroad to cover a particular storyline. I just don't know what to think about it.'

Jack rose and walked over to the carved sideboard on which sat the silver platter, glasses and bottles of spirits.

'A drink?' he asked, unscrewing the top from a whisky bottle.

'No thanks, Jack, I'm driving,' she said, conscious still that her car was perhaps not totally free of incriminating evidence and that she had placed a bag of her clothes in the boot for disposal away from the house. She made a mental note to get rid of the bag and get a get the car thoroughly cleaned as soon as possible.

Jack sat down again, nursing his whisky in the crystal glass.

'That's odd,' he said, looking pensive, 'I wonder what has changed his mind. I suppose the most likely thing is that he is unwell or out of the country, as you say, but that's a bit disconcerting, isn't it? I was looking forward to the news that you had seen him and paid him off. It is peculiar that he hasn't phoned your office to rearrange his appointment.'

'Your cheque is still in my office safe. I haven't deposited it yet and wasn't planning to do that until I had handed him his money. Do you think I should phone the Star? After all he was legitimately going to write an article about me. It wouldn't be too ridiculous for me to get in touch with them and ask them when I might expect a follow-up visit, would it?' she asked.

'Well, the Star would certainly know where he was, I suppose, but isn't that tempting fate a little? He would then be under the impression that you are really worried about him and what he knows, and might see that he could ask for more money.'

'Yes, and really I have no desire to see this man at all, so I'm not rushing to do that,' she agreed.

'If he is in hospital, presumably he will return home eventually and give you a ring. If he doesn't recover, then we would see an announcement in one of the local papers, most likely in the Star. Do you get that regularly?' he enquired.

'Not everyday, but my secretary does and I'm quite sure she would tell me if she had seen that he had died. She can't stand him; calls him Ratty.'

Jack smiled, 'Not an inappropriate tag. I don't know what else to suggest, Nicky, I suppose we will just have to wait and see.'

Nicky was wondering how else she could pursue this subject with Jack and try to push him into telling her something incriminating about Ratcliffe's death. She knew details which only the killer would know, so she asked him, 'I could drive round to his house and see if he's there. Do you think that would be sensible?'

Jack sat pensive for a while and then said, 'Again, it would look as though you were a bit desperate, wouldn't it? It is frustrating but we have to be cautious. He does not sound like the sort of man who would forget about this money-making scheme and I'm sure he will appear when he is ready. Do you know where he lives?'

'I think I mentioned to you before, it is in the Wheatfield estate but that's not an area of the town that I'm familiar with. Do you know it?' she asked, watching his reaction.

'Wheatfield, yes, that's close to the town border. I knew the builder, Jeff Vickers, who planned and built it but I couldn't say that I would find my way round in it. I hear that it is rather a wild place nowadays, anyway, so maybe you should avoid it.'

Nicky wasn't convinced that she had extracted any clues from Jack. If he had murdered Ratcliffe, he was hiding it pretty well. She rose, shook his outstretched hand and said, 'Until the 3rd of May, then.'

'The third of May,' he repeated, nodding.

Nicky drove slowly down the long drive and turned left away from town. Several miles on, there was a large dumpster at the side of the road. She stopped, took the bag of clothes which she had worn on the night of her visit to Jeremy Ratcliffe, from the boot and tossed it inside. Closer to town, she noticed a garage offering car washing and valet facilities. She pulled in, approached the counter and booked in. In the small waiting area, she picked up a paper and then, seeing a Star magazine on the small coffee table, she read it from cover to cover, gleaning absolutely nothing about Jeremy Ratcliffe, nothing to indicate that he was alive or dead. It was almost an hour later that she took possession of her gleaming car with its fragrant interior. She drove home, all the while wondering if she would ever know who had killed Jeremy Ratcliffe.

28

Two more weeks passed and there was still no news of Ratcliffe. Nicky put it to the back of her mind and knowing that the momentous meeting with Jack, Alex and Christopher was only a week away, she gave considerable thought to the possible conversation and determined to do her best to ease the tensions.

She felt certain that Alex would not be confrontational or judgmental. He was a diplomat, after all, and although he must have strong feelings still, and concern for Felicity, she thought that he would be trying to draw a line under the past and move on, for his own sake and for Christopher's. Felicity's situation was hard to take but she was getting the best care it seemed and little more could be achieved there. Alex and Christopher were in constant communication and both seemed quite thrilled about finding each other. Christopher would also behave impeccably, she was sure. He was, like his father, a gentleman and Nicky knew that he would also try to make the best of this meeting with his grandfather. It was important to him.

Felicity would be a topic of conversation and Nicky wondered if Alex and Christopher would broach the subject of visiting her. It was impossible to predict how she would react to seeing them and Jo was right, they would have to discuss the potential problems with her doctor before embarking on that course. The more Nicky thought about it, the more she began to think that she should visit Felicity and get a feel for her state of mind without mentioning Alex or Christopher. She mulled on this thought for a day or two and then, deciding that it might be useful to know something more about Felicity before the 3rd of May, planned a visit to the Fairfax Clinic.

She easily found the address on the Internet. It was described as a modern and well equipped facility offering specialised care in a variety of situations, including drug and alcohol dependence as well as a variety of nervous disorders. On the following afternoon, she drove over to the clinic. There were numerous cars lining the road outside the building and she carefully checked them to make sure that her visit was not coinciding with one from Jack or Sylvie. Jack's Jaguar was one she could spot easily as she had already memorised his new plates which were JKR 015 and had earlier chosen the acronym JK Rowling Owl 5 and kept an eye open for the plate. There was no sign of it, nor any grey four by four like the one Sylvie owned, so she parked on the opposite side of the wide street and walked casually up the driveway to the castellated building. It was an impressive edifice with a wide stairway up to the entrance hall. A large sign showed that she was at the right place. It bore the bold writing, *Fairfax Rehabilitation Clinic.*

The ornate glass door swished open almost noiselessly and immediately the black and white marble reception desk was evident. A young dark haired girl, wearing a smart, pale blue uniform, and a name badge with Mandy inscribed on it was on duty.

'Hello,' she said brightly, giving Nicky a charming smile.

'Hello. My name is Nicky Partington. I am Mr. Jack Randall's lawyer and I was wondering if it would be possible for me to talk with Miss Felicity Randall for a few minutes.'

'If you could wait for a moment, Miss Partington, I will see if Miss Randall is available,' the girl said, leaving her post to climb the short staircase to the next level.

Nicky stood in the foyer, taking in the simplicity and cleanliness of the place, the black and white rubberised tiles which created a dramatic effect, like a draughtboard, on the entrance floor, and the luxurious white, leather chairs which had been strategically placed in a corner by the door, presumably for visitors. She was a little apprehensive about meeting Felicity and hoped that she would be able to see her, now that she had prepared herself mentally. As she waited, she wondered what the receptionist had meant by *I'll see if she is available.* Did this mean that she might already have visitors or perhaps be involved in some therapy?

Mandy reappeared a few minutes later, and said, 'Yes, that will be fine. Miss Randall is in Room 12 at the top of the stairs. If you go up there and turn immediately to your right, you will see the door facing you, at the end of a short corridor. If you require a lift, it is over there.' she said, pointing to a glass fronted elevator, tucked in behind the white upholstered chairs.

'Thank you,' Nicky said smiling. 'Have you told her that I'm coming?'

'Yes, she knows,' replied Mandy.

Nicky climbed the flight of stairs, her shoes sinking into the thick pile of the black and white carpet. At the top, she turned right and as Mandy had indicated, the door to number 12 was facing her. It was ajar. She took a deep breath and advanced, knocking lightly as she stepped across the threshold.

'Come in,' said a quiet voice.

Nicky found Felicity Randall sitting on a large, colourful beanbag and watching a huge plasma screen TV. She knew that Felicity was 38 but this slim, fair haired girl looked younger than her years. Her straight hair was not in a ponytail but hanging loosely at her shoulders. Her dress was also more appropriate to a teenager than someone approaching 40, Nicky thought, as she took in the loose, white design with its high hemline. A delicate gold bracelet hung daintily from her wrist and she wore a matching gold chain at her neck. There was no doubt that this was the girl in the painting hanging in the entrance hall of Beaulieu. The initial impression was one of innocence, femininity and a little nervousness and shyness.

'Hello,' Nicky said. 'My name is Nicky. I'm a friend of your father's.' she explained, speaking slowly and clearly.

The girl stared at her and Nicky wasn't sure whether she had understood or not.

'I'm sorry if I am interrupting your television programme,' she quickly continued, perching on the end of the bed, there being no seat other than the beanbag in the room.

Felicity switched off the movie that she had been watching. It had involved something with a lot of noise and violence. Perhaps she had not heard Nicky's voice.

'How are you?' began Nicky, 'I hope you are making progress here. It seems to be a nice place,' she commented, looking round at the high quality of the furnishings and the dominance of the colour pink, with so many aspects similar to her bedroom at Beaulieu. It crossed Nicky's mind that the patients, particularly the long staying patients, might be permitted to choose the room colour scheme and have their own pieces of furniture.

'Yes,' came the expressionless reply.

'Felicity, I wanted to talk to you about something that happened a long time ago. Do you mind if we talk?'

'Is Sylvie with you?' the girl suddenly asked, almost whispering.

'Sylvie? No, she is not with me. I came alone. Do you

want to see Sylvie?' she asked.

'No.'

'Does Sylvie come to see you often?

'No'

'How long have you stayed here, Felicity?'

'Yesterday.'

'You came here yesterday?' Nicky was confused and wondered if she was wasting her time.

'Sylvie came yesterday.'

'Oh, I see. That was nice. I expect she wants to see that you are being cared for properly.'

'I hate her,' Felicity whispered, smiling inappropriately.

'Why do you hate her?'

No reply.

'You must miss your mother. Alice, wasn't that her name?' Nicky tried again.

'She should be here.'

'Yes, it is sad that she died so young,' Nicky said.

'Everybody has to die,' Felicity continued, calmly and still smiling. Nicky found her a little disturbing and for a moment paused, trying to direct the conversation elsewhere. 'Do you remember when you came here first, Felicity?'

Felicity didn't seem to be listening and her responses were slow. She started to hum. It wasn't clear if she just didn't want to talk about her first admission to the Fairfax, had no memory of it, or whether she just didn't want to converse at all. Nicky tried to continue as calmly as possible. 'Eventually we all die, that is true, but you are still young and have a lot of life to look forward to. Tell me, what do you do in here? Have you hobbies, games, books, things to do?'

'School,' said Felicity, blandly.

'You go to school?' Nicky asked incredulously.

The girl smiled. 'Cooking, computers and art classes.'

'That's good. That must be interesting. What do you like best?' she asked.

'Art, maybe.' she replied after a pause. Nicky noticed that Felicity had not moved since she came in, her thin legs tucked up underneath her, her hands in her lap. It was like talking to a much younger person and she didn't seem to be making much headway.

'Do you ever go back home? Maybe for a day?' she asked.

'Yes.'

'Wouldn't you like to live at home again one day?'

'No.'

'Why is that, Felicity?'

'Home is not a happy place.'

'What do you mean? Do you mean because Sylvie is there?'

'I like it here,' she said picking up the remote control and rotating it repeatedly in her hands, humming again.

'That's nice. I'm glad you're happy here.'

'Perhaps some day you will meet a handsome man and get married,' Nicky suggested, hoping that talking about men might kick off some conversation about boyfriends and her father, but that idea failed.

Felicity smiled.

Nicky decided that she had learned enough to judge Felicity's state of mind. It would be hard for Alex or Christopher to converse with this girl who had monosyllabic, flat answers with a built in delay and a permanent fixed smile, regardless of the subject. Whether their presence would affect Felicity, she could not tell. The girl continued to rotate the remote control more quickly and Nicky felt that it was time to go.

She didn't feel welcome and Felicity was growing agitated so she stood up and looked out of the window. It wasn't much of a view, several parked cars, two enormous dumpsters and a notice which read *Furnace Room*. She turned back to Felicity and said, 'Well, thank you for seeing me, Felicity. Perhaps we'll meet again some day. Good bye.'

'Good bye, Miss Partington,'

For a few seconds, Nicky hesitated. It was odd that the girl had so accurately recalled her name.

She turned and asked, 'Do you know who I am?'

The girl smiled that disconcerting smile again and said 'Yes, Sylvie told me.'

'Sylvie told you what, exactly?'

Felicity shrugged but gave no reply. Momentarily Nicky wondered if the smiling mask had exhibited a transient look of alarm, but still the girl stared at her and hummed an unrecognisable tune.

'Good bye, then,' Nicky repeated and left the room. She jumped when she heard the sudden explosion of gunfire behind her. The television programme had resumed immediately.

She hadn't known what to expect from Felicity but it had been rather disconcerting and Nicky felt confused. Of course, the girl had suffered a breakdown and had never been the same it seemed, since that time. She certainly exhibited a strange effect and perhaps that was why she felt no empathy with the girl. She was ignorant of mental disorders and found it hard to understand and she was no further forward in knowing whether a visit from Alex or Christopher would be useful or just a waste of time. If Christopher was hell bent on seeing his mother, he might be very disappointed, she thought.

She reached the bottom of the stairs where a middle aged, suited man was leaning on the reception desk chatting to Mandy. He turned when she had reached the draughtboard floor and asked politely, 'How was your visit with Felicity?'

'A bit weird, actually,' she said, wondering if this were a fellow patient or visitor.

'I'm Dr Robertson. I look after Felicity,' he said, moving away from the desk and shaking her hand with a rather limp handshake and accompanying her through the door.

'My name is Nicky Partington. I am one of her father's lawyers.' she said, trying to sound matter of fact.

They shook hands and Dr Robertson said, 'Felicity is a bit better this week but she goes through spells where she becomes uncontrollable and needs to be sedated. In fact, she has just passed through a bad phase and that is the reason I asked you how your visit was. It's important for me to see what impression she is giving to other people who don't know her as well as we do.'

'Is she manic depressive, then?' asked Nicky.

'No, nothing like that. She has brain damage from drugs she took when she was young.'

'She was a junkie, then?' she asked, thinking that this was not something she had heard from Jack.

'No, not exactly,' he said, stopping in the stony drive. 'Her father probably told you about the miscarriage when she first came here.'

'Yes,' Nicky said, remembering Jack's version of events.

'She didn't want the child and took every pill she could get hold of for several months to try to get rid of it. In the end, she caused herself a great deal of harm, kidney failure and some permanent brain injury. She'll never get any better, I'm afraid.'

'The child, then. Would the child have been affected by all these drugs?' Nicky asked, her mind on Christopher's well being.

'Well, of course, the child died. She did miscarry at the time. If it had lived, who knows? It might have been affected. It depends on whether or not the drugs passed through the placental barrier or not. It's amazing how children survive their parents, but in her case, the baby died.'

'That's terrible. So you think she will be here for a long time?'

'Yes, I guess so, but she's not a prisoner here. She has everything she needs and she can go home for a visit if she wants to. We don't restrict her movements and strictly speaking, she would be capable of taking a bus or a taxi independently, should she wish to do so. As it is, she seems happy to stay where she is cared for and safe. She has been settled here for many years now.

Nicky was surprised that Felicity was permitted to leave the premises but didn't say anything.

'It is a lovely place, obviously somewhere where she will be well cared for.'

'It belongs to her father, as you will know, being his lawyer, so she will certainly be cared for, spoiled even, that's for sure,' Dr Robertson smiled.

'Of course,' said Nicky, unaware that Jack Randall owned the Fairfax. She knew his portfolio well and there was certainly no mention of ownership of a nursing home. Perhaps it was one of Jack's tax dodges.

'I hope you weren't trying to get her signature on any documents. We try to steer people away from that. Sometimes Felicity can behave almost normally but a great deal of the time she could be considered to be *not of sound mind*. Consequently, in a court of law, her signature could be challenged.'

'No, it was nothing like that. The purpose of my visit was something else entirely. I hadn't met Felicity before today, only heard about her from her father and step mother, and I wanted to see her for myself. You see, a friend of hers from the time she was about twenty years of age, is coming to see Jack Randall on Saturday. He will be travelling with his son and I believe they would like to visit Felicity. It occurred to me that I might try to assess her to see if that would be at all sensible or not. Obviously I'm not a professional in this matter and, quite frankly, I think I am more confused than ever having spoken with her. What would you advise in this situation? Do you think it would be beneficial or perhaps inadvisable for visitors to come and trigger old memories?'

'It's hard to say. She might handle it quite well. If she has happy memories in relation to this person, then she could behave well. On the other hand, she may become frustrated trying to remember the old times and then she could become agitated and aggressive. If I were you, I would give it a shot. If she starts to get out of control then they should leave. We will keep a special eye on her that day if you can tell us when they plan to come.'

'It will be Saturday, 3rd of May,' she said. 'I think we will come in the afternoon, if that suits you… maybe three or four o'clock?'

'That's fine. I'll make a note to let the staff know about that so they are prepared, but actually she will probably be OK.'

'That's very helpful, Doctor. When you say she becomes aggressive, *how* aggressive does she get?' asked Nicky.

'She lashes out at people from time to time, throws things around… that sort of thing but she probably is more inclined to hurt herself. She has scars up her arms where she has cut them with nail files and other sharp instruments. We have to watch out that she cannot easily get hold of anything which might be used to harm herself. You didn't give her anything, did you?'

'No, nothing at all.'

'She doesn't get along very well with her step mother

and it's probably best that they keep out of each other's way but hopefully this visitor and his son will bring back only happy memories and she will be fine. Both anger and alcohol can trigger or worsen her mood swings and we want to avoid both of these. If she does get out of control, we are ready to handle it, so don't worry about it.'

'Well, thank you for being so forthcoming. That has been helpful and I shall try to dissuade her step mother from accompanying us to the Fairfax on Saturday.' Nicky said, shaking Dr Robertson's outstretched hand and walking to the car.

29

Saturday arrived in a blaze of sunshine and Nicky was buoyant at the thought of seeing Alex and Christopher again. Jo was flying home to Virginia to see the family while Alex confronted Jack Randall so she would not be accompanying her husband on this occasion.

Christopher was first in the door just before nine o'clock, having taken the train home from university. She hugged him and told him how pleased she was to see him. He seemed more grown-up and better-looking every time she saw him.

'How's university, then?' she asked.

'Good, yes, pretty good. We have exams coming up soon so I've brought my books back with me this weekend. Do you think there will be any time for studying?' he asked her.

'Well, you'll just have to use what time is available. I don't imagine our visit to the Randalls will take up the whole day and tomorrow should be quiet.'

Nicky went into the kitchen to switch the coffee percolator on and Christopher followed her, bringing his rucksack with him.

'Could I pop in some things for washing, Mum? I haven't had time to do everything.'

'Just put them in now. That's fine,' she said, helping to load the machine and noticing the large tomes and notebooks he was carrying.

'Well, maybe you'll get some time to study on Sunday depending on how things go with Jack and how long Alex is staying. I am a bit anxious about the meeting and hope that it does not turn out to be an unpleasant experience.'

'Me, too,' he said. 'Alex e-mailed to say that he would only be staying until Sunday morning, so Sunday afternoon might be free, and I can stay until Monday as our Monday lectures won't start until the afternoon.'

'Well, that's great. I can have you to myself for a wee while,' Nicky said, giving him a cuddle.

'I'll go and shower and get ready. Have I got a clean shirt here, Mum?'

'Yes, in the wardrobe.'

Shortly before ten am, a taxi drew up outside and Nicky watched as Alex entered the apartment block. She opened the door and awaited his arrival. Looking dashing and handsome, he emerged from the lift, a small valise in his hand.

''Hello, Nicky. How very nice to see you again,' he said, giving her a warm hug.

'Please come in, the coffee is on and Christopher is in the shower.'

Alex put his case on the floor, gave her a brief hug and followed her into the kitchen.

'Black or white?' she asked, pouring the coffee.

'Black, thank you. I'll need to be wide awake for our visitation with Jack.'

They went through to the sitting room where Alex complimented her on her lovely apartment and sat in one of the large armchairs.

'You have been pretty busy, I expect?' Nicky asked, sitting in the adjacent seat.

'Yes, it has been a long and hard few months. However, there is just a debriefing meeting on Monday and then I can have a few days at home to see Jo and find out what the kids have been up to.'

'Christopher tells me that you are staying until Sunday. You would be very welcome to stay here for the night if you would like. I have plenty of room and the cupboards are full, in preparation for Christopher's homecoming. Please stay,' she said.

'That's very kind of you and I would be very grateful if I can stay here. It will be good having Christopher and you here with me. You know he is in regular contact. We have great discussions by e-mail and text. I feel that I have become closer to him in the last few weeks. You know, we share a lot of things in common and I am constantly amazed at his knowledge and his sensitivity about other people. We have talked about today's visit at length and have come to some conclusions about how we should deal with Jack. You can rest easy. We will be as agreeable as it is possible to be. We have decided that there is no point looking backwards and criticising Jack. We have to move forwards now and get on as best we can.'

Nicky laughed. 'Yes, Christopher is a different person now that he has you. I know how much he appreciates your interest and the time you take to keep in touch. Thank you for that.'

Suddenly the door opened and Christopher appeared, wearing his dark suit, white shirt and a blue and silver striped tie, and looking very smart.

'Hi, Alex' he said excitedly, his face lighting up as he saw his father. Alex rose and the two men embraced.

'You look ready for the fray; very impressive if I may say so,' Alex said, stepping back to admire his son.

'I'm the lucky one,' said Nicky, 'escorted by two dashing men today.'

They laughed together and sat around the coffee table. Nicky looked at her watch. 'I think we have about ten minutes before we set off. Let me tell you what has been happening here,' she said.

She went on to relate the details of her recent visit to see Jack Randall, his affability and wish to make amends as far as it was possible. She didn't mention her horrific experience at 47 Wheatfield Crescent but did tell them that there had been no communication from Ratcliffe.

'That's very odd, isn't it, Mum?' Christopher said, frowning.

'Yes, I don't understand that at all but have decided to be glad for the time being. I suspect he will appear in due course. Bad pennies usually turn up, don't they? Meantime, there are other things to tell you,' she added, and went on to describe her meeting with Felicity at the Fairfax and her chat with Dr Robertson.

'So Dr Robertson would be in favour of us making a visit this afternoon?' asked Alex.

'I told them that this was the most likely day for a visit and he said that the staff would keep an eye on her, so if you choose to go along today, they will be prepared. If she becomes excited or uncontrollable, we have to leave and the staff will sedate her if necessary. Of course, we don't have to go at all. I told Dr Robertson that you were an old friend, Alex and that you were here with your son. He believes that Felicity had a miscarriage and is quite unaware that she has a son. You may feel that it's too soon to visit. It's entirely up to you. Jack Randall has no idea that I went to see her nor does he know of your wish to go to the clinic and it would be courteous if we tell him what we are proposing when we go this morning. He will definitely want us to ask his permission. He sees himself very much as her guardian and likes to control what happens with her. I should probably explain my visit, too.'

'You have been busy, Mum. I certainly would like to meet Felicity but I wouldn't like to trigger any problematic behaviour. What do you think, Alex?' Christopher asked, turning to his father.

'I hadn't been expecting to see her so soon, but you're right, Nicky. We do need to see her, ourselves, and there's no time like the present. I have been thinking a lot about her and it would be good to have a firsthand impression of her situation. I suggest we do go, if we can, this afternoon, when we leave the Randalls.'

'Right, that's settled then. Now I think we should get moving. Jack will be worried if we are late. He is, as you might expect, a bit wary of meeting you two, and although he is looking forward to seeing his grandson, he has serious concerns about raking over the old coals.'

They drove in Nicky's car to Beaulieu and there was continuous conversation as each of them related how they felt about the pending meeting. As Nicky pulled into the drive, the loose stones crunching beneath her wheels, Christopher commented, 'One very impressive house and some expensive motors in the yard.'

'Yes, Jack is not short of money, as you will see, and his wife, Sylvie is rather good at spending it so they are well suited. It is a lovely house,' Nicky said.

Peters was at the door almost immediately and welcomed them in.

'Nice to see you again, Mr. Sanderson.' he said, almost smiling.

'And you too, Peters. Are you still living at the lodge?'

'Yes, Sir.' he replied and turning to Nicky, he added, 'Mr. Randall asked me to take you into the sitting room, Ma'am,' and led them through the newly decorated foyer into a magnificent spacious room with polished parquet flooring, white furnishings and thick white fluffy scatter rugs. There were three large settees and two individual chairs, their heavy white fabric contrasted with several black furry throws. An abstract black lamp holder with a white, frilly shade sat on a small black table on each side of the marble fireplace, a warm glow emanating from the artificial coal fire. On the walls were hung four pictures with a modernist look, all featuring black and white colours. The white flimsy full length curtains framed a massive window which looked out over the front lawns and the familiar fountain. The whole room looked as though it had just been decorated and had rarely been in use. It was more modern than Nicky would have expected in Jack's house and she concluded that Sylvie had been the one to choose the decor.

They had barely entered the room when Jack and Sylvie Randall appeared. 'Good morning, Nicky,' Jack said. 'Thank you for coming and thank you so much for bringing Commander Sanderson and Christopher.'

He stretched out his hand and shook the hands of Alex and Christopher warmly, his gaze focussing predominantly on his grandson.

'This is my wife, Sylvie. Alex, I think you two met a long time ago, but Christopher you will not have met Sylvie.'

Sylvie was looking very stylish in a figure hugging green dress with a high rounded neckline and short sleeves. An emerald necklace and bracelet sparkled as she moved. Her plain, high heeled shoes were a dark green colour. Her over-bright eyes and flushed cheeks suggested that she had already had a few drinks to help her through the day.

The introductions over, Jack ushered everyone further into the room.

'Please have a seat and make yourselves comfortable. I thought we should all have a drink first before lunch and get to know one another. Esther, will help with the drinks,' he said, sitting himself in a single chair to the left of the marble fireplace, and nodding to the young maid who was waiting, a silver tray in her hand.

'It must be eighteen years since we met, Commander,'

said Sylvie, trying to get the conversation started, 'and you look just the same as ever and your son looks just like you.'

'I visited this house on several occasions at the beginning of 1995 and I believe we met briefly then.' Alex replied, omitting to return the compliment that she hadn't changed over the years either and Nicky felt sure that she was disappointed.

'A lot of water has run under the bridge since then. You have had a most successful career. I see pictures of you in the papers on a regular basis. It must be very gratifying,' Jack contributed.

'Thank you. I have been lucky in my choice of career and I enjoy every minute of it. Not everybody can say that,' Alex said.

'Where do you stay, now?' asked Sylvie, sitting herself on the arm of Jack's chair and swinging her elegant legs.

'I stay in Virginia with my wife, Jo, and our three children- Joseph who is fifteen, Caroline who is fourteen and Clementina who is twelve but of course, my job requires considerable travelling and I don't get to spend as much time with them as I would like.'

Nicky felt that the conversation was stilted and unnatural, veering away from the focal point of the meeting. At some point, they had to address the issues which were foremost in everybody's mind and she wanted to clear the air and move on from trivialities to the main purpose of the meeting. Esther had handed her a gin and tonic, so she gulped half of it down and then said, 'Jack, forgive me for making an opening gambit but we all know the reason for this meeting and it is my opinion that the sooner we dispense with the formalities and launch into discussing that reason, the easier it will be. Perhaps I can begin.'

She looked at Jack and he nodded, resignedly. Standing up, and, holding her crystal glass in one hand, she said, 'I just want to recap everything so we are all singing from the same song sheet. Eighteen years ago, Alex and Felicity were in love. When Alex left to go back to sea in April 1995, he was unaware that Felicity was pregnant. In October, Christopher was born in this very house. Sadly, Felicity is not here today to tell us what was going on in her mind but we can surmise that she went through a difficult time that summer because she did not confide in Alex, Jack, Sylvie or anyone else that she was indeed pregnant and the first you knew of it, Jack, was when you received a frantic call in Switzerland begging you to come home and help her.'

'I didn't know anything about it. Jack told me that he had urgent business to attend to. I wish he had involved me then. I could have helped and maybe things would have turned out better,' Sylvie interrupted.

'My daughter was in trouble. She sounded hysterical and desperate that night. We had always been close but after Sylvie and I got married, Felicity was a bit jealous I think, and our relationship had suffered. I was aware of that, felt a bit guilty and so when she phoned in that distraught state, I had to go and sort things out for her. Our closeness had suffered after Alice died and I remarried. It was natural. She was lonely and perhaps looking for support from me and I wasn't there for her. So I feel very responsible for her failure to communicate. She must have gone through a personal hell all by herself.'

'Jack, I don't think we need to go over every detail of that night, but I want to let you know that I visited Felicity at the Fairfax this week and although it was obvious that she wasn't quite normal, she did talk to me.

Afterwards, Dr Robertson asked me how I had found her.'

'You really had no right to visit her,' interrupted Sylvie rather angrily. 'Jack doesn't like her to have visitors. It disturbs her.'

'You're right. I should have mentioned it to you. My plan was to see whether or not she was able to meet Alex and Christopher. I had never met her, only heard about her problems and I felt that I really needed to see her for myself. In any event, Dr Robertson divulged that Felicity had taken drugs towards the end of the pregnancy, perhaps to expedite the baby's delivery and it was the drugs which damaged her kidneys and her brain. You said that Felicity was desperate and in a frightful state, Jack, when you saw her that night and I am beginning to think now that the drugs she had taken had already made her behave oddly. You took control, looked after her and later on took her to the clinic where she was admitted to the Intensive Care Unit and given every possible therapy to make her better. Unfortunately, the damage had been done and sadly, Felicity suffers from permanent irreparable brain damage.'

Nicky looked round. Jack was slouched forwards cradling his whisky and Sylvie still looked somewhat disgruntled. Alex and Christopher sat together and both looked down-hearted.

'I am usually pretty good in a crisis, or I thought I was, until that night. Finding Felicity on the bed and out of her mind was awful and I was panicking. I attributed her bizarre state of mind to the trauma of delivering her child alone at home, but you're right, she had taken drugs, according to Dr Robertson's blood tests, and it's possible that she already had brain or kidney damage at that time. Coming into that situation was horrific and my main concern was for my daughter. Everything that happened that night was done in a haze of anxiety and fear-fear for my daughter's life.'

Jack put his glass on the small table beside him and looking at Alex and Christopher, he said, 'Felicity was behaving strangely but I put it down to the hormonal upset of the pregnancy and the fact that she had endured a difficult labour all on her own. I had no idea that she had been taking drugs. It was Dr Robertson who told me that later and it explained a great deal. I had no experience of babies and I saw that the baby's cord had not been tied. I thought that he had bled to death. He wasn't moving or breathing.'

He paused to sip some whisky and then continued, 'She wanted to put the baby in the woods and although I thought it was an odd suggestion, she was screaming and insisting that I took her. There was no placating her and I did what she asked in the hope of calming her down. Then, we were no sooner back home than she wanted to go back and get him.'

'And you did go back,' Nicky said.

'We did and by that time you had found him and taken him away. All Felicity found was an empty box. That triggered the most alarming screaming and yelling. I couldn't control her and had to take her to the clinic right away. It was a nightmare.'

Jack looked beaten as he poured the story out and suddenly he fell forwards on to his knees in front of Alex and Christopher and begged them to forgive him.

'I'm sorry for what happened. We thought the baby was dead, believe me. I know it sounds like a strange thing to do, taking the baby to the woods but that night was all so strange. Nothing was normal and I have regretted my actions for eighteen years. I let Felicity down; I let Alice down and I let both of you down. I am sorry, deeply sorry,' he said, sobbing.

Nicky noticed that Sylvie was looking very ill at ease. She had probably never seen her strong, controlling husband behaving in this way. Christopher had tears in his eyes and Alex sat impassively.

Nicky leaned down and helped Jack to his feet. She

went over to the sideboard where the drinks were standing and brought him a whisky as he sat down.

'When I heard that you and Felicity went back to get the baby, I was rather unnerved myself. I thought that by taking him away, that I had denied him a family, a life here in Beaulieu with his mother, because he would have started to cry or move and you would have known that he was alive. At the time, I was under the influence of sleeping pills and painkillers too, but even later, I thought that I was the best person to bring him up because I needed him and I loved him.'

Jack had poured himself another whisky and Sylvie had risen to offer more drinks all round.

'We are talking about you, Christopher, as if you weren't here and I'm sorry. I felt badly about keeping you to myself when I heard that Jack and Felicity had gone back but now that I have met Felicity and chatted with Dr Robertson, I don't feel so badly. It is my theory that you weren't breathing or moving much because you were affected by the pills she had taken. And maybe you had lost some blood, too. So it seems likely that you would have seemed dead at that time. At first, I thought that Jack and Felicity had deliberately tried to do away with you but I have revised that theory and now I don't blame Jack. He did his best in very difficult circumstances. Felicity had decided to tell no-one of the pregnancy but in the end she was struggling to cope with it all and in an effort to get it all over, she resorted to the drugs. If you had returned here, Christopher, I suspect that Felicity would not have been able to look after you herself. I'm sure, Jack, that you would have ensured he had all the care in the world but I feel better thinking that I gave him as much of a mother's love as any mother could have. Whatever the truth is, it is a long time ago and you survived unscathed, Chris. I have a wonderful son, if I may still call you my son, and I am so proud of you.'

'I should have agreed to the marriage. If I had, this would never have happened. I was prejudiced and proud. I'm sorry, truly sorry. In the end I was the one who lost out. I lost my lovely daughter and I almost lost my only grandson. There is no way to change the past, much as I would love to. All I can do now is apologise and try to make a better job of the future,' Jack said, tears streaming down his face.

Alex then spoke, 'You had a dreadful experience and you have obviously deep feelings of guilt. I do too, Jack, because if Felicity had not been pregnant, she would never have suffered in the way she has. So I must share some of the blame here. I wanted to marry your mother, Christopher, I loved her very much and if I had known about the baby, I would never have left her to bear the pregnancy alone. Jack, I want to see her if you don't mind. If I could help at all, I would.'

'There's no point raking over the ashes any more,' said Sylvie suddenly. 'What happened happened. Christopher has had a healthy, happy life and a loving mother. Children are resilient. It was better that you brought him up, Nicky. Jack and I would not have been able to give him the same unconditional love that he has had from you and Felicity would certainly not have been able to contribute at all. So you shouldn't feel badly about taking him away.'

'May I speak?' Christopher asked, rising from the settee.

'Of course,' Nicky said, taking a seat opposite Jack.

'I have been very fortunate to have had a wonderful upbringing, oblivious to all of these goings on. My mother, Nicky, has given me everything I need to face the world, endless love, support, moral guidelines and a good education. I always respected and loved her but since hearing about my birth and her finding me in the woods, I have an even greater admiration and love for her. That has opened my eyes and I have learned a lot from that.

I'm so glad that she did find me, not just for my sake but for hers. She deserved a much happier life, too. It hasn't been easy for her. She has had to bend the rules sometimes and now she is being blackmailed so Mum is paying a price for finding me, still.

But in spite of all of that, I just want to say that I have now found my father and that has been a phenomenal gift at this stage in my life, I have two half-sisters and a half-brother, and now I have met my grandfather. I bear you no grudge, Mr. Randall. I appreciate that you arranged this meeting today and I hope very much that you can accept me for what I am. I'm sorry about Felicity and with your permission I would like to see her, too. Although Nicky will always be my mother, Felicity is my birth mother and I need to know what she is like.'

Christopher sat down. For a few seconds there was a pause in the conversation and then Jack said, 'Thank you for making this easier for me today. Please feel free to visit Felicity, both of you, and Christopher, I would very much like you to feel that this is every bit your home as it is Felicity's. If you can accept me as your grandfather, I would be thrilled, and Alex, may I also ask if you could try to forgive me and start to build a better relationship?'

Alex, Christopher and Jack all rose then and shook hands.

Sylvie then announced that dinner would be ready in the conservatory and they all made their way through the house, the ice well and truly broken.

The afternoon passed without further melodramatics and conversation was almost normal as Christopher chatted about his university course and Alex talked about his activities abroad.

As they left Beaulieu, Christopher, Alex and Nicky felt

that something had been achieved. There were still feelings of unease but the worst was over. They had all managed to speak openly and freely. Alex was right. He and Christopher had been tolerant and forgiving. Nicky felt very proud of them both.

They drove along the streets towards the Fairfax and chatted about the day.

'He has aged considerably since my last visit,' remarked Alex.

'It was eighteen years ago,' said Nicky.

'Yes, he has lived with this for all that time. You have to feel sorry for him. All this money and no kids to share it with,' said Alex.

'I'm a bit old to play in the fountain or climb the trees but it is a palatial residence and a houseful of kids would have transformed it, and Jack, I suspect.' Christopher said. 'Funny it looks almost familiar to me. I don't know why that should be.'

'Well, a long time ago, when you were almost three years old, I brought you up Cherrybank Avenue to look for the house. I had just discovered who owned the car which brought you to Mansion Hill and I came just to see where it was. We watched that very fountain together. Perhaps you have a memory of that occasion.'

'I felt Jack was trying very hard to bond with us, particularly with Christopher. The whole visit was much easier than I had imagined; certainly much easier than any of my previous visits, I can tell you,' said Alex.

'Yes, I believe he is genuinely pleased to have found you, Chris, and I hope you can give him a little of your time,' Nicky said.

'Yes, I plan to visit and keep in touch with him. He is my grandfather. I think we'll be OK.'

The car pulled into the park at the Fairfax Clinic and they entered the glass portals to speak with the receptionist.

'Oh, hello,' she said. 'Yes, Miss Randall is expecting you, or at least Dr Robertson spent some time with her today to tell her about the visit. Whether she appreciates who you are, we won't know until she sees you. Do come this way.'

She led the way up the stairs and turning right, she knocked on Felicity's door. There was loud music coming from inside and no-one answered. The nurse knocked again and opened the door. Felicity was watching a rock concert on her plasma screen and seemed totally absorbed in it.

'Felicity, your guests have arrived,' said the nurse, taking the TV control from her and switching off the noise.

Felicity hit out at the nurse and then, seeing she had company, resumed her relaxed position on the bean bag. The nurse left the room, and on her way out, said, 'If you have any problems with her, just shout to me. I'll be in Reception.'

Felicity looked at the TV screen as though there was still a show to watch and paid little attention to her guests. Nicky went to her, crouched down on the carpet and said, 'Hello Felicity, do you remember me? I came to see you. Nicky Partington is my name. You can call me Nicky.'

After a few seconds, the girl faced Nicky and smiled in the inane way she did, but said nothing.

'I would like you to meet two friends, Alex and Christopher. A long time ago, you met Alex. Perhaps you remember him.'

Alex sat in front of her and tried to hold her hands but she hastily withdrew them and frowned at him. His soft words fell on deaf ears and it seemed that she was not able to recognise him. Christopher then tried, sitting cross legged on the floor. He told her that he was Alex's son. For a while she sat unmoving and silent, and then she blurted out, *'Son, son, son.'* Christopher smiled at her and said, 'Yes, Felicity, I am your son too.'

She stared at him for a long time, stretched out her hand to touch his hair and then hit him on the face.

Christopher backed off but made light of it. 'It's OK, Felicity. You didn't mean to hurt me, I know that. You just wanted to show me that I meant something to you.' He stood up and let her settle, but shortly afterwards, she started to bellow and shout. She hit the television and would have lashed out at all her visitors, but Alex held her tightly while Nicky called the nurse. Restraining her made things worse and she became uncontrollable.

Dr Robertson was summoned to sedate her and to take her to the hospital wing for a spell. 'We expected that the visit might provoke an outburst but it was worth a try and actually you may find that she remembers part of the visit. She could behave quite differently on another occasion.'

'I would like to visit again, Dr Robertson; not for a few weeks but sometime in the future, if that's OK with you,' Christopher said.

'Of course. Best let us know when you are coming. We may be able to increase her medication to cope better. Today, perhaps there were too many new people for her to handle.'

They left the clinic, all feeling downhearted, but it had been what they expected.

'She's still very pretty,' Christopher said.

'Yes, she looks much the same as she did eighteen years ago but she is not the same person. She was sweet and gentle. It's a tragedy.' Alex said. 'Still, I'm glad to have been here today to see for myself exactly what the situation is.'

In the evening they chatted easily and Nicky noticed how close Alex and Christopher had become in a matter of weeks.

'Nicky, Jo and I would very much like Christopher and you to visit our home in Virginia. Our three kids are falling over themselves with excitement that they have found a big brother. You have no idea. I was wondering when would be a good time. I'm going to be away until September but after that, there is an opportunity for a visit, if that is any good for you.'

'That's very kind of you, Alex. At present I believe that September will be good for me and Christopher will be finishing up the term. Let's plan for that,' she said happily.

'I'll keep in touch with Christopher and we can sort out the dates and let you know, OK?'

'That would be great.' she said, anticipating Christopher's joy at finding his kin. She was so happy for him.

Alex left on Sunday morning and Christopher studied all day, taking breaks only to share meals with Nicky.

He left early on Monday morning to return to his course.

30

DEAD FOR 7 WEEKS; WELL-KNOWN JOURNALIST MURDERED, were the headlines on the morning papers. Nicky dropped Christopher off at the station, made no comment to him and on the way out, picked up a newspaper and went straight to work, her heart in her mouth.

'Have you seen this?' Marilyn exclaimed, thrusting a newspaper under Nicky's nose as she entered.

'It's him; it's Jeremy Ratcliffe. That's why he hasn't kept his appointment. The man is dead.'

'Is it really Ratcliffe?' Nicky asked, 'I saw the headlines on the billboards but I didn't see the name.'

Marilyn followed her into the office and shut the door. She held the paper up to her face and read from it. 'The decomposing body of journalist, Jeremy Ratcliffe, was found today when police broke into his bungalow home in Wheatfield Crescent, Edgerley. Star Magazine, with whom Ratcliffe had a contract, had asked the police to investigate the journalist's prolonged absence from work.

Mr. Ratcliffe, who made his name a few years ago when he wrote a series of articles on the top celebrities in the fashion industry in this country, had been missing for 7 weeks. At first it was thought that he was sick and then it was suggested that he had a family problem but the Star editors felt that it was unlike Mr. Ratcliffe not to inform them of such a long absence from work.

'The police made the gruesome discovery when they forcibly entered his home on Saturday. The police have not revealed the manner of his death and are appealing for witnesses who may have seen Mr. Ratcliffe approximately 7 weeks ago. Residents of the Wheatfield estate have been asked to wrack their brains and try to remember any stranger, an unfamiliar car or any unusual goings-on in that area around the time of the murder.'

'Oh, my God,' said Nicky. 'How dreadful!'

'He was a real sleaze bag and I didn't care for him, but nobody deserves to be killed and not found for 7 weeks.'

'You're right. It's horrible.'

'Do you think we should tell the police that he didn't come for his appointment?' asked Marilyn.

'Do you think that would be of any help?' asked Nicky, hoping that Marilyn wouldn't pursue the matter.

'It might help them to pin down the time of the murder. We know that he phoned here on the Thursday before you came back from Southampton and that he made an appointment for the following Friday so he must have been killed that week.'

'That's true.'

'I wonder if he managed to submit his article about you to the Star Magazine before he was murdered, otherwise that won't be going ahead as we expected. I suppose another journalist will be assigned in due course.'

'I doubt he will have done it because I was supposed to go over it with him before he submitted it. Perhaps he sent in a draft, of course. We will have to wait to hear from them.'

'I could ring them this morning,' she suggested.

'No,' said Nicky. It is too soon and I don't want to seem totally uncaring about Ratcliffe.'

'Oh, you're right. It wouldn't be appropriate so soon. No doubt they will get in touch in any case.'

'You know, I've kind of gone off the idea of that article anyway. If it is written, so be it, but if not, I think I would like to forget about it.'

'Are you sure?' Marilyn said disbelievingly. 'Don't you want your fifteen minutes of fame?'

'If the article was written by someone else, I think it would always be associated with Ratcliffe's murder. I don't think we should pursue it,' she said. 'However, you are right. We should tell the police. Check out the dates of his phone calls so that we can be accurate, then if you would like to phone the police station and tell them, that would be fine. After all, you may have been one of the last people to talk to him, Marilyn.'

'Gosh, that's right. I'll do that right away.'

For the rest of the morning, Nicky read and reread the newspaper she had picked up at the station, looking for hints that someone had left clues in Ratcliffe's house. She was in a terrible fluster. She couldn't get the thought of Ratcliffe out of her mind. Marilyn entered the office at 10.30 a.m. bearing a cup of black coffee for Nicky and related her conversation with the police.

'There will be someone round to take a statement shortly,' she said. 'Isn't it exciting?'

Nicky didn't feel at all excited, more nervous and worried but she tried not to show it.

At noon, Marilyn came into the office, and ushered in two plain clothes policemen. They showed their warrant cards and explained the reason for their visit which was an investigation into Jeremy Ratcliffe's murder. The senior officer, smartly clad in a dark suit, white shirt and dark woollen tie, was Detective Inspector Barry Ryan and the younger colleague, less stylish than his boss, wearing a sagging grey suit, black shirt and tie, was Sergeant Josh Avery.

It was Detective Inspector Ryan who asked the

questions.

'Miss Partington, I believe you were in contact with Mr. Ratcliffe some weeks before his death. Can you outline for us the reasons for that and tell us exactly the last day you saw him?'

'Yes, of course. Mr. Ratcliffe was writing an article about me for the Star.'

'Why was that, Miss Partington?'

'Recently my success in the business sector had been recognised by the Law Society and I was appointed to a prestigious position on a national committee. The Star Magazine editor wanted to write about my rise to the top because I am a single mother and they believed that I was a good role model and an example to others that with hard work, one can be successful. Jeremy Ratcliffe had been assigned to the job. That was the gist of it.'

'So he came to see you?'

'Yes, he came on the first occasion. It was a Thursday, about two months ago. That visit was simply to ask my permission to write the story and to set up another meeting to take photographs and have further discussions.'

'So he came on a second occasion?'

'Yes, he came a week later, again on a Thursday, with a cameraman and I posed at my desk for a few pictures. We discussed the content of the article.'

'Did he then set up a further appointment?'

'No, he said that he would phone my secretary to make a further appointment when he had completed the article. He was to let me read it and to check that all his facts were correct and that I approved of the photograph they had chosen.'

'And he did phone your secretary to make that appointment?'

'Yes, he phoned when I was on business in Southampton and set up an appointment for the following

Friday afternoon at 6 p.m. Marilyn, my secretary can give you the exact dates and times of the appointments.'

'Yes, she has already given us a list.'

'So on that Friday, we waited for ages. Marilyn was here with me until around 6.30 p.m.and then I stayed on, working until about 10.30 p.m.'

'Were you expecting him to come as late as that?'

'No. I often stay late to work. I was simply mentioning that because he definitely didn't phone and we received no mail requesting a change of the appointment. It wasn't a question of him arriving late and there being no-one here. If he had arrived late, I would have been here.'

'Your secretary gave us the impression that you didn't like Mr. Ratcliffe. Is that the case?'

'Neither of us took to him. He was a rather unkempt and smelly individual, with longish hair and an ingratiating manner. I suspected that he had an alcohol problem. He was rather brusque and a little rude to Marilyn on the phone when he couldn't get the appointment date that he wanted. That was all. I hardly knew the man.'

'Do you know the Wheatfield estate, Miss Partington?'

'I know roughly where it is, near the outskirts of town. I have seen signs to it but I have never driven through it,' lied Nicky, worried that someone had taken note of her car while she was parked near the Crescent. Was he testing her reaction? She tried to relax and look as calm as possible.

'Did he ever suggest to you that he had enemies… that he was frightened of something?'

'No, not at all. His visits here were purely professional and he did not talk about himself at all.'

'Right, Miss Partington. Thank you for telling us about the dates. It is helpful in pinning down the exact time of his death.'

The two men rose. Then the older man turned as he reached the door.' Do you know what sort of car Mr.

Ratcliffe drove, by any chance?'

'I'm afraid not. I don't know if he came here by car or on foot.'

'He did have a car and a neighbour saw it parked outside his house about the time of the murder.'

'I see.'

'It's not there anymore. Looks like someone took it.'

Nicky frowned, 'How odd.'

'No, in the Wheatfield estate, that is the norm. Cars are damaged and stolen on a regular basis. Perhaps when we find the car, we will find the killer,' he said, nodding to her.

'I hope so. It's a horrible business.'

The detectives left and Nicky found herself perspiring and hot. She went to the water fountain and drank a large carton of ice cold water.

Luckily she had thought about the sort of questions she might be asked by the police. It had occurred to her that they should know about Ratcliffe's debts and the possibility of a debt collector killing him but if she had mentioned that, the police would have wondered why he should divulge such information to Nicky and might subsequently consider that he had been asking her for money. She had, therefore decided to say nothing of that conversation. Still she felt very uneasy and guilty for the rest of the afternoon and wondered if Jack Randall had read the paper. She thought about phoning him but then she thought that Marilyn might think it odd that she made the phone call so soon after the police had visited. She waited until Marilyn had left for home, still high on the excitement of the day, then opened the safe to retrieve the cheque she had made out to Ratcliffe as well as Jack Randall's cheque, and closing the office, decided to drive to Beaulieu.

All the way there, she was watching cars around her, trying to see if she was being tailed. She took a round about way to the house and was fairly sure that she had not been followed. She could always say that she had business with Jack if she was interrogated. He would corroborate that, she was sure.

When she arrived, Peters asked her to wait in the sitting room while he told Mr. Randall of her visit.

She could hear Sylvie's voice coming from the study. It seemed unnaturally high pitched and Nicky concluded that the news had already spread.

A few minutes later, Jack appeared and ushered her into his study. Sylvie was running up the stairs and did not look back or acknowledge Nicky. She was clearly upset by the news.

'Hello, Nicky, I was expecting you to call or to come round. I trust you have read the papers?' Jack said, sitting down behind his desk.

'Yes, that's the reason I came. I've had the police to my office, too. Ratcliffe was in touch with the office, as you know, to make an appointment which he didn't keep and my secretary felt that the police would like to have this information. It may help in pinpointing the time of his death.'

'Did they say how he died or whether they had any leads?' Jack asked.

'No. They asked the questions and told me nothing. I just wanted you to know about Ratcliffe's death because we had been surprised at his failure to turn up. Now we know why. It looks like he was dead before the time of his appointment.'

'I suppose he may have information about you on his computer or in his paperwork. If the police discover that, we are back to square one,' he said, playing with an empty glass which was sitting on his blotter. Another empty glass stood on the silver tray on the sideboard. Nicky concluded that Sylvie and Jack had both had a drink to help handle the news.

'Yes, that's a possibility, of course. He may have already written the article he was preparing for the Star about me and so I would expect him to have some documentation in the house or on his computer.' Nicky said, ' However, the police did not say anything about that, so perhaps they have not as yet discovered what he was up to,' she added, knowing that the police would not find any paper trail to her in his house. She had checked and disposed of some papers but the killer had taken what relevant files were there and also the laptop. The main worry was the laptop, where it was and who was in possession of it.

'The police gave no indication that they had found anything?'

'No. I suppose it will take them time to work their way through his things and of course, they may have held back information in an effort to see what people tell them.' Jack Randall sat pensively, still rubbing his hands together.

'Sylvie is very distraught about it. She is very anxious that none of this rubs off on us.'

'Naturally, I'm a bit anxious myself,' she said, extracting the two cheques from her bag.

'I won't be requiring these any more,' she said, handing them to him, 'Thanks, anyway.'

Jack looked at the cheques and then, rising to go to the shredding machine sitting in a corner, he inserted them. The grating noise somehow seemed appropriate to the circumstances of Ratcliffe's death and Nicky shivered.

'I'll not keep you, Jack. Just wanted to touch base.'

'While you are here, Nicky, there's some business I need to discuss with you,' he said, moving over to his filing cabinet and extracting two buff coloured files.

Nicky wasn't in the mood to discuss business after her experience with the police, but she listened to what Jack was saying.

'I have been thinking about Christopher. He is constantly on my mind. What a fine young man he is! You have brought him up well and I'm very grateful to you for that as well as for bringing us all together again under such difficult circumstances.'

'There was no other way, Jack.'

'Yes, there were other ways of dealing with it but you chose this way and that was the best possible outcome. I was thinking that if Felicity could understand what has happened, she would want me to look after him. I told you that he would be looked after. Well, having met him, I am very happy to support him and I have made a few changes to my portfolio. You need to know that, anyway.'

He picked up the two folders and handed them to her.

'I am a rich man, Nicky, and have more money than I will ever need, a house in Zurich, another on the Cote d'Azur and plenty of money in foreign bank accounts. Felicity has the trust fund which you know about and she is sorted for life. I have been making transfers out of this country in case this Ratcliffe business destroys my life, and I am disposing of some assets.

The Manilaw Pharmaceutical Industry has been a tremendous source of income for me over the years. It is booming and I have decided to split my shares in that company between you and Christopher. You will each have a 12.5% holding so together you will hold a controlling hand and you will both be secure for life. I am anxious to see that you are secure, too. If anything happens in the investigation regarding Ratcliffe, you may lose your position and I can't see you in difficulties.'

'Jack! What are you thinking of?' she said, amazed at his kindness.

'I'm thinking that without you, Christopher would not have turned out to be the wonderful grandson he is and I'm thinking that if Ratcliffe's story should emerge and destroy your career, you will need some income. That's the reasoning behind it. It's big thank you, Nicky.'

'I don't know what to say. You didn't need to do this. It is so generous.'

'Perhaps you will pass on the news to Christopher next time you see him, explain something of the company to him and guide him in its management. I know you can do that.'

'I'll certainly do that. He will be in touch with you.'

Jack rose from his chair and gave Nicky a hug.

'Don't let this Ratcliffe business get you down. You are OK now and you won't have to worry about Christopher.'

'Thank you from both of us.'

'Thank you for keeping me informed about Ratcliffe. We will just have to wait and see what happens. It is possible of course, that Jeremy Ratcliffe was blackmailing other people too, you know. It may have absolutely nothing to do with us. '

'Yes, that's quite possible.' she said, thinking that another blackmailer would have no reason to steal information about her, unless, of course, they wished to take over the blackmailing. She shivered at the thought.

'I should feel easier to know that Ratcliffe won't be bothering me and you and I can carry on as before without any public embarrassment, but I have to admit that I'm a bit anxious about it all.'

Jack put an arm round her shoulders and walked her to the door.

'Come any time, Nicky, and keep me informed.' he said as she left, clutching the two folders tightly.

31

During the weeks that followed, Christopher made several visits home. He always phoned Jack Randall to say he was in town and without any hesitation Jack invited him for a meal and a chat. Christopher knew how generous his grandfather had been and although he knew what part he had played in his own early life, somehow that was put behind them and an easy relationship developed between them. Jack's wealth of experience in business had given him a strong understanding of money and he never lost an opportunity to advise Christopher with regards to his finances and help him in his career in a willing and interested way.

Sylvie stayed very much on the sidelines, extremely busy with her hectic schedule of coffee mornings, fashion shows and redecoration.

Christopher also visited Felicity on a couple of occasions but she was reluctant to engage in conversation and he felt that his visits upset her. Thinking it would help if she went along too, Nicky accompanied Christopher on one of these visits.

Felicity was, as usual, watching a DVD or television programme. For some reason she liked the volume to be very loud and it seemed to Nicky that the types of films she watched were full of violence and horror. Christopher tried to talk to her about the movies or the actors and actresses but sustaining any kind of conversation proved impossible.

'Perhaps you could show us the school room, Felicity, where you do your computer work and art?' Nicky asked, hoping that a change of scene might help.

'Yes, I can do that,' she suddenly answered positively, and jumped up, leading the two of them downstairs. They passed the reception desk and turned acutely right along a wide corridor, passing three doors before Felicity turned into a room with the sign *Classroom* on the frame.

Nicky and Christopher followed in her wake and found that there was a middle aged lady perched on a stool in front of a desk, teaching a young girl what seemed to be the rudiments of the computer.

'Hello, Felicity.' she said, looking round at the visitors.

'Hello' said Nicky, My name is Nicky Partington and this is my son, Christopher. We are friends of Felicity and she kindly offered to show us where she did her studies. I do apologise for bothering you. You are obviously very busy.'

'No, no, that's quite all right,' the lady said standing and smoothing her dress, approaching Nicky.

'I am the teacher of computer studies here. My name is Beryl Stanwick.' Nicky noticed the firm handshake and could see that the woman was smartly clad in a black dress, her matching jacket hanging over the back of a chair beside her.

'Jacqueline and I were just having a preliminary look at the computer to see if she would like to join the class.'

The girl was young, perhaps only sixteen but looked poorly nourished and had a pasty face. Her dress was loose and drab, the khaki colour doing nothing at all for her appearance.

'I would like to s- s - start, Miss Stanwick,' the girl said timidly, stuttering a little with the words.

'That's excellent,' exclaimed Miss Stanwick,' I'll see you in here tomorrow then at 10 a.m., OK?'

The girl nodded and scurried away with a backward glance at Felicity.

Turning to Nicky, Miss Stanwick said, 'Perhaps Felicity can show you her paintings. Are they in your desk, Felicity?' she asked.

Christopher followed Felicity to her desk and Nicky watched as she opened the drawers to show Christopher her latest achievements. From a distance, Nicky saw only large black shapes and wondered what she had been painting.

Miss Stanwick drew Nicky aside and asked, 'Is she better today? She has been very contrary this last week or so.'

'She is not very communicative but that is not new. Perhaps Christopher's presence upsets her. She seems better when I am on my own,' Nicky remarked.

Miss Stanwick pulled Nicky a little further away from Felicity and Christopher who were busy looking at pictures together. 'Some days she is quite hysterical. There is another girl here called Kirsty Muir. She is a drug addict and spends her life in and out of this place. She winds up Felicity. I try to keep them apart. The other person who seems to wind her up is her step mother, Mrs. Randall. I have suggested that she minimises her visits and now she doesn't come in frequently, thank goodness.'

'That's a pity, isn't it, because I'm sure Mrs. Randall would like to help her.'

'I doubt that,' said Miss Stanwick. 'She always shouts at Felicity as though she was just an idiot rather than a sick, young woman.'

'What does she shout at her for?' asked Nicky, curious.

'Well the last time she came, which was about a month ago, she was upstairs in the bedroom. The door was open and everybody could hear her. She kept telling her that it was all her fault, that something Felicity had done was threatening to ruin everything, and something about money.

She said that, because of Felicity, her father could lose a lot of money.'

'Did you speak to Mrs. Randall later?'

'I tried to but she didn't want to talk, and I'm not really in a position to criticise her. She is the owner's wife after all, and she pays my salary.'

'Was Felicity upset?'

'Very. She huddled in a corner, sucking her thumb and curled up in a ball, making whining noises. It took a long time before she settled again.'

'I'll try to talk to Mrs. Randall about it,' she said, wondering what she had been divulging to Felicity. Ratcliffe's blackmail activity? How strange. If that was the case, she clearly had no insight into how detached and distant Felicity really was.

Miss Stanwick left and Nicky joined Felicity and Christopher at the desk where the pictures were on display and Christopher was making complimentary remarks about them. There were no recognisable objects in any of the paintings, just a mass of black. Only in one, did there seem to be long strands which had a suggestion of a tree. For a moment, Nicky thought how disturbed the girl was and was about to comment that one resembled a tree when it struck her that perhaps this was her memory of Mansion Hill woods, a black night in the trees. She shivered and kept her thoughts to herself.

Later in the evening, Christopher looked depressed. Nicky asked him

'Did you find the visit to the Fairfax a bit dismal today?'

'Yes, it's a tragedy. She is not old and could live for a very long time in this state. There doesn't seem to be any hope of her getting better, does there?'

'No, the doctor says there is unlikely to be any major improvement.'

'I had hoped, you know, that seeing Alex and me, she might have had a memory of the past, but she doesn't seem to have changed at all since I first visited.'

'I'm sorry, Chris. I understand what you're saying but perhaps her memory of Alex and her baby are submerged somewhere and there may be more understanding than you imagine. It's disappointing, I'm sure, but there's not a great deal more we can do.'

32

The newspapers continued to print stories of Ratcliffe's demise, leaking titbits of information gleaned from the police, each week. It became known that he had been stabbed and that drugs were involved, the police having discovered several packets of Class A drugs in his home. Various neighbours, friends and colleagues had helped the police with their enquiries but the case remained a mystery. They had not made any arrests and had not been able to locate the drug supplier. His ex-wife was remarried and lived in Spain. She had nothing to add to the story but she appealed again for people to come forward with anything at all which might help in the apprehension of his killer. The forensic team had found no fingerprints and the laptop which Ratcliffe used was now being sought as it was thought that it might yield important clues. The police appealed to anyone who might have been offered a cheap laptop or who had seen one in a rubbish dump, to come forward.

However, as time passed, it became relegated from the front pages to the inner ones and gradually it was no longer news. Nicky was relieved that no-one had been arrested. She didn't want anyone to be found in possession of the laptop either, because it most certainly would hold the key to Ratcliffe's murder. Jack Randall always asked Nicky if there had been news but after months, even his interest seemed to fade.

Nicky felt safe again although there was always an undercurrent of guilt, a nervousness which was not far from the surface. She could live with it. In the meantime, she was thoroughly enjoying her work and was very relieved to have been given additional time without being exposed.

At the end of September, Nicky and Christopher were invited to stay with the Sandersons in their gracious mansion in Virginia. Alex had generously purchased the flight tickets and arranged to meet them at the airport. They were made very welcome and a bond was formed between Christopher and Alex's other children. Nicky felt like one of the family. She enjoyed Jo's company and there was a lot of laughter and fun. Nicky knew that this trip would be the first of many for Christopher and that he would always be one of their family. She wasn't sad about sharing him. Indeed, she felt a great sense of relief that he would be all right in life and have plenty people who would look out for him. He couldn't have found a nicer family.

A year passed and Ratcliffe's murder was almost forgotten. Peace reigned again.

However, in May of the following year, another article on the subject appeared in the newspapers. All the previous details were given once again but a new development had emerged. Nicky read on with growing concern.

It seemed that a man who lived on the Wheatfield estate had been found to be dealing drugs and admitted that he had supplied Jeremy Ratcliffe periodically. In order to avoid a harsh sentence, the man said that he knew something about Ratcliffe that might interest the police. He told them that Ratcliffe had been on the point of receiving a large sum of money. He had told his supplier that he had discovered an important secret and was making the most of it. He said that he was expecting to receive the money the following week, and had remarked that his worries were

over, *that the bitch was filthy rich* and would be keeping
him in luxury for the rest of his life. The police were now
reviewing their leads and focussing on the women who
knew Ratcliffe, as it seemed likely that the killer could be a
woman.

Nicky's heart was in her mouth. The office bell rang
and immediately she jumped to the conclusion that it was
the police returning to ask more questions, but it was only a
package being delivered to one of her colleagues.

It was Jack Randall who made the communication on
this occasion.

'Have you a few minutes to spare today? I was
wondering if you would come by the house?'

'Yes, around 6 p.m. Does that suit you?'

It did, and Nicky drove to the house after work,
wondering if Jack wanted to discuss the latest
developments about Ratcliffe's murder. When they were
cloistered in his office, Jack said, 'What do you make of
this revelation in the papers?'

'I don't know. It's been a year and I was beginning to
think that the investigation was going cold. I have been
feeling more relaxed but suddenly we are catapulted back
to square one, and I'm worried that I'll get another visit
from the police.'

'Nicky, I don't know a tactful way to put this but if you
had anything to do with Ratcliffe's death, I would support
you wholeheartedly. You know that, don't you?'

'Jack, that's generous of you but I honestly had nothing
to do with his murder. Believe me, I have felt that I would
be a prime suspect if the police knew what Ratcliffe had
discovered, but I did not kill him.'

'It sounds as though this drug dealer does not have a
name or any clues as to who Ratcliffe was referring to, or
the police would be at your door pretty quickly.'

'They might follow me or bug my phone, I suppose.'

'We must never talk about it on the phone. I know we have been careful but I am just reiterating it. I'm sorry that I asked if you had something to do with it but now that it appears a woman may have been involved, I added two and two and made five. Sorry.'

'It's OK. It's natural that you should think that. The police have never found the murder weapon or Ratcliffe's computer. I wonder where they are.'

'Who knows? Destroyed, well hidden by this time.'

'I am coming to the conclusion that he must have been blackmailing someone else. The murderer could not come forward with the computer now because it is evidence and incriminating. If someone came to try to blackmail me again, I would know who had murdered Ratcliffe and that would put the blackmailer in even more jeopardy.'

'Yes, let's hope that the computer is never found, and let's hope that this drug dealer really doesn't know the name of Ratcliffe's apparent benefactor.'

As the weeks passed and there was no visit from the police and no further revelations in the papers, Nicky became resigned to having this black cloud following her around. It was never far away from her mind. She began to think that it would be better to know who had killed Ratcliffe; at least then she would feel safe from suspicion of murder. She had, of course, helped to disturb the crime scene and could well face a stiff sentence for that offence. It was, however, the not knowing which seemed to be the problem. Her initial thoughts that Jack had committed the deed, had waned as he had given no indication of his involvement and indeed, seemed to be looking at others, including herself.

Towards the end of June, Jack phoned to tell Nicky that Felicity was behaving hysterically again and suggested that she avoided the Fairfax for a day or two until she had settled.

'What triggered this episode?' she asked, wondering if Sylvie had dropped by and accused Felicity of something.

'There has been some petty stealing in the place, small things mainly but recently the staff had lost wallets and jewellery so the police were called in. They didn't interview Felicity at all but she saw them and that seemed to upset her. I don't really know why. Perhaps she knows who is pilfering things.'

'Thanks for phoning, Jack. I'll bear that in mind but we have been getting along quite well recently. Felicity even gave me a hug a few weeks ago. Maybe I could help to relax her; a friendly face, you know.'

'Well, I'll leave that to you. I just wanted to warn you in case you were planning to visit. I know you go quite frequently.'

'Thanks, Jack.'

As the afternoon wore on, Nicky found herself worrying about Felicity more and more. She had felt that there was a bond developing between them and so she decided that she would go to visit her in case she could help.

The Fairfax was quiet as she drove in and parked alongside the front door. Even the reception area seemed calm. When she asked if she could see Felicity, the nurse at reception told her that Felicity was indisposed and not available for visitors at the moment.

'Mr. Randall telephoned to say that she was upset. I thought I might be able to help calm her down.'

The mention of Jack Randall was enough to change the nurse's attitude.

'Well, if you feel that it would help, go on up. As long as Mr. Randall knows you are coming. He has given us strict instructions not to allow her visitors at the moment, but if you have discussed it with him, I'm sure that will be fine.

Nicky climbed the stairs and saw immediately that there was a problem in Felicity's room.

Dr Robertson and a colleague were standing at the door. Dr Robertson had a syringe in his hand, clearly prepared to administer its contents in an attempt to quieten the girl. Felicity was cowering in a corner, her large eyes peeping out from behind her knees, giving the impression of a terrified rabbit caught in the headlights of a car. As Doctor Robertson advanced, Felicity let out a blood curdling scream which penetrated Nicky's very soul. The room was a mess with scraps of paper all over the floor and on the table. Felicity held a pair of scissors in her right hand, trembling in fear and poised to strike.

'Excuse me, Dr Robertson. I wonder if I might help here,' Nicky offered, trying to avert the pending injection which was clearly disturbing Felicity.

Dr Robertson turned to face Nicky and said 'I don't see what help you could be right now, Miss Partington, but thanks for the offer.'

'Please let me have a few minutes with her. Perhaps she will calm down.'

Dr Robertson had retreated from the doorway and came to speak with Nicky in whispers.

'She's armed with a small pair of nail scissors and she is quite dangerous when she is riled up like this. I would advise you to steer clear. We really don't want any accidents.'

'I understand your concern but perhaps your presence is making things worse. If I go in, calmly and without any syringe, she might see that she is in no danger from me.'

'She could injure you, you know, and she may also injure herself. We really need to get these scissors away from her pronto.'

'Five minutes; let me try.'

Dr Robertson didn't seem at all pleased with the

suggestion but eventually heaved a sigh and said, 'Clive, come out for a minute.'

A doctor in a white coat backed out of the room.

'We'll stay out here, so please call if she behaves aggressively.' said Dr. Robertson. 'At the least sign of any threatening behaviour, we will be right in there.'

'Thanks.' said Nicky, wondering if she were mad to even attempt to talk to Felicity.

When the two doctors had moved away, Nicky slipped in and closed the door behind her.

'Hello, Felicity. Don't be alarmed. I'm your friend; you know that.' She sat down on the beanbag and watched Felicity's response. The wide eyes followed her but the feral keening lessened to a murmur.

Nicky talked about the doctors, saying that they wouldn't touch her and reassuring her that all would be well. She continued with all the platitudes she could come up with and Felicity became silent, although still hanging on to the scissors for dear life. 'Felicity, what was it that upset you today? Was it the policemen?'

No reply.

'Some things have gone missing in the house, and the policemen were here today to try to find out who has been taking things. No one blames you in any way.'

No movement.

'Do you know who has been pinching things, a wallet, some jewellery, that kind of thing?'

'Martha,' came the swift reply.

'Martha has been stealing things?'

'Martha.'

'Are you sure it's Martha? Is she staying here, too?'

'Martha.'

'That's very helpful, Felicity. The policemen will be able to search Martha's room and if they find the stolen things, they will go away. I'll tell Dr Robertson that it was

Martha,' she said and rose to open the door where Dr Robertson and his colleague were obviously doing their best to eavesdrop.

In earshot of Felicity, she said, 'Dr. Robertson, Felicity tells me that Martha is the thief. Have you searched her room?'

The two doctors peeked in. 'There is nobody called Martha living here at all, Miss Partington. If she is referring to Martha Wright, she was a patient here some months ago and, having responded to treatment, she has been discharged,' Dr. Robertson said firmly.

'Do you mean Martha Wright, Felicity?' Nicky asked the cowering girl. Felicity nodded.

'Yes, it is Martha Wright. Perhaps she has been visiting old friends. Have you considered that?'

'We'll ask around, but I fear she is talking nonsense,' Dr. Robertson said resignedly.

'Please ask around,' said Nicky and closed the door. Felicity had been listening to the conversation and her head was now fully visible.

Nicky sat again and smiled at Felicity.

'They will ask the others if anyone has seen Martha. Don't worry. If she took things, she will be found out.'

Felicity sat rigidly, still armed with the scissors.

Nicky looked around at the mess in the room.

'Shall I help to clear this up? It looks like confetti, as though there has been a wedding in here,' she said, smiling and kneeling on the carpet, picking up the green and white paper. There was a small silver coloured rubbish bin in the corner, lined with a polythene bag, and she brought it into the centre of the room and occupied herself collecting all the small pieces of paper. From time to time she looked up to smile at Felicity and to check that she wasn't preparing an assault on her with the scissors. She hummed a song as she worked, hoping that Felicity would relinquish the scissors voluntarily.

As she handled the bits of paper, she caught parts of the words written there and suddenly a word caught her eye- *hospital*. She paid more attention to the words and found another bit with the part word- *hysterec..* . , and then she knew exactly what Felicity had been cutting up. It was the hospital notes documenting Nicky's operations in 1994. All at once, the green colour of the files in Ratcliffe's office, came to mind. It was the same colour. Her humming stopped and she looked up at Felicity. Tears were falling down her cheeks and she had put the scissors down on the bed beside her.

Nicky sat back on her heels and thought hard about Ratcliffe's murder. It was a woman. It was carelessly executed. Felicity could take a bus or a taxi on her own. Or could someone else have put them here to incriminate Felicity? Sylvie?

Nicky resumed the tidying up, making sure that every bit was in the bucket. Then she turned to Felicity and said, 'Felicity, have you any more paper from this green folder? It's important that I destroy it all.'

The girl unfolded her legs and went to the chest of drawers. Fumbling about in numerous undergarments, she pulled out a sheaf of white papers. Nicky looked at them. They were copies of hospital records, names of births and deaths around the 30th October 1995. Ratcliffe had been doing his homework. Nicky folded up the papers and forced them all into the rubbish bag. Then she faced Felicity and asked, 'Do you have the laptop, Felicity?'

For a few minutes, Felicity stood with a vacant expression on her face, perhaps realising that Nicky knew what was hidden in her room. She wiped her face with her hands and then, standing on the edge of the wardrobe, she reached up and pulled out a brown paper bag. Coming down from the chair, she turned to Nicky and hesitantly handed it to her. It was heavy. The bag contained a black, Sony laptop.

'Thank you, Felicity,' she said. 'I'll take care of these for you. Don't worry about it.'

Nicky emptied the wastepaper contents into the brown paper bag containing the laptop and pushed in all the sheets of paper. She removed her jacket and folded it round the bag, so no-one would see it.

'Is there anything else you want me to take care of, Felicity?' she asked the pale woman with tear stains on her cheeks.

Felicity shook her head and started to cry again.

Nicky put her arms round her to comfort her and whispered, 'You must have been very frightened. I'm sorry that all this happened. I would like to have known you and been your friend. We share something very important, don't we? We are both Christopher's Mum. He so wants to know you and love you. We can make things better. We can work at this together. I'll help you in any way that I can. What you did that night a long time ago doesn't matter. You weren't right. You were sick from the pills. What you did, Felicity, saved my life because I found him. Please listen to me. No-one will ever know what happened to Ratcliffe. I'll make sure of that.'

Felicity clung to her and started to hum quietly. They stayed like that for a long time.

Suddenly Felicity stopped humming and jerked back her head, banging Nicky's chin.

'Will the police come?' she asked with a worried look on her face.

'Not for you; maybe for Martha.'

Felicity began to tremble again and Nicky hugged her close.

'You don't have to worry. I went to Ratcliffe's house and cleaned it all up. I took the knife and threw it in the river. They will never find it.'

Felicity looked at her wide-eyed and frightened. 'You need to get some sleep now. Don't worry about anything, OK?'

Felicity clearly didn't want Nicky to leave, clinging on tightly for a while but eventually with some persuasion, she went over to her bed and lay down.

Nicky picked up the scissors, dropped them into her shirt pocket, and said, 'You're not alone, Felicity. I'll always be here for you. Don't be afraid.' She kissed her lightly on the forehead, carefully picked up her jacket with its hidden contents and making sure no-one could see anything, she left the room.

Finding the two doctors leaning on the banister, she said, 'She is better now. I think she will sleep without an injection. The police seem to have frightened her but I have reassured her that all is well and that Martha will be interrogated.'

'Thank you. You did well. She obviously trusts you. We have telephoned the police about the allegation that Martha is the culprit so they are planning to visit her at home and see what, if anything, is going on. I find that a bit far fetched but you never know.'

'Well, hopefully, things will settle down now,' she said, 'and by the way, I removed the scissors from her.' She headed quickly down the stairs to the car, clutching her jacket and the concealed paper bag very tightly.

She drove home, filled with sadness for Felicity. Nicky surmised that Sylvie had told her about Ratcliffe and she had been driven to kill him. As if the girl didn't have enough worries without Sylvie burdening her with the news of the blackmailing! Felicity had moments of apparent understanding but it did worry Nicky that she had been able to find Ratciffe's address and get there by bus or taxi. Why had a taxi not been seen in Wheatfield Crescent? Why had the taxi driver not come forward? He should have remembered a fare from the Fairfax to Wheatfield Crescent and he couldn't forget an odd passenger like Felicity. How did she get back to the Fairfax? Where did she get the money? Did she ask the driver to wait while she killed him?

The more Nicky thought about it the more she believed that Felicity had not acted alone. Someone had driven her there and back. That person was someone she knew, someone she would go with and it was someone who must have thought it didn't matter or perhaps thought that it was better if she was caught. That person could not have been Jack Randall for he adored his daughter and would never hurt her, but Nicky was coming to the conclusion that Jack's wife knew more about this than she had said. How would Jack feel if he knew his wife had been involved in Ratcliffe's murder?

Nicky drove home carefully, all the while wondering what had happened to upset Felicity this particular day and trying to piece everything together. Sylvie had not been visiting Felicity this afternoon and so she could not have been blamed for the outburst. She was so fragile and sporadically volatile from all accounts. It maybe hadn't taken much to trigger her reaction, a word, a suggestion, perhaps reading the details contained in the green folder.

Once inside, Nicky removed the laptop from the paper bag and scrunched up the bag with its contents. She left the flat and walked down to the street, looking out for a rubbish bin. A few hundred yards along, there was a dumpster. She lifted the lid and tossed the bag inside. She hadn't eaten all day and bought a takeaway Hungarian goulash dish at the deli before walking back to the apartment. Clutching her meal, she headed home but suddenly someone touched her shoulder and said, 'Hello, Nicky.' Nicky turned to find Catherine Jepson, one of the secretaries she had worked with at Bradbrook, Kemp and Armstrong all these years ago.

'Gosh, how nice to meet you after all this time! How are you? Are you married yet?' she laughed because Catherine had always been looking for the right man to come along.

'Well, on that front there's bad news and good news. Which would you like first?'

'Both' said Nicky laughing.

'Well, yes, I got married to a good looking bloke called Mitch Hyland. After two years we couldn't stand the sight of each other so we are now divorced.'

'Oh, I'm sorry' said Nicky, 'but there's still time and you will be more cautious now.'

'I'm still madly totally infatuated with Mr. Amos, of course. Did you hear the news?'

'What news is that?' she asked, pretending that she was not hanging on to every word about John Amos.

'He is divorced now. That marriage was a sham from way back when. He only stayed because of the kids but now they are away, he has upped sticks and left her.'

Nicky hadn't known that. He had tried to contact her but she had not responded. Perhaps he had wanted to convey the news of his divorce to her. It was her fault. She had dissuaded him so many times, but now it hurt.

'No, I didn't know that. Well, there you are, you can make a play for him now that he is free.'

'It's not so easy now. He's left the firm, gone to be a director of something. Rumour has it that he has bought a penthouse over in Riverside Drive, so he must have plenty of money.'

'What else has been happening at the firm since I left?' she asked, her mind entirely on John Amos's divorce and change of job.

'Well, Miss Gladwyn left and we have a new girl called

Isabella. She's quite nice. Everything else is much the same. Listen, we must meet up again for a chat. Give me a call at the firm any time you are free.' Catherine said, 'I'm on my way into the deli too. It's great here, isn't it.'

Nicky said good bye and suddenly her longing for John Amos was rekindled. Why couldn't she have allowed herself to get close to him? She had ruined it all now, and he was free after all this time. Despondent, she hurried back to the flat.

Picking at the goulash, she unplugged her own laptop and exchanged it for the one she had found in Felicity's room. Unfortunately, the files were locked with a password and try as she might, she was unable to open them. There was no way that she could ask for help to open it so she decided to dispose of it safely. She deliberated as she ate her dinner thinking of a secure place where she could dispose of it. If she tossed it into a dumpster, chances were someone would think it was a great find and get help to open it. No, it had to be destroyed. She thought of the bridge where she had disposed of the knife but if she was seen at that spot behaving oddly, divers might be sent down to investigate. That was very undesirable. It was then that she remembered the view from Felicity's window. At the rear of the building were several parking places, two enormous dumpsters and a sign which had said *Furnace Room*. As she finished her meal, she decided that would be the ideal place for the laptop.

She would burn it.

It was now after 11p.m. but she decided that this had to be done as soon as possible. The laptop was vital evidence in the investigation of Ratcliffe's death and she should not be found with it in her possession. Just looking at it made her feel nervous. Finding a large, used brown envelope, she squeezed the laptop inside and sealed the edges with cello tape. She put on one of Christopher's hooded anoraks which swallowed her small frame easily and set off for the Fairfax, taking a long, indirect route through side roads and away from public scrutiny. She parked almost a mile from the clinic and walked, carrying her package under her arm. The streets were quiet and only three cars were parked by the building. These, she assumed, belonged to the staff. She skirted past the vehicles, glancing up at darkened windows to check for prying eyes but no-one was paying her any heed. She rounded the dumpsters and reached a shady corner where the furnace room door was visible. For a few minutes, she stood there waiting to see if there would be any movement in or out of the rear of the building but no-one was about. She quickly ran to the door and turned the large metal handle. Nothing happened. The door was securely locked. She was cursing herself for not anticipating this eventuality when suddenly she heard a door opening at the back of the building, and darted back to the cover of the dumpsters. An elderly porter, white haired and bent, dressed in a navy boiler suit emerged, dragging behind him two chain-linked and rattling trolleys on which numerous rubbish bags of differing hues, were piled. The man approached the dumpsters but luckily was concentrating on tossing the trash and didn't think about checking to see if anyone was hiding behind the containers. He stood on a long pedal and the lid of the dumpster flew up. He selected all the black bags, two at a time, and threw them to the back. With only the orange bags left, he redirected his noisy trolleys to the furnace door. Here he extracted a key from his overall pocket and pushed the door open. Nicky heard the clanging of metal and then the sound of scraping as though the man was clearing out the base of the furnace. She deduced that the orange bags had to be disposed of in the furnace. Since the man seemed pre-occupied, she ran over to the rear of the second trolley and tried to open one of the bags. There were strong plastic ties holding them tightly and she couldn't undo the tie. The porter came out of the furnace room and heaved two large bags inside. Nicky ducked down and frantically thought of some way to open the bag without raising any suspicion. Suddenly, she remembered that she had Felicity's scissors in her pocket and so she quickly cut through the ties and slipped the laptop inside. She had just managed to knot the ends of the bag when the porter appeared again and lifted another two bags. Quickly, she ran back to the cover of the dumpsters and hid, breathless with worry more than exertion, wondering if the porter would notice the missing tie and hold back the bag from incineration. She didn't need to worry in the event, as he hefted the two remaining bags and disappeared inside with them. She heard a metal clanging noise again and hoped that it signified that all the bags had been disposed of in the furnace. The porter locked the furnace door and trailed his empty, clattering trolleys back into the building. Nicky waited to see if anyone else would venture out but it was all quiet. Looking up, she saw that the pink curtains at Felicity's window were drawn. As she had watched the porter disappearing back inside the building, she noticed that the broken plastic tie was lying on the tarmac. She waited for a few minutes and then went over to retrieve it before sneaking past the cars again and making her way back along the road, the hood of the anorak pulled well down over her face. She tossed the tie into the first wheelie bin she passed.

Driving home, she worried about Felicity, wondering whether she would relax now that the incriminating evidence had been removed from her room. She hoped that she would revert to her previous, so-called normal state. There was nothing to remind her now. She wouldn't have to worry if the police came back. The more Nicky thought about Ratcliffe's murder, the more convinced she was that Felicity could not have killed Ratcliffe alone. She had to get to his house and that meant someone had to take her there in a car or a taxi. She also had to come back again. The careless murder, leaving the weapon and probably leaving fingerprints suggested that the attack was not planned well. Someone had scoured the files and removed the offending one; someone who knew what to look for, but was Felicity able to concentrate to that extent? Nicky thought that was unlikely. Could Sylvie have gone with Felicity? Could they have done this together? Nicky couldn't imagine why Sylvie would take a disturbed girl with her when she had to deal with Ratcliffe. Who knows what Felicity could have done, and in any event, Felicity didn't like Sylvie, from what she had heard. The only alternative seemed to be that Sylvie had carried out the whole thing and then concealed the evidence in Felicity's room deliberately. If the police had found the laptop or the file, Felicity would have been the prime suspect even if she was considered insane or unfit to plead. She had the evidence and she had motive. In her disturbed state of mind, she would be placed in an institution but not sent to prison. Sylvie would never have her at home again. Was that at the back of this? Was she so jealous of Jack's love for his daughter?

For the rest of the evening, she paced around, drinking coffee and tossing about her theories as to how Jeremy Ratcliffe was murdered. It occurred to her that she could tell Jack about the discovery of the laptop and the file. What would he make of that? Could he have driven to Ratcliffe's? Was he the murderer? She dismissed this theory because the police now thought it was a woman they were looking for, because Jack would have planned the murder much more carefully and he would never have left the evidence in Felicity's room. No, that was not Jack. Hard man as he was, he did love his daughter and looked after her in every way.

Nicky's thoughts turned to Alex Sanderson and she wondered what he would do in her situation How she wished she could talk to him about it and unload her concerns, but at the end of the day, she knew that she couldn't discuss this with anyone. Perhaps she attracted problems like this. It seemed to her that her whole life had been spent as the sole person who knew the truth about certain events. It had all stemmed from that night when she found Christopher and even now, after she had spilled the beans to Alex, Christopher, Jack and Sylvie, there were still more secrets which were burdening her and she could not share them. Would this ever end?

Weeks passed and the newspapers gave up on the story of Ratcliffe. Nothing new had emerged and the story had gone stale. Nicky had heard of no further histrionics from Felicity.

It was the university holidays and Jack invited Christopher and Nicky for lunch. The weather was fine and lunch was served in the back garden on a wide patio surrounded by ornate pots filled with strongly scented red roses. In answer to Jack's questions, Christopher talked at length about his course, his enthusiasm for the work and his future. Sylvie drank a great deal of white wine and became increasingly talkative. She asked Christopher about Bobbi and about the possibility of marriage. Christopher laughed and said, 'We are both too young to get married and Bobbi wants to do so much in her own career. We both know that our relationship is not nearly ready for a permanent commitment.'

'Quite right,' said Jack. 'There's a time for marriage and if she is the one, she will still be there when that time comes.'

'I was just thinking how nice it would be to have a marquee in this garden. When you do decide to get married, we would love you to have it here, wouldn't we, Jack?'

Sylvie slurred.

'If that is what you want, of course, we would love that.' Jack answered.

'That's very kind and I will bear it in mind,' said Christopher,' but as I said, that is something for the future. So don't order the marquee just yet.'

He smiled and hoped the conversation would alter course.

Peters approached the table and quietly informed Jack that there was a phone call from the Fairfax. Jack excused himself and walked smartly into the house, looking serious.

'Oh, I hope Felicity hasn't been acting strangely again. She seems to explode sometimes and behave rather bizarrely. Jack gets so upset when he hears bad news about her. Perhaps the doctors need to increase her medication,' remarked Sylvie, pouring herself another drink.

'I went along to the Fairfax a few weeks ago when she was giving a bit of trouble,' Nicky said.

'Did you?' asked Sylvie, staring at her, accusingly.

'Jack had telephoned to let me know that it wasn't the best day to visit, but I have felt recently that we were developing a sort of bond, and so I went along to see if I could get through to her.'

'And did you, Mum?' Christopher asked, clearly interested.

'Yes, I just talked to her, tried to explain that all was well, the usual platitudes and she eventually relaxed.'

'What do you think had triggered her mood?' he asked.

'I don't know exactly but there had been police at the home that day. There has been a bit of thieving going on and the police went along to see if they could solve the problem. Felicity had seen the two policemen, it seems, and then she started screaming.'

'Why would the police worry her? Do you think she had anything to do with the thefts?' he asked.

'I don't know. Felicity told me that someone called Martha was the culprit but I didn't hear any more about it.'

'Perhaps she feels guilty about something?' suggested Sylvie, finishing her large glass of wine.

'She has been cloistered in there for years. What could she possibly have done?' asked Nicky.

'Well, she can go out if she wants to. We don't know her every movement.'

'I asked the staff about that and they told me that she only came here to Beaulieu on any outings and then she was picked up in the car either by Jack or by you, Sylvie. So she doesn't seem to make much use of her freedom,' Nicky added.

Jack Randall returned to the table, looking concerned, with deep furrows running across his forehead.

'Felicity is a bit upset, apparently. I think I'll pop along to see what is happening.'

'May I come too?' asked Christopher, rising.

'Yes, if you want to.' Jack replied.

'Nicky and I will enjoy our coffee out here until you return then,' said Sylvie.

'There's no point in all of us going, is there?'

'No, that's fine. We'll not be long,' Jack said, and the two men walked off.

Sylvie drank the dregs of wine in her glass.

'More wine?' she enquired of Nicky.

'No thanks, I think I'll wait for the coffee.'

'Peters, we are ready for the coffee,' she waved at the butler who bowed politely and disappeared into the house.

'Felicity's tantrums do get rather boring, I must say,' said Sylvie. 'Jack is forever dashing back and forth to that blessed home. She has been there all of our married life, you know. It just gets tiresome.' Sylvie slurred.

'It's a great pity, such a waste of a life. Jack has lost a great deal because of her illness.' said Nicky.

'That's true, and he might have lost a great deal more if …if Ratcliffe hadn't been murdered. That was a blessing if ever there was one,' she replied.

'No-one has been arrested for that. I saw an article suggesting that a woman might have been involved. Did you see that?' Nicky asked.

'Yes, but they didn't release any details, did they?' Sylvie said.

'No, but that doesn't always mean that there aren't any details. They might be keeping snippets to themselves to see if they can trip someone up.'

Sylvie reached for the wine again as Peters arrived with a tray laden with coffee cups and a large glass pot from which steam emerged.

'Thank you,' said Nicky.

Sylvie's hands were very unsteady. She laughed and joked that she had had too much to drink. Nicky took over the pouring of the coffee and handed her a cup. She placed it on the table in front of her and filled her wine glass again. For a few minutes they sat silently and then Sylvie said, 'I think Felicity killed him.'

'Why would you think that? What motive would she have?' asked Nicky.

'She had all the same motives as you and Jack, but she isn't normal, so really, she doesn't need a motive. She could just see him on the television and take a dislike to him, for all I know.'

'That's a bit far-fetched,' said Nicky.

'I dare say that she didn't want the revelations which Ratcliffe would make, to come out. What light would that put her in? She tried to murder her unborn baby by taking drugs and then tried to dispose of him in the woods. That wouldn't be very nice publicity, would it? She may have thought that she was protecting Jack from all of that.'

'But do you really think that she knows about Ratcliffe?

Does she read newspapers and how would she know where he stayed? How would she get to his house? She doesn't have a car and frankly I don't think she has the mental capability of doing such a thing.'

'You might be surprised. Sometimes she has surprised me, I can tell you. Besides, she watches a lot of television and there has been so much information about Ratcliffe's house in the Wheatfield estate, that it wouldn't take Einstein to work that out.'

'Well, his whereabouts have only come to light *after* his murder, not *before*.' said Nicky.

'She could have looked at a telephone directory. Surely his name and address will be there for anyone to read.'

'Yes, but then someone had to have told her that Jeremy Ratcliffe was a threat to her. Someone must have informed her of my connection to Ratcliffe. Who would do that?'

'I suppose that I might have discussed the matter with her. Perhaps I did mention the connection,' Sylvie confessed.

'So, what you are suggesting is that after hearing about him from you, Felicity looked up his address and set off to kill him?'

'Yes, she would not want him to make the connection to her.'

'So, how did she get the knife?'

'It's probably one from the kitchen at the Fairfax. It's not so hard to get a knife. She could have bought it.'

'What colour are the kitchen knife handles at Beaulieu?'

'Why do you ask that? I don't know. I'm never in the kitchen.'

'So, Felicity bought a knife and set off to Wheatfield Crescent?'

'I suppose so.'

'How did she get there? She doesn't have a car.'

'She could have taken a taxi.'

'No taxi driver has come forward to say that he took a young girl from the Fairfax to Ratcliffe's address, and she behaves in an odd way. A taxi driver would remember a trip like that.'

'She might have just asked to be dropped off on the main road, not in the estate.'

'She would have to be an amazingly well organised person to have thought all of this out.'

'She's not as deranged as you think she is,'

'Obviously not. She had to check through the files in Ratcliffe's house and had the presence of mind to take the laptop too. What about her fingerprints? Did she wear gloves?'

'I expect so. The police haven't found any, have they?'

'No, or perhaps they have, but at the moment, they don't have the murderer's on record.'

Sylvie stood up. 'I think I should go to the Fairfax and see what is happening. I'm not going to be able to settle until I know Felicity is all right.'

'Dr. Robertson seems to think that Felicity is disturbed by your visits and I think the computer teacher, Miss Stanwick, spoke to you about that too. Perhaps we should just let Jack handle her.'

'That's nonsense,' retorted Sylvie, standing up unsteadily, 'Just because I take a firm line with her, and don't mollycoddle her like everybody else, doesn't mean to say that I don't care for the girl. I certainly don't set out to disturb her. God knows, she has everything she could possibly want there. I find that very insulting and hasn't a thing to do with Miss Stanwick or Dr. Robertson for that matter.'

'Very well. If you insist on going, I'll drive,' said Nicky.

.Sylvie didn't look too pleased. 'It's not necessary for you to come too. Why don't you just get off home? I'll see that Jack drops Christopher off when we leave,' she said.

'You've had quite a lot to drink, Sylvie. I don't think you should be driving. It's no trouble for me to take you and I can check the situation too.

'Peters could take me,' Sylvie persisted.

'Let's not bother Peters. I really want to go, in any case. Occasionally, I have managed to get through to Felicity and maybe I'll be of some use; you never know.' said Nicky firmly, walking to the car.

It didn't take long to get to the Fairfax Clinic. Sylvie said very little on the journey, clearly tossing over the previous doubts which Nicky had voiced.

'Hello, Mrs. Randall, Miss Partington. You will be looking for Felicity?' the pleasant nurse on reception said. 'I'm afraid she has been taken down to the treatment room. She was very agitated this afternoon and the doctor thought it best if she was sedated, I believe your husband and another gentleman are with her there.'

'Do you know why she was so upset?' asked Nicky.

'I'm not too sure but the police were here again today, just to follow up on their enquiries about the stealing that is going on, and it may have been the sight of them. That seemed to have something to do with it last time,' she said.

'Did the police find the thief?' Nicky asked.

'Yes, it was Martha, a patient who spent some time here before. She had kept copies of the keys, and had been popping back to take things. Lots of stolen property was found at her home apparently. So she was arrested and that's all sorted, thank goodness,' she answered.

'I would like to wait in Felicity's room,' Sylvie said.

'Yes, go ahead,' the nurse said. 'I'll tell Mr. Randall that you are here.'

As they walked up the stairs, with Sylvie holding on to

the banister for support, she turned to Nicky and said, 'Why don't you just go home, Nicky? I'll have Jack take me home and he will drop Christopher off at your house. There's no point in your wasting time here. It could be a long time before we know what's happening.'

'I'll wait for a little while to see that Felicity is all right, if you don't mind.' she said, getting the clear message that she wasn't wanted.

Sylvie resigned herself to Nicky's presence and entered Felicity's room.

'We must get her a larger place. She has so much furniture in here, there's barely room to swing a cat. The television is far too big and she has all these horrid videos. Have you seen the titles? All violent or creepy films. No wonder she is disturbed,' she said, picking up the DVDs one by one and reading the labels.

'It's a cosy room with all the pink colours.' said Nicky.

'It's just like her bedroom at home. That was Jack's idea, to make her feel at home. She always loved pink things but she is older now and it is rather girlish, isn't it? Maybe a more mature decor would be better.'

Sylvie opened the doors of the built-in wardrobe and started to look through all the clothes.

'This is stuffed with expensive outfits and she doesn't wear any of it, only her jeans and a variety of tops,' she commented.

'Once when I was here, she had on a white dress, a frilly, soft material. It made her look very young and innocent.' Nicky said, remembering her first visit to Felicity.

Sylvie closed the doors of the cupboard and started opening the drawers in the dressing table. She fumbled about in all of them, tossing undergarments around, and then became more frantic as her hands did not find what she was looking for.

'Why don't you sit down and relax?' suggested Nicky, beginning to see that her suspicions about Sylvie were correct. She seemed to be searching for the incriminating papers which had now all been disposed of.

Sylvie sat on the edge of the bed, twisting her hands and looking anxiously around.

'I'm worried about her.' After a few restless minutes, she stood again and started to go through the drawers again. 'I'll just occupy myself by tidying her things,' she said.

Nicky stood too and moved over to the window, leaning on the sill. Down below, a large dumper truck was reversing into the yard, its bleating warning signal heralding its arrival. The elderly porter she had seen previously trailing the bags to the dumpsters and to the incinerator, was waving to the driver, helping to guide him close to the two large black containers. Eventually the driver stopped and hopped out of the vehicle. The two men heaved the first container into position alongside the truck and with the press of a lever, the huge bin was lifted slowly up and its contents tipped into the back of the lorry.

'Maybe Jack killed Ratcliffe? Have you considered that, Sylvie?' Nicky asked.

'It wasn't Jack.'

'He had the motive, the weapon and the opportunity.'

'Jack couldn't kill anybody. He is a gentle person. It wasn't Jack.'

'You sound very sure about that.'

'I am sure. He didn't do it.'

The second rubbish container had been elevated into position and soon was pouring its bags and boxes into the lorry. Nicky watched as the two men then went to the furnace room and together wheeled out a long coffin shaped metal box full of ashes. They had almost reached the lorry when the driver turned and picked something out of the mounds of grey ash. Nicky could see what it was and held her breath. It was a mangled, charred laptop.

The two men examined the object together, turning it this way and that and then, shrugging his shoulders, the driver tossed it nonchalantly into the back of the truck.

Nicky breathed again. The ashes were deposited into the lorry and the rattling metal crate returned to the furnace room.

'The last time Felicity became hysterical, I came to speak to her. She had got hold of some scissors and the doctors were concerned that she would hurt herself.'

'She has done that several times.' said Sylvie, folding a pair of white silk pyjamas.

'She didn't want the scissors to harm herself. She was cutting something up. There were millions of little bits of paper, like confetti, all over the floor.'

'What was it?'

'It looked like a green folder and white paper.'

'Sylvie stopped folding the clothes and looked at Nicky. 'Could you read any of the papers? Do you know what it was?' she asked tensely.

'No, she had made sure that it was unreadable.'

Sylvie's shoulders seemed to relax and she resumed her drawer tidying therapy.

'I asked her what it was and she could only say one word, again and again.'

'What word?'

'Your name- Sylvie, Sylvie.'

'She blames me for everything. She has always resented me for taking her father away from her. That's how she sees it. What could I do? I was in love with Jack and he with me. I tried to befriend the girl but she was having none of it. I wasn't her mother and that was that.'

Nicky came back to sit on the beanbag, crossed her legs and wondered about Sylvie. She had as much motive as Jack and Felicity. If Jack were to lose his standing in the community and possibly his money, she would suffer. She would not be able to enjoy the expensive lifestyle which she loved so much. She had known where Ratcliffe lived and she was much more capable of formulating a plan to kill him. Was all of this drinking to excess, this restless hyperactivity, a sign of stress because she had committed the murder? Nicky was beginning to come to that conclusion.

'I suppose you might be considered a suspect too, in Ratcliffe's murder, after all you have a lot to lose too,' she suggested.

Sylvie turned angrily to her and shouted, 'I haven't done anything. How can you even think such a thing?'

'I'm just going through the possibilities. You have more motive than I have,' Nicky replied angrily.

Sylvie turned her back on Nicky and pulled out another drawer.

'You're right, of course, but I didn't kill him. I can't say that I'm sorry he is dead, however.'

'We are all happy that he is dead,' Sylvie answered, reaching into the back of the drawer.

'If Felicity was found guilty, she would be placed in a secure unit of some sort. She wouldn't be allowed to stay here in the Fairfax. She would be considered a danger to others.'

'I suppose.'

'Jack would be devastated.'

Sylvie began to cry and kept her back to Nicky.

'You killed him, didn't you, Sylvie?' Nicky asked softly, 'and then you planted the file and the laptop here to incriminate Felicity.

Sylvie shook her head and sobbed, 'No, no.'

'Felicity had cut up that green file into smithereens. I picked up every bit and dumped it,' she explained to Sylvie. 'You can stop searching in there. You won't find anything and the laptop is not there, either. I think Felicity understood what you had done, that you planted the evidence here to entrap her for the killing of Ratcliffe, and every time she sees the police, she fears that they have come to charge her. I think that this is the reason for these hysterical outbursts.'

'You can't prove any of that,' Sylvie said, sitting on the bed now, her shoulders slouched.

'You weren't very careful at the crime scene,' Nicky continued. 'All your fingerprints must have been on the files. The knife, too. That would have been covered in fingerprints. Did it come from the kitchen at Beaulieu, or did you take one from the Fairfax to incriminate Felicity? If it matches the other knives here, that would be a significant breakthrough for the police. Didn't you worry that the forensic examination would find your prints?'

'I didn't take the …' she began, and then realised that she had all but admitted that she had done it. She dissolved into tears, buried her face in her hands and her whole body shook with fear.

Nicky waited, watching Sylvie's patent distress and then said, 'It wouldn't serve any purpose for me to tell the police about this now and I don't plan to do that.'

'How did you know about the knife?' Sylvie asked, tearfully.

'I guessed,' she said. 'Tell me about it. You took a tremendous risk driving to the Wheatfield estate in your car and no doubt, dressed in one of your designer outfits. Somebody must have noticed you in that environment.'

'You take me for a fool. I may not have your education but I'm not completely thick and I did think about it a lot beforehand.'

She sat looking angry and insulted, but then started again. 'After you left on Wednesday morning, Jack had to tell me the story. I shouted at him until he gave in. He eventually broke down and it all came out, piece by piece. I found it incredible and felt that we were so vulnerable if this horrible man, Ratcliffe, told the police. I just couldn't get it out of my head. I could see Jack's name on the front page of every newspaper, his photograph on the television, and that journalist spelling out all that Jack and Felicity had done.'

'Jack said that you had taken it badly at first.'

'He made me take some sleeping tablets to calm down, but all that night and on Thursday, too, I thought about what should be done. We couldn't just let it be, let Ratcliffe dictate what was happening. Something had to be done. By Friday morning, I had worked out a plan. Jack was going out of town that day on business and I didn't want to drive my own car to the estate. I'm not totally mad.'

Nicky waited while Sylvie dabbed her eyes and changed position on the bed. 'There was a potted plant, an orchid in the dining room. I took it to my car, lifted it out of its pot and scattered earth all over the passenger seat. Then I called the garage and asked someone to pick up my car for valetting, explaining that I had had an accident and had dropped a potted plant all over the seat. A man came almost immediately to collect it. Then I asked Peters if I might borrow his Astra for an hour or so. Of course, he agreed.'

'Did you park outside Ratcliffe's house?' Nicky asked.

'No, of course not,' she said grumpily. 'I was dressed in one of my *designer* outfits, as you call them, but I had rummaged through Felicity's wardrobe and found a pair of jeans and a duffle coat and a pair of leather gloves. I wore my trainers and planned to stuff all my hair into a beret. So, I left the house looking my usual self, but I was carrying a bag with all of these things in it, as well as a kitchen knife. It wasn't part of a set. I found it in a drawer along with lots of other knives. I'm sure it had been there for a long time and there were so many others, I didn't think Esther would miss it.'

'It took a lot of courage to embark on this route,' Nicky said, thinking that maybe she had underestimated Sylvie.

'I pulled into a quiet side road about two miles short of the estate and changed my clothes. Then I parked at one end of Wheatfield Crescent and walked down to his house, carrying the knife in a newspaper. When I rang the bell, he appeared at the door, looking pretty dishevelled and I saw that he was much bigger than me. I must say that I was quite frightened at that point. Anyway, I made up a story to tell him. I had been reading a novel about a girl called Carol Barnaby and so I told him that my name was Carol Barnaby and that I was your cousin.'

'What did he say?'

'At first he didn't say anything. He just stared at me. His eyes were wide and sort of glazed over and I wondered if he had been taking drugs.'

'He seemed to have that habit.'

'Yes, well, I prattled on that I knew all about Christopher and how he came to be your son, and asked if we might discuss the matter, implying that I might have some useful information for him.'

'What did he do?'

'He opened the door wide and invited me in. He led me through to a small study and offered me a seat. His laptop was open on the desk and it looked as though he was busy writing an article or something. He asked if I would excuse him for two minutes while he saved his work and shut down the computer, so I sat and waited, wondering what on earth I was going to say. Luckily the phone rang just as he was finishing, and he picked it up and started to talk. I had the impression that someone was asking him when his story was to be ready. It seemed like an opportune moment. He wasn't expecting me to attack him and had his back to me. I took out the knife and rammed it into his chest just as he put the phone down.'

Sylvie held her head in her hands and sobbed again. 'It was horrible,' she said, shivering. 'He tried to move his arms and looked up at me with a surprised look on his face. Then he just fell forward onto the desk. I staggered backwards and fell over a coffee table, knocking a lamp down and landed next to a filing cabinet. I hurt my arm on the corner of it,' she said, rubbing her left shoulder.

Sylvie composed herself again and went on, 'I quickly flicked through the files in the cabinet and found one with your initials on it, N.P. There were quite a few sheets of paper so I just picked up the whole folder. Then I noticed that his laptop was making a funny noise. His hand was leaning on the keyboard, so I removed it and unplugged the laptop. I wrapped the folder and the laptop in a newspaper and got out of the house. I did have gloves on all the time, Nicky, so I don't think there would have been any fingerprints.'

'That's a relief.'

'I walked back to the Astra, drove to the quiet street again and changed into my proper clothes. On the way home, I dropped Felicity's clothes, the beret and the gloves into a clothes recycling box outside a charity shop.'

'Well, you covered your tracks but I suppose someone might recall a well polished, blue Astra.'

'I thought about that too, and I would hate to involve Peters in this mess, in any way. He is retiring in six months' time and he and his wife are going back to live in Dorset where they have a son, Michael. Jack and I want to give him a substantial present for his long service, so I suggested that we buy him a new car. Jack agreed and asked me to approach him on the subject. He has had three Astras in a row and it took some persuasion to choose something else. After a lot of talking, I persuaded him to give his Astra to his son, Michael, and buy a new Honda

Accord, which was one of the designs he said that he liked. To cut a long story short, he drove down to Dorset last weekend, gave the Astra to Michael and came home by train. The Honda was ready to be picked up on Thursday, so he is now proudly driving that around.'

'You did well, Sylvie. At least now, that is unlikely to be a problem. Well, I suppose we just have to sit it out now and wait to see what emerges.'

'You won't tell Jack, will you?' she begged, 'I wanted to protect him. He doesn't deserve all of this and I love him so much. He would lose his reputation and a great deal of money. Our names would be mud if everybody knew about Christopher. We couldn't have it come out, don't you see?' she pleaded, 'Please don't tell. I know it was wrong. I was in such a state, all the repercussions whirling round in my brain. It was unkind to involve Felicity with the evidence but she was the cause of all this trouble. Somehow I felt that she was to blame. She should shoulder the responsibility for all of this heartache,' she said.

'No, it wasn't a good move. Felicity's behaviour is already drawing suspicion. Even the receptionist has realised that the police make her uncomfortable.'

'It was shocking. I wasn't thinking properly. I've been out of my mind with worry,' Sylvie said, dabbing her eyes with her handkerchief. 'I promise never to do anything to hurt Felicity again. It has been so hard. You, of all people must know what a disaster it would be if the circumstances of Christopher's birth were known. I'll promise anything if you can just keep this to yourself. Am I asking too much, Nicky? We are going to live in Switzerland. Jack has made that decision, so we won't be in this country. He is almost 65. Could you please at least keep it a secret for a few years longer? It doesn't matter about me. I just want to protect him. Could you keep it a secret for a while?' she beseeched Nicky, tears streaming down her face.

Nicky sighed deeply and turned to face Sylvie whose face was red and blotchy, her whole body trembling uncontrollably.

'Won't you tell Jack what you have done?' she asked.

'Oh, God, no, I can't do that. Don't make me, please. He would leave me if he knew.'

'Do you think that you can carry on in this marriage knowing that there are such massive secrets between you? What sort of marriage will it be?' Nicky asked her.

'All couples have secrets. It is fantasy to think otherwise. There are lots of things I don't discuss with Jack. He's a busy man and he wouldn't want to hear all about my petty bits and pieces. What I did, I did for him. People think that I married Jack for his money, but I didn't. I had admired him for years and fell head over heels in love with him. After his first wife died, he was lonely and he needed me. Felicity was a constant worry for him. We have a solid marriage and this won't change things. I'll say nothing and hopefully it won't ever come to light. It all depends on you now,' she said, her eyes anxiously seeking reassurance.

'Can you find it in your heart to keep quiet, Nicky? I would be so grateful,' she said beseechingly.

Nicky stood up in front of her for a few moments and then said, 'When it comes to keeping secrets, I'm an expert, Sylvie. I have a few of my own.'

Sylvie looked up at her and stretched out to take her hand, 'Thank you so much. I know that I will have to live with this for the rest of my life and, you're right, I didn't think enough about it. I made mistakes and the police could still name me as a suspect any day, but my marriage is everything to me and if I can hold it together, that will be wonderful. Jack doesn't deserve all of this worry. All he ever did was help Felicity.'

'I disposed of all the documents in the green file,

Sylvie, and the laptop too, is now out of harm's way. That evidence at least, is no longer a concern.'

'Oh, thank you. I have been so worried about it. I was planning to remove it all by myself but you have beaten me to it. I've been so silly. If anyone else had found it, the truth could have been discovered.'

'I'm going to head off home, now. Will you wait for Jack and Christopher?' Nicky said.

'Yes, I'll wait,' she said quietly.

Jack dropped Christopher home later that evening and Nicky sat up with him discussing the day's events but omitting her conversation with Sylvie. Christopher had witnessed Felicity's manic behaviour and had been affected by the experience. He seemed sad and quiet. Nicky tried to talk about other subjects, reminding him of his second forthcoming visit to Virginia to visit the Sanderson household and soon he brightened up.

'You seem to be in good spirits,' he remarked as they sipped hot chocolate together that evening.

'Well, I'm happy to have you home and glad that you have so much to look forward to. Although Felicity has her problems, I think she is well cared for and I have a feeling that she will settle down now. Something triggered her anxiety, maybe the police visit, and hopefully now the trigger has gone, she will be OK. The police won't need to return, having arrested the person responsible for the thieving.'

'Have you seen anything of John Amos recently?' he asked innocently, changing the subject and surprising her.

'Not for a while. I believe he has left Bradbrook, Kemp and Armstrong. I shall have to renew my contact with him. Why do you ask?'

'He is a nice guy and I know you like him; that's all,' he said, setting his mug down on the table and rising.

'Have a bath, Chris, if you want. I'll just watch the

news for a while before I turn in,' she said.

He bent down to kiss her goodnight and went off to bed.

Nicky relaxed in her large armchair and tucked her feet under her, still cradling the remains of her hot chocolate. She felt relieved to have extracted Sylvie's confession but it still worried her that some clue could have been left behind. The evidence had been disposed of and hopefully the trail would not incriminate Sylvie. There was nothing further she could do about Ratcliffe. Sylvie really did love Jack. Perhaps she also loved the life she led, but she really did love him. She had killed for love. Her intention to involve Felicity was nasty, most likely driven by jealousy, but ultimately she had seen the error of her ways and as time passed, it seemed less and less likely that an arrest would be made. There was no way that she herself could inform the police. She had disturbed the crime scene, destroyed evidence and would merit a custodial sentence. The entire story would be exposed and while, before Ratcliffe' death, the truth was damaging, the consequences were now much, much worse. There seemed to be some innate flaw in her temperament, she surmised. Looking back over the last seventeen years, she had carried out some extraordinary and even criminal acts, all done to protect Christopher, all done for love. She didn't consider Sylvie a risk to others and she didn't really feel she was a bad person either. How long would she be allowed to continue without all hell breaking loose?

She switched on the television and turned the volume down low. The news stories were old and of no major interest to her and she wanted to think a bit more about something Sylvie had said. *All couples have secrets. It's fantasy to think otherwise.* Maybe she had been wrong in distancing herself from John Amos. She had heard about his divorce and he was never far from her thoughts.

33

The following day, Christopher caught the train to university and Nicky returned to work, switching off her thoughts about Ratcliffe. There was nothing further she could do on that score and it was just a question of waiting to see if some further evidence emerged.

Somehow, Sylvie's remarks had rekindled her thoughts of John Amos. He had left Bradbrook, Kemp and Armstrong after years in the firm and his marriage had finished too, so he was making life changing decisions. Nicky couldn't help wondering what he was doing. He hadn't informed her of his latest moves and it did concern her that he might have found someone else, someone who could return his love and someone who had less baggage than she had. There had been so many secrets. Now, some of these were much more out in the open than before. She had been in love with John Amos as long as she could remember and she still wasn't sure what he would make of her past, but she owed it to herself to give it one last shot. She had nothing to lose. It was Sylvie who had said, All *couples have secrets.* Maybe it could work. She had to try.

As the day progressed, she ploughed through the work on her desk but from time to time, she paused to plan what to do. At first she had considered giving him a ring but finally she decided to visit him in his new apartment. The luxury Riverside apartments were not far and although she didn't know exactly where he stayed, she was sure she could find out. There couldn't possibly be two people called Amos. She left the office at around 6 p.m. with a plan forming in her mind.

She showered, doused herself in her favourite perfume, Joy by Jean Patou, spent some time getting her hair and makeup perfect and then dressed in her cream silk suit which had hardly been worn.

As she closed her front door, she found herself saying *Good luck* to herself. It was roughly four miles to the new Riverside apartment blocks. It was dark as she circled around searching for the main entrance but eventually she located the well illuminated reception area. As she entered the plush foyer, a smartly attired security man scrutinised her and said, 'Good evening, Ma'am.'

'Good evening,' she responded. 'I have come to visit Mr. Amos, John Amos.'

'Oh, yes, that will be the penthouse, number 5 elevator, just behind you, Ma'am.'

'Thank you,' she said.

She seemed to sail up the twelve floors without noticing and alighted outside his door. Nervously, she raised her hand to press the buzzer but suddenly heard a female voice from inside.

'You need a maid, you're so untidy' she heard, and then some girlish laughter. Her heart sank. He had found someone else. She was too late. She was on the point of leaving when the door burst open and a lively bright eyed young girl barged out, carrying several bags.

'Sorry,' said Nicky as the two almost collided.

'It's OK. It's Miss Partington, isn't it? I recognise you from the newspapers. I'm Gillian Amos. Dad is in the shower, please go in and make yourself at home. I'm sure he will be pleased to see you,' she said cheerily, and bounced off down the corridor.

Nicky's spirits rose and she tentatively entered the

elegant apartment, her sandals sinking into the deep pile of the white carpet. She walked into the sitting room, impressed by the size of it and the tasteful decor. Along one side was a huge window which afforded one a panoramic view of the town.

On a small coffee table, there was an opened bottle of champagne and two half empty glasses. She lifted the glasses and went to explore the kitchen, fully fitted with every conceivable gadget. She rinsed the glasses and took them back to the sitting room, refilled them from the large champagne bottle and carried them with her to find John Amos. There was the sound of a shower running, coming from somewhere so she followed the noise. It led her to the master bedroom, situated alongside the sitting room, the large window again offering spectacular views. There were unpacked cases and boxes lying around. It was clear that he hadn't moved in long ago. She placed the glasses on the bedside table and lay down on the king size bed, kicked off her shoes and gazed out at the display of lights. A few minutes later, the shower stopped running and John emerged, only a towel round his waist.

For a moment, he was startled to find her there.

'Hello, stranger. How are you?' he then said, laughing. 'Some security system I have here. How did you get in?'

'Gill let me in as she was leaving.' she said, sitting up and admiring his bare chest.

'It's good to see you, Nicky. I've missed you.' he said, coming to join her on the bed.

'I've missed you, too, and someone told me that you had been making some changes to your life lately. I wanted to see that you were all right.'

'I've left Bradbrook's and my marriage is over. The kids are all grown up and we felt that it was time to be decisive about our situation. It has been a facade for years and we both knew that. The whole separation thing has been fairly amicable as these things go and frankly it is a great relief to me to sever that bond.'

Nicky ran her hands over his chest and slowly slid them downwards.

'You didn't come for coffee, then?' he asked as she pulled the towel away.

'Maybe later,' she whispered, loosening her top.

They made love passionately and eagerly, both releasing pent up feelings of need and love. It had been a long time since they had been together but nothing had changed. The longing, the wanting was still as strong as ever.

Lying on the bed, nestling together, John explained, 'You know that living here is a fresh start for me. Perhaps Carol and I should have separated earlier but we felt the kids were most important so we waited. The kids are not kids any more. Both of them are making their own way in life and they accepted the split without too much angst. Christopher is moving on, too, isn't he? You must feel that you are not required quite as much as before.'

'Yes, I miss him a lot but it is good to see him standing on his own two feet.'

John leaned over to kiss her forehead and said, 'I know that you have always kept your distance from me and perhaps that was entirely because of my marriage. Maybe there is some other reason, but you must know, Nicky, that I have always loved you. What we have is so special and over the years I have known you, my feelings have never changed. I was frightened to approach you again; frightened that you would send me packing again. Having you turn up like this is something I didn't expect.'

Nicky wrapped her arms round him and whispered, 'I fell in love with you that first day we met at Bradbrook's and I have struggled with my feelings for a long time, not because I didn't love you and not entirely because you were married. I had other personal reasons for distancing myself.'

John ran his hand over her hair and then lifted her chin up to kiss her. It was a soft long and deep kiss which elicited strong emotions and desires. He pulled away and looked into her eyes, 'Nicky, marry me; please marry me,' he said, longingly.

'I would love to marry you, but there are things I have to tell you before we lose all sense of reason,' she said, lying back and looking up at the ceiling.

'Just tell me you love me. That's all I want to hear,' he said. They caressed each other and Nicky knew that her confessions would have to wait as they made love again so tenderly. They lay together, his head nestling on her shoulder.

'OK, I'm ready,' he said, breathing heavily, 'I guess I'm not as young as I used to be. Sorry if I don't match up to your previous beaux.'

'There have never been any other men in my life, John. I have never made love with any other man,' she said.

'Objection, your Honour, we have proof that the plaintiff has had previous lovers,' said John firmly, leaning up on his elbow to study her.

'And what proof is that?'

'Christopher,' he said, simply. 'Your son, Christopher.'

'And have you DNA proof that Christopher is my son?'

He looked at her quizzically and asked, 'What are you saying?'

'You have just lost the case, my learned friend, because you didn't do your homework. Christopher is not my son.'

John sat up on the bed and continued to stare at her, puzzled.

'You have a bit of explaining to do, Mrs. Amos.'

She smiled at him. 'Shall we have coffee while I tell you all?'

'OK, but only if you promise to return here, later.'

'I promise,' she said, pulling him to her.

They sat side by side on the long sofa in the sitting room, wrapped in white towelling robes, his arm around her shoulders, sipping coffee.

'Fire away,' he said. 'This has got to be good.'

She began again from the beginning, the day of the accident and her own injuries, including the hysterectomy.

'You should know, John, that I can't have children. If you are set on having more, then this is not your girl.' she said candidly.

He hugged her and kissed her hair. 'I have two great kids but I don't need any more. I'm too old to start all that again in any event,' he said reassuringly. 'Go on with your story.'

She relived again the night on Mansion Hill, the story of Christopher's beginnings, how she found out, knowing the number plate, that Jack Randall was his grandfather and Felicity his mother. She related her experiences in Southampton, her meeting with Alex Sanderson and the blackmail threats from Jeremy Ratcliffe. Much of the story came out in a condensed and heavily censored version. John listened attentively but did not interrupt her. She knew that he would interrogate her when he was ready. She omitted telling him of her visit to Ratcliffe's house and the disposal of the laptop and green file. No mention was made of Sylvie's involvement or Felicity's disturbances at the Fairfax Clinic.

When she had concluded, she said, 'I rest my case. You have to be judge, jury and executioner. As a practising lawyer, you may not wish to be associated with a criminal; you may even feel obliged to turn me in for the crimes I have committed. I'm in your hands,' she said, and turned to look up at his face.

After a pause, he said, 'Actually, I'm not a practising

lawyer any more. I haven't told you but I have become a Director of the Manilaw Pharmaceutical Company with a 15% shareholding. If you look out of that window,' he said, pointing through the glass panes, 'you will see the multi-storey monolith which belongs, in part at least, to me. That is why I bought this flat, so I could gaze at my assets.'

'That is amazing,' Nicky said, thinking that her story, which was so personal and so meaningful to her, had not had the same impact on John. He was caught up in his own dreams. Here she was lying beside him and holding another 12.5% of the shares in this thriving business and he didn't seem to know.'

'Funnily enough, it was Jack Randall who first introduced me to the company. It was a large part of his share investment and he was always going on about how successful it was. Well, you will know, as his lawyer, that the company made a lot of money for Jack. Unknown to him, I bought shares when I could and more recently, was able to amass a lot more. Jack holds a large percentage and I don't think he knows yet that I have become his partner. I hope that one day I will be able to buy him out. That would be something. Strange, isn't it, that he is Christopher's grandfather? However, there is a board meeting in a couple of weeks when the facts will be presented. All the major shareholders will be present. He will be attending and will learn exactly what has happened. It will be interesting and now that you have told me about his daughter and her son, I shall look on him with new eyes.'

'John, do you understand why I couldn't tell you all of this before now?' she asked.

'I wish you had told me. Perhaps I would have been able to help you more. It's incredible what you have overcome. I had no idea but, you know, life moves on and what happened all these years ago, well, it's ancient history. What you went through must have been horrendous and you have certainly excelled yourself as Christopher's mother and as a lawyer. I see what problems you encountered and you did well to deal with it all. It's surprising that you have managed to keep it secret for all of this time. I can only admire you for what you have done and it doesn't affect my feelings for you. In fact, I respect you even more. Whatever happens now, you won't be alone. I will help you deal with anything else which presents itself. You don't need to worry about me letting the cat out of the bag. Your secrets are safe with me.'

Nicky kissed him and snuggled into his arms, so pleased that he would be there to help her but anxious too, knowing that she was still holding back, that he still didn't know the whole truth.

'If you marry me, you don't need to work any more. If you want to become a lady of leisure, that's fine with me. Don't worry about your job. You can work if you want to but you don't need to. We can enjoy the profits of the company together and put all of this behind us, start again. I'll share my fifteen per cent with you. I'll even give you five per cent as a wedding present. How about that?' he said jokingly.

'That would be very nice, but it would be a mistake,' she said.

'Why?' he asked.

'Because then I would have control of the company. Jack may not know about your holding in Manilaw Pharmaceuticals but he does know that he split his twenty-five per cent between his grandson and me.'

'What? So you are my partner?'

'Yes, I'm your partner and so is Christopher.'

John laughed uproariously and rolled off the sofa. 'We must drink to this.' he said, still laughing and went to retrieve the bottle of champagne. When he returned and sat, pouring the drinks, she asked,

'John, seriously, are you sure that you want me, knowing what you do now?'

He pulled her towards him and took her head in his hands. 'I want you with all my heart, Nicky. Please say *yes*.'

She smiled and looking into his dark eyes, said, 'You just want me for my money.'

He tickled her and she ran to the bedroom with John in hot pursuit. This time their love making reached heights of ecstasy previously unattained, and Nicky whispered, 'Yes, Yes, Yes.'

In the small hours of the morning she lay awake, unable to sleep as she mulled over the revelation of Sylvie's involvement in Jeremy Ratcliffe's death. She had misjudged Sylvie, underestimated the thought that she had put into his murder and realised for the first time, how much she loved Jack. She didn't condone what Sylvie had done, not in the very least, but she understood how she had felt driven to eliminate Ratcliffe in an act of self preservation and love for Jack. What had she herself done for her own self preservation and love for Christopher? It hadn't ended yet, some clue could yet be unearthed, the Astra could have been observed in Wheatfield Crescent and, one day, a diver could make a telling find in the waters under the Channing Bridge. Christopher needed to be dissuaded from changing the information on his birth certificate because sight of the original document would then raise all manner of embarrassing questions. Even discounting that, Alex's acknowledgment of his son could herald an unwanted interest in his origins. There were fifty nine relatives, according to Jo, all of whom would be very curious about Christopher's appearance on the scene. Sylvie's liking for alcohol also worried her. She might let slip some crucial information when she was under the influence. There were so many possibilities and too many potential pitfalls. Sleep would not come. The weight of all of her anxieties seemed overwhelming.

Aware of John's rhythmic breathing by her side, she rose quietly, slipped on a white towelling robe and went to the balcony outside. She sat on a black wrought iron chair and pulled the robe around her. The air was cool, the sky overcast. For a while, she gazed at the panorama of a million lights across the town, the twinkling stars and the massive Manilaw building with its familiar beacon pulsing out its red signal as it had done all these years. Tears spilled down her cheeks, blurring the bright lights, as she remembered another dark night when she had looked back at the same scene from the woods of Mansion Hill. Gazing through the interstices of the ornate railing, she could see to the ground level, the hard grey concrete slabs of the forecourt. It was a long way down and certain death for anyone who should fall over the guard rail. Death would be quick. This feeling of desperation was familiar to her but now, in spite of the minefield ahead, she felt that she had reached a watershed in her life. For seventeen years, she had put her heart and soul into caring for Christopher, ensuring that he lacked for nothing and for seventeen years, she had worked night and day to further her own career in an effort to provide him with the best of everything. He was a young man now, intelligent, good looking and charming, and had a balanced point of view. He was also rich thanks to his grandfather. His future was secure. She didn't need to worry about him any more. Her own career had flourished, had reached heights she had not dreamed of and if she were to lose that now, she would still have the satisfaction of knowing that she had been a success. John was there for her and it looked as if they would have a future together. He knew a lot about her past and was accepting and rational about it. There would always be an underlying concern about decisions she had taken, things she had done, but for the time being, she could live with that. She wasn't alone any more. Sliding back the glass doors to the balcony, she shut them firmly behind her before dropping her robe, and gently slipping into bed beside the man she loved.

Lightning Source UK Ltd.
Milton Keynes UK

176323UK00003B/3/P

9 781616 672706